ECHO SIX:
BLACK OPS 2
ERIC MEYER

First published in the United Kingdom in 2012 by Swordworks Books.

ISBN 978-1-909149-13-7

Typeset by Swordworks Books
Printed and bound in the UK & US
A catalogue record of this book is available
from the British Library

Cover design by Swordworks Books
www.swordworks.co.uk

ECHO SIX: BLACK OPS 2

ERIC MEYER

CHAPTER ONE

They stared out to seaward, but as ever there was only the crash of the waves. Spume frothing and breaking on the fine, white sand, lit only by the moonlight. Nothing. The air was warm, as it always was in the Caribbean. A light breeze, barely detectable, gave the two men a little relief from the stifling humidity, a very little relief. Jorge, the older man, wiped his brow and dried his hand on his jeans. The sweat trickled into a man's eyes on these hot, damp nights and made it difficult to see any distance. He tracked around and took in sprawling main building. Clustered around it were the bungalow suites where the wealthy guests stayed. To one side of the resort, and perched on the edge of the cliff, was another set of buildings, windowless, but these were closed to visitors. He smiled, all they'd needed was to label them 'staff only', and even the most adventurous guest quickly lost interest in seeing how the lowly servants lived. He scanned along the high wall that separated these buildings from the guest areas, noting that the security gate, the only point of access by land, was shut tight. A red warning light blinked regularly to indicate the gate was locked. If the light ever went out, armed guards would rush to investigate, but during his fifteen months on the Cay, he'd never seen the light go out at night. He doubted if it ever would.

Who the hell would be interested in this flyspeck of land?

The government of Turks and Caicos was well recompensed, by way of taxes and huge bribes, to stay away. So they never came near; it was in their interest to keep the bribe money flowing. He did another sweep of the area, not that he expected to see anything. This was the remotest part of the island, Pelican Cay, set on the northeast tip of the remotest island chain in the Caribbean, the Turks and Caicos Islands, and there were rarely, if ever, any surprises. The company helicopter brought in wealthy tourists from JAGS McCartney International Airport, also known as Grand Turk, landed on the resort helipad and flew them out again when their vacation was ended. In the harbor, there were a number of pleasure craft, expensive yachts. Rich men's boats, fast and luxurious. They were the property of the guests. And if you wanted something more, high-octane thrills, girls, boys, drugs, it was yours for the asking. No matter what your requirement during your vacation at Pelican Cay, the owners would find a way to provide it. The guests were impressed with the security too. Guards like him; all of them armed with the latest TEC-9s, made of molded polymers and stamped steel parts. Twenty round magazines, and the ability to fire on full auto, these 9mm machine pistols were not the watered down variants available to the American market. They could spit out bullets at a rate fast enough to empty the magazine in two or three seconds, and devastate anyone foolish enough to tangle with the guards at Pelican Cay. No one had been that foolish.

They watched over this little piece of paradise and the bloated, pampered bodies of the guests as they lounged on the silvered, fine sandy beaches. Guests who had no idea that the guards' primary task was very different from looking after the millionaires and billionaires who came to Pelican Cay. And they never guessed the real reason. Jorge smiled to himself. It was better they stayed in ignorance, if they wanted to live.

He saw his companion Cristobal coming toward him. As ever, he envied his trim, muscular body and flat stomach. Maybe Jorge should cut down on the booze and the pastries when he got home, his wallet stuffed with cash. The pay was good, that was true, and he'd want to find a pretty girl with whom to spend some of it. He knew his paunch did not make him as attractive as Cristobal. His companion was much younger too, a mean looking youth, just twenty years old, and also desperate to spend some of the cash that weighed down his pockets each payday. Pelican Cay Resort was a generous employer, so it was a pity there was so little for the guards to spend their money on in this place.

"Hey, Cristobal, you see anything?"

"Nada! Do we ever see anything, Jorge? This job is a total fucking waste of time."

"Better than peddling dime bags to the tourists in Cockburn Town, my friend."

Cristobal shrugged. "Maybe, but at least there was some action in the capital. Hey, Jorge, did you see that waitress, the new one? She has a room on the floor below ours. That girl is really something. I tell you, she's a real princess. Do you think it's true what they say about the young women that work here? I'd sure like to sample a couple of them."

"You mean that most of them are whores who put out to the guests for money?" Jorge replied with a grin. "Sure it's true, my friend. But there are two problems you need to consider. First, even you haven't got that kind of money. Those whores are a thousand dollars a night. And second, you know the rules. The girls are for guests only, and if any of the staff touches one of them, they get fired."

Cristobal grunted. "For that new one, it'd be worth getting fired. Mother of God, she's a real angel."

"Maybe she is, but what would happen if you were caught? The management here is not likely to forgive something like that, not easily. You may find yourself swimming home to Cockburn Town."

"Fuck that, Jorge, it's fifty miles! No man can swim fifty miles."

"Exactly. So keep your dick in your pants, my friend, and save it for when the contract is ended. And remember, there's a new consignment coming in tonight, so stay sharp."

The younger man scowled and strutted away to find a quiet place to have a smoke, maybe catch up on some sleep. Jorge would call him if anything unexpected happened. And it never did.

* * *

"Target in sight, range five thousand meters. I can see the harbor clearly, Skipper. Sea is calm, and we have a half moon."

They all looked at the LCD repeater screen, which relayed the image from the camera on the electronic periscope to the control room. They could just make out the yacht harbor, with the buildings housing the resort complex onshore, and above them, the anonymous, walled compound with the windowless buildings that was their objective.

"Very well, bring her up slowly until the sail is clear. Make sure the hull doesn't breach the surface."

"Aye. Down scope, bringing her up to ten meters, no, belay that. Hold your depth. Skipper, I see a patrol boat on the surface. She was stopped in the water with her engines off. I guess that's why we missed her, but she's moving now. Her track is taking the vessel between us and the beach."

The overhead speaker came to life. "Con, sonar, small craft, moving across our course. Intercept point is fifteen hundred meters dead ahead, six minutes at our current speed."

They looked at the Captain expectantly.

"Keep on it, sonar. Let us know when he clears the area. Raise the ESM mast. Let's take a look. I'll take the con."

"Aye, aye. Captain has the con."

He looked at the officer stood next to him. An American, sure, but his unit wasn't US military, so this was a first for the USS Virginia, the boat normally carried Seals on their highly secret operations. "What do you want to do, Lieutenant? If we launch the RIBs now, he's sure to see us. They're pretty primitive in these parts, but not that primitive."

"Is it a Turks and Caicos naval vessel? Or something

else?"

"You mean like the traffickers?" He thought for a couple of seconds. "My guess would be traffickers, yeah. Government vessels in this area are few and far between. The crews like to be tucked up in a nice warm bed at night. No, it has to be 'narcotraficantes'. Probably a guard boat watching for someone just like you."

"We'll have to go in from further out. Would you take us out to ten thousand meters, Captain? And get those RIBs to take us in to five thousand meters. That should do it."

"It's a long swim, Lieutenant. It'll cut into the time you have ashore."

The officer shrugged. "We'll manage."

We always do. That's our job.

"Exec, you have the con. Take out to ten thousand meters."

"I have the con," he agreed. "Ten thousand meters, aye."

The men waited, tense and silent as the sub reversed its course and headed back out to sea. The exec looked at the Captain.

"We've reached the ten thousand meter point, Skipper."

"Very well, take her up to ten meters."

"Ten meters, aye."

He looked at the other man. "Let's hope this'll be far enough to clear that patrol boat. They carry some heavy hardware."

The other man reassured him, "It's far enough. We're good."

"Hatch is one meter below the surface, Sir."

"Very good. On my order, put the hatch out of the

water and hold her steady."

It was quiet, very quiet for such a large warship, one that carried so many men and such a mighty complement of devastating armament. Captain Ed Dawson, Skipper of the USS Virginia, stood in a relaxed position in the control room, listening to the low hum of the ship's systems, his ears attuned to the familiar sounds and alert for anything unfamiliar. He glanced at his executive officer, Lieutenant Commander John Waltham, who was monitoring the boat's status boards. He squinted at the lights and indicators, like a jealous mother guarding its young. The water off the coast of the Turks and Caicos Islands, or more specifically here, the Caicos Island, was shallow, especially for a boat like theirs. The nuclear powered craft, motto 'Sic Semper Tyrannis, Thus Always To Tyrants', was modern by most standards, commissioned in 2004. Powered by an S9G nuclear reactor, the USS Virginia was one hundred and fifteen meters long, and weighed seven thousand eight hundred tons. Almost silent in the water, and with a crew of one hundred and thirty-four officers and men, the vessel was already a veteran of the United States war on terror. The boat was equipped with four VLS tubes, the vertical launching system that could propel Tomahawk missiles from under the sea to their targets. She was also unique in having a pressure chamber to deploy Navy Seal divers or other Special Forces units while still submerged. This time, the boat was carrying a NATFOR Special Operations unit, part of NATO. The pressure chamber would not be needed. The SpecOps unit on board would travel the last part of their journey on the surface. A pair of RIBs was ready to be launched; silent, powerful, low profile rubber raiding craft that would not attract the attention of any watchers gazing across the calm, clear sea above them. At least, that was the theory.

The Skipper of the Virginia turned to the man dressed in a black wetsuit standing next to him.

"Lieutenant Talley, this is where we part company. We're set to launch the RIBs. You have everything ready in the sail?"

Talley nodded. "We're ready, Skipper."

Dawson nodded. "Very well. The hatch will be clear of the surface soon, so you can proceed. Good luck, Lieutenant. We'll remain on station as long as we can for the pick up. Don't forget, I can give you until dawn, no more. This is a large vessel to stay hidden for too long in these waters. In daylight, the water is clear enough to spot a rowing boat. If you're not back, we'll return tomorrow night and wait for you. But if you're…"

Talley nodded. "I get it, Skipper. But if we're not back by dawn, we won't be coming back. There's nowhere to hide on that flyspeck island. Don't worry, we'll be there."

"A pity about that patrol boat, it's thrown our schedule to hell."

"Yeah. We'll get by."

They shook hands and Talley went forward into the sail. He entered a large steel chamber, crowded with men and equipment. Above him, in the top compartment just under the main hatch, he could make out the legs of the two sailors preparing to launch and navigate the RIBs that would carry his assault party most of the way to the objective. There was little room to maneuver. The steel compartment was crowded with the men of Echo Six, like him wearing wetsuits ready for the long swim to the beach. He nodded a greeting to Sergeant Guy Welland, his second-in-command. When he'd first made Welland his Number Two, there'd been a couple of objections, not least because some of the team were commissioned officers. But the protests quickly died when they saw the hard, tough, SAS trooper in action. Guy got the job done, no matter what. He was almost an elemental force, immensely skilled, diamond hard, and unstoppable. The success of Echo Six owed much to Sergeant Guy Welland, and success inevitably meant fewer casualties. His methods were hard and brutal, often raising more than a few eyebrows. But Echo Six was the SpecOps unit that their NATO bosses sent for when they needed to get results fast. Toughness and brutality was their 'Modus Operandi', and there were few after-action complaints. From the enemy, there were inevitably none, only a long eternal silence. NATFOR operatives were selected from member countries for one reason only. They were the best of the best.

"We all set?" he asked Guy.

"Yep. The sailors up top say as soon as the hatch is opened, they only need a minute to inflate the RIBS and start the motors, no more. They seem pretty slick, so as soon as they go out the hatch, we'll follow."

Talley looked around at his men. Vince DiMosta, formerly Delta Force, was a unit sniper who resembled a Mafia hit man, with his dark Mediterranean looks. The other sniper stood next to him, Jerzy Ostrowski, known to all of them as Jerry. He'd served in the Polish Special Operations force GROM, and NATO had selected him just like the rest of them; he was at the top of his profession, and the best. For a pilot, it would have been the astronaut program that was the pinnacle of their ambition. For a

SpecOps soldier, it was NATFOR. Lieutenant Domenico Rovere watched closely. An Italian, and the unit joker, Rovere was a typical Italian, dark haired, olive skinned, and dark eyed. He was well built, bigger than Guy Roland, with a baby face that made him appear almost ten years younger than his twenty-five years. Rovere's specialty was chasing the ladies, when he wasn't playing practical jokes on other members of the unit. There were twenty operatives in all, including Talley. They were the men of Echo Six, NATO's secret weapon of last resort.

The Skipper gave a quiet order. The boat moved up a fraction, and the sail ascended so that the hatch cleared the surface. A seaman flung it open, and Talley looked up as a cascade of seawater showered down over them. As the hatch opened, the pressure equalized, causing his ears to pop. Already, Guy was hurling himself up the ladder, and the other men followed close behind.

"Fuck!"

Domenico Rovere cleared the seawater from his eyes. He spoke the curse with an Italian accent. A veteran of the 4th Alpini Parachutist Regiment 'Monte Cervino', the man above him had banged a compressed air bottle against the Italian's head as he moved.

"Sorry about that."

The Italian grimaced. "As a great man once said, 'I would challenge you to a battle of wits, but I see you are unarmed.'"

He shook his head to clear it as the men chuckled, and he continued climbing up to the hatch. Sergeant Roy Reynolds, a Delta Force operative before he'd joined NATFOR's Echo Six, followed him. The black sergeant grunted as he hauled a heavy, waterproof bag after him.

14

Talley knew it contained the unit's two Minimis, the lethal SAWs. Squad Automatic Weapons, lightweight machine guns that were issued to most NATO units. In the US, the Belgian designed weapon was designated the M249 Machine Gun. The men all carried their personal weapons in bags strapped to their chests. Like Special Forces across the NATO countries, many of the men preferred the Heckler and Koch MP7 for CQB, close quarters battle. The radical new carbine length submachine gun fired lethal, undersized 4.6mm rounds. The bullets were specially designed to penetrate most body armor where a larger caliber round would fail to penetrate. Talley took a last look around, hefted his air tanks, and followed the men up to the deck where they were checking their gear.

"We're all set, Boss."

He looked at Guy. "I'm not happy about the moonlight. We'll need to be careful when we hit that beach."

"Maybe. I doubt they're expecting trouble. We'll catch them in bed with their senoritas."

"Maybe. I'll take the first boat and lead the swim inshore. You follow in the second boat, and watch out for stragglers, I don't want anyone falling behind."

"Copy that. They won't fall behind."

No, they won't. Guy will make sure no man lags behind.

Talley stepped into the first RIB and hunched next to the sailor manning the console. The men followed, distributing themselves around the boat. He nodded and the sailor pushed the throttle forward. The boat purred away toward their embarkation point, five thousand meters offshore. The target was known to have a ring of subsurface sensors that could pick up propeller noise from a craft that came within five hundred meters, and so the plan was to enter the water at one thousand meters. But extending their swim to five thousand meters would slash the time they had to complete the operation. If they weren't out by daylight, well, it was best not to think about that. The island was small, too small for concealment during daylight.

"I always enjoy a voyage in a small boat," Rovere smiled at him.

"You may change your mind when the shooting starts on the island," Guy pointed out.

"Is that 'the way to dusty death'?" Domenico fired back at him. "Life's but a walking shadow, my friend, a poor player, that struts and frets his hour upon the stage."

They grinned. Rovere was hard to put down and hard to ignore. Talley shut him up. They had work to do.

"I'd enjoy it more if that patrol boat wasn't in the area. It's going to be a long swim, Domenico, and an even longer night, so save your breath for later."

Rovere shut up. If the gunboat came across Echo Six, the mission would be a bust, no question. The RIBs were almost silent as they sped across the water. The powerful Mercury gas engines were specially silenced, to give the best compromise between speed and stealth. It was only minutes before they were approaching the five thousand meter mark. In the distance, Talley could see the navigation lights of the patrol boat. If it was one of the traffickers' boats, it would have the best and most sensitive equipment money could buy. But equipment did not mean the people who manned it would be alert, and the undersea sensors suffered from the same problem. If the operator was asleep, drunk, or maybe even having sex with a local whore, they wouldn't be alert for an attack. It was the best they could hope for. The boats slowed as the sailors cut the power.

"We're at the spot, Sir."

"Right. Return to the Virginia. We'll call if we need you."

He pulled down his mask and sucked in his mouthpiece. With a last look around, he slid backward into the warm sea and swam down, turning around to watch as the rest of his unit entered the water and joined him. Roy Reynolds and Virgil Kane were towing the waterproof bags with their heavy equipment, the Minimis and the stores of two hundred round magazines. Jerry Ostrowski and Vince DiMosta were pulling overlength bags with their sniper rifles, the British Accuracy International Arctic Warfare Super Magnums. Known as the AWM, the bolt-action rifles, outfitted with a Schmidt & Bender PM, had proved outstanding in the field. Equipped to fire the heavy .338 Lapua Magnum rounds, they had scored kills at a range of a mile or more. The AWMs and SAWs were the iron fist of Echo Six, and they had demonstrated their ability to kill the enemy in large numbers and at great distances on several previous operations.

It was a long swim, and they had to watch for the unknown; defense systems that may have been changed since the last intelligence sweep. They heard the patrol boat in the distance, but it never came close. As he got into the constant rhythm of pushing himself through the water, Talley thought about that letter, back in his locker. His wife had asked the court for sole custody of his kids, and then written to him trying to justify it.

'You're never there, Abe, you're a stranger to them. And besides, look at the kind of work you do. I don't want my kids to be brought up by someone who's little more than a government assassin.'

He'd almost torn it up in an uncharacteristic fit of anger.

Her kids? What about me? And why does she think the kids can go to bed safe at night, without having to worry about a second nine eleven? I loved her when we first married, but she's become the kind of schemer who'd be behind that kind of a letter. Kay knew when we married I'd be away for long periods of active service, but the arguments soon started. Then she began the affair. Maybe they're thinking of getting married. That's fine by me, but using my kids as a weapon against me, is not. I'll fight it, but how? Ask the Islamic fanatics to hang fire while I deal with the custody battle?

With an effort, he put his troubles out of his mind and kept an eye on the progress of his unit.

They finally made it to the beach after the exhausting swim. The twenty men of Echo Six went ashore at the foot of the cliffs and began preparations for the assault. Guy Welland came toward him, festooned with ropes and karabiners, and with his NV goggles strapped to his helmet. He smiled; they were askew, almost like decorations on a Christmas tree.

"Any problems?"

The SAS man shook his head. "None. We're good to go."

Talley nodded, looking at the height of the cliff above them. "Not an easy climb, Guy, and we're already running late. It would be useful to find a shortcut."

"We went over that before, Boss. It's this or nothing. One shot from those guards up there and the shit really hits the fan. There's no time to discuss this. We have to move off now."

"Yeah, okay, we'll keep to plan. My unit will circle around to the harbor. As soon as you call in, we'll move in and secure the resort. Once you're in, get those charges set fast and get out. We'll block any reinforcements from the outside, but even so, it's going to be a close run thing."

"Aren't they all?" Guy smiled.

"Yeah."

Welland jogged away and assembled the rest of his task force. Eight men, including him, all expert climbers who would scale the cliff, kill the sentries, and capture their objective, then hold it long enough to prepare the demolition charges. He watched as Guy reached the foot of the cliff. Guy took a last look the ascent of the sheer, rocky cliff face, sixty meters high, and started to climb. Talley's unit, twelve men in all, would skirt around the base of the cliff and establish a blocking position in the main resort area. There were at least forty heavily armed hostiles at the last count, stationed outside the walled, windowless compound. When they realized they were under attack, they'd come pouring out to defend the main complex, and Guy's group would be hard pressed to hold them off. Talley's group, with the two SAWs and the AWMs, had to be in position before the trouble started, or they were lost. He looked around. His men were ready.

"Domenico, get moving now, take some men to cover the harbor. Roy, cover our rear. Remember, time is definitely not on our side."

Domenico sped off along the narrow strip of sand toward the harbor, and a minute later Talley led his own squad toward the resort that lay just above it. Jerry Ostrowski took a last look back at the men scaling the cliff before they rounded the headland. It was slow going, incredibly difficult. He looked aside at Talley as they jogged along the beach.

"It's going to be a bitch, getting up there. It could slow us down if they're late."

"Guy will make it. He always does."

"Maybe, but that sub won't wait around."

Talley looked at the Pole. "What's up, Jerry? What's bugging you?"

"I don't know, Boss. Something about this place, I've got a strange feeling about it."

"Like what?"

He shook his head. "I don't know. Like there's something waiting for us we haven't foreseen. These traffickers, they're not stupid, and with the billions of dollars they can spend, I just don't think we've seen everything they have to offer. There's something else, too. This whole operation, it looks too big for just a bunch of gangsters."

"It's well defended, Jerry."

"That's right, and well organized, those electronic sensors, the patrol boats."

"We'll deal with them. What more could they throw at us?"

Ostrowski fixed him with a stare. "At lot. A helluva lot."

The commo interrupted him. "Echo One, this is Three. I can see the entire harbor. We're almost there, and it looks quiet."

Domenico Rovere, his Italian accent strong.

"Copy that, we're moving forward. Echo Six, anything happening back there?"

"All clear, Echo One," Roy reported in. "No, wait, something's going on. There's a patrol coming from the other direction, several men. They've stopped just below where Guy's group is climbing."

Shit!

"Have they seen them? Do they suspect anything?"

"No, but if our guys make any noise, they're toast. I'd guess they're only halfway up, about thirty meters above the beach."

"Any idea what the patrol is doing, Roy?"

"They're just waiting for something. Yeah, I see it now. It's some kind of a boat, low in the water, about twenty meters offshore. It's weird, like a submarine, or a semi-submersible. They're wading out to pull it onto the beach."

Interesting. Semi-submersibles aren't new, but the intel weanies will be interested. It's something they missed while they focused their surveillance on the compound and the harbor.

"Understood. Stay where you are and keep an eye on them, Roy. Keep it quiet, but use the Minimi if you have to."

"Copy that."

He tried calling Guy. "Echo Two, this is One."

The murmured reply came back to him. "This is Two, we heard. We'll keep climbing. As long as they don't look up, we're okay."

"I've deployed one of the Minimis to cover you, in case you're spotted."

"Not necessary. You'll need everything to fight with when you get inside. It'll be like stirring up a hive of angry bees."

"Yeah, I copy that. I'll leave Roy where he is, but I'll call him forward when he sees you're in the clear. Good luck."

A click of acknowledgement sounded in his earpiece, and then there was silence. Talley took a last look around, but it was clear, and he signaled his men to keep moving.

21

They cleared the headland, and there was the yacht harbor with dozens of luxury yachts tied to pontoons. He could see Domenico ahead, hunched behind a pile of rocks with his men deployed in a defensive formation.

"This is Echo One. Domenico, everything quiet?"

"It looks good here, Abe. But we're falling further behind schedule."

"Can't be helped. We have to keep going. You can move up to the quayside, and we'll head straight for the resort complex. It's only another fifty meters, and if nothing goes wrong, we'll join up there in ten minutes or so. That should sync with Guy's climb up that cliff."

Domenico acknowledged. Talley heard him say, 'something always goes wrong, my friend', just before he signed off.

He couldn't argue with that. Rovere started to move, and Talley gestured for his men to follow him. They stopped between the quayside and the resort, close to hundreds of millions of dollars of leisure craft. Ahead of them, the complex was still quiet, and beyond that, the mysterious, walled compound was in darkness. They removed their NV goggles. The place was lit at intervals by ornamental lamps strung from palm trees, enough to disrupt NV. Talley took a last look around. Still nothing.

"Let's do it."

They charged toward the resort, and still there was no sign the defenders had twigged to them. They passed the main hotel building, skirted around the side of one of the luxury bungalows, and in front of them was their objective, the high-walled compound across a clear, empty space. He saw Roy Reynolds running up to join them.

"Deploy the Minimis on the flanks. Vince, Jerry, cover

them, you know what to do. The rest of you…"

He stopped as powerful floodlights flared into life. The area was suddenly brightly lit, almost as if it was daylight. Someone had switched on the banks of overhead security lights; they were fastened to the tops of the buildings and on the high, concrete wall. As their eyes adjusted to the light, they saw armed soldiers running just below the top.

So they've got a parapet allowing them to fight from behind cover. Shit!

Talley skidded behind a low concrete loading ramp. Domenico joined him, and they looked over the top. The defenders had ducked down behind cover, and so far none of them had showed themselves to open fire, so it would be impossible for the snipers to take them on. He looked behind him as a powerboat sped into the harbor. The boat stayed a few meters out from the quay, and Talley could see armed men moving on the deck, two of them were preparing a heavy machine gun.

How the hell did they react so fast? And why didn't the surveillance I was given warn us about the parapet?

He tensed as the single door to the compound opened, and a man walked out. He stood in the open, waiting. He seemed relaxed, smoking a cigar, looking around with interest.

"You want me to take him?" Vince called on the commo. He was eager to take the shot.

"Negative. Let's see what the bastard wants. I'll go talk to him, cover me."

Talley got to his feet and walked into the open. The man stared at him, smiled, and walked forward to meet him. He was a Latino, maybe in his late twenties, and powerfully built. He was dressed simply, in a heavy, cream silk shirt and designer denim jeans, with what looked like hand-tooled loafers on his feet. The effect was money. This was a guy with wealth, everything expensive, the best. His long, glistening black hair was tied in a ponytail, showing off his strong, olive skinned face. The eyes were dark brown, intense. They faced each other, waiting. Finally, when he realized Talley wouldn't break the silence, he spoke.

"I am Miguel Rodrigo, and I have the honor to be the manager of this facility. And you are?"

"Lieutenant Talley."

"American?"

"Something like that."

"This is a legitimate business operation. Why are you here, Lieutenant?"

Talley smiled and didn't bother to reply. The man nodded.

"I wondered when you'd come," the he said thoughtfully. "Did you think you could invade my privacy without us knowing? We have sensors and security systems here that you could only dream of. We saw you come up from the harbor. I assume you swam ashore under cover of the pleasure boats?"

Talley stayed silent.

So they don't know about Guy's group.

"You must lay down your arms, Lieutenant Talley. Surely you can see it is useless to try and fight us all."

"I've got a better idea, Rodrigo. You tell your men to lay down their weapons. Give it up, and you won't get hurt. This time, you've bitten off more than you can chew."

Rodrigo chuckled. "I think not, Lieutenant Talley. You are surrounded. You see the men on the wall, and on the boat in the harbor. I even have men up on the cliff." He unclipped a radio from his belt.

"Jorge, come in. Have you got these soldiers covered from up there?"

There was only the hiss of static.

"Jorge? Cristobal? Report in, what is your status?"

He looked at the radio in irritation, shrugged and went to clip it back on his belt, when there was a muted reply, with an English accent.

"Hey, Pal."

He snatched up the radio. "Who is this? Jorge?"

"Jorge's not here."

"Who is that? Cristobal?"

"Cristobal isn't here either. They went for a dive, over the cliff."

Rodrigo tossed the radio aside in anger and ran back for the doorway into the compound. "Shoot! Kill them all!"

Echo Six opened fire, and the Latino staggered as a shot hit him in the back. Then another, but he must have been wearing an armored vest, for he carried on and dived through the door that closed behind him. Gunfire shattered the peace of the night, and flashes showed above the wall where the defenders were firing at them. But Echo Six was behind cover too, and they returned fire with a vengeance. MP7s, and a couple of HK416s fired short bursts. The snipers opened up, and the AWMs hurled their precision rounds at any enemy stupid enough to offer a target. The Minimis added their voice, hurling lethal volleys of bullets at the enemy. Lights were coming on all over the resort as the pampered guests woke up to the reality that their Caribbean paradise was turning into a nightmare. Talley ignored them, peering out from behind the low wall where he'd dropped into cover.

What the hell is Guy up to?

He keyed his mike, but the answer came before he could speak.

"Holy shit!" Domenico Rovere's awestruck comment came as the charges detonated, and the compound was engulfed in smoke and flames. The earth moved as if in an earthquake, and it seemed the entire cliff top shook. Great chunks of masonry fell away from the wall and the building behind, as if it was in danger of disintegrating. Talley opened fire and knocked down one of the more determined of Rodrigo's gunners. He was leaning out, trying to rake Talley's group with an M60. He dropped the machine gun and went over the wall with a scream, plunging to the concrete below. Two men rushed to pick up the gun, took aim, and died even before they'd pulled the trigger. Talley reloaded and called Guy. It was time to regroup.

"Echo Two, come in. Where are you, what's going down?"

The reply came a few seconds later. In the background, he could hear sporadic gunfire.

"This is Two, after we detonated, we abseiled down the cliff to chat to those guys standing around the submersible. We're clearing them now. Give us a few minutes. Out."

A burst of machine gun fire chipped stone from the wall inches from his face. He lurched to the side and looked around. It came from the patrol boat in the harbor. They'd opened fire at last, and he cursed himself for not taking care of it. He needed a machine gun, and fast. He remembered Reynolds.

"Echo Six, this is One, where are you, Roy?"

"This is Six. I'm holding a position by the headland."

"Copy that. Can you see the gunfire from the harbor? That patrol boat, a few meters off the quay."

"I see it. You want me to dust them off?"

"Quick as you can, Roy. We're pretty exposed here."

"I'm on it."

The gunfire from the wall of the compound had slackened as the defenders rushed to cope with the fires and wreckage caused by the explosion. But there was still enough incoming fire to damage Talley's squad, and his operation had only achieved a part of the objective. They'd dealt a heavy blow to the infrastructure. Now it was time to go in and take out the men who did the real work of drug trafficking. Otherwise, they'd simply move elsewhere and start again.

We've done well. If we can finish this fast, we can get back in one piece. We may not be so lucky next time.

"Domenico, we have to get inside that compound fast. As soon as Roy opens up on the patrol boat, we're going in. We'll have to blow the door. I'll give you covering fire, be ready to move."

"I'm on it."

Talley called to the men still firing at the few men on the wall.

"Pour it on, Rovere's going in. He needs cover."

The firing increased to a furious intensity, and Talley saw the return fire from the defenders slacken as the hail of bullets from the submachine guns, the sniper rifles, and the Minimi reached a crescendo. Roy opened up with the second Minimi, and the shooting from the patrol boat stopped as they searched out the new threat. Domenico was almost there. Talley jumped to his feet.

"That's it, let's go!"

The run across the open space seared the breath from his lungs, and he winced as bullets pinged all around him, but he reached the wall without injury. The rest of his men made it safely, and he saw Sergeant Heinrich Buchmann, their demolitions specialist, preparing a charge.

"Heinie, I want that door opened now!"

"Jawohl, I'm on it, Boss."

The German, a veteran of the elite German KSK Kommando Spezialkräfte, was almost ready. He looked around and nodded at Talley.

"Fire in the hole."

They hit the dirt, and Buchmann detonated the explosive. It was a small explosion, but the door was punched backward inside the compound. Talley was already up and running through the smoke and debris.

"Move, move, before they recover. Domenico, take the other side. Don't give them a chance to regroup!"

They followed him through the smashed portal. He dived right, and troopers hurtled to both sides of the entrance as a hail of gunfire from the defenders' submachine guns tore through the open doorway. He was already facing the threat. There were five men with TEC-9s, spraying poorly aimed bullets at Talley's squad, and missing. The weapons were notoriously inaccurate at anything other than point blank range, and the hail of fire from Echo Six scattered them. Four more defenders went down, and the fifth ran into the main building. Talley glanced around for another way in, but there was only one entrance, an iron door that clanged shut even as he watched.

"Buchmann! Open it."

"Ja, ja, Lieutenant, I'm on it."

The German trooper ran forward and began to place charges against the massive iron hinges. Another burst of gunfire made Talley whirl around. A man was on the wall, aiming at the demolitions man. He clutched his chest as at least one of the bullets found a target. Every gun pointed upward at the shooter, and he was hit by a score of bullets that riddled his body. He stood up as the shock of incoming bullets made him jerk like a marionette. Then he tripped and toppled to the concrete below. His body hit the ground with a meaty 'thud', but there was no scream; the man was dead long before his feet left the roof. Talley ran toward the German.

"Heinrich, where are you hit?"

The trooper looked up at him. He was breathing heavily. "My vest, it stopped the bullet, Herr Leutnant. I'll be okay. I just need some time to get my breath."

He slumped back down, gasping in shock and pain. Talley looked around for one of his men to take Buchmann's place.

"I want someone who can handle it to blow that door. The rest of you watch out for squirters up top."

"I can take care of it."

He nodded at Vince as the sniper put down his rifle and finished placing the explosive. He looked at Talley.

"That should do it. I'm not certain of the amount, so I used all of it."

"Good enough. When you're ready, Vince."

"Fire in the hole!"

They flattened to the ground. A single shot ricocheted off the concrete, close to where Vince had hunkered down, and then the charge exploded. It was massive. Enough to shake the entire building, and Talley felt him lifted a few inches into the air. He looked up as he heard a scream and a nearby 'thump'. A body had fallen from the roof. The guy who'd shot at Vince had been blown clean off as the blast wave knocked him off his feet and over the edge. This time, he'd been alive all the way down, hence the scream.

Maybe it would've been better if he'd been killed first.

The man gasped out his last breath and died. Talley looked up. The blast had blown a massive rent in the side of the building, fully three meters wide. The blast must have been paralyzing for the defenders. Talley jumped to his feet and started running.

"Charge, men! Let's wrap up these arrogant bastards and go home."

He meant one arrogant bastard in particular, Rodrigo. Smug and secure in his drug trafficking headquarters that he thought was safe from international sanctions. Comfortable and confident in his expensive designer clothes, surrounded by what he thought were impregnable defenses.

He was wrong, badly wrong.

As he ran, he heard Guy call him.

"Echo One, this is Two. The beach is secure, repeat, the beach is secure."

"Copy that, Echo Two. Did you take any prisoners?"

One of their primary objectives was to take away at least two prisoners.

"Negative, One. They're all dead. They wouldn't surrender."

"Copy that." The SAS never did have a good reputation for taking prisoners. "Destroy anything of value, and come around and wait for us at the harbor. Look out for Roy as you fall back. He's up there with the Minimi."

"Copy that, we'll be there soon. How's it going?"

"We're good, no serious casualties so far."

"Give it time," Guy warned.

"Yep. We'll see you at the harbor. Out."

Talley was still running, and so far there was no fire coming from the defenders.

"Domenico, take two men. I want a couple of prisoners while there're a few left alive. You know what we're looking for."

"Copy that."

Rovere shouted two names, and the troopers followed him into the wreckage of the building. Talley led the rest of his squad up the staircase to the upper levels. They ran from room to room, clearing out the last of the defenders. The hallways echoed to the sound of gunfire and ricochets as Echo Six relentlessly pushed the enemy back, slaughtering the defenders, giving them no quarter. He was satisfied. His men had a job to do, and they were doing it ruthlessly well. In this kind of close quarters battle, it was the law of the jungle, kill or be killed. He heard more shooting from the first floor, and keyed his mike.

"Domenico, I said take prisoners, not kill them all."

"We're working on it, Boss. We've kept one of them alive so far. He's the guy that came out to talk to you. I guess he's the 'Jefe'. He was unarmed."

"Understood, but be careful. Watch out for an ambush. These people are not giving up without a fight."

"Copy that."

At the end of the passage, Talley could see an open doorway. He signaled his men to spread out behind him and walked carefully toward the entrance.

"Whoever you are inside there, come out. If we have to come and get you, we'll come in shooting, after we've tossed a grenade in first. It's your choice, dead or alive."

After a few seconds hesitation, a voice shouted to them.

"I'm coming out! I'm unarmed."

"Just make it slow, buddy. Make sure we can see your hands, and they'd better be empty."

The man appeared in the doorway, his hands held high, and palms open to show he was unarmed. Behind him, Talley heard someone say, "Jesus Christ!"

The comment was understandable. The man who emerged was a heavily bearded Muslim Arab. Yet by his clothes, his robes, he was more than just a Muslim. They'd all seen men like this in the newsreels, and occasionally in the field, on clandestine operations. He wore a black turban, long black robes, and a white, collarless shirt, Iranian style. That was interesting. The Iranians banned ties after the 1979 revolution, as a symbol of American decadence.

"I guess you're an imam. Iranian?"

"I am the Imam Rashid Fard." The man scowled as he spoke, his words hissing out in anger. "You have no right to take me prisoner! I hold diplomatic immunity from the Islamic Republic of Iran. You must release me immediately!"

There was something wrong, something about the guy. Talley couldn't pin it down. Behind the bluster, there was something else, guilt. The guy was red faced, sweating, as if he'd just emerged from a heavy session in a brothel.

What the hell has he been up to?

Talley mentally shrugged it off. It would come out later, in the interrogation.

"Yeah, right." He turned to the nearest trooper. "Cuff the bastard, and make it good and tight."

The Iranian reddened. "You cannot do this. I am accredited to the Iranian Embassy in the capital, Cockburn Town, on Grand Turk. I must return there at once."

Talley stood over him. "Here's the thing, Imam Fard. Since the Siege of the American Embassy in Iran, I reckon your people have given up all rights to diplomatic protection. Let's call this a little payback, shall we? Take him out!"

His earpiece came to life. Rovere.

"Go ahead, Domenico."

"We have our prisoner secure, and we're exiting the building. You want us to cover your exit from here?"

Talley looked around, the place was little more than wreckage. They'd done what they came to do, and the shooting had died out. The defenders were either all dead or they'd run.

"No, go down to the harbor and choose a boat to take us out of here. Get the engines running and everyone aboard. We'll join you shortly."

"What kind of a boat?"

"Anything you like, but make it something big and fast. We'll deep six it when we meet up with the sub, so we won't need to risk the RIBs on the outward journey."

"Copy that."

He clicked off and looked around.

"Vince, does Heinrich have anything left in his pack to finish this place off? Something that'll go off with a big bang?"

He nodded. "Sure thing. Jerry here was carrying a pile of his spare charges, so I can rig something good." He indicated the Pole, who was close by.

"Do it. I want to leave this place a heap of rubble. There's a helipad close by, so find it and make sure their helo never gets off the ground again. When you're done, come on down to the harbor."

Vince nodded, and he sped off with Jerry to finish the job. Talley followed the rest of the men into the open space that separated the compound from the resort hotel. The hotel wasn't quiet, not anymore.

He looked at the crowd of people who were watching him, had probably been rubbernecking the battle.

It reminds me of those old photos. Civilians who'd ventured out to the hilltops to watch battles during the Civil War. To watch men being slaughtered. Ghouls.

Most were still clad in their nightclothes, women in filmy, silk negligees, men in striped PJs, and Ralph Loren monogrammed robes. He walked up to them.

"Show's over, folks. If I were you, I'd make arrangements to leave. The service here ain't gonna be so fast from here on in."

One man stepped forward, older, in his sixties. Tall, gray hair, expensively trimmed, the security lamps showed off his Caribbean tan. He had the look of corporate America, a man accustomed to getting his way, to shoving people around. A bully.

"Who the hell are you, soldier? What gives?"

"Name's Talley, Sir. I'm the guy who came to destroy the drug traffickers who own this resort; the guys who've been using it as a cover to flood America with illegal drugs. Our job's done, so we're leaving. If you don't want to spend several days in a Caicos prison, explaining where you were when this went down, I'd get out of here. If you can, that is."

The man grimaced. "I don't like this, not one bit, Mister. I reckon you have a lot to answer for. We ought to call in the cops to talk to you."

Talley smiled. "That's a great idea, you go ahead and call the cops. They'll just love talking to you. In the meantime, we have places to go, so I'll say goodnight."

The man ignored him and turned to someone in the crowd behind him.

"Billy, get onto the manager! Tell him to have my helicopter standing by. I'll take care of..."

He stopped. They all looked toward the other side of the compound where the helipad was sited. The explosion lit up the sky for a few, brief moments, and many of the civilians ran screaming for cover as chunks of broken metal rained down over the resort. They were beginning to realize that the squalor and detritus of war was no respecter of wealth and position.

"Maybe you'd better consider going by boat," Talley advised him as he walked away.

Guy and his men were waiting on the quay. They'd prepared a defensive position, in case the enemy had more soldiers ready to join in the defense of the resort. It wasn't necessary. The battle had ended, the hostiles were either dead or on the run, and only civilians remained. He looked back at the chaos in front of the resort hotel. They were hurrying to pack their things, no doubt taking his advice and getting out before the police arrived looking for answers. Domenico shouted from a nearby pontoon. He'd chosen a thirty-six-foot Chris Craft Corsair. Fast, luxurious and very, very expensive.

It'll be a shame to sink it when we're done, but it's too bad, this is war. Maybe some of those wealthy vacationers may even thank my unit when the supply of cocaine dries up, and the danger to their kids from illicit narcotics is lessened. But I doubt it

He noticed two men helping Heinrich Buchmann along the quay. He was still stunned by the force of the bullets that had impacted his vest. The Frenchman, a new man, Robert Valois was watching.

"Give them a hand, Robert. Buchmann is hurt."

"He can take care of himself, Lieutenant. That arrogant Kraut bastard thinks he's so tough, he can manage without my help."

Talley sighed with frustration. The row between Valois and Buchmann had been brewing ever since both men, veterans of the conflict in Afghanistan, had joined the unit. It was something to do with an action in Helmand Province a couple of years before that had suffered heavy casualties, but it didn't make his job any easier.

It's time they buried the hatchet. They're in the same unit, brothers in arms.

He fixed the Frenchman with a hard stare.

"That's an order, Valois. He's your comrade-in-arms. Either you help him, or you can transfer out as soon as we get home."

He grimaced. "As you wish, Lieutenant."

The Frenchman cursed beneath his breath, but he went to help out. A quote rushed into his mind, JFK's address. 'United there is little we cannot do in a host of ventures. Divided there is little we can do.' He grimaced, thinking of another incident, when Valois had waved at someone stood behind Buchmann and the German thought he was giving him a mock Nazi salute. It had taken six of them to pull them apart that time.

Maybe I should direct Valois to that inaugural address. It's time the man realizes, in Echo Six, everyone counts. No man is left behind. No one. If someone ever asks me what my job really amounts to, it's that simple. To get my men back, no exceptions.

"Let's get aboard, men, time to put some distance between us and this place."

They ran along the pontoon and boarded the luxury craft. Less than a minute later, Vince and Jerry appeared, running like crazy from the hotel. They were pursued by a screaming, shouting horde.

What the fuck is this?

"We need to get out of here," Vince gasped as he jumped aboard. "Jesus Christ, get this tub moving."

Talley unslung his MP7 again and began searching for threats.

"What is it?"

"It's those women, the wives! They're going fucking crazy, threatening us with everything under the sun. I swear to God, they're more vicious and aggressive than their husbands. I thought they were going to attack and tear us to shreds for wrecking their prized vacation. They sure are a bunch of tough old birds. I'm not staying to tangle with them."

Talley laughed and lowered his gun. "I hear you. Domenico, take her out."

The trim, fast craft sped over the calm sea. They were unopposed. No one tried to stop them, no patrol boats fired on them, nothing. Talley called up the Virginia. The sub was keeping a radio watch with the communications aerial on the top of the periscope, which was kept just clear of the water while they waited submerged.

"Virginia, this is Echo One. We've left the harbor, and

we'll be at the ten thousand meter mark in approximately twenty minutes. Acknowledge."

"This is USS Virginia, Echo One. Skipper says we're waiting for you," the radio operator replied. "Captain Dawson asked how you are managing without the RIBs."

"Tell him we borrowed a Chris Craft."

"Nice. That's the way to travel, in style."

"It sure is. She's going straight down when we leave her. We don't want to leave any navigational hazards floating around the ocean."

"Shame. They're a beautiful boat. Have a good trip, Echo One."

They transferred the shocked and cowed prisoners to the brig of the Virginia. The two men were clearly awestruck at the quiet, understated power of the huge, nuclear powered missile sub manned by quiet, professional crewmen, manning their consoles and stations. It gave the impression of power, a force that was unstoppable. Which was mostly true. When they'd been locked away, Ed Dawson glanced at Talley.

"Did you lose the boat? I don't want some enraged vacationer making a claim on the US Navy?"

"All done, Captain. She's on the way to the bottom, but only with great reluctance. She was a beautiful craft."

Dawson grunted, "Yeah, and I'll bet the owner thought the same thing. Pity." He looked around the control room. "Prepare to dive, Commander. Make your depth fifty meters. It's time to take these people home."

"Aye, Captain. Fifty meters it is. Chief, how are we looking?"

The Quartermaster and Chief of the Boat concentrated on the board in front of him. "Hatches are secure, we have a clear board. Ready to dive, Sir."

"Dive. Make your depth fifty meters."

"Fifty meters, aye."

Talley watched them go about their business. They were competent, focused, professional, and almost casual, at least to the uninitiated. It was easy to forget the complement of Tomahawk cruise missiles they carried, which could be launched from underwater and guided to a target two and a half thousand kilometers away with pinpoint accuracy. The Tomahawks generally mounted conventional warheads, but could also carry nuclear tips when required. There were also the stores of Mk 48 torpedoes, which could be launched against enemy vessels up to a range of forty kilometers. She had a speed of twenty-five knots, and maybe a little more the Navy wasn't making public. They were notoriously shy about giving away everything to do with their nuclear boats, for the attack sub was indeed an awesome machine of war, more so when the enemy were unaware of its capabilities. He glanced at Dawson, who was watching everything in his control room with a keen eye.

"How long to get us home, Captain?"

"We'll be putting in to King's Bay, Georgia. The Navy will have a Chinook standing by to transfer you back to MacDill Air Force Base. I guess you're all looking forward to some R&R, Lieutenant. The Florida sunshine takes some beating. "

Talley shook his head. "Our bosses keep us pretty busy, Captain. We'll get a few days at most, and we may have to take that in Europe if they call us back to NATO Headquarters. Maybe I should consider a transfer to submarines. I used to be Navy."

Dawson looked him up and down. He saw a man who was tall, narrow, and long-limbed, with curling, but short dark brown hair over a smooth face with intelligent, dark brown eyes that seemed to be everywhere at once; eyes that were calculating, assessing, and constantly working out the odds. His skin showed the effects of wind and weather, so he was an outdoorsman, unlike the pasty skinned submariners. Dawson guessed some people would write off Lieutenant Talley as Mister Average. Except that his build, his stance, his bearing, all hinted at an innate and barely hidden toughness, and a propensity for violence. It all added up to only one thing.

"I guess you were a Navy Seal. Coronado Base?"

"Yep, you got it."

"Why did you transfer to a NATO unit?"

Talley smiled. "It seemed like a good idea at the time."

"And was it?"

He considered that question.

Kay and the kids, back home in the US. Has my career cost me my marriage, my wife and kids Probably. It's a high price to pay. But I often think of the quote, 'all that is necessary for the triumph of evil is that good men do nothing.' Someone has to do it.

He quickly changed the subject.

"NATO has only half the resources of the US, Skipper, and a good chunk of the world to cover, so it keeps us pretty busy. I guess your long, peaceful cruises in the Virginia are more relaxing."

Dawson stared at him. "Relaxing! You can't be serious! We're a nuclear-powered attack boat, and sometimes we're ordered to carry nuclear warheads. We have to be ready at a moment's notice to respond to threats of mass destruction any point on the globe that would make nine eleven look like a minor skirmish. It's not as physical as what you guys do, but it sure isn't relaxing. And the headaches take a lot of getting used to." Then he stopped as he saw Talley's expression. "You were kidding, right?"

Talley chuckled. "I was. Besides, at least we get plenty of fresh air."

"Yeah, I forget what it tastes like after a month underwater."

Talley grimaced. "You're right. I'd sooner have people shooting at me. I'll stay where I am."

"Good plan, Lieutenant."

It's when I get back that the troubles start, Talley thought.

He watched the well-oiled machine that was a nuclear attack boat going through the complicated maneuvers of conning the ship through dangerously shallow and congested waters, as it sped toward its destination on the East Coast of the US. After a short time, he went to find his unit. They were in the galley, wolfing down chow from the impressive buffet. Maybe the air wasn't too fresh, but the food was good. Guy looked up and nodded a greeting.

"Everything okay, Boss?"

"Everything's fine." He helped himself to a plate of food. "Are those prisoners comfortable? I'd like to think we deliver them in good condition. Plenty of people will want to talk to them."

"They're okay. The imam is whining for diplomatic privilege, and that Latino is protesting his innocence; surprise, surprise. Who're you going to hand them over to? CIA, or our NATO intel guys?"

"It'll have to be CIA. MacDill is their territory, and this is their boat, so they'll have the final word. The best we can hope for is they'll let our NATO people sit in."

"I guess so. When do we return to Europe?"

"Feeling homesick, Guy?" Talley grinned.

"Yeah, I miss the cold and the rain, can't wait to get back. But seriously, we're beholden to the Americans at MacDill. I mean, no disrespect, Boss, you're an American, and they're the main force behind NATO. But I'd like some sort of independence from them."

Talley looked around the spacious, well equipped cafeteria. "I'm not sure I'd agree with you. I've never seen the Europeans have chow facilities like they do on the Virginia."

"True, the food on British subs is not in this league. Just the same, I'd like to be able to call the shots. Like the prisoners, they'll whisk them away to Guantanamo when they find there's a terrorist link, and..."

"Terrorist?" Talley stared at him. "What are you talking about? This operation was to take down a drug pipeline."

Guy grimaced. "You haven't spoken to the prisoners we brought back, have you? The Latino, he's just a creep, a thug. He was hired to run the Caicos side of the business and keep the shipments moving. It's the other one, the Iranian imam, Rashid Fard that worries me. I had a long talk with the guy, and I get the definite impression that the trafficking operation on the Caicos is more than just a few Colombians and Iranians on the make."

"What exactly do you mean, Guy? I don't get it."

"He has close links to the movers and shakers in the Iranian government. While you were in the control room, I took a look at the computer in the ship's library. I put the name Imam Rashid Fard into the browser, and I got several hits, including several images of him with Ahmadinejad. He's well connected. And I mean VERY well connected."

"You mean THE Mahmoud Ahmadinejad? The clown who runs Iran?"

"Yes, him."

"Christ, I know the Iranian government is as crooked as they come, but I can't see them behind something so overt and criminal as this drug operation."

"I asked him the same thing, and he just laughed it off. He said he would be protected, no matter what we think we have on him. He kept saying that, 'no matter what'. It was strange. He got angry at one time when I pushed him hard, and threatened him with Guantanamo, and he said Arash would look after him. When I pressed him about this Arash, he clammed up."

"What is this Arash? One of their organizations, or is it a man?"

"I don't know. He obviously shouldn't have let the name slip. He looked pretty nervous after he'd blurted it out, but it all adds up to something, and whatever it is, I think it's something pretty high level. And bad, very bad."

Talley frowned. "Like what? We need more than supposition to take back to our intel guys."

Rovere joined them at the table, smiling broadly. Talley groaned.

"Not now, Domenico, I can't take another quotation."

"Be not afraid of greatness, friends. Some are born great, some achieve greatness, and others have greatness thrust upon them."

"Shakespeare again?" they groaned.

"Who else? But I think I have an idea. What are the Iranians desperate for? Vast sums of cash, dollars and euros to prop up their economy. What better than to join up with the South Americans? They help them organize their drugs shipments, and in return, the Latinos fill the state treasury with cash, and put a dagger into the heart of our young people. Simple!"

Talley mulled it over. "It's a possibility, I grant you that, but there's something you haven't considered. The Iranians are desperate for another commodity, and it's not hard currency."

They both looked puzzled. "What would that be?" Rovere asked softly. "What could they possibly want more than the money for their regime to survive, to keep them in power?"

Talley stared at them. "Nukes."

Their eyes narrowed; the big Iranian bogeyman, nuclear weapons that would arm the Islamic Republic and enable them to destroy their enemies in a nuclear firestorm.

"Nukes are the big item on their shopping list," Talley continued.

Rovere grimaced, "God help us, the world's greatest criminals join together to obtain nuclear weapons. If it's true, they'll keep us pretty busy."

"There's one thing for sure, there has to be a terrorism angle to this," Guy pointed out. "It's Iran's number one export."

Talley mulled it over all the way back to King's Bay.

Arash, who is he, or what does it mean? Nothing good, that's certain.

He went ashore with his unit escorting the two prisoners, and found a phone to report to Admiral Brooks in Brussels. The fiery NATFOR chief was quiet for a few moments after he'd given a brief report. When he did speak, his reaction was not exactly what he'd expected.

"You haven't discussed this with anyone else,

Lieutenant?"

"No, Sir. Only within the unit, and the two prisoners, obviously."

"Good. This name, Arash, does it mean anything to you?"

"No, Sir. Have you heard it before?"

Brooks hesitated for a couple of seconds. "Don't mention that name to anyone, Talley, no one! Not even God, clear? I'll arrange for someone to debrief you when you get back to MacDill. We'll talk some more later."

"Yes, Sir, but I wondered…"

"No, don't even wonder, Talley. Not another word, between any of you. Not until you're debriefed at MacDill. That's all."

They flew to MacDill in a Chinook, and he thought about his conversation with Brooks the whole way.

What is it about the name Arash that seemed to spook him? Well, if it's important for me to know, they'll soon tell me. After all, this is a military operation, and 'need to know' is more than just a buzz phrase.

Then he put it out of his mind. Going back to the States meant he was closer to the kids, and closer to the battle that was coming with his ex-wife. He thought briefly about giving up his military career to spend time with James and Joshua, his two sons. And then he thought about what they may be facing, a rogue Iranian nation with nuclear warheads, perhaps pointed at the US.

I have to keep going, and maybe when the boys are older, they'll understand. Maybe.

He was still working it all out when they started their descent.

The moment their wheels touched down on the

concrete of the helipad, a Navy Hummer with MP markings screeched to a halt right next to them. A petty officer jumped out of the passenger seat and came across to the Chinook. He was an MP, a naval military cop.

"Lieutenant Talley?" His voice was as hard as his expression, tough, no-nonsense.

He nodded, "Yeah, that's me."

"You're to come with us, Sir. Just you."

He watched the last of his men climb out the door of the Chinook. The twin turboshafts roared as the pilot throttled up and flew the heavy craft back up into the sky. Its nose dipped as it headed due south, and it was soon lost in the heat haze. Then it dawned on him.

Fard and Rodrigo! I didn't see them leave the helo.

He looked at the cop. "Where are you taking my prisoners?"

"Prisoners, Sir? I don't know anything about that."

Talley looked around. There was only his unit standing on the tarmac. The Chinook had spirited the two prisoners away, as if they'd never existed.

CHAPTER TWO

He was seated in a windowless room, with only the hum of the air conditioning for company. The table was bolted to the floor, gray, steel-framed, and steel-topped. The three chairs were also steel, except they were not bolted to the floor. The walls were gray too, with no adornment, no posters, no signs, and no warnings. Not even 'no smoking'. There was only one way into the room, through a solid-looking gray painted door, a steel door. When he'd walked in, they closed it, and he'd heard the key turning as they locked him in. It was a room without a soul, a room designed to demonstrate to a man his impotence, his weakness, and his vulnerability to the 'system'. A room designed to leech out a man's will to resist, to protest. Whoever had designed it was an expert in interrogation techniques. How to break a man, using only a simple, locked room to demonstrate the futility of resistance to the men with power, the men who held the key to this room. He closed his eyes and tried to doze, but the forbidding place made even this simple act difficult. He opened them when he heard the key turning in the lock, and the door opened. Two men walked in. They could have come from the same mold. White shirts, button-down collars and ties, dark pants. They both sported buzz cuts, metal rim glasses, and were clean-shaven. And mean. Their cold eyes glinted behind the lenses of their glasses. They were the backroom boys, the analysts, not field operatives. CIA, Langley. They carried no briefcases, no pads or clipboards, nothing. He understood immediately; the room was bugged. It would be video monitored as well, of course.

Spare nothing in the quest to explore a man's soul.

"Thank you for waiting, Lieutenant Talley," the first man said softly. He was a little older, maybe in his late thirties. His shoulders were slightly stooped; too long behind a desk. Talley waited. Protest would be pointless. They controlled him; they were all aware of that simple reality, and the room reinforced it if he ever forgot. The man looked up and into his eyes.

"Tell us about your last mission."

"Who are you? CIA?"

The other man nodded. "The Director sent us down here straight away, as soon as we got word of the Iranian. Now, tell us about your mission."

I don't like the way this is going. They seem to assume that CIA is some part of my chain of command. They're wrong.

"What are you, counterintelligence?"

The man looked irritated. "I guess there's no reason for you not to know. Yes. Our brief is specifically the Mideast. Tell us about your mission."

"I want your names. I don't work for you. I'm with NATO."

"Either you start talking, Lieutenant, or we get up and

leave. We won't be back until tomorrow, or maybe the day after that. It'll be a long wait. We've told you everything we're authorized to tell you. Now we need to hear what went down in the Caicos. And before you ask, we've been authorized by your new boss Vice Admiral Brooks to conduct this debrief. If you want to call him, we'll facilitate that call. But only him, you talk to Brooks, no one else."

He thought for a few seconds, deciding they were on the level.

Besides, the US is part of NATO, so these guys aren't exactly the enemy.

He told them everything, and they listened without pause until he got to the part about Rashid Fard, and his impression that the imam was holding something back.

"Like what? Go on, Lieutenant, what was your impression?"

He held up his hands, palm up. "I honestly don't know. Their operation on Caicos, I guess."

"What do you know about Arash the Archer?"

"The Archer? That's the first I've heard about Arash being an Archer. What is he, some kind of a terrorist, a missile shooter maybe?"

There was no reply, and they shifted the conversation back to Fard.

I'm certain they know more about Arash than they care to tell me. The Archer? What's that all about?

"Did he have blood on his robes?"

"Fard, blood? No, he wasn't hurt, not that I could see."

Both men nodded. They didn't smile. "Uh, huh. Go on, Lieutenant."

Talley had the uncomfortable feeling there was something they weren't telling him, something big, some undercurrent that would put a different twist to what happened over there in the Turks and Caicos. Something that had the CIA worried, as well as his own people at NATO. He told them the story, right up to where his prisoners were whisked away south in the bird that had flown them from King's Bay. They made no comment, just kept nodding. Finally, he'd had enough.

"Look, why don't you guys level with me? What the hell's going down? We completed the operation as ordered. If there're any more questions, you need to talk to my people at NATO headquarters. That's in Belgium, if you didn't know. The address is Boulevard Leopold III, 1110 Brussels."

"Uh, huh." They ignored his protest completely. "Tell us about the boy."

"What boy?"

"They found a young man, about fourteen or fifteen years old, in the rubble of that compound. An Iranian kid, did you see him?"

"No."

"You sure? None of your guys roughed him up, or anything like that?"

"What the hell is this?"

One of them nodded. "Thought not."

"Tell me about this kid. What's the story?"

They looked at each other. Finally, the younger man started to explain.

"Here's the deal, Talley. They found the body of a boy. It showed evidence of repeated anal rapes, and other sexual, er, assaults. I guess that's the best way to put it."

Talley shuddered. "We saw nothing like that."

"No. It seems this kid was strangled, not killed in the

assault. They say it looked kind of like some sex game between two homosexual males. After your explosives destroyed the place, his body was pretty mangled, but a couple of guys from the Iranian Mission in Cockburn Town rushed over early in the morning to search the place. The coroner was already on scene, that's how we know about the rape, but the Iranians are screaming the Americans killed him. Apparently, this kid was well connected, or his family was, to Ahmadinejad's government. I guess you can imagine that when his parents wake up to discover their golden boy was found dead, and after a raid they presume to be American, they'll go ape. The Great Satan murders innocent Iranians again, and the shit's going to hit the fan like you wouldn't believe."

Talley shook his head. "Listen, buddy, you'd better believe it, no Echo Six operative was involved in anything like that. Jesus Christ, it's disgusting just to talk about it."

"We know you're in the clear," the older man said quickly. "In fact, we already know who assaulted and murdered the kid. We just wanted to talk to you and confirm a few details."

"So who was it?"

"It's no secret. That imam, Rashid Fard, he brought the boy with him from Iran. Maybe he offered to give him a free vacation, or some kind of religious instruction. He sure gave him some instruction, but it wasn't anything religious."

Talley was almost sick as he digested what they'd said.

"So you're going to send him back for the Turks and Caicos to prosecute him?"

Both men shook their heads and smiled. Suddenly it all came clear to him. They'd spirited him away, imposed a veil of secrecy. "You're going to turn him."

"It's a possibility," the older one replied with a smile. "What matters to you is what we've pieced together already. It's likely to become the basis of your next operation."

"Since when does CIA direct a NATO unit?" he snapped, beginning to feel serious anger with their 'we know more than you' line of questioning. But their smiles only widened. "Oh, we won't direct anything," the older agent countered. "We just pass on information. Other people make up their own minds about these things."

Yeah, right. That'll be a first.

"As it happens, it dovetails nicely with the opinion of your boss in NATO," he continued. "And yes, Lieutenant, I do know where to find Boulevard Leopold III in Brussels. I've been there more than a few times. They've asked you to head back there. They need to brief you ASAP."

"About what?"

"About an operation inside Iran. We know they're mounting a strike against the West, a hit that could upset the balance of power in the Mideast. They want you to find the guy behind it and deal with him."

So that was it. Arash. Had to be him. The Archer?

"What kind of a strike?"

"We're not sure, but the name Arash isn't new to us. They've been searching for a line on his operation for a long time, and then along comes Imam Rashid Fard. The plan is to use pretty boy to get to him."

"And if Arash is someone senior in their government? Even Ahmadinejad?"

They both shrugged. The younger man said, "If he fits the bill, he goes down, buddy. It's that simple."

Talley nodded. So he was going back to Iran, the most

brutal regime in the Mideast. The home of religious lunatics, tyranny, the executions of women hung from cranes in public squares, and despite their oil wealth, a population that was sliding into poverty and despair since the coming of the Islamic Revolution, and Mahmoud Ahmadinejad.

Is it possible he is Arash the Archer?

* * *

The flight over the Atlantic was long and boring. He'd been called back to Belgium by the next available flight. He'd got the short straw; the rest of Echo Six were allowed a few days R&R in the California sunshine. But it wasn't as an uncomfortable journey as it could have been. Shortly after takeoff, the Air France cabin attendant, a chic, twenty-something Parisienne, "my name is Nicole", offered him an upgrade to first class. Okay, she was hitting on him, but he was more than happy to go with it, and it meant he'd have something good to look at through the mind-numbing transatlantic flight. The inflight movie rated a poor second to her trim body, attired in a fitted uniform that clung to every curve, and her pretty, red-lipped smile every time she went past him was enough to get any man hot under the collar. And elsewhere. When she leaned over him to retrieve a glass from the passenger in the next seat, he smelled her perfume. Expensive, very expensive, and it seemed to blend with the natural female scent of her body, so that he realized he was getting aroused. He hastily put his book on his lap to cover up his crotch, but she was no stranger to the powerful effect she had on men.

"Is there anything troubling you, Sir?" she smoldered.

"No, Ma'am, I'm just fine."

Her eyes met his own. They were huge, dark and moist, with more than a hint of female mystery in their dark depths, and a lot of promise.

"Good," she breathed. "If there is anything I can get you, just ring the bell. I'd be more than pleased to," she hesitated for a second or two, "serve you."

He couldn't speak, just nodded his thanks. She glided away in a cloud of fragrance and musk, and he managed to settle down and relax. Eventually, he got some sleep in the comfortable first class seat. When they landed at Brussels, he felt better. As he walked to the forward exit, Nicole was waiting to see her passengers off the aircraft. Her smile widened when she saw him.

"Mr. Talley, I trust you enjoyed your flight?"

"Thank you, it sure was pleasant."

"Good. If you are at a loose end while you are in Brussels, give me a call." She pressed a small card into his hand. He looked at it, Nicole Rochat and a cellphone number.

He nodded his thanks, "Maybe I'll just do that." And he meant it. He walked down the steps and found his way into the busy terminal, forcing himself not to look back. He realized he was shaking.

Jesus!

When he'd gone through immigration and collected his case from the carousel, he spotted a soldier, wearing sergeant's chevrons and holding up a card that read, Lieutenant Talley.

"I'm Talley."

"Could I see some id, Sir?" His nametag said Williams, and his accent was British.

At least we'll understand each other. Some of the NATO personnel are not as fluent in English as they'd like to think.

"Sure." He showed his passport and NATO id.

"Thank you, Sir. Please follow me."

The guy took his case and went at a fast pace through the door. Out in the car park, he led them to a Mercedes saloon. Talley noted it was an S430, the luxurious corporate model, although the olive paintwork did little for its aesthetic appeal.

Nothing but the best for NATO personnel, except junior lieutenants don't normally warrant this kind of treatment, he reflected. The soldier put his case in the trunk and opened the rear door. Talley shook his head.

"I'll ride up front."

"You sure, Sir?"

"I'm sure. I'm no Admiral, Sergeant, and never will be."

The man smiled, and his formality relaxed a little. They purred out the car park, the powerful engine almost inaudible, and cut into the Brussels traffic to drive the short distance along the A201 to the gray office block that stood in its own grounds off the Boulevard Leopold III. As they pulled up, Talley smiled at the rows of flagpoles bearing national flags of the member countries, as if proclaiming to the world their unity.

Tell that to the French!

The Sergeant climbed out and retrieved his case. Talley went to grab it but he held on.

"I'll leave this with reception, Lieutenant. They'll have it sent on to your quarters."

"I don't have any quarters, Sergeant."

"You do now, Sir. It's all organized. Follow me, please."

He followed the man into an elevator and got completely

lost in a maze of corridors, bustling with legions of men and women, many wearing the uniforms of a dozen different nations. He'd been there before when he joined NATFOR, and several times since, but he'd never got the hang of the layout. They entered another elevator. The Sergeant used a keycard to operate it, and they descended several floors, emerging into a windowless corridor. They walked past several more offices until they came to a closed door. The Sergeant knocked.

"Come."

They walked in, and Talley stiffened to attention. The man sitting behind the desk wore the uniform of the US Navy, with the insignia of a Vice Admiral. He saluted, and the man waved his hand by way of a return. The Sergeant backed out of the room and closed the door. He stared at the Admiral. The officer was black, a well-muscled man with a trim, fit body. He had a sculpted face almost like a Roman god, with close-cropped black hair, and the overall effect was of a man accustomed to wielding a great deal of power. Right then, his demeanor was hard to decipher. The man's eyes bored into him, curious, almost intense, and his expression was flat, neutral. Talley waited, Brooks had a reputation that preceded him. He was a professional, a veteran of countless engagements, and a man who meant business.

"Sit down, Lieutenant. I guess you're wondering what gives?"

"Yes, Sir."

Brooks handed Talley a sheaf of documents.

"Those are your orders, Lieutenant, with the new chain of command. First off, I'd better explain who I am," he grinned. "My name is Vice Admiral Carl Brooks, and I've taken overall command of NATFOR." He waited while Talley absorbed the new information. "As you know, Admiral Alexander only sat in this chair while they were looking for a replacement, following the debacle with his predecessor."

Talley grimaced. *'Debacle' was a delicate way of putting it.*

Talley had been the man who'd arrested Colonel Hakim, the previous NATFOR supremo who'd sold out to a group of Islamic terrorists holding his family hostage.

"I remember, Sir."

How the hell could I ever forget that nightmare? It cost the lives of many innocent people, including some of my men.

"I'll bet you do, Son. Poor bastard, that Brit colonel, he was torn between the devil and the deep blue sea."

"He went with the devil, Admiral. He should have chosen the deep blue sea and jumped in."

"You don't have any sympathy with him?"

"He caused a lot of deaths, some of them men in my unit. No, I don't have any sympathy."

The black man nodded. "I hear you. Okay, that's history. Moving forward, that raid of yours on Caicos Island, it sure stirred up a hornets' nest."

"You mean with the Iranian connection?"

"Exactly that. I gather that CIA told you part of the story. With this Iranian imam onside, it means we can go right in and take out the man at the top, this so-called Arash. At a stroke, it'll put an end to a helluva lot of trouble they're causing us in the NATO member countries. America, of course, but Europe is feeling it too. He's already begun a systematic program of bombings and assassinations, financed with the drug money from the Caicos operation."

Talley recalled what the CIA men at MacDill told him, and felt cold. They'd hinted that Arash was high level. He could even be the President of the Islamic Republic.

Jesus Christ!

"Surely, you can't think it's Ahmadinejad? I mean, Admiral, he's the President! We're soldiers, not assassins."

"Yeah, tell that to the Iranians," Admiral Brooks muttered. He took a breath. "We don't know for sure who it is, but I don't think it's Ahmadinejad. He's just a bag of piss and wind. He says what he wants people to hear, but behind it all, he's another politician on the make, doing what's best for himself and fuck what his people really need or want. Forget him for now. This name, Arash, it's almost an honorary title, designed to appeal to Iranian sympathizers. I gather you hadn't heard it before?"

"No, Sir."

He nodded, lifted a paper off his desk, and quickly scanned it.

"Arash is a character from Persian mythology. After a long war between the Persians and their enemies, they agreed to decide the future national boundaries by means of archers, one from each side, who would fire an arrow. Wherever the arrow landed, that was the new boundary, and as you can imagine, Arash fired his arrow one hell of a long way. He became a national hero. In modern times, there was a poem about Arash the Archer. It's based on ancient Persian myth and depicts Arash's heroic sacrifice to liberate his country from foreign domination. Whichever way you look at it, the name is intended to whip up the Iranians to a heap of trouble. I guess the theory is this modern Arash will fire his symbolic arrow and enable Iran to dominate the Mideast. The problem is which country he'll aim at first."

"Israel."

Brooks nodded. "Yeah, it's possible. It's the obvious one. But whichever way you look at it, the Mideast is about to become a powder keg, and this Arash is sitting on the keg with a lighted match stuck in his ass." Talley smiled at his choice of words. "Arash is your target. I want you to uncover his identity, locate his whereabouts, and take him down. Clear?"

"Yes, Sir. How do we find out who he is?"

"Imam Rashid Fard, that's how. He'll help us. He knows the alternative."

Brooks sat back and leafed through another folder on his desk. He looked thoughtful.

"We're pretty certain the guy at the top is not a politician, so you can almost certainly forget Ahmadinejad. Quite the opposite, we think that Ahmadinejad will be one of the first casualties when their organization becomes strong enough to make a play for power. The Fard interrogation points in another direction."

"It has to be someone wealthy, and with business ties, I guess," Talley nodded. "He'd need a bundle of money just to get started in the drug trafficking business."

"Normally, I'd agree with you, except that this is Iran. Everything in that country is upside down. Who do you think controls every move the oil industry makes?"

"The military, I'd guess. No, wait. It would be the militia. The Revolutionary Guard?"

Brooks nodded. "Yep, the militia, the Army of the Guardians of the Islamic Revolution, the Revolutionary Guard. Right now, they have a hundred and twenty-five thousand troops, comprised of ground, air force, and navy. They also control the Basij militia, which has about ninety thousand troops. What many people don't know is that they've become a multibillion-dollar business empire, the third-wealthiest outfit in Iran."

Talley whistled. "So they're not just the bunch of heavily armed religious nuts people see them as."

"Not at all, Lieutenant. Their leaders, the Revolutionary Guard generals, have a very tightly defined agenda with a precise set of targets. Israel first, and when they've sewn up the Mideast, the NATO countries will be picked off one by one. "

Talley nodded. "You think this Arash could be a general?"

"Maybe, but it could just as easily be a wealthy sponsor of the Guard. We're hoping that Fard will lead us to him. Either way, the Revolutionary Guard will protect this guy with their lives, and they're not all patsies. The Supreme Leader, Ali Khamenei, has given huge powers to the Guard, and their leaders are some of the most feared and brutal men in Iran. Arash could well be a religious leader, an Ayatollah. It's a scenario we've considered."

Talley stared at him. "Admiral, this just gets worse."

Brooks smiled. "It does that, but it's the reason we put together NATFOR. No other SpecOps unit could even consider going in there to undertake this kind of job. You were a Seal, so you know we have people like DEVGRU who could do the job."

Talley nodded. The United States Naval Special Warfare Development Group was also known as DEVGRU. Their Seal Team Six had come to the notice of the public after their spectacular raid, Operation Neptune Spear, when they'd finally turned Osama bin Laden into fish food.

Talley nodded as Brooks continued.

"We can't use them for this one. We have to have the consensus of all of the NATO nations for a job like this with so many different countries involved. That's why it's in your lap."

"I see. Who else knows about the plan?"

Brooks was thoughtful for a few moments. "You mean have we consulted with our NATO partners? The answer is no. SACEUR has been kept informed, of course, but in the strictest secrecy."

The Supreme Allied Commander Europe, SACEUR, was the head of Allied Command Operations. He was responsible for the conduct of all NATO military operations.

"What about those CIA guys at MacDill? They knew we were mounting an operation."

"Well, yeah, they had to know what we were looking for, so they could extract the right information out of Fard. By the way, we're letting him go home."

"You what!"

"I know, it sounds crazy. But his ass is ours, now that we have evidence of his predilection for abusing and murdering young boys. Turns out it's nothing new to the CIA. They have quite a file on him, including photos. Once they showed it all to him, he was more than willing to help us. He'll be your contact in Tehran, and we hope he'll lead you to the man at the top."

Talley thought about that. "I find it hard to believe he doesn't know the identity of this man. Especially, as he was part of the Caicos operation."

"He says he was never told. Either it's the truth, or he's too frightened to come clean. We think it's genuine. The head honcho is very, very careful to hide his identity. Even so, we're confident that Fard knows enough to lead you to him."

Talley nodded, his mind whirling as he calculated the chances for the operation to succeed. They weren't good. He stared at Admiral Brooks.

"Sir, to be clear on this, you want Echo Six to infiltrate Iran, make contact with Imam Fard, a pervert and murderer, and he'll help us identify an unknown man at the top of a supposed terrorist organization. Then we locate him and take him out. Don't you think the Iranians will have something to say about it? They'll be after us from the moment we arrive in country."

Brooks smiled. "Putting it like that, it does seem like a tall order. But you'll be going in under deep cover."

"What kind of cover?" Talley asked suspiciously.

Brooks grinned. "You'll be with an archaeological group. They're on a research project to uncover hidden qanats close to the Garden of Niavaran, about fifteen klicks from Tehran. They're short of money, like these people always are, so we offered to help them with enough grant funding to pay for their research for an extra year. In return, they'll allow you to use their operation as a cover." He grinned. "Be sure the Iranians don't find out, those scientists would be pretty pissed."

"Admiral, what the hell is a qanat? I'm no archaeologist. You know that. None of us are."

He chuckled. "Yeah, I had to read up on it too. A qanat is an underground tunnel, designed to carry water from the mountains to the towns and cities. The Persians built them three thousand years ago. Some of them are still in use today, but many have been lost, and archaeologists believe there's a wealth of history hidden in some of the forgotten ones. Folks used them to hide valuables, documents, and so on during times of war."

Talley nodded his understanding. "So how do we join this outfit?"

"The helos will take you in at night from our base in Iraq. You'll land somewhere quiet out in the desert, and they'll meet you, or you can walk in if the helos can get you close enough."

"When do we go in?"

You have seven days to prepare, Lieutenant." Brooks looked at the file on his desk again. "Today is Friday, so you can get straight down to Ramstein in Germany and meet up with your unit. They'll arrive there early tomorrow, so they'll be ahead of you. We're flying Professor Wenstrom in too. He's the director of the dig. We'll bring him in from Iran to Ramstein for a quick visit to meet you guys. We found a pretext to get him away from the dig, something about needing to consult with experts and look at some research in Berlin University. So you'll have a chance to get acquainted before you go in. The following Friday, we'll transport you and your men to Balad Airbase in Iraq. The 160th Special Operations Aviation Regiment will be waiting for you with a couple of their modified MH-60M Black Hawks. They're the new silenced helos for launching SpecOps missions."

"We've traveled in them before, Admiral. And the Night Stalkers, you don't need to sell them to me. Those guys could snatch the devil from hell if you tasked them to do it."

"They would at that," he agreed. "They're the best in the business."

"But seven days, Admiral? It's not a lot of time. It looks patched together to me. We'll be going in on a wing and a prayer, with almost zero intel. It may not be time to locate and take out this guy. Sir, I respectfully suggest you delay the mission, at least for a few weeks until we can go in better prepared."

Admiral Brooks stared at him for a moment. Then he sighed, "Yeah, I hear you, Lieutenant, but the truth is we don't have time on our side. You see there's something else that I haven't mentioned yet. Under interrogation, Fard revealed some information that caught us unaware. You're aware of the ongoing row over the Iranian nuclear program, of course."

"It's no secret. The whole world knows they want a nuke. Always have, always will."

"That about sums it up, yeah. And they're close, real close, but close isn't good enough for some of them, and they still have a lot of ground to make up. Here's the kicker; Iran borders onto Pakistan, and they have close ties to the Pakistanis. According to our tame imam, the Revolutionary Guard has made a deal with their allies in Pakistan. They plan to divert two live nuclear weapons and transport them across the border. Once the Iranians have them, they can clone the technology. It'll be the final link they need to own their own nuclear arsenal in months, rather than years. Remember, this is not the regular Iranian military we're talking about. It's much worse, the nutjobs in the Revolutionary Guard. We're staring a nuclear holocaust in the face."

Talley shook his head in disbelief. The nightmare scenario was hard to believe. "Are you sure this Imam Fard was telling the truth? Not just giving us stuff he thought we'd want to hear, to get a 'get out of jail free' card.

"We're as certain as we can be. He knows there's no going back to the way things were. We have him on tape, his confession, the photographs of his earlier transgressions, and pictures of the kid's body on Caicos. He just wants to survive, and he's walking a very thin tightrope right now. So yeah, we're pretty certain. To put it bluntly, Lieutenant, what started as a straightforward raid to take out a bunch of drug traffickers opened a can of worms, or perhaps more accurately a nest of vipers, and one viper in particular, this guy at the top, Arash. You have to find him, and toast his ass, Talley. This craziness has to come to an end."

Brooks glanced down at the file again, but Talley could see he wasn't looking at the documents it contained.

"We can't delay for a few weeks, not even a few days. You fly to Ramstein tomorrow to meet up with your men. In one week, you travel to Iraq and infiltrate Iran. You'll have a week in the country to complete the mission."

Talley went to object again, but he held up his hand.

"You won't be on your own. CIA has an attaché in the Tehran Embassy. He's their Head of Station. His name is Miles Preston, and he'll be your primary contact when you're inside Iran. He'll help you any way he can. As soon as you have a name and a face, you take him out. The critical path is the transfer of the nukes, and it's due to take place two weeks from today. That's your deadline, there's no alternative. You have to make this work."

"What you're asking seems almost impossible, Admiral. There isn't enough time."

Brooks' eyes drilled through him. "Nevertheless, Talley, those are your orders, or are you telling me your team is not up to it? I can always get someone else. Delta Six is between missions right now."

Talley weighed up the odds.

If I turn the mission down, maybe the recently reformed Delta Six, under the command of that fiercely competitive Frenchman, Sous-Lieutenant Michel Dubois, will be sent in. No way! Echo Six is proven in a number of bloody engagements. Like the famous English general, the Duke of Wellington, my outfit has never lost a battle. This mission will be a hard and bitter fight, and we'll need every ounce of our skill and strength to win. Maybe it's stubborn pride. Maybe it's our duty. I can't say which.

"We'll do it, Sir."

"Good. In that case, let's get down to the details."

They spent the next hour going over every scrap of intel that Brooks had to show him. Both men looked up when there was a knock at the door.

"Come!"

Sergeant Williams came into the office. "Sir, you have a meeting in twenty minutes with SACEUR."

"Okay, Sarge, I'll wrap this up." He looked at Talley, "You'll stay in Brussels overnight. Sergeant Williams has accommodation arranged for you. You can take the opportunity to meet one of the archaeologists. We invited Doctor Frost over here to discuss the details of the research grant. I understand you're in the same hotel as the Doctor. It'll save time if you get acquainted now." He relaxed and smiled. "There's just one thing I need to cover. You're getting your promotion. When you return from this job, you're moving up a grade to O-4, Lieutenant Commander, that's NATO code OF-3. Between you and me, you're fast-tracked for early promotion to O-5, the rank of Commander. Congratulations, you've earned it."

Talley felt mixed emotions.

Commander Talley? It sure sounded good. Except…

"Sir, what about my unit, Echo Six?"

"All told, you'll be in responsible for eight units, including Echo Six. Delta Six too, who I believe you worked with in the past."

"So I lose my field command of Echo Six?"

"Yeah, your new rank will mean you'll be more of an administrative position. You'll be coordinating operations at times, but you won't actually be leading missions in the field. You'll be too senior."

"I see."

Brooks stared at him. "There a problem with that?"

"I'm not happy about leaving active operations, Sir."

"It happens to us all, Talley. Someone has to direct things behind the scenes."

"What if I refuse the promotion, Sir?"

The Admiral's face lost its smile. "Don't do anything stupid, Son. You'll go where you're ordered. This isn't the Boy Scouts."

"No, Sir, I realize that."

"Good. Believe me, working behind the scenes can be every bit as rewarding as being out in the field. A successful operation is just as satisfying, no matter what part you play in it."

"I understand that, Sir."

"Fine." He stood up. "Good luck. I guess you'll need it where you're going."

They shook hands, exchanged salutes, and Talley left.

Jesus Christ, they're taking my unit from me! It's not what I signed up for! How the hell can I stop it?

He waited while Williams called the hotel, speaking in fluent French, the lingua franca of Brussels. He ended the call and turned to Talley.

"It's the Brussels Marriott Hotel, Lieutenant. Rue Auguste Orts, in the center of Brussels, just ask your driver. I'll call for a pool car to take you out there. You'll need to grab your case on the way out," he reminded him.

"No Mercedes Benz this time, Sergeant?"

"I doubt it, Sir. They're using mid-range Peugeot saloons; they're a compact. Not as luxurious as the Mercedes, but it'll get you there."

"What about this Doctor Frost? How will I recognize him?"

"Good question. When I made the booking, I arranged for dinner at 2000 hours this evening. After you've gone, I'll call them back and ask them to put you at the same table. You can talk over dinner."

Talley nodded. "Sounds good to me. Except that I know nothing of archaeology, so I doubt the conversation will be exciting. What's he like, this academic?"

"I haven't met him, Sir, but I can well imagine."

"Yeah, it's going to be an interesting evening."

Williams smiled and escorted him through the labyrinth of NATO Headquarters. He retrieved his case, and Williams said goodbye. Several minutes later, he was sitting in a compact car with his knees almost up to his chin, driving through the tortuous traffic of Brussels on his way to the Marriott, and the certainty of an awkward, long and boring evening with Doctor Frost.

He took the stairs down to the lobby. He felt like he needed exercise after the transatlantic flight and the briefing with Admiral Brooks. Maybe he'd checkout the hotel gym if there was time. He smiled wryly to himself.

Time is one thing I don't have. Right now, it's more precious than gold.

He barely noticed the room even though it was opulent compared to normal officers' quarters. The furnishings were plush, Euro-chic, and a fine wrought iron balcony overlooked the central courtyard. The building itself was a fine example of solid, traditional European architecture, set in downtown Brussels, but Talley had no eyes for its undeniable charm. His thoughts were on the operation that would take him and his unit into a country with one of the harshest regimes in the world. He reminded himself of that country's harsh brutality if the worst came to the worst. Yet his fate was as nothing compared to what was at stake. If they failed, and the Iranians managed to produce nuclear weapons, it could mean the end of any safety and stability for the West. The threat posed by drug trafficking was minor, compared to the threat of an Iranian sponsored nuclear holocaust.

What was it Admiral Brooks described Ahmadinejad as? Full of piss and wind, yeah, maybe he is. But if he commands a nuclear arsenal, the fallout from his missiles will be carried by the winds to spread over a huge area as they impact the territory of Israel. Or any of his neighbors he feels like wiping off the face of the planet.

He reached the lobby and saw the restaurant in front of him. The maitre d' guarded the entrance, and he approached him.

"My name is Talley. I have a table booked with a Doctor Frost?"

The man inclined his head gravely. "Certainement, Monsieur Talley. If you would follow me, Doctor Frost has not arrived yet."

Maybe the crusty old academic won't show. Perhaps the lurid delights of Brussels were too much for him, and he's gone out to get laid in one of the city's many brothels. Maybe the academic life isn't so bad after all.

He took his seat and studied the menu. After less than a minute, he looked up as a shadow loomed over him.

"Excuse me, is this table taken?"

He caught his breath as he stared at the vision standing before him, a girl, or more accurately a young woman. Her hair was medium length, dark brown and lustrous, and styled in waves that cascaded over one side of her forehead. He noticed she had a mannerism of continually pushing it back while she waited for him to reply. Her skin was mid-cream, hinting at some exotic bloodline in her ancestry. Her eyes were wide-set, thick-lashed and dark brown, the same rich color as her hair. She didn't appear to be wearing makeup that he could see. Not that he was an expert, but her beauty was clearly a part of her, not painted on from a bottle. She had a hint of mystery about her, something dark, exotic. But the overwhelming effect was like physical jolt, and he felt a pang of regret that she wouldn't be sharing his table.

"I'm sorry, Ma'am, but yeah, it's taken. I'm waiting for a Doctor Frost."

She looked at him for a few moments, weighing him up.

"I am Doctor Frost."

Jesus Christ!

He scrambled to his feet. "I'm so sorry, Ma'am, I mean, Doctor. Please, take a seat. I'm Talley, Lieutenant Talley."

She gave him a smile that enveloped him like a warm ray of sunshine.

"Please, call me Anika, Lieutenant."

"I'm Abe. I was just trying to work out the menu. It's

all in French."

She looked at him curiously. "Would you allow me to order?"

"Sure, go ahead."

I'd allow you to anything, anything at all.

Her English accent seemed to make her more exotic, more interesting, and more desirable. She called a waiter and ordered the food and wine in what sounded to him like perfect, fluent French. They chatted, and he waited to ask her about the archaeological dig. It was all he could think of to say. He felt awkward and tongue tied, like a teenager on his first date. There was a silence for a few moments, and then they both spoke at once. He smiled. "Go ahead, you first."

She grinned back at him. "I was curious about you, Abe."

"Curious, in what way?" He took a sip from his wine.

"I've never been on a dig with a spy before. How do you get into that kind of work?"

He almost choked on his drink.

"I, er, well, I… What makes you think I'm a spy?"

She chuckled. It was a tinkling, musical sound that sent shivers through him.

"They've asked Professor Wenstrom to help a military unit stay out of sight of the authorities, so what else would it be? Or are you planning to assassinate Mahmoud Ahmadinejad?"

He laughed to hide his discomfort. "That's crazy, of course we're not planning to assassinate Ahmadinejad, or anyone else."

"That's good to know. My boss Professor Wenstrom isn't happy about it. I spoke to him on the phone before

I left London, and he's mortified that the only way to extend his research is to help the military. I doubt he'd believe you about the President. He's something of a conspiracy freak, especially about the military. If it weren't for the money, he'd have refused outright. To be honest, he dislikes anything American."

"But we're NATO, not American."

She smiled. "He doesn't see much difference. He just needs the money."

"Right. It always comes down to the money, doesn't it?"

She nodded thoughtfully. "It sure does in the archaeology business."

"We have budgets too, in the military, in NATO."

"A bit bigger than ours," she grinned.

"I guess. But look, we'll be there to gather intelligence, that's all. Not to kill President Ahmadinejad."

She nodded. "That's a shame. I've met the President on two occasions, and he's a slimy little misogynist as well as an anti-Semite, who deserves to have his ass kicked. I loathe all racists, they're a bunch of bottom-feeding parasites." She suddenly smiled, "Forget it for now, I'm ranting on. You'll be talking to Wenstrom before you go out there? I gather he's traveling to Ramstein on a NATO flight."

"That's right. Tell me about yourself, Anika, and this project you're working on. What's it all about?"

He was fascinated by her and just wanted to keep her talking, and maybe something more.

No, I can't get that lucky.

She looked surprised. "Me? What can I say? I finished my doctoral thesis two years ago. It's about the impact of ancient cultures on art during the golden era of Persia. You'd probably find it boring."

She could recite the Brussels tram timetables to me, and I'd find them interesting.

"Not at all. Tell me about this project at Niavaran."

She launched into a long and detailed explanation. "You know about the qanats."

"Not much, I've heard of them, that's all."

"Okay then, you know why they were built. In 400 BC, Prince Cyrus the Younger rebelled against his brother, King Ataxerxes. Cyrus was killed in battle, but it laid bare the weakness of the Persian Empire, which until then was considered impossible to conquer. And then Alexander invaded."

He felt confused. "You mean THE Alexander?"

"Alexander the Great, exactly. During the invasion, many of the qanats were destroyed to deny fresh water to the invaders. In addition, they were a place the population could use to store their possessions; the time honored tradition of burying your valuables when soldiers march across your land. Our dig, at least in part, is to discover these long forgotten qanats, and try to excavate some of the lost artifacts from that period."

"Sounds interesting. How far do these qanats stretch?"

"History tells us that the Caliph Mutawakkil constructed a qanat system, using Persian engineers that brought water to his residence, which was three hundred miles from the source."

"Christ, that's really something. So is there a qanat that runs from Niavaran all the way into the city of Tehran?"

"Without doubt, yes, there'll be several. Why do you ask?"

"Just interested, that's all."

The food arrived and they began to eat.

"Now it's your turn. Tell me something about yourself, Abe," she smiled.

"There's not much I can say. Most of my work is classified."

"They told me you're due for promotion, to Lieutenant Commander, is that right? But you're still a Lieutenant?"

"Yeah, something like that."

"You don't sound very enthusiastic."

He shrugged. "It's complicated."

So how accessible are the qanats? Are they a back door into Tehran? If so, it could make the task of Echo Six that much easier. I'd best be patient and get it out of her another time. I don't want her knowing everything.

He thought he'd missed something when he heard her ask him, "Where shall we go?"

"Excuse me, you mean which airport? I thought you were flying out to Iran tomorrow."

"Yes, I am," she smiled, "but I meant tonight. I thought maybe we could go somewhere, a nightclub, something like that. How about it? The city is alive right now. It seems a shame to just turn into bed."

It all depends who you turn into bed with, he thought, but he kept his face neutral.

"I'd like that, yeah, a club would be fine."

"Somewhere with a floor show," she said happily. "I'll ask at the desk. They're bound to know."

They trawled the Brussels nightspots, and he spent half a month's pay having the night of his life with this beautiful, effervescent girl. He even told her, to peals of laughter, how he'd envisioned a dusty academic, creeping off to find some back street brothel to satisfy his frustrated lusts. Eventually, they made it back to the Marriott and stood awkwardly by the elevator as the attendant waited for them to make a decision.

"Which floor are you, Anika?"

"I'm on the sixth. You?"

"I'm on four. I just…"

She made the decision for him. "Take us both to the fourth floor, please." She turned to him, "Okay with you?"

He didn't trust himself to speak. Instead, he just nodded.

CHAPTER THREE

He awoke early the next morning. She was gone, and only her lingering fragrance remained on the pillow. Anika had explained she would be taking the early flight to Tehran. He smiled to himself, thinking of the night before, and the lust they'd shared.

Maybe the prospect of going to Iran made it so good; you never know whether you'll get out of that flea-infested sandpit, so you take what you can when it's on offer. Whatever the reason, it's an experience I'll be a long time forgetting.

He checked his wristwatch, it was 0600 hours, time for a shower and then grab something from the buffet as he went past. The car was due at 0630 hours to carry him back to the airport, in time to board an Air Force C130 headed for Ramstein. They drove through the gray, misty streets of the Belgian capital. The people of the night had already left. He saw a pair of teenage prostitutes making their tired way home, walking unevenly after yet another busy night. Even from inside the car, he could feel their despair at the relentless treadmill they walked every night, a slow descent into a pit of drug fueled decline and early death. The only other people on the sidewalks that early were the street cleaners, busy preparing Brussels for another day. By day, it was the center of both NATO and the European Union. The city was a busy hub for both military and government. By night, it was time for the bureaucrats and armchair soldiers to come out to play in the many lurid clubs, bars, and brothels. And so the cycle went on, it was a depressing sight.

He brightened as they reached the airport and drove straight out to the cargo area where the C130 was on the tarmac, loading the last of its cargo for Ramstein. He breathed in the stink of kerosene, jet fuel, as he looked around the bleak tarmac. It was familiar, comforting, almost home.

It makes me think of the kids, James and Joshua, and THAT letter. When this is over, I'll get back to the States and talk it through. I have to make Kay understand they're my kids too. Still, there's nothing I can do now, not here.

He found the crew chief, showed his papers, and went aboard. Twenty minutes later, the aircraft lifted off, and he relaxed, as much as possible on the canvas jump seat; looking forward to linking up with his unit. They bumped down onto the tarmac in Germany, and Talley walked down the rear ramp. His second-in-command, Guy Welland, was waiting for him beside a Humvee with no unit insignia. The SAS Sergeant greeted him with a handshake.

"How was Brussels, Boss?"

"Great, really good," he replied, realizing he'd spoken with too much enthusiasm. The image of Anika had flashed through his mind when he heard the word Brussels, almost enough to give him an erection.

"That good? It must have changed since I was last there. I found it a depressing place. Too many bureaucrats," he paused, "and they speak French."

"Yeah, that's about it. Is everyone here?"

"Yep, but they're pretty upset at having their leave cut short. What's so important? You look like you have something on your mind."

For starters, the bastards want to replace me as leader of Echo Six and dump me behind a desk. There's a crazy mission someone thought up, which could end with us having to whack Ahmadinejad. And a vicious ex-wife back home who's trying to take my kids. Apart from that, everything's fine.

He shook his head. "I'm fine."

They drove past lines of aircraft lined up on the ramp, and he forced himself to calm down and explain the operation to Guy. Fighters, F/A 18s, cargo aircraft, C130s and the bigger C17 Globemasters, four engine turbojets, were lined up; ready to fly out wherever they were needed. Parked next to the helipad, he caught sight of a flight of Little Birds on the tarmac. Armed with twin electric Gatlings, .50 caliber GAU19s, they were a formidable machine, often used to carry Special Forces into battle, and to support them with lethal curtains of heavy gunfire during the action. He recalled the times he'd gone into battle, clinging to the side of one of the tiny helos.

Soon, it may be all I have left, my recollections.

As Guy drove them to their quarters, he told him about the link from the last mission that had led all the way to Iran, and the nukes. The Brit's face went pale.

"I thought it looked pretty bad at the time. Iran! Jesus, if that bunch of crazies gets a shortcut to a nuclear weapon, it'll be a disaster."

"It's even worse, Guy. It's not the regular military who're doing this. It's the Revolutionary Guard."

He raised his eyes. "God save us all. The asylum goes to war."

They reached the building assigned to Echo Six, and Talley greeted the squad, twenty troopers, and all skilled specialists. There was no time for celebratory drinks, no let-up, no time off. They went straight to work and spent the remaining part of the Saturday and all of Sunday checking out equipment and running through scenarios in the Kill House. The rambling basement underneath Ramstein Air Base had once been a nuclear bunker. Now it was used for more everyday purposes, and was known as the Kill House. Simply put, it was where the men practiced the craft of killing. He sat on a chair in a dark basement room and watched the team burst in and start shooting at dummies ranged around him. Some were in the guise of terrorists. Some were civilians, some of them children. And there was him. He closed his eyes as the flash grenade sent white light searing around him, and listened to the sound of suppressed weapons as the men swept through, shooting down the targets and sparing the hostages. Except that Sergeant Reynolds, the black ex-Delta trooper miscalculated and shot an unarmed civilian. It was a deliberate misdirection. A guy in Arab dress similar to the terrorists, but he carried no weapon, hence he rated as a civilian. The debrief was not pleasant.

"I'm real sorry, Boss," Reynolds apologized to him. The rest of the men knew what was coming next. The expressions of anger on their faces were eloquent.

"You know the way it works, Roy. One mistake and

ERIC MEYER

we do it all again. Except that the second time, we fill the room with smoke and do the exercise wearing respirators, which should make it more interesting."

"Aw, shit, Boss," Roy groaned. "We've been working flat out. We need a break before we go in."

"That's a pity. You won't get one tonight either. The Germans have sent us an archaeology expert to help us understand some of what's going on at that dig. It could be useful to us, so I want you all present. At 0600 hours tomorrow we're back here, and we'll run through that exercise again and again until we get it right."

There was utter silence. They knew it had to be done. In five days time they'd be going into an alien country; one where every hand would be turned against them. Where the penalty for failure was unspeakable cruelty and a very hard, agonizing death.

"Any questions?"

There was complete silence. Finally, Talley nodded.

"Good. Let's get some chow."

When should I tell them the rest of it, that I'm being replaced? No one likes change, especially in a tight knit unit like this one. Is there a way around it? That's something I need to think about, how far can I push my bosses before I piss them off so bad I wind up guarding an airfield in Nowheresville, deepest darkest Africa.

The archaeology expert was as boring as any of them expected. Quite why anyone would want to know about the way a baked clay brick was laid next to another baked clay brick was beyond any of them. The only light relief was the part about the qanats.

"Are you telling us that you could cross large parts of Iran underground, through these qanats?" Rovere asked him.

The academic, Herr Doktor Walther Messerschmitt nodded enthusiastically, pleased that Domenico had asked a question. "In the dry season, yes. During the rains, of course, they are flooded, but for much of the year they carry a trickle of water. Yes, theoretically, it should be possible. But why would anyone wish to travel that way? Only a fool would do that. It would not be wise."

"The fool doth think he is wise, but the wise man knows himself to be a fool," the Italian said gravely. The German stared at him in confusion.

"I'm sorry, I…"

"Shakespeare," Rovere explained. "A man who knew himself to be a fool, and was wise enough to know the difference."

He stared at the Italian, his face creased in puzzlement. Clearly, humor was not a part of his repertoire. Finally, he cleared his throat.

"What is most interesting is the cumulative effect of changes during the Achaemenid period, 550-330 BC, sometimes known as the First Persian Empire. Founded in the 6th century BC by Cyrus the Great, who of course overthrew the Median confederation. This was a time when…"

Talley went to sleep. Someone kicked him when the lecture has ended, and he flexed his legs and got to his feet. Domenico Rovere stood in front of him, grinning.

"Is it over?"

"He went away a few minutes ago. Shame on you, Abe. You should have set an example."

Talley shook his head. "I'd sooner have root canal treatment than listen to any more of that. I'm off to bed. We've an early start in the morning."

He lay awake for hours, thinking about the dark mysteries of those qanats.

Movement inside Iran will be difficult at best. It's just possible that the irrigation tunnels will come in more than useful.

He had a strange dream. He was trapped in a dark passage, and he could hardly breathe the stale, suffocating air. There was water at his feet, a few inches, and he was heading toward someone calling to him for help. He recognized the panic-stricken voice, Anika Frost.

"Where are you? I'm coming to find you. Tell me where you are!"

"The water level, Abe. It's rising. Help me!"

"Water level? Fuck the water level, where are you?"

"At the end of the passage. But the water, it's too late. You won't make it. Save yourself."

"No, I'm coming, I'll get you out. I'm nearly…"

He looked behind him. The wall of water was hurtling toward him, thousands of gallons of cold, clear water, so desperately needed in the parched deserts of Persia to sustain life. But this water brought only death, a relentless torrent that hammered toward him. He reached her. She was lying injured on the floor of the tunnel. Her clothes were torn, her face bruised and bloody, but still her beauty shone through like a star in the night sky. He had to save her, had to.

"Anika, can you walk?"

"No, I'm sorry. My leg, it's broken."

He bent down and pulled up her pants leg to inspect the broken bone. "I'll help you out. If you stay down here, you'll die."

"But Abe…"

Something in her voice made him look up. Her face

was serene, but the color had disappeared. The skin was alabaster in color, as if she'd been underwater for some time.

"What is it, what's happened?"

"The children, they were trapped. I came to save them."

"The kids? Joshua and James, where are they? Show me where they are, for Christ's sake. I'll go find them."

"It's too late, they've gone. You shouldn't be here. You're not a soldier, Abe. You work in an office."

"But, the kids!" he shouted. "You have to take me to them."

"You're too late. They're already dead. We're all dead."

Her eyes became deep, black pits, and her flesh began to decay in front of him and peel away in long strips of gray skin. Then the wall of water hit. That sound, what was it? Was this the afterlife, a peal of bells, music?

And then he opened his eyes, someone was banging on the door, and both his cellphone and the bedside phone were ringing. He shook his head to clear it. Somebody wanted him in a hurry. He left the phones ringing and went to the door.

"Boss, are you okay?"

He checked his wristwatch. 0420. "I would be if I could get some sleep, Domenico."

"You were shouting. I thought you were with someone at first."

"Just dreaming. What's happened?"

"We're needed. The Germans have a hostage situation, and they want us to handle it."

"Tell 'em to call Grenzschutzgruppe 9. It's their gig, hostage rescue. There's no call for NATO to become involved in a domestic situation."

"It was GSG9 who called us, Boss. They can't handle this one."

Talley looked at his wristwatch again, and at his bed, still warm and inviting. With a sigh, he pulled on his pants and shirt, laced on his boots and followed Domenico out of the room and along to the temporary briefing room they'd been given while they were at Ramstein. Half a dozen of the men were already there, and others were trickling in. A hard faced German cop; immaculately uniformed and clutching a briefcase, stood in the center of the room, staring with contempt at Talley's bleary-eyed disarray.

Well, fuck him, Talley thought. *He was probably on night duty, not dragged from his bed at some ungodly hour.*

"Lieutenant Talley?"

He nodded. "Yeah, that's me."

The man nodded. "I am Hauptmann Werner Baumann, GSG9. I apologize for asking you to help us out, but we have a serious problem."

The German's face was pale, almost square, rock hard, with small, watery blue eyes under thick, pale blonde eyelashes. His buzz cut hair was also pale blonde, so he was almost a caricature of the German model of Aryan perfection from the days of the Third Reich. Broad shouldered, and his uniform perfectly cut over an athletic body, this was clearly a guy who looked after himself. As he should, the reputation of GSG9 was legendary. Talley shook his hand.

"How can I help you, Captain?"

The German paused for a few moments, almost as if he was embarrassed.

"We have a serious problem. One that may be more than we can handle, Lieutenant."

For God's sake, spit it out! What did you drag me out of a warm bed for?

Someone passed Talley a mug of strong coffee, and he sipped it as he looked at the German. He started to feel better as the caffeine entered his bloodstream.

"I thought GSG9 was capable of anything. That's your reputation, anyway. Has something changed?"

Baumann reddened.

Yeah, he sure is pretty embarrassed about something. It has to be serious. He waited for him to continue.

"It's in Saarbrucken. It's er, a…"

Some politician caught with his dick out in a brothel?

They were all staring at the German, willing him to explain himself.

"It's a synagogue," he began at last. "A group of Palestinian terrorists took it over. They went in late last night. A group of worshippers were about to leave. They took them hostage, and have threatened to kill them if we don't release the leader of their terror cell, a man we arrested last month."

"I still don't get it, Captain. It's a standard hostage rescue mission; exactly what your outfit was set up for back in 1972. That Black September business at the Munich Olympics, wasn't it?"

"That is correct, yes. A unit of our Bundespolizei attempted to rescue the Israeli hostages and failed. They all died."

"Yeah, that was tough, but you're better trained and equipped for that kind of thing now. What's the problem?"

"They're Jews."

"Who?"

"The hostages, in the synagogue. They're all Jews."

Talley had to work hard not to smile.

For Christ's sake! Who would you expect to find in a synagogue, Buddhists?

"Well, yeah, of course they're Jews."

"That business in 1972, they were Jews back then, as you know. My men are afraid of a repeat. We Germans have an unfortunate history with our Jews."

Unfortunate! That sure is one way of referring to mass murder during the Second World War. Like calling the Wall Street Crash a bank overdraft.

"The Second World War was a long time ago."

"Yes, so was the Munich Olympic fiasco. My men are, shall we say, reluctant to undertake this mission. Even if I order them in, I fear they may not give of their best. If any of those Jews die during a rescue attempt, it would be a disaster."

"It sure would be for them, Captain," Guy snapped out.

Talley realized that Welland was staring at the German, his face a mask of hatred.

"What is it, Guy?"

"Why does he call them Jews? If they weren't Jews, would he call them Christians, Catholics, Protestants, or atheists, whatever? They'd just be fucking people. These bastards never learn, do they?"

There was a tense silence in the room as they digested what he'd said. Captain Baumann reddened even more, if that were possible.

"If I have offended you, I apologize, Sir."

Guy didn't reply. Talley made a note to speak to him later. It had never occurred to him that any of his men were religious. There was no reason to ask, and he sure didn't give a damn one way or the other. He guessed that if a man was of Jewish descent, and a lot of Brits were descended from German Jews who'd fled to England during the Nazi terror, any life or death problem that linked Germans and Jews could be pretty emotive. Talley switched his attention back to Baumann.

"Okay, Captain, let's cut to the chase. Saarbrucken is what, fifty klicks from here?"

"Sixty kilometers, I would think."

"Okay. These Palestinians are holding a group of people hostage in a synagogue, and you want us to go in and get them out. Forget the politics, does that about sum it up?"

Baumann looked relieved. "It does, yes."

"Do you have maps, diagrams, a building layout?"

"I have everything with me." He gestured to his briefcase.

"Okay then." He turned to Welland. "Guy, get the men ready. We'll leave in twenty minutes, prepare for close quarter battle. Domenico, arrange transport to take us to Saarbrucken. Find who's in command of those Little Birds on the pad. We could use at least one for an overhead assault. I'll go in with the helo. Guy, I want you to lead the rest of the team in on the ground assault."

Even as he was giving orders, his mind was ranging through the options for a successful assault and hostage rescue; they were always tricky. There never was an easy one. And for the hostages, they had no body armor, no training, and no weapons to protect them. They were at the mercy of their kidnappers, and the Palestinians had a record of shooting their hostages when a rescue mission went south. Mercy and compassion was not a part of their make up. Guy and Domenico had disappeared to make preparations for battle. He turned back to Baumann.

"Right, Captain, turn out your briefcase. Show me what you have."

They traveled the sixty clicks to Saarbrucken in a Chinook. A Little Bird flew alongside them, and they would transfer when they were close to the target. The MD MH6 Little Birds were fitted to carry four SpecOps operatives on seats fitted two to each side. Talley carried his MP7, the lightweight Heckler and Koch submachine gun. Domenico was to go in with him on the Little Bird, and Roy Reynolds and Virgil Kane would occupy the other two seats. Guy Welland would lead the ground assault, and from an early read of the documents Hauptmann Werner Baumann had given to him, Talley believed it would be possible to get the hostages out; hopefully alive. They landed in a school playing field a kilometer from the synagogue and used the school hall as a temporary operations room to prepare the assault.

"Domenico, we'll go in loud and hard with the Little Bird. I want those guys to be looking up when Guy goes in on the ground with his squad. Buchmann, you're our demolitions specialist. I want you to blast through the outer wall, and make a breach the rest of the unit can enter through."

He stopped and looked around the school hall. What had been empty space, with wooden gymnasium equipment festooned around the walls and a headmaster's lectern on the stage at one end, was transformed into the chaos of men and women running to set up the necessary equipment for the forthcoming operation. On one side, a group of disconsolate men, wearing uniform were stood talking quietly, and smoking. He guessed they were the GSG9 Operatives.

Too bad, they should have taken the mission, and to hell with the politics. The Germans are still sore about the Second World War, and rightly so, but there are lives at stake here.

He turned back to the men and continued.

"We'll be firing tear gas and smoke, so we'll need respirators, and…"

The German, Buchmann, had a sour look on his face.

"What is it, Heinrich? Is there a problem?"

"You want me to blast through the wall. This is a synagogue, Lieutenant. These Jews, if I destroy a sacred part of their building, they'll…"

"Jesus Christ, not you! Buchmann, you'll do it. I don't have time to argue."

"You want to blow up the Jews' synagogue, get that damned Frenchman to do it. He doesn't have a conscience to worry him."

"Stop! Right there! It's your job, and Valois has his own duties. Heinrich, these are people, period. A building can be rebuilt, no matter how holy, sacred, or anything else. I don't give a damn if it's the roof of the Sistine Chapel; it's still the same principle. People come first. Clear?"

He nodded reluctantly. "Very well, I will do as you order."

"You'd better. If you blow a hole through some sacred Jewish shrine, they'll be pissed. But if you stand by and do nothing, and allow the terrorists to kill innocent people in that synagogue, we're likely to find the Mossad mounting an operation to destroy the Reichstag."

Domenico looked at him sharply. "I wouldn't go there, Abe. It happened before."

"The Reichstag fire in 1933? I couldn't give a goddam. This is now and that was then. Let's get the job done and get those people out. So, plenty of smoke, and make sure you use the red dot sights, and be careful about who you shoot. Any questions? We need to start moving before those terrorists up the ante. Guy, are you set to go?"

"All ready, Boss. The local cops have laid on a couple of trucks to carry us and our equipment to the target. I'd suggest we leave now, and we'll call you when we're in place."

"Good. We'll be ready to come in like a bat out of hell."

Guy led the men out. They loaded their gear, boarded the trucks, and drove away to the synagogue. They'd infiltrate the grounds of the synagogue in silence and lay their charges ready to go in. When Talley's group of four men landed on the roof in a clatter of engine noise, rotor blades, and shouted orders, Heinrich Buchmann would detonate his charges. Immediately, Guy Welland, who was designated Echo Two, would lead his squad inside the building in thick, choking smoke and tear gas and take out the hostiles. The stakes were high. Thirty-three Jewish worshippers held prisoner, and a lethally dangerous group of terrorists that had to be stopped from committing an act of mass murder. He led Domenico, Roy and Virgil over to the Little Bird. The pilot, a Marine Captain with a Louisiana accent nodded a greeting.

"How long before we get the go, Lieutenant?"

"Any minute now, you all set?"

"Just about. You want me to spool her up?"

"Yes. Captain, I don't want to land on the wrong roof. I asked our guys to use a laser target designator to light up the target. Is that okay?"

"That suits me. I don't want to put you guys down to start shooting up the local convent school. Yeah, we can read your laser designator, no problem."

"Good. Stand by to leave. When we get the call, we go in like a bolt of lightning. I want us to dazzle those guys with everything we have. They have to look up at the roof while my ground assault team goes in."

"You want me to use the high-intensity search light slung under the fuselage? That'll get their attention."

"We'll be using Night Vision gear, so it would blind us. But thanks anyway."

"No problem."

He heard a murmured voice in his earpiece and held up a hand for the pilot to wait.

"This is One, go ahead, Echo Two."

"We're in position. Buchmann has set his charges in what he believes is a good entry point. Laser target designator is on."

"You got any audio or video from inside?"

"That's a negative. The walls are very old, a couple of feet thick, I'd guess. It would take too long to bore a hole for a probe. The local cops have infrared cameras and as far as we can tell, we've isolated the part of the building we need to hit. But once we're in there, we'll have to wing it."

"I hear you, Echo Two. We're leaving now. As soon as we drop onto that roof, start your attack. Good luck."

"And you, Echo One. Two out."

The pilot had got the message. The engine roared as it built up power, and the rotors spun in a dizzying arc.

"Let's mount up."

Talley fixed his respirator in position and sat on the seat fixed to the side of the MH6. It was a short journey of one klick to the synagogue, and even before the helo lifted off the ground, they were making their final preparations for the assault.

"Radio check, do you read?"

A chorus of 'five by fives' came back to him. He looked down, and he could see the synagogue already looming, lit up by the flashing police lights surrounding it. He'd ordered them to keep their searchlights switched off. The pilot's voice came into his earpiece.

"We're thirty seconds out, Lieutenant."

"Copy that. Switch to NV."

He saw the whole world turn green, with pinpoints of light where the cars and roof lights of the local cars on the scene tried to burn through the sensitive optics. He could see cops all around the perimeter, but there was no sign of Guy's group, which was as it should be. If he could see them, other people could see them too."

"Ten seconds."

"We're ready."

The helo dropped like a stone, and Talley experienced the familiar feeling as his stomach tried to push up into his chest. Then they were over the roof, and he looked down. It was less than a meter below them.

"Bravo Two, blow it in five seconds! Let's go!"

He jumped down onto the flat concrete rooftop and saw the other three operatives land close to him. He shot out a glass skylight and armed a tear gas grenade, lobbing it through the hole. Around the rooftop, the other men did the same. Four tear gas grenades exploded, and clouds of the gas began to permeate the building. Each man then hooked a rope to the nearest smashed skylight framework, looped it around, clipping the end to a karabiner.

"Smoke grenades!"

They threw the missiles, and even before they'd detonated, the four operators were making their rapid descent down the ropes, and then the smoke grenades exploded. Talley's feet touched the floor. He looked around and saw they were in an attic storeroom. A flight of steps led down to the second floor of the synagogue, and he sped over to them. Along the corridor, the smoke was drifting in clouds.

Up the staircase from the first floor, he could hear a man screaming, "Don't come any nearer. We'll kill them all. These Jews will die! This is your last chance. Get out of the building, or we kill them. We are…"

The explosion overrode his shouting as Heinrich Buchmann's charge detonated and blew out a section of the synagogue wall.

"Go now," Talley shouted to the men. "Hit them before they recover!"

One of Guy's squad tossed in a stun grenade. They heard the shout 'fire in the hole' and covered their ears, but the shock was still enough to slam into them, temporarily disorienting them. Talley shook his head to clear it. He was already halfway down the stairs, and the scene that greeted him was like one of those gruesome medieval paintings, a depiction of hell; terrified people milling everywhere. Some lay on the floor, men and women screaming, tendrils of smoke and tear gas floating around the room. He focused on the action, which now seemed to occur in slow motion. They'd trained hard and relentlessly for this moment. The snarling shouts of the terrorists, and the automatic scan for who was a threat, who carried a weapon or a bomb and who did not. He saw the red dots lighting up the targets and heard the 'phut, phut' as the silenced rounds slammed into their targets. A hostile recovered and aimed his assault rifle, a German G3.

The German armament manufacturer Heckler & Koch developed the 7.62mm battle rifle in the 1950s. An accurate and powerful weapon, it could be fired in full-auto mode, and the shooter managed to loose off half of the 20 round magazine. Thankfully, the man's eyes were smarting from the smoke, and his brain confused from the effects of the stun grenades. His shots went wild, tearing chunks of plaster from the decorated ceiling. Domenico hit him with a short burst from his MP7, and the man skittered to the floor. A group of hostiles gathered themselves for a concerted fightback on the NATO unit. In the center of them, Talley saw a man arm a grenade. He shouted a warning.

"That group of hostiles by the Ark, one of them has a grenade!"

The Ark, the holy chest, occupied a key place in any synagogue. The valuable artifact was placed in a niche, opposite the temple's door. The synagogue always pointed to Jerusalem, and the Ark stored the Holy Torah, a worthwhile terrorist target.

A half-dozen guns switched aim, and the red dots cut through the haze, targeting the hostiles. The man with the grenade went down, shot through with enough rounds to take down an elephant. The other hostiles were milling in confusion when his grenade went off, tearing the entire group into a bloody ruin. It was almost ended.

"The Torah! We must save the holy books!"

Talley looked around to where the voice was coming from. An elderly man with long black hair and beard, wearing a prayer shawl, was running toward the destroyed part of the synagogue. Flames and smoke were licking out of the wooden structure.

"Save them, we must hurry."

Another man got to his feet and ran to help. Out of the darkness at the other end of the synagogue, a figure materialized and ran toward the people who were getting to their feet, believing the trouble to be over. It wasn't over. He carried a weapon. Talley recognized the folding stock AK-47S, the Russian built rifle intended for paratroopers and Special Forces, and beloved of terrorists around the world. He wanted to open fire, but the worshippers blocked him, shielding the man whose rifle was positioned ready to sweep the building and riddle the hostages with bullets. His mouth was half open, and his lips pulled back in a snarl. His teeth showed white against his olive, Arab face, and he screamed a word alien to this holy place.

"Allah A…"

A red dot had appeared on his forehead, and then the dot blossomed into a gaping wound as a pair of 7.62mm sniper rounds smashed into him, hitting him in almost exactly the same place. He was tossed backwards, as if a truck had hit him. Talley searched for the man who'd fired. It could only be one of the snipers, Jerry or Vince. It had been a dangerous, almost impossible shot and easy to hit one of the hostages by mistake, unless you were a world-class shooter. A sniper whose skills had been honed in hundreds of training sessions, thousands of marksman hours spent on the range, and scores of live operations. Both the Echo Six snipers were such men. He saw Vince get to his feet and lower his rifle, the Accuracy International Arctic Warfare Magnum. It was loaded with .338 Lapua Magnum rounds, capable of pinpoint accuracy to a range of almost a mile. Inside the building, range was not a consideration, and Vince had taken the shot at a target less than an inch from the nearest hostage. Talley pulled off his mask and sighed with relief. The worst of the smoke had cleared. The civilians were coughing and red faced with the effects of smoke and gas, but they were alive.

"Nice shooting, Vince. We were worried about the civilians. How'd you do it?"

"See that woman there, the elderly lady?"

Talley looked over at the group of civilians.

"Yeah, I got her."

"She'd put out her arm against the younger woman next to her. I shot underneath her elbow. It was the only window open to me."

"Yeah, what if she'd moved? At the last second, I mean."

Vince looked at him steadily. "But she didn't move."

Talley nodded. Some things were best left unsaid. "No, she didn't."

The rest of his Echo Six troopers were roaming around the synagogue, making sure of the hostiles.

"They're all dead," Rovere said, coming up to him.

Talley nodded. "I hear you. Good work."

Both men looked around as the guy with the black hair and beard ran toward them, shouting.

""It is destroyed, our Ark, it was blown to pieces by that grenade. This is terrible, a catastrophe."

Another man, younger, was trying to pull him back. "Joshua, no! We are alive. It is all that matters. These people have saved us."

They reached Talley. The older man had stopped

shouting, and now he was weeping, his shoulders hunched over and shaking with emotion. The younger man nodded a greeting.

"We are deeply indebted to you and your men. Take no notice of Joshua. He is our Rabbi, and to him, matters of religion are more important than people."

"But they are, Israel, do you not understand?" the Rabbi shouted. "They have stolen our heritage, which is priceless."

"They did not steal our lives, Joshua. We can rebuild everything. We cannot bring back the dead. And you have not yet thanked these men who risked their lives to save ours."

The Rabbi nodded. "You are correct. We will rebuild everything." He turned to Talley. "Sir, you have my thanks. I apologize. I was just upset. I was very young the first time that happened to me, and it brought back memories. It was a long time ago."

"There's no need to apologize. You were in a camp?"

He nodded. "Auschwitz."

It was almost as if the temperature of the room had dropped by several degrees. The mere mention of the name in a synagogue, a German synagogue, was enough to sober men's minds. There was little more to be said. Rovere looked grave.

"It's about time these people gave up and left you alone. No sooner do you rid yourselves of the Nazis than along come the Muslims."

"At least the Muslims are hard at work killing each other," Guy remarked, as he joined them. "It takes their minds off killing Jews, for some of the time at least."

Israel looked at him strangely. "You are Jewish, my

friend?"

"I'm not anything, not anymore. But my family is Jewish, some of them. What difference does it make?"

"Refugees from Nazi Germany?"

"Yes, I suppose they were."

"Then I trust they have found what they were looking for. You are English, are you not?"

"That's right." He looked around the devastation, the damage, the bodies on the ground, and the smoke still hanging in the air. "How can any of you as Jews find peace as long as these vermin keep trying to kill you?"

"It is a long fight." Joshua had begun to recover his composure, and his voice sounded calmer, more measured. "They have been trying for thousands of years to kill us. But we are still here, and will always be here. We are God's chosen people, and we will prevail, even if it takes ten thousand years."

Guy went to reply, but Talley interrupted. "In ten thousand years, Rabbi, everyone here will be long forgotten. Best take care of the living, and worry about the rest later. Be thankful for what you have."

The Jew wearily inclined his head. "Perhaps you are right. Again, you have my thanks."

He plodded back to the Ark where German police were trying to put out the last of the flames. Talley called Echo Six to be ready to move out. Their job there was finished. It was time to get back to Ramstein and continue preparing for the real work of stopping the Islamic lunatics from acquiring a weapon that could turn the whole of the Middle East, if not the world, into a glowing, radioactive fireball. The men assembled outside in the fresh air.

"Lieutenant!"

He looked around. Hauptmann Werner Baumann was running up to him.

"Yeah?"

"You did a good job, my friend. A wonderful job."

"Thanks. Maybe you could keep an eye on these Islamic troublemakers. Make sure none of the scum try something like it again."

"We do our best, but our resources are limited."

"They weren't limited when the Nazis were killing them. There's not that many left, so maybe it's time you started working to keep them alive."

The Captain's jaw dropped. He started to bluster, but Talley stopped him. "And next time, if there is a next time, maybe you should do the job you're paid to do and fuck the politics. Goodbye, Captain."

They walked out to the waiting Chinook and climbed aboard. Only as the engines started, and the rotors began whirling, did Rovere chuckle.

"You told that German where to get off. Shakespeare said, 'For when the noble Caesar saw him stab, ingratitude, more strong than traitors' arms, quite vanquished him, then burst his mighty heart.' It'll give that pompous German something to think about."

"Rovere?"

"Yes, Lieutenant?"

"Shut the fuck up."

"Yes, Lieutenant."

They rode in silence until Guy spoke to him. "That Rabbi back there. It's attitudes like his that get people killed. It wasn't until the Israeli Jews started fighting back that people began to think twice about kicking them around."

"It is difficult for us Germans," Buchmann interjected. "We have a tarnished history that is not easy to live down. Those GSG9 guys, I can understand their reluctance. If anything goes wrong, there's an international outcry, like after the Munich Olympics."

Talley called for their attention. "Men, I'll say this, and I'll say it once. Religion has no part to play in the job we have to do. We fight for NATO, for the democracies of the US, UK, Europe, against anyone who tries to attack them. It means we'll encounter two types of humankind in the field. People, who deserve to live their lives in peace and security, and terrorists, murderous scum who prey on their own people. People we leave alone and protect when necessary, and the scum, we put down like rabid dogs. Religion has no part of it. There's only good or bad, and that GSG9 Captain was wrong. We do our job regardless of religion. Period."

There were several raised eyebrows, but they sensibly left it at that. When they put down at Ramstein, they began to walk down the rear ramp of the Chinook. A civilian was standing nearby, watching them. Abruptly, he stomped up to Talley.

"What's this crap about Jews? You were supposed to be here to meet me a couple of hours ago. I've been sitting on my ass here while you go charging off on some idiot rescue mission, like a bunch of boy scouts! It's a stupid waste of my time. I'm inclined to cancel the arrangement."

The men stood staring at the stranger. He was a tall man, even taller than Talley, dressed in cord pants tucked into cowboy boots and a battered but expensive and still stylish bush jacket. His hair was long and wavy, dark with streaks of blonde that looked very contrived. Most women would undeniably find his face attractive, clean-shaven, tanned, and perfectly proportioned. A good-looking guy, and he knew it, reveled in it. Talley disliked him on sight, apart from his racist rant, which he chose to ignore. This was clearly Professor Wenstrom, their passport into Iran. He couldn't be anyone else. Talley opened his mouth to greet him, but Guy pushed him aside in his eagerness to reach the academic. He was shorter than Wenstrom, but the SAS man possessed a raw, elemental strength that obviously shocked the Professor.

"What the fuck did you say, asshole? You have a problem with Jews?"

"No, no, it's not that." He tried and failed to push Welland away from him. "I have to be back at the dig, you see. My time is too precious to waste while you chase around the countryside. Much too precious."

"More important than people's lives?"

"Well, it's not that. Let me go, man!"

Talley pulled him off. "Leave him, Guy. It's not worth it."

"I'll break his fucking neck, he starts that again."

"Sure, sure. He'll be okay now. Professor, I'm Lieutenant Talley. Come with me, and let's talk about how we're going to play this when we arrive at the dig."

The man recovered some of his composure and straightened his clothes. "I'm not sure this is altogether a good idea, Talley. I mean, that man of yours, he's a savage, attacking me like that."

"Maybe you'd be something of a savage if almost your entire race had been murdered by racists. It kind of makes people pretty sensitive when you suggest your travel arrangements are more important than their lives."

Wenstrom nodded and pursed his lips. "Okay, point taken. What do you want from me, Talley?"

He's going to back down, thank Christ. He sure is anti-Semitic, but he won't be the first, or the last. A second-in-command of Jewish descent, and a rabid Jew-hater running the project we're counting on to shelter us from the gaze of the Iranian authorities. Great!

"I want what they told you we'd need, for you to provide cover for my unit. We'll just blend into your archaeological dig. It shouldn't be too difficult. We'll be coming and going a lot, mostly at night. During the day, we'll just need to bed down and stay out of people's way."

Wenstrom grunted. "I suppose I can organize that. Why are you coming to Iran, what's your mission?"

"That's classified, Professor. Sorry, but you're not cleared for that information."

"Is it an assassination? Is that what you're planning?"

Talley considered his reply.

If there is going to be an assassination, I'd like to put this odious creep at the top of the list. Except we need him.

"I told you, it's classified. But no, it's not an assassination."

Wenstrom nodded. "In that case, I'll go along with it. When will you arrive?"

"We're flying out Friday, direct to Iraq, and we'll fly over the border and join you during the night. We'll need space for our gear and somewhere to sleep."

"Yes, I can provide that. You'll be in tents, like the rest of us."

"We're used to it," Talley smiled. For some of their operations, a tent would be a considerable luxury. "Make certain there is some distance between us and the rest of your people. As I said, we'll be coming and going during the night, and they may be curious."

"Oh, they'll be curious all right. You'll just have to find a way to deal with it."

"Just be sure our tents are separate from your people, that's all. We'll take care of the rest."

"Very well," he muttered. "I'll try and have it all ready for you."

Talley stared at him. "You do that, Professor. As you've seen, some of my people get really pissed off when they think someone's screwing around with them."

Wenstrom ignored the warning and looked at his watch. "I have to go. They're sending transport for me. It should be here shortly."

"I'll walk you out."

There was an air taxi laid on by NATO waiting on the tarmac, a Piper twin. It would take Wenstrom to Frankfurt where he'd pick up a connection to Tehran. Talley walked with him across the tarmac. Wenstrom turned to him just before they reached the aircraft.

"I hope you'll rein in that man of yours, Talley. I don't want any trouble with him when we're on the site."

"He'll be fine, Professor. He just has this little problem."

"What problem is that?"

"It's with anti-Semites. They make him violent."

Wenstrom snorted. "He'll have a problem in Iran. They're all anti-Semites over there. Some of my best friends are anti-Semites, but we still get along. He'll have to learn to control his violent tendencies."

"They're what we pay him for. Guy is ex-British SAS. He happens to be very good at what he does. Very good, and believe me, he can get very, very violent. I'd remember that if I were you."

They came to the Piper Seneca, and Wenstrom stopped.

"You'll have to keep him under control when he's inside Iran."

"It doesn't work like that, Professor. You stay away from him if you can't avoid making racist comments. It's safer that way."

This time Wenstrom flushed, so he'd understood the warning. Talley handed the academic over to the waiting pilot, who took his bag and stowed it in the aircraft. Wenstrom boarded, and the pilot climbed in and closed the door. Talley could see the Professor staring back at him as the Piper taxied across the apron and turned onto the runway. The engines roared, and it shot forward to climb into the sky.

That guy is capable of making trouble, that's for sure, even though NATO is paying him well to turn a blind eye. I hope it's enough to shut him up. If it isn't, there are other ways of dealing with the arrogant little shit. I'm sure Guy will be more than happy to shut him up.

"It's good to see the back of that sonofabitch," Guy murmured. He'd walked up behind him.

"I agree, but we're relying on his project to give us cover, so we'd better not upset him. Not too much, anyway."

"Maybe it would be better to give Mossad a heads up about the fool. I don't trust him, and I don't like having to use him for cover while we're in country. He could blow us to the Iranians at any time."

"Not while there's money on the table, Guy. His precious project is all that matters to him. Besides, we have to look after him, he's important to us."

"And if he sold us out to the Iranians for more money?"

"I think he knows he'd find a world of pain fall on his head if he tried it."

"Does he?" Guy asked, looking at Talley intently. "A total ass like that, I'm not so sure."

Talley was thoughtful. *I need to keep a close watch on Wenstrom, but how? Of course, Doctor Anika Frost, and talking to her about her employer will mean being close to her again. Yes, she'll be able to watch him.*

* * *

The desert night was balmy and dry. He realized with a pang what he'd miss if they went through with their plans to promote him. He resolved to fight them every inch of the way before he gave in tamely and sat behind a desk.

They were watching the spectacular view of the sands as they rushed past, seated next to the open doors of the MH60. The helo, the stealth variant of the venerable Black Hawk, had become the workhorse of the US and certain NATO military forces. The aircraft was the property of the 160th Special Operations Aviation Regiment, the special operations unit of the United States Army that provided helicopter aviation support for special operations forces, and was frequently sidelined by NATO for their own operations. They'd taken off from Base Balad, formerly Balad Air Base and before that, Logistics Support Area Anaconda. Since it had been returned to the Iraqi Air Force in 2011, the US had maintained facilities at the base, which meant that Echo Six could arrive, transfer to the MH60s after dark, and take off again without arousing undue attention. They had plenty of space. They'd been loaned four MH60s, part of a 160th training flight that had been diverted. Talley could see the dark outlines of the other three helos as they flew fast and low over the undulating landscape of ancient Persia. His headset clicked.

"This is the pilot. We just left Iraq. We are now over enemy territory. Stay sharp, people. This is Iran. Home of the big, bad bastard dictator, Ahmadinejad."

Talley watched the pinpoints of light that had to be a city, grow nearer. He was curious, and he clicked his mike to transmit.

"Pilot, what's that place down there?"

"That's called Kermanshah, Lieutenant, plenty of history all the way back to the Stone Age. Lots of archaeological stuff going on down there."

"Copy that."

It was a name worth remembering, Kermanshah, in case they were ever questioned. Any archaeologist would look bad if they hadn't heard of the place.

"I wouldn't take this historical thing too seriously," Guy said. He was seated next to him in the body of the helo, and like him was watching the landscape rush past, dimly lit in the light of a quarter moon. "We'll be in and out of here fast, so I doubt we'll have occasion to talk to anyone about ancient civilizations."

"Maybe, but we could be stopped by the cops in a random roadside check."

"In that case, we'll have to deal with it in the time honored way."

"You mean kill them?"

"I mean deal with them the way they'd deal with us."

Talley nodded. *So he meant kill them. The SAS is not known for its gentle handling of those who opposed the Regiment, and surviving prisoners of the SAS are something of a rarity.*

"Let's save that for the last resort, Guy."

He heard the man grunt, but it didn't sound like

ECHO SIX: BLACK OPS 2

agreement. He remembered his response to Wenstrom's racist rant.

It's true, Guy is good, the best Special Forces operative I've ever known, but his extraordinary skills need to be kept within bounds. He's a deadly weapon. Then there's Kay and the kids. There's another fight and one that could devastate my life, and the lives of Joshua and James if it goes wrong. As if it isn't enough to fight the Iranians, I've NATFOR in Brussels to go to battle with, and Kay back in the US. Fuck it, a war on three fronts. Whoever said life isn't easy had it bang to rights.

"Heads up, Iranian Air Force flight, ten kilometers to the south. It looks like a pair of MIG 29s. They haven't picked us up, but if they do, it could get interesting. Hold tight, I'm going lower."

The helo dropped down until it was skimming the surface of the sand barely fifteen meters below them, and the other three helos kept station, dropping down to stay alongside. Everyone held his breath. Tangling with MIG 29s from a helo was a strictly shut end operation. If they did attract their attention, their only hope would be to land and fight it out. He watched the desert rush past, and at times it seemed only inches below them. They were looking south, waiting for the flash of navigation lights that would announce the arrival of the enemy fighters; fast movers that could finish them in a single pass, a missile launch or shattering burst of cannon fire. But they never came.

"This is the pilot. We're all clear, people. They've headed in the opposite direction, but I intend staying at low level. There's no need to tempt them to look our way."

There was no disagreement there. They flew on, and even out in the desert and away from the cities, Talley began to experience the smells, the atmosphere of Iran. He found it difficult to describe, a dry, spicy tang, and yet over it all, something dark and sinister, a tinge of corruption and decay that tainted the air. As if reading his thoughts, Guy leaned toward him.

"It's a funny old place, Boss. Something not quite kosher about it, even though we haven't got our boots on the ground yet."

"It definitely isn't kosher, Guy."

The men close to him roared with laughter.

"Iraq doesn't seem so bad," Talley went on, "but here, I dunno. What did George W Bush call it, part of the Axis of Evil?"

"When he said that, he included Iraq, as well as North Korea. At least Iraq has been knocked off the list."

"Mission accomplished?" Talley grinned.

"I wish," the Brit shook his head ruefully, "but you know we're working on it. A lot of people would like Ahmadinejad to get a kick in the balls. I'd guess our masters in NATO are watching this operation carefully, with an eye to the future."

"I hope not too carefully," Talley replied. "It's supposed to be top secret, eyes only. If it isn't, well…"

"We're all fucked?"

"Yes."

They landed ten klicks from Niavaran, a longer walk to the archaeological dig than they'd planned. The pilot had received intel from an NSA satellite overpass, which suggested there were Iranian military maneuvers taking place in the area. The nightmare scenario for the pilot would be to land forty million dollars of secret American helicopter technology in the laps of the Iranians. The rotors still turned as they unloaded their gear, and the MH60s immediately took off for the perilous low-level flight back to Iraq. Talley formed up the men, put Guy at the rear, and Domenico and Vince at point. After a last look around, they moved off into the almost silent desert. They could feel the heat coming out of the sand, in marked contrast to the chill night air. The sky was cloudless, with only the waning moon to light the way, and they relied on their NV gear to navigate. They trekked across the dunes, and Talley felt himself beginning to sweat under the weight of the heavy load and the soft, cloying pull of the sand; then the desert was no longer silent.

"Boss, I hear engines," Guy murmured. "It sounds like they're headed toward us."

He stopped and listened. It was the high-pitched sound of jeep or light truck engines, and the lower, diesel throb of something bigger, probably an APC, or a tank.

"Everyone stay out of sight. I want spotters out front and back. Vince, Jerry, climb those dunes. Try and pinpoint those guys and find out what they're up to. What the hell are they doing out here at this time of night?"

Domenico looked at him. "There's always the obvious reason."

"They knew we were coming? No, that's impossible. How the hell could they know that?"

"Because someone told them, my friend. It seems the devils are here."

"A traitor? I doubt it. This is super-secret, need to know."

His earpiece clicked. "Echo One, this is Five, we have several vehicles in sight, making their way over the sand. They're a couple of dunes away from our OP. If they hold their position, they'll head away from us. A jeep, three truckloads of infantry, and a tracked APC, looks like one of those old Soviet BMPs."

"Copy that."

He looked around. The men had gone to ground, and unless someone was searching for them, there was no way they'd be found.

But what if they are searching for us? Or is it just a sweep for smugglers?

"Roy, Virgil, prepare the Minimis. I don't think we'll need them, but I'd like to be sure."

"Copy that."

He saw the two men climb up out of the sand and remove the machine guns from their canvas bags. They unfolded the bipod legs, each loaded a mag, and within a minute, they were ready to fire. They used their camo nets to cover them, and when they lay down, they were little more than a natural feature of the desert. He remembered the Iranians would almost certainly have NV gear.

"They're going past, Echo One. No, wait, the jeep, it's turned toward us."

In the desert, sound traveled a long way, and it wasn't difficult to make out the different noises. The diesel engine of the BMP, the squeak and clatter of the tracks, the engines of the infantry transports, almost inaudible behind the roar of the armored vehicle. And the sharper, higher pitched noise of the jeep's gas engine as it plowed across the soft sand.

"Echo One, that jeep, it's definitely headed toward us. Four men inside, looks like the driver, an officer and two infantrymen."

"Copy that. Snipers, are you on them?"

"Echo Five, ready."

"Echo Six, ready."

"Copy that. Hold your fire. Let's hope they roll straight past us. Machine gunners do not shoot until I give the order, not on any account."

He could hear the noise of the jeep, louder as it drew nearer, and the engines of the rest of the vehicles growing quieter as they moved further away. Then the jeep burst out in front of them. It crested the dune nearest them and stopped. They froze, waiting. The soldiers and the officer climbed out, only the driver stayed in the vehicle. The officer, Talley could see he was a captain, began quartering the area with his own night vision binoculars. Talley hoped they were as crap as people said they were. His men were searching too, walking along either side of him, prodding the sand, as if looking for something concealed.

"What do you think?" Guy asked him.

"They're searching for something. Could be rebels, smugglers, deserters, who knows?"

"Or us."

"Yes, there's that. Us."

They heard a shout. One of the infantrymen had discovered something. The officer walked over and bent down to examine it.

"Fuck it," Guy swore. "One of our guys left boot prints in the sand."

"Damn. They were supposed to cover their tracks."

The SAS man shrugged. "We all make mistakes, Boss."

"Mistakes get people killed. Now we'll have to take them."

"At least it'll be less to fight in the future."

"We're not here to fight, Guy. We're here to take down

a bunch of renegade lunatics who want to make Iran a nuclear power, not to take on the Iranian Army."

"What about Ahmadinejad? He could become a target if we find he's involved."

"If he proves to be one of this group, he goes down too, but I doubt he is involved." He called up Vince. "Bravo Five, we're going to have to take them."

"We're ready to take all four, on your order, Boss," Vince acknowledged "What about the jeep? They'll wonder who killed them."

"You're right. Hold on." He looked around for Buchmann. "Heinrich, could you rig something to look like an IED?"

The German chuckled quietly. "Ja, give these people a taste of their own medicine. I can do that."

"Get your explosives ready. We'll pile the bodies in the jeep and rig it to look like a rebel ambush. They'll never know the difference."

"Boss, they'll find the bullet holes, sooner or later," Guy objected.

"Right, and it'll take 'em time to conduct an autopsy. If we're still in country when they're done, we may as well put up our hands and surrender. I want…"

"Bravo One, this is Six, one them has disappeared."

Damn! We don't need a wild card blundering into our position.

"This is One, anyone see that trooper? Jerry just reported he lost sight of him."

"This is Five. He disappeared into a fold in the ground between two dunes. By my reckoning, he's coming toward you."

"I'll take him," Guy murmured. Before Talley could answer, he took out his huge combat knife, put down his assault rifle, and started to crawl forward into the dunes. Within seconds, he'd disappeared out of sight of even their night vision gear, swallowed up by the timeless ocean of sand.

"Bravo Five and Six, listen up. Guy is out there hunting that guy. Keep a bead on the other three, and don't lose them. I don't want you to shoot, not yet. It would alert the missing soldier. But if you have to, if they look like they're wandering away from your line of fire, take them down. And if any of them look like using a radio, take them down. We can't afford to have any floaters, not with that armor in the area. Clear?"

"Copy that."

They waited, and he watched the remaining soldiers continue their search. The driver of the jeep had dismounted now to help his comrades, and the three men were following the boot prints that led directly to their position, and toward where he knew Guy must be stalking the fourth man. It was going to be tight. He keyed his mike.

"This is…"

He didn't finish. The sand fifty meters in front of him erupted in movement as a soldier catapulted to his feet, unslinging his assault rifle to open fire. He never stood a chance. A dark shape leapt up beside him, like a charging panther. Guy dragged his prey down to the sand, with one hand fastened over his mouth to prevent him shouting, and the other on the Iranian's hand that was trying to work the trigger. He ripped the man's fingers out of the trigger guard and bent his body over double. Talley heard a muted, agonized squeak as Guy broke the man's fingers; a squeak that was cut off as the Brit switched his grip to the man's neck, and brought up his knee to hammer it into his groin. Another muted gasp of agony carried across the dunes before Guy freed one hand, pulled his combat knife from his belt, and slashed once across the man's neck. The loudest sound that reached Talley and his men was the sigh of air escaping from his ruined throat. It also reached the officer and two men who were still out searching the dunes a short distance off. The three Iranians stopped, listening. He gave the order.

"Take them, now."

The sound was soft, just a few quiet, sound suppressed shots from the AWMs, but it was enough. The three Iranians went down, tossed to the dark sands like rag dolls by the impact of the .338 Lapua Magnum sniper rounds.

"That's it, get those bodies and throw them into the jeep. Heinrich, rig that IED. You'll need a timer. Make it thirty minutes. That'll give us time to get away. Guy, are you okay?"

The Brit materialized out of the night, right next to him. "I'm fine."

"Go with the men and make sure there're no visible bloodstains. It shouldn't to too difficult. The NV gear shows up blood pretty well. When the IED explodes, they'll swarm around like flies on a jam pot."

He noted the smears of blood on the Brit's camo gear. It showed up as a dark smear that stood out clearly from the rest of the confusing Multicam pattern.

Thank Christ he's on our side!

"I'll backtrack now," he replied, "and make sure it's wiped clean."

Guy waded back through the sand, and Talley went up to the top of the nearest dune and scanned around.

The Iranian column had disappeared, which in the desert could mean they were anything from five to fifty klicks away. There was nothing near, nothing he could see. In the distance, he could make out the wink of navigation lights from a low flying aircraft, but they were at least twenty kilometers away, so it was no threat. Satisfied, he walked across to the Iranian jeep. The four bodies were already piled inside, and Buchmann was lying on the ground, setting the fuse and detonator to his explosives underneath the chassis. He quickly crawled out and got to his feet.

"Everything is ready. As soon as you say the word, I'll start the timer."

"Do it now."

He took a last look around, but it was still clear.

A pity the soldiers died for almost no reason, but maybe they should have voted for a different President.

"Let's go."

They went swiftly across the desert without encountering any further opposition. Talley had called a brief halt when the explosives detonated, but there was no sign the Iranians had any suspicions about how their men had met their end. The back trail remained clear. They reached the outskirts of the dig, and Domenico went forward with Vince to check out the encampment. It was clear, and to one side they saw a group of four tents pitched and pegged out on the sand that Talley knew had been earmarked for his unit. They were white canvas, a color intended to reflect the sun's rays and stave off the worst of the heat. The point men checked them out, going from tent to tent, and called it in.

"Echo One, this is Three. We're clear in here. There's no one about."

"No sign of Wenstrom? He was supposed to be waiting for us."

"Nothing at all. He's not here. There's nobody."

Talley knew he would have done that deliberately. He was that kind of guy.

"Understood. We'll have to take a chance and occupy the tents. We can't stay out in the open when it gets light. Let's move in, men. At least we can get some sleep."

They reached the tents and Talley called them together.

"I want one man from each tent to stand watch. We'll take two hours each. Split up, I'll take the tent nearest the camp. Guy, you take the next, Domenico and Jerry, take the end two, five men to each tent. We'll set up the Minimis to cover the approaches at each end. Stay sharp, but try and get some rest. We'll be moving out tonight, and remember, during the hours of daylight wear your civilian gear. You're supposed to be graduate students, not hired killers."

Hired killers, assassins, it reminds me of Kay's view of my work. Maybe she'd prefer wearing a burqa!

He watched as they disappeared under the canvas.

"Domenico, that Minimi in your tent. I can see the barrel poking out through the front canvas. It needs to be hidden. Put something over it."

"Copy that."

"And make sure the sentries wear civvies. If they catch sight of an armored vest and a Kevlar helmet, these folks will have kittens."

He made sure they all understood, kicked off his boots and helmet, and lowered himself on his cot. Almost immediately he fell asleep, despite the closeness of his enemies. When he awoke, he was momentarily confused.

Where am I? Oh yeah, Iran.

But it was the sound of motor vehicles that had awoken him. He peered out of the canvas flaps of his tent, looking toward the dig. Outside, it was a bright, sunlit dawn. Vehicles had just appeared, military vehicles, two trucks and both carrying troops.

They must be carrying an entire platoon. And an armored car, fuck!

He whispered into his mike.

"This is Echo One. Heads up, the Iranian Army is here!"

"What do you want us to do?" Guy replied almost instantly. His voice was icily calm. "We can take them, but it will have to be quick."

"And the mission would be over. No, make sure everyone is in civilian clothes. Let's try and bluff this one out."

"Copy that."

He looked again at the armored car. The turret had revolved, and the gun was pointing at them. The troops had dismounted, formed up, and started to advance toward their tents.

So there'll be no working it out, no bluff.

He heard the rear tent flap open, and Domenico Rovere slipped inside.

"Boss, you've seen them? They're heading straight for us. They know we're here."

"Yeah."

"What do we do?"

"We'll handle it, Dom. Then we go find this Arash and boil his ass."

CHAPTER FOUR

He watched the Iranians move at a slow, relentless pace across the narrow strip of sand.

We have two minutes, no more. I have to decide. If we fight, the mission is over. If we let them come on, the mission is over. Which do we do?

"Boss, one of the archaeologists is here."

He looked around. Anika, Doctor Frost, had slipped inside the tent. She looked as lovely as he remembered her from Brussels, even in her working gear, khaki shorts and shirt, sandals, and a bush hat on her head.

"Anika! You've seen them coming? I'd get out of here if I were you. This may get ugly."

"Abe, there's a way out. I came to tell you. I had the tents positioned close to a qanat, and it's right behind your tent. Come with me. They're nearly here. Get the rest of your unit moving right away, and make sure they stay out of sight. You'll have to take your military gear with you. If they see that, you're finished."

"But…"

"Abe! Just do it, there's no time."

He nodded and clicked his mike. "This is Echo One. I want all of you to come to the rear of my tent. Don't let them see you, and bring your weapons and equipment. Only leave civilian gear. Move it, we only have seconds before they see us!"

"Let's go," she ordered as he finished speaking. It was a different Anika, tough and in command. Not the soft, sensuous lover he'd known in Brussels.

Who is she?

He followed her out, and Domenico came behind him with the men who'd shared his tent. Other troopers were crawling out from their tents, keeping the canvas structures between them and the Iranians. Anika pulled aside a sheet of ply board, underneath was a row of timber planks.

"This used to be a well. There's an old qanat under here. It's dry right now, so you can hide down there, and I'll cover it up. Hurry!"

As if in a dream, or more likely a nightmare, Talley responded fast. He and Domenico ripped the boards aside. There was a square opening with a ladder leading down, a new ladder.

How come? How did she know we'd need this?

"What's this all about, Anika?"

"Later! Get in there. They're nearly here."

They threw themselves down the ladder. The shaft was about six meters deep, and at the bottom, they saw a low tunnel that ended after a couple of meters. It was a tight squeeze for twenty men and the gear, and some had to cling to the ladder. The shaft went dark as Anika threw the boards over the entrance. All they could do was wait.

"Who's up there on the ladder?" he murmured quietly.

"I'm at the top. It's me, Roy."

"Good. Someone pass him up a Minimi. If those boards are removed, and you see Iranian soldiers looking down at us, blast them."

"Copy that. Who has the Minimi?"

"Coming up, the clip is loaded ready." Guy gave it to the man at the foot of the ladder, and they passed it from hand to hand until it reached Reynolds. He positioned it ready for use."

"If they try anything, a few grenades would quiet them down," Guy suggested.

"You're right. Who's carrying an HK 416 with a launcher?"

"It's in the gear bag, Boss." He recognized the voice of Virgil Kane. "I'll find it right away."

"Yeah, do that, and pass it up to the man behind Roy."

"Buchmann here, Boss. That'd be me."

"Very well, Heinrich. If Roy starts shooting, I want you to send out four grenades, one for each quadrant. Enough to catch any troops clustered around the shaft."

"Jawohl, Herr Leutnant."

Talley grinned. It was a measure of the tension they were under. Buchmann showed it by reverting to his native German.

We all know what he means, so what the hell?

They waited for an hour. They couldn't see or hear anything outside the shaft, and Talley felt his nerves stretched to breaking point, knowing there was a heavily armed enemy force just meters away. Then they heard the sound of the boards being removed.

"It's me, Anika."

"Hold your fire, men."

Light streamed into the shaft, and he saw her peering down at them.

"It's okay, they've gone. You can come up, but keep the guns out of sight. They've started work on the dig."

They climbed back up the ladder and into the open air. Anika was standing close by, her expression grim.

"I think they may have been tipped off about you, but I can't be sure. They went through your tents pretty thoroughly, but they didn't find anything. I told them you were exploring an area closer to the city."

"Who would have tipped them off?"

She stared at him but didn't reply. He nodded his understanding. Wenstrom. He'd kept his part of the bargain, and provided the tents for them as cover. But then he could have reported them to the Iranians. Not the entire truth, he wouldn't have told them Special Forces were hiding in his camp, for if that was the case, there'd have been a battalion of troops looking for them. He would have made up some tale about thieves or maybe terrorists. There were plenty of those in Iran. It would have been so easy, a call to the local militia, send in a couple of truckloads of troops to arrest them, a quick trial, and a public hanging; a long drop from a crane in Sabalan Square, in the center of Tehran. He could still have claimed the rest of his money from NATO, maintaining he'd carried out his part of the bargain. Yes, it was masterful, a way to get keep the Echo Six operators out of his hair, win some Brownie points with the Iranians, and secure funding for his dig. Except that Anika had foiled his plot. It was as if she'd known something like this would happen. They slipped back into their tents, careful to keep out of sight of the diggers. Anika Frost joined him in the tent, with

Guy and Domenico. The Italian always hated to let a pretty girl out of his sight. Talley turned to Anika.

"What happened, how did you know they were coming? And how come you prepared that bolthole? Who are you?"

She hesitated for a few moments and then nodded. "Okay, I guess it has to come out. I work for the British Secret Intelligence Service, MI6. They like to have someone on these Iranian projects to keep an eye on things, and on this one, well, I'm that someone."

"Yeah, you're too damned sneaky for just an archaeologist, having that back up plan. Are you really an archaeologist, by the way?"

"I am, yes. I was recruited at Oxford while I was an undergraduate, and they asked me to specialize in Iran for my doctorate so I would have the credentials to come here."

"I see, and Wenstrom? Was it him who snitched to the Iranians?"

"Probably. He used his satphone to make a call, and he was very careful to make sure no one overheard him. He would have called the local militia barracks. That's where those troops came from."

"I'd like to rip the bastard's head off," Guy snarled. "Boss, let me take care of him. I'll make sure he never does anything like that again."

"No, we can't touch him. He's the project leader here, and he holds the license from the Iranian Antiquities Office. If you knock him off, we'd have to pull out. We have to leave him alone, for now."

"As you wish," the SAS man muttered, "but when the time comes, he's mine."

"Maybe, Guy. We'll see. We have to get our operation

off the ground, that's the important factor. To do that, we need to meet with Imam Fard as fast as possible."

"I can help you arrange that," Anika said. "I have my own satphone, and I can use it to call him."

Talley stared at her, appalled. "You mean his number's in the phone? You realize if you're caught, it would lead them straight to him?"

She smiled. "We're not that stupid. All I do is dial a number with a prefix assigned to Fard. They connect me to him. It's very simple, very safe, and can't be traced to him."

He nodded. "I suggest you fix it up, and ask the good Professor to come see us. I think we'd better meet him for a little chat."

She smiled. "I'll contact Fard."

A half hour later, Talley was talking to Guy when Wenstrom entered the tent. The academic smiled and held out his hand.

"Talley, good to see you…"

Guy whipped out a knife with one hand, grabbed Wenstrom's neck with the other, and pressed the blade to his skin. Talley watched and didn't intervene. The Professor needed a lesson in manners.

"I want you to listen to me, and listen good. You hear?"

The man gurgled in shock and terror. Guy ignored his choked protest.

"The next time you pull a stunt like that, I'll come and find you, and kill you. It'll be very slow, very painful, and you'll die screaming in agony. You got that?"

"Uurrghh…" He was trying to nod his head, but the razor edge of the blade made if difficult.

"I think he understands," Talley said gently.

Guy let him go, and the Professor massaged his neck. He looked equally terrified and angry.

"How dare you threaten me! I did nothing, Lieutenant, you have to…"

Talley held up his hand to stop him. "No, you still don't get it. We know what you did. You do it again, and if Guy doesn't kill you, I will. Understood?"

His expression changed, and his head drooped down. "I understand," he muttered.

"Good, now get out. If we need anything, we'll let you know."

He stumbled out of the tent. Guy stared after him, then looked at Talley.

"You think he'll behave?"

"Yeah, I'm pretty sure he will. You had him terrified there. Anika will keep an eye on him."

They turned as she walked into the tent. "I saw Wenstrom stalking away. He didn't look so happy," she chuckled.

"I can't imagine why. Maybe it was something he ate."

Her grin broadened. "Probably something you rammed down his throat, more like. The good news is I've fixed up a meeting with Fard. We're meeting him in two hours time, and I asked him to arrange for a truck with a canvas top you can ride in out of sight. He'll point out the location of the people who recruited him. He doesn't know the address, but he can direct us there. Once he's shown you where it is, he wants you to take him back to his home before you go in. I imagine he's worried if things go wrong and he's implicated."

"Yeah, we'll see about that. You'll bring the truck right here?"

"Yes, if you wear the same style of clothes as the others on the dig, and hide your gear in canvas bags, you can just climb aboard the truck as if you're off to explore another part of the area. It's quite natural. I'll put the word around you're searching for a hidden entrance to the qanat system. There's one more thing. I want to bring in our local Head of Tehran Station. We're going to need his local knowledge. I had hoped we could use Professor Wenstrom to advise us, but obviously he can't be trusted."

"And this guy can be trusted?"

There are altogether too many people who know we're here. And now she wants to include another one.

"Abe, he's the MI6 Head of Station! He's worked for the British Secret Intelligence Service since 1979, and is considered their top man in the Middle East, so yes, he can be trusted. You know we're short on time, so we have to use all the help we can get."

"Okay, but no more, the security on this operation has already been shot to pieces."

"Very well," she checked her watch, "I have to go. I'll be back later with the truck."

"You be careful."

She smiled and nodded. Then she ducked out of the entrance. Domenico looked thoughtful.

"You know that girl."

"Of course, I met her in Brussels."

The Italian smiled. "Please, my friend. I meant 'know' in the biblical sense. I was planning on dating her at some time. She's a nice piece of tail."

"A what?"

"It's an Americanism, I heard it somewhere."

He smiled.

126

"So, do you know her, or can I try my luck? You know she'd find me impossible to resist."

"Stay away, Domenico."

The Italian nodded glumly. "Merda! I thought so."

"You and Guy, get the men ready, and make sure they look innocent. Remember, we're archaeologists, not hired assassins. Keep the weapons out of sight."

Hired assassins, Kay's label, he shuddered.

Talley checked his own gear and settled down to wait for Anika to return with the truck. He felt a growing tension in his gut. They'd only just arrived in country, and already things were starting to go wrong, even before they'd started to hunt.

Arash, who is he? If he turns out to be Ahmadinejad, what then? The guy could already have changed his location if he suspects a NATO SpecOps unit is hunting him. If we fail to find him, what's next?

He tried to relax, but two hours later when he heard the truck bumping across the sand, he was still trying to work out possible contingencies. Anika's face appeared through the canvas.

"You all set?"

"Sure."

"Come on out and meet the good Imam Fard. The MI6 Head of Station is here, so any questions you have, ask away. He knows this area backwards."

* * *

The truck drove along the dusty road toward Tehran. Talley was in the passenger seat while Anika drove, and the SIS Head of Station sat uncomfortably in the center.

His name was Jeffrey Petersen, and he was dressed in local clothes, including a collarless shirt, so that he looked more Iranian than some of the locals. He wasn't an imposing figure, short, somewhat wizened, with a short, gray beard. His hair was also gray, and his tanned skin was dry and wrinkled, giving him the look of an ageing college professor who'd lost little of his wisdom and cunning. His eyes, which were questing and curious, clear and bright, dominated his face, and Talley suspected the brain behind them had lost nothing of its sharpness over the years.

"Don't worry about the clothes. It's all show, old chap," he'd beamed when he saw Talley eyeing him with concern. "I try to blend in, and not to stand out too much when I'm trying to chat to the local movers and shakers. They know I'm a Brit, but it means they're not seen with an obvious Westerner, which in Iran is always a cause for suspicion."

"So you haven't always lived here?"

He smiled. "Good God, no. I was born in Dorset, England. Educated at Charterhouse, and read Greats at Oxford."

"Greats?"

"Classics, old chap. Literature, Greek and Roman history, Philosophy, Archaeology, and Linguistics. You must know the kind of thing."

"Yeah."

"I came over here in 1979," he continued, "to keep an eye on things, if you know what I mean."

"Khomeini, the Islamic revolution."

"Just so. Never been back. My cover is as a journalist. I do a column for a couple of newspapers back in the UK, and it pays well, on top of my, er, other activities."

"So you like it here?" Talley asked incredulously.

"Not that much," he replied quickly. "But it gives me a chance to keep up with my hobby, the study of antiquities, amongst other things."

Talley nodded.

He doesn't like Iran that much, except he likes it enough to stay for the past thirty years.

The fruit and vegetable truck they rode in had a canvas back, which hid the men while they made last minute checks on their weapons and equipment. As far as they knew, there'd be no trouble, but they were in Iran, and so they always expected trouble. He watched the houses and industrial buildings grow more numerous as they reached the outskirts, and the increasing evidence that they were in a totalitarian state. There were at least two cops or militiamen stationed at every intersection, and posters of Ayatollah Khomeini, Mahmoud Ahmadinejad and Ayatollah Khamenei, the current 'Jefe' of the Iranian Muslims. The traffic thickened, much of it military, and Talley realized that if things went wrong, the place could prove difficult, or impossible, to get out of.

Imam Fard leaned through from the back. "The place you seek is close to here. Two blocks further you turn right, and it is halfway down the street."

"You mean the old cinema?" Petersen asked him.

"That is correct, yes. It was destroyed shortly after the Islamic Revolution, for showing films that displayed Western decadence." His voice dripped contempt.

Talley turned around to look at him. "You mean decadence like pedophilia, Fard?"

The man flushed and stayed silent for a few moments. Then he indicated they were almost there, and he pointed to the next street.

"Okay, stay sharp. Anika, stop when you turn the corner, and we'll take a look."

"Will do."

"If this goes well, you may get home sooner rather than later, Lieutenant," Petersen smiled.

"Maybe."

They turned the corner, and Anika braked sharply, bringing the truck to a stop. They could see the old cinema three hundred meters away from them. Opposite, a half-dozen military vehicles were parked outside a gaunt, new, concrete structure. Several soldiers strolled along the sidewalk.

"What the hell is that place?" Talley asked, turning to look at Fard.

"It's the rear of the headquarters of the Revolutionary Guard. The main entrance is the other side, in Martyr's Square."

"You don't think you may have mentioned it?"

He shrugged. "It makes no difference. It's the last place they'd expect foreign soldiers to operate, so it could even help us."

Talley looked across at Guy. "What do you think?"

"Hard to tell. It's a hell of a risk, operating so close to a Revolutionary Guard barracks, but maybe he's right, they wouldn't expect us to be right under their noses."

"Okay. Anika, drive up to the old cinema and we'll go in. Men, keep those weapons out of sight. If those gomers see us carrying heat, they'll be all over us like Aladdin and his fucking lamp. No, wait, hold it."

A convoy of trucks had turned the corner and was driving along the street. They stopped outside the Revolutionary Guard building and militiamen started to dismount, all of them armed with modern assault rifles.

"I think we ought to leave," Petersen murmured. "It looks like there's something big happening. There are more militiamen than I'd expect to see."

"I could go in there with a small squad, say four of us in all," Guy offered. "We'd just wander down the street and take a recce inside that cinema. That way we'd know what was going on inside, without risking the entire unit."

"Don't underestimate those people," Petersen warned. "They may act like clowns, but they're not entirely stupid."

"We have to know what's inside that building. It's the only way. Boss, you see that, surely?"

Reluctantly, Talley nodded. "You're right, Guy. We have to keep moving forward, and until we find out about that place, we're at a standstill. Go ahead, but remember, you're archaeologists, that's all. And keep those guns well hidden."

"Copy that. I need three men to go with me. Roy, you up for it."

The black former Delta operative grinned. "I'm always up for it, you know me."

"Count me in."

He nodded to Jerry Ostrowski, one of their snipers. "Good man. I need one more."

"I'll go."

It was Robert Valois, the former Brigade des Forces Spéciales Terre, BFST, French Army Special Forces Brigade operative. A veteran of Afghanistan, Valois was a recent addition to the unit. A tough Frenchman from close to the German border, he'd already proved his worth in a previous operation. Of medium height and build, he was very Gallic in appearance, with carefully styled blonde hair, blue eyes, and a carefree grin that attracted females like a magnet. A typical Frenchman, except that he was also a likeable guy who got on well with the rest of the unit; most of the unit, all except for Buchmann, who hated him. It was mutual.

"Very well. Guy, if you see anything you don't like, get out fast. If it looks bad, we'll pull out and wait somewhere close but out of sight. We don't want to attract untoward attention."

"Copy that. We'll be fine, Boss. We'll stay in contact and let you know what we find inside."

The four men dropped off the back of the truck. Four operators all dressed innocently in casual clothes, jeans, chinos, and T-shirts. Valois wore short pants, a polo shirt, and carried a backpack, looking for all the world like a graduate student. The other three men were in denim jeans and T-shirts. Guy wore a baseball cap. They were fit and tanned, so they looked the part. The men disappeared into the building. He nodded to Anika, and she started the engine, turned the truck around, and parked on a piece of waste ground in the next street. All they could do was wait. They sat in the hot morning sunshine, and Talley willed the commo to come to life. Petersen smiled across at him.

"Not easy, is it? The waiting."

"No, it is not. Tell me, Sir, what's your real interest in this operation?"

"What do you mean? I'm here to advise you, that's all."

"No, Mr. Petersen. The MI6 Head of Station doesn't sit in a truck in downtown Tehran just to offer advice. What gives?"

Anika turned to look at the Brit. "Is there something I

should know, Sir? Some operation we're mounting behind the scenes?"

He shook his head emphatically. "It's nothing like that, Doctor Frost. We normally have intelligence operations in progress, but nothing that relates to this mission."

She stared at him for a few moments in disbelief. Then she looked back at Talley. Petersen couldn't see her raised eyebrows. He understood immediately, there was something going on, but what?

"Echo One, this is Two."

"Go ahead, Two."

"We've got problems, Boss. The first floor was empty, so we moved up to check out the upper floors. Militia coming in, and it looks as if they're about to search the place. How do you want us to play this? I think we can take them, but it'll be close."

"How much time to you have before they know you're there?"

He waited for Guy to come back to him. "They know we're here. They've just shouted up the stairs for us to surrender."

"In English?"

"Yes."

Shit. Do they know who we are, and why we're here?

"How many of them?"

"I'd guess about twenty or thirty. They're carrying assault rifles, and they have AKMs."

Talley thought rapidly. *Twenty or thirty Iranian fanatics, armed with automatic weapons, facing Guy and three other operatives armed with pistols. It's a trap!*

"Guy, you have to give up. Try and lose the pistols and bluff it out. You're just innocent researchers, in the country for legitimate reasons."

"But, Boss, we could…"

"That's an order, Guy. We'll work at getting you out from the outside, but don't start a bloodbath. Confirm you understand."

There was a short pause. Then he murmured quietly, "Understood."

Talley turned to Anika. "Come with me, I want to see what goes down. A guy with a girl won't attract too much attention."

They slipped out of the truck and walked to the corner. They were in time to see a strong contingent of troops emerge from the old cinema, with Guy and his three men in the center. Talley held Anika's hand, to keep up the pretense of a Western couple out for a stroll in downtown Tehran. Guy and his people were all in handcuffs, and they were marched across the street and through the door of the Guard barracks. He turned to Anika.

"I guess about now would be a good time to test your local knowledge. How do we get them out?"

"The Pasdaran, the Revolutionary Guard, are a law to themselves, Abe. It won't be easy. It's probably impossible."

"Do you think your pal Petersen may be able to help us?"

"I don't know. Maybe, but I'm not sure I trust him, not entirely."

"I thought you worked for the same organization?"

"We do, but someone is leaking information, and until I know who, I don't trust anyone." She looked thoughtful. "Jeffrey's been different lately, strange."

"In what way?"

She shook her head. "It's nothing, maybe he's just under

pressure. Abe, we need to contact the Embassy, surely? They'd be suspicious if we didn't."

"Embassies. Guy is a Brit, Robert Valois is French, Buchmann is a German, and Reynolds a US citizen."

"Ouch."

"Yeah. It would be a lot quicker to break them out."

"It would make it worse for them if it backfired."

"I guess it could," he grinned, "so we'd better make sure we do it right. We've seen enough. We need to clear the area before they take too much interest in what we're doing."

They reached the truck, and Anika drove slowly and carefully back to the dig. They crammed into a single tent, and there was only one topic under discussion. Talley turned to the MI6 man.

"Jeffrey, you're the resident expert, how do we get our guys out?"

"You're going about it all wrong," he man replied. "You have an important mission here in Iran which must take precedence. You have to locate the target and destroy it before they get hold of those nukes from Pakistan."

"And what about my men? What'll happen to them?"

Petersen thought for a few moments. "They were found in a suspicious location. They'll be treated as spies, so that means they'll be tried in front of a Revolutionary Court. I imagine they'll be transferred later today to Evin Prison, that's at Darakeh, a few miles west of here. It's where they conduct the main interrogations of political prisoners. It could take a couple of years before their case is heard in a court. But listen, this group that's about to bring in nuclear weapons from Pakistan, that has to take priority over four soldiers. I'll help you investigate. I mean, I feel sorry for them, but…"

"What's the route?"

"I'm sorry?"

"The route they'll take, from Tehran to this jail."

"Well, the transport will take the main highway, the Vali Asr. It runs all the way from Tehran to Evin. It will be a heavily armed prison convoy with plenty of troops, and they'll likely have an armored car in support." He sighed. "This is idiocy, Talley."

"We'll locate those Iranians, Petersen, and we'll complete the operation. But first we get our people out. I don't leave my people behind, not for anything. If they wind up inside this Evin prison, they may never get out. What's the penalty for spying in this country?"

"They hang them from a crane in Sabalan Square in central Tehran."

"Not these guys, they don't. I'm going to need this truck. Anika, take your boss where he wants to go and bring the truck back here. Can you do that?"

She nodded. "Yes, I'll do it. What about Imam Fard?"

"We'll keep him with us. He'll be our technical advisor."

She smiled and nodded to Petersen. "Sir, we'd better go."

Talley looked for Rovere. "Dom, I need to raise Carl Brooks. We're going to need support for this one."

"I'll use the secure commlink."

"Make it as quick as you can. The rest of you, start preparing your gear. We're going to hit the prison transport on the road before it reaches Evin Prison."

"What kind of attack are we looking at?" DiMosta asked him. "I mean, it's daylight, and we'll be tangling with a well-equipped force."

"Shock and awe, Vince, shock, and awe. No bastard takes our guys prisoner and gets away with it. We're going to hit them so hard, they'll shit their pants from the word go. It's the only way to get our guys out without them being hurt. Make sure everyone is in full kit with body armor."

He smiled as he walked swiftly out. "Copy that."

"Abe, I have Admiral Brooks on the commlink."

Talley took the headset from Rovere. "Admiral, did Lieutenant Rovere explain the problem?"

"He did." Even over the neutral tones of the decrypted audio, Talley could hear the curt, cold tone of Brooks' voice. "But you'll have to shelve it until your mission is completed, Talley."

"I can't do that, Sir."

"What do you mean, you can't?"

"If they disappear inside the Pasdaran jail, they'll be there for years, and they could wind up swinging from a crane in the main square. I won't sacrifice them, Sir, not when there's a chance of saving them. It's not negotiable."

"Talley, the mission has to take precedence."

"It does, Sir, and those men are a vital part of the mission. As soon as we have them back, we'll carry on and locate our target."

He heard Brooks sigh. "I don't like it, Talley."

"No, Sir, but I doubt you got to be an Admiral by leaving your men behind in the shit."

Talley heard the chuckle from the other end, "No, I guess not. What do you need?"

"An armed drone, Sir."

"Over Iran, in daylight? The hell you do! No way!"

"It can be done," he persisted. "What about the new

drone, that Lockheed Martin developed? The Avenger, I think it's called."

"You know about that? It's supposed to be classified, Lieutenant. It isn't even in service yet."

"Even better, Sir. It'll be a chance to iron out the bugs."

The Lockheed Martin Avenger was an advanced vertical take-off reconnaissance and attack drone. With a maximum payload of more than a thousand kilograms, no exposed rotors, and a service ceiling in excess of eight thousand meters, the Avenger could carry a variety of payloads to distant battlefields. It was also the first of its type to be built with stealth capability. Fitted with Lockheed manufactured Hellfire missiles, the drone was able take off from a limited area, like the deck of a warship or a jungle clearing, and deliver a massive punch to the enemy, yet avoid being picked up by hostile radar. Brooks was silent for a few moments. Finally, he signaled his reluctant agreement.

"Very well, Lieutenant. I'll put your request to SACEUR, that's Admiral James G. Stavridis. I can't guarantee he'll go for it. He'll be pretty pissed if it crash lands inside Iran."

"He'd be even more pissed if those nukes found their way across the border, Sir."

"Yeah, he would at that. You're telling me that you have to have those men to complete the mission?"

Talley smiled. The message was clear. They needed to make a powerful case for the drone.

"Absolutely, Sir. It can't be done without them."

"He's no fool, Talley. He'll know what you're up to."

"He's also military, Sir. Not the kind of guy to cut and run when your men are in trouble."

"That's true. I'll get back to you."

"Thank you, Sir. We'll continue with our preparations and begin moving toward the intersect point."

"You'll continue even without drone support? I can't guarantee they'll go for it."

"Yes, we will. We'll continue if we have to throw rocks at them, but those men are not going inside that Iranian prison. Just make it clear to the Admiral that without the drone, our job will be that much harder, maybe even impossible. Which means…"

"I hear you, Talley, and he'll understand it too. Brooks out."

Talley changed into his camo gear, armored vest, webbing, and helmet. He checked his weapons, the MP7, Sig Sauer P226 9mm automatic, and his combat knife and spare mags. He managed to slide into the next tent without being seen by the workers on the dig. The rest of the men were crammed into three tents, all of them armed and ready for action. He looked at Rovere.

"Any sign of Anika? She should be back any moment now."

Domenico smiled and shrugged as they heard the sound of a truck engine approaching. One of the troopers looked out through the tent flap.

"It's the truck coming back. It must be her."

Anika reversed toward them so they could climb into the truck without being seen. Talley pushed Imam Fard into the back. He was trapped between two troopers who dwarfed the cringing Iranian, so he looked even more miserable. He ignored him, went around to the cab, and spoke quietly to Rovere on the commo. There was no need to give anything away to Fard, especially data about a super secret stealth drone.

"Domenico, switch on the satcom, and listen for Brooks' call. If we don't get that drone, it'll be a damned hard fight. And don't let Fard know anything about it."

"Why is he coming with us, Abe? He could be a serious security risk."

"I want him where I can keep an eye on him. You don't think it was an accident those Revolutionary Guards went into that old cinema?"

"You think it was Fard?"

"Well it sure wasn't Bigfoot. I'm not sure about him, but I want to cover the bases."

"Copy that. I'll let you know if I hear anything from Brooks."

He saw Anika staring sideways at him. She looked puzzled.

"Drone? What's that all about? You can't have drones flying around over Tehran. They'll go crazy if they find out."

He explained about the stealth drone. She looked dubious.

"I doubt they'll wear it. The Iranians have already shot down an American drone. The Pentagon won't want to risk another."

He looked at her grimly. "They have to, if they want us to carry on. Either way, we get those men out."

"But Abe, you'll be attacking a heavily defended prison convoy. Without air support, the casualties are likely to be heavy."

"As long as it's their casualties, that's fine by me. We'll manage."

We'll manage, because we always do. And when we stop managing, we die. It's a simple equation.

They reached the highway, the Vali Asr, and drove along it until they reached what Talley had concluded was their most likely ambush point. It was the Parkway Bridge, a huge, busy intersection, with traffic crossing from several different directions. Close to the bridge, they found an abandoned factory building next to the Vali Asr. Vince DiMosta dropped off the truck and ran inside to set up his stand on the roof. Anika drove out again and headed for the road the led underneath the bridge where they could wait without being seen. It was a simple plan. Vince would shoot the driver of the prison transport, causing it to crash. His Accuracy International AWM was a rifle that could to do the job at twice the distance. They'd just have to hope Guy's men weren't hurt if the vehicle collided or turned over, but it was a chance they had to take. It should look like an innocent traffic accident; maybe the driver suffered a heart attack. The rest of the convoy would naturally stop to help the stricken vehicle, and Anika would drive the truck alongside and stop to help, as people would normally do with a traffic accident. Talley's men would climb out, take the guards by surprise and cover them while they freed the prisoners. It wasn't a plan without flaws. If the convoy did have an armored car in support, it could prove to be a tough nut to crack. And if there were too many guards, they'd quickly realize they had the advantage and could strike back hard at Talley's force; too many ifs. They needed the drone, and so far, Brooks hadn't come back to them; time was running short. Their best estimate was the convoy would be along in the next hour.

"We're almost at the bridge," Anika said. "Does the assault go ahead?"

"We go, whatever."

"Echo One, the prison convoy is in sight."

"Copy that, what's their strength?"

A slight pause, "It's not good, Boss. They have an armored car up front and another at the back, the old Soviet BTRs. They also have two truckloads of troops to look after the armored prison transport. It'll be a bitch. What do you want me to do?"

He turned to Domenico. "Any word on that drone?"

"Nothing."

Shit! Where's Brooks when I need him? Where's that drone? They'd better make up their minds. If they want Arash, they'd better come up with the goods. We're almost out of time.

CHAPTER FIVE

He cast around for alternatives, but there were none. He had to make a decision, right now.

"Vince, you got a shot?"

"Just about. The view is obscured when other vehicles go past, but yeah, I can take him."

"Copy that. Wait for my word. Attention men, the operation is a go. I repeat. We are go. We move as soon as that prison transport goes off the road."

He took a last look around. He could see the convoy in the distance, the ugly, squat shape of the Russian APC leading. In the center was the prisoner transport, a closed steel truck with tiny barred windows. It carried no markings. At front and back, the infantry trucks kept station, the troops seated in the rear. Apart from the convoy, there were no other threats in sight. No cops, no militia, nothing.

He smiled to himself. *That convoy will be more than enough to deal with.*

"This is Echo One. Echo Five, take the shot. Everyone,

stand by."

It took a few seconds for Vince to line up on the driver. Talley saw the windshield fracture into a thousand cracks as the bullet drove through and into the driver's brain. The transport slewed across the roadway, lifted up on two wheels, almost as if it was about to overturn, and dropped back down. But the vehicle was also starting to spin around, and as it came nearer to Talley's position, he could see the driver slumped in the cab, his forehead a bloody ruin. The guard next to him was wide-eyed with panic, as he fought to regain control of the stricken vehicle. The infantry trucks were pulling to a stop, and then the APC at the front braked hard so that the truck behind ran right into its back, catapulting the soldiers into a tangled panic. It was enough.

"Let's go get 'em. Vince, stay on that APC at the rear. Try and knock out the driver. Anika, start up and go alongside that prison transport. We're just friendly passers-by, folks, good Samaritans. We're just offering to lend a hand at a road traffic accident. Heinrich, make sure you have the charge ready for that APC, or we're in trouble. Let's go, people!"

He looked at her as she fired up the truck. He hadn't wanted her to come on the desperate rescue mission, yet he acknowledged the fact that her local expertise could tip the balance between success and failure. Between life and death. After just one night in a Brussels hotel, she was on his mind, almost constantly. And for a soldier, that was dangerous. He was fighting for his life and the life of his men. And he wanted the delectable Anika Frost to be a major part of his life.

She slammed their truck forward and accelerated to

cross the short strip of roadway that separated them from the convoy, and braked to a stop. They were American troops in camo gear and armored vests, but Talley counted on shock and confusion to blind them to that reality until it was too late. They tumbled out of the truck, and the men of Echo Six went to work. To do what they did best. Anika was shouting at them in Persian that they were there to help. Unnoticed, Heinrich Buchmann darted forward and threw an improvised satchel charge below the hull of the stationary APC.

"Fire in the hole!"

He made 'fire' sound like 'feuer', but they got the message. The troopers threw themselves behind cover, and seconds later the bomb detonated. The blast was enough to disable the armored car, but the Russian BTR was laden with ammunition, and it literally blew apart as the munitions exploded in a massive secondary explosion. The Iranian militiamen had just dismounted from their truck, shocked and bruised, and they were hurled off their feet. It meant they were out of action, for a minute or two at least.

"This is One, take care of the second infantry transport. Heinrich, get the prison truck open. Vince, how're you doing with that second APC?"

"Not good, Boss. The bastard swerved just as I fired. He's out of my line of sight now. No, wait, he suspects something's up. The turret just started to move. It's turning and lining up on the prison transport. Shit, he's…"

Whoever was in command of the armored car had quick reactions. A stream of machine gun bullets hammered into the tarmac just inches from the side of the prison transport. Maybe he'd noticed the unfamiliar uniforms, or maybe he had orders to shoot first and ask questions afterward. Whatever it was, he'd recovered fast, and the rescue plan was in danger of becoming a massacre almost before it started.

"Vince, can you do anything? We need to waste that APC."

"Negative, Boss. The bastard has closed the hatches. It would take a rocket to prize him loose from there."

"We don't have a rocket. Heinrich, can you do anything about that armor?"

Talley ducked as more soldiers opened up on them. They were from the rearmost truck. His men were shooting back, firing furiously, and the area had come to resemble a major battle as hundreds of bullets ripped through the air. The situation was bad and getting worse by the second. He realized he could lose the entire unit.

Damn that drone!

He turned to Anika. "Keep the motor running. We may have to pull out of here if things get any worse." He keyed his mike. "This is Echo One, prepare to fall back. If you can't reach the truck, make…"

"Boss, this is Rovere. I'm patching the drone controller through to you now."

His earpiece crackled.

"Echo One, this is Creech Control. Do you copy, NATO?"

Creech Airfield in Nevada. The drone!

"Go ahead, Creech."

"I have orders to vector a drone to your location. How the hell did you swing it, Echo One? You know this baby is the latest stealth drone. It's not even supposed to exist."

"Put it down to my personality. What are you packing,

Creech?"

"We're carrying a full load of Hellfires, and with orders to fire on your command. What do you want to hit?"

"We're at the junction of Val Asr and the Parkway Bridge, Creech."

He ducked, rolling away as a stream of heavy slugs ripped up the tarmac close to him.

The bastards are getting too accurate.

"There's an APC, a Russian-built BTR. We need to lose it, and fast."

"I copy that, Sir. We're over Evin right now. Hold tight, I'll just…Yeah, I see him. Can you light him up for me? I'd hate to get this wrong."

"Wait one." He shifted to their local net. "Echo Five, do you have a Laser Target Designator?"

"Sure do. You want me to light up that BTR?"

"Sooner rather than later, Vince. It's getting pretty hot around here."

"Hold on. Yep, it's done. Tell 'em to hit it."

"Creech, target is lit, I repeat, target is lit. Fire your missiles."

"It'll only take a minute, NATO."

Talley saw Buchmann take a hit; a pair of bullets punched into the pack strapped to his armored vest. The German pitched forward, and every man who saw him winced, waiting for the explosives and detonators in his pack to ignite. But he crawled forward, uninjured, apart from a few bruises, and there was no blast of smoke and flame from his pack. Then the BTR exploded, as the Hellfire missile struck and detonated on target. The Revolutionary Guard armored vehicle was almost vaporized in the immense heat and blast of the exploding missile. A wall of flame leapt out from the APC and engulfed the infantry who'd been sheltering close by, as they exchanged shots with the NATO force. The soldiers from the lead truck stopped firing, shocked by the awesome power of the explosion that swallowed up their comrades. The massive blast, on top of their collision with the forward APC, and the astonishing appearance of NATO troops in their midst, threw them into a state of mental fugue. Talley knew they'd either go crazy, and renew their attack on Echo Six with even more savagery, or they'd run. But there was a third option, and he took it.

"Heinrich, get that prison truck open. Vince, watch our six. The rest of you, charge!"

He snapped in a new clip, leapt to his feet, and ran toward the enemy, firing short, three round bursts from his MP7. In front of him, the startled faces of the Iranians stared at him in terror. Behind him, he heard the shouts of his men as they followed him, and they began to pour a curtain of fire into the Iranian position. A single shot came back at them, and then another. The Guard was still in a good defensive position, and he knew if they decided to fight back, he stood to take casualties. The battle was finely balance on the cusp of victory or defeat. But in his soul, he knew they could take them, could shock and terrorize them with the face of imminent death, enough to turn a disciplined force into a frightened rabble. For several seconds, he kept running and firing, waiting for the hail of lead that would hammer toward them. He saw one Iranian, braver than his comrades level a machine gun toward him, but Virgil Kane tipped the balance. He'd set up the Minimi, the M249 light machine gun, and opened fire. As he kept going forward, Talley saw the Iranians stop shooting and look around for an escape route. A couple of them shouted at a man standing behind them, their officer. An argument developed, and the officer strode forward, pointing at Talley and his troopers who were almost on them. He shouted again, and then his head burst open as Virgil's stream of 5.56mm rounds found their target. He was tossed to the ground in a heap of broken flesh and bloody wounds. That was the end. They stared for a brief moment in horror at the bloody corpse. They then ran, tossing their weapons to the ground in their haste to escape the horror that had engulfed this normally peaceful suburb of Tehran. Talley signaled for his men to stop, and Heinrich shouted for the second time, "Feuer in the hole."

There was a loud blast, and the door of the prison transport went spinning through the air to land with a 'clang' onto a concrete driveway almost a hundred meters away. Guy clambered out of the back of the truck, turning to help his troopers down. Talley ran up to them.

"Guy, is anyone injured?"

The Brit shook his head. "A few cuts and bruises. Jerry is the worst. They gave him a hard time. They may have broken something."

"I hear you. We'll have it looked at as soon as we can. Get the men over to our truck. We're leaving, right now."

"No problem." He looked around the devastation of the ruined vehicles, smoke rising from the destruction and bodies strewn on the ground. "You sure stirred up the ragheads, Boss. They're gonna be mad when they see this."

The last trooper struggled to climb down from the prison transport. "Jerry, take it easy now. Roy, Robert, help him. He may have a break to that leg."

"I'm okay," Ostrowski shouted defiantly.

"Yeah, sure," Guy grinned. "Get into the truck, and fast. The cops will be here soon. It's time we were outta here." He grimaced when he saw Imam Fard seated between them in the back. He hadn't moved a muscle during the firefight, just sat frozen with fear.

"What's he doing here?"

"Lieutenant Talley likes to keep him where we can see him," Rovere answered. "It is a matter of trust."

"Yeah, I can see that," Guy nodded, "or lack of trust."

The Iranian scowled at him but averted his gaze as Guy stared back with loathing. They packed into the truck, and Anika drove away from the scene of devastation. In the distance, they could hear the sound of sirens. The emergency services were approaching the scene of the ambush.

"Keep your speed down," Talley told her. "Anything fleeing the scene is likely to be suspect."

"Will do."

"Anika, you're the MI6 specialist on the Iranians, what do you think about us hiding out at the dig? Will they link this attack to what's going on at Niavaran?"

"I doubt it, but there's always the possibility of a tip-off."

"You mean Wenstrom?"

"Him, yes. Who knows?"

"In which case, maybe Niavaran is the best place to be. We can keep an eye on the bastard."

"That's one way of looking at it."

"We don't have any other options for now. Take us to the dig, and we'll lay low while we work out our next move."

"What will that be?"

"Nothing's changed. We need to locate Arash. As soon as we get back, I'll contact our man at the Embassy."

"Miles Preston?"

"Yeah, you know him?"

"I know Miles, yes."

"What's he like?"

She paused for a few moments and concentrated on negotiating a street market that spread across the roadway. Then she turned to him.

"It would be best if you made up your own mind about Miles."

"You don't like him," he replied. It was in her tone, the sound of distaste. "Or is you don't trust him?"

"Let's just say we've had our disagreements in the past."

"I hear you, but can we trust him?"

Again, the pause as she phrased her reply carefully, "I'd trust him as far as it suited his own interests."

"By his interests, you mean the CIA?"

"I mean Miles Preston."

So she doesn't trust him. Just great.

She drove a circuitous route back to Niavaran, preferring to negotiate the suburbs of Tehran where there would be plenty of traffic around, than to use the less traveled roads to the north of the city. They passed through a wide variety of streets. Closer to the city there were many scabby buildings, and sidewalks thronged with black-clad women busy with the day's chores. There were vehicles abandoned at the roadside, many stripped of all their parts, and others burned out during some previous unrest. Groups of feral-looking youths sat idly in the squares, waiting for the spark that would ignite their anger and stir them into the next violent protest. The cause probably made no difference. It was violence that drove them, and anger was the detonator that would set them off.

Maybe they should just get off their butts and find some useful work.

In contrast, further from the city center, there were quieter tree-lined streets, with decent, middle class houses in good repair. Most of the women wore Western style clothes, except they had their heads covered with scarves. But it was a surprising side of the city, and one rarely seen in the Western newsreels.

It won't last. When the crazy Islamists take over the area, they'll begin their protests. Then the streets will be torn apart by fanatics, protesting, burning and looting, in the name of Islam.

Anika drove out of the suburbs, and they entered the countryside where the built up areas became large swathes of sand. So far, there'd been no signs of any pursuit, and Talley began to relax a little. They reached the dig at Niavaran, and she backed the truck up to their tents, so they could slip inside undercover. She joined him inside the tent. Rovere was already there.

"Domenico, I need you to contact Admiral Brooks. We need a meeting with Miles Preston, but I want him to come here. I think the streets will be a little too hot for us right now."

"You're don't say," he grinned. "Shakespeare said that, 'pleasure and action make the hours seem short.' You should be more grateful."

"Dom, can it."

"Okay, but we kicked their asses today, that's for sure. They're not going to forget that in a hurry."

"No, that's what worries me. Roy, I want you and Virgil to change into civilian clothes. Take the truck away from here and get rid of it, somewhere it won't be found. Drive it into a river, something like that. I don't care, then get back here any way you can."

"Copy that." He walked out as Guy entered the tent. "What are your orders, Boss?"

"First, are the men changing into civilian gear?"

He nodded.

"Good. We're back to being archaeologists for now. Make certain Jerry is okay, and find out if we need to get him to a doctor. The CIA guy is sure to be able to arrange it if it's needed."

"I'll get changed and check on Jerry."

He slipped out and crossed to the next tent. Talley began stripping off his armored vest and camo gear before realizing Anika was still there.

"I'm sorry, I just…"

She chuckled. "Hey, it's not like I haven't seen you naked before."

Rovere looked up quickly, and then bent back to the radio.

"Domenico, take that radio and find another tent."

He picked up the equipment and walked out, whistling to himself. Talley felt his face redden.

"Can I help you with anything?" she asked him.

I can think of a few things, yes.

"I'm okay, thanks."

Her eyes narrowed. "Abe, you have a nasty bruise low down on your left side. I want to take a look at it."

"A stray bullet hit me, but I was wearing my armored vest, so it's nothing."

"Let me look."

He was almost naked, wearing only his shorts. She

touched his skin, and he flinched. As much to the feel of her cool fingers, and the memories they invoked, as for the soreness of his wound. He felt the warmth of her closeness, and to his horror realized he was becoming aroused. So did she.

"Abe, you're feeling randy," she accused, her face split in a grin. "I can do something about that, you know."

"Anika, no, not here."

But she gently pushed him down to the cot and eased down his shorts. She put one cool hand on his throbbing penis while she used the other to pull off her own shirt and short pants. Underneath, she wore cream silk underwear, bra and panties, and she removed them almost as if by magic. Overcome, he touched her stomach and let his fingers drift down between her legs. He could smell the scent of her, a heady mix of healthy perspiration, female musk, and soap. The he felt her vagina and she shuddered. She was damp with her own arousal, and he slid his fingers into her easily. She began to writhe and buck.

"Abe, oh, my word, this is unbelievable. Is it always like this after a fight?"

"I don't normally have a beautiful partner with me, so I wouldn't know," he replied drily. "But I'm more than happy to find out."

It was true, the relief of knowing you were still alive after a clash with death was a heady aphrodisiac. She climbed over him and lowered herself down over his hard organ, slipping him inside her. They made love, an urgent coupling of need between two lovers who'd experienced the reality of imminent death. It was fast, furious, and intense. Afterward, they lay together, holding each other. He didn't care if someone came into the tent. He cared for nothing except this precious moment of life in the midst of death. He later found out that Domenico had warned them all to stay away from his tent.

As they lay dozing, he heard a vehicle approach. He quickly put on his short pants and a T-shirt with 'NYU' emblazoned on the chest. Then he strolled outside, carrying his hiking boots, and a battered, wide brimmed Fedora to finish dressing as he watched the newcomer draw near. He hoped he looked like a postgraduate student rather than a warrior; apart, that is, from the 9mm Sig Sauer P223 tucked into his waistband. The vehicle, an SUV braked to a halt. It was a shiny new Toyota Land Cruiser that had once been gleaming red, but was now covered in a fine layer of sand from the journey out of the city. The driver's door opened and a man climbed out. It could only be Miles Preston. No one but a CIA desk jockey would come so ill equipped for the desert. He was a tall man, over six feet, wearing an off-white linen suit that was sufficiently rumpled to look used, but not enough to hide its obviously expensive bespoke tailoring. He wore what looked like hand-tooled boots, similar to desert boots, but these were dark brown leather with the sheen of polish and money. His shirt was a paler cream than the suit, heavy silk, and he wore a bow tie. His head was bare, but he carried his hat, a cream Panama, in his hand. The man was like a caricature from an old black and white movie, or maybe an Indiana Jones flick. He came forward and offered his hand.

"You must be Talley."

"Lieutenant Abe Talley."

Close up, the CIA man had the look of a heavy drinker. His handsome, patrician face bore the telltales of spidery, red veins, and his eyes were slightly bloodshot. Even so, he still was a good-looking guy, and Talley had no doubt he thought himself something of a ladies' man. But his bloodshot eyes told the real story of his life.

So this is our contact. A pompous, arrogant asshole, if looks are anything to go by.

He didn't offer to shake his hand or introduce himself. "I gather you're holding Imam Fard here, is that correct?"

"That's right."

"You have to let him go, Lieutenant. He's a friendly, or hadn't you noticed?"

"He stays with us, Preston. He's a turncoat and a pedophile, or hadn't you noticed?" Talley fired back, "And I don't trust him."

"Even so, he has to make contact with his people. Otherwise they'll grow suspicious. And if they're suspicious, they won't tell him what we need to know to find the location of their leader."

Talley thought about it for a few moments, and finally he nodded. "Okay, you can take him with you."

"Good. About this other business, the fuck-up close to Evin prison. You know that half the Iranian Army and the Revolutionary Guard are searching for you, as well as the cops? And the CIA asked me to find out how come our latest top-secret stealth drone was revealed to the enemy. I doubt you could have screwed up any worse if you'd tried. I've already asked my people to contact NATO and have your unit replaced. You're finished!"

Talley looked away while he got his thoughts together.

It's no use telling this man about Guy and the other three troopers held prisoner, and likely to be executed; at the very least, they'd have been left to rot, maybe for decades, in some stinking Iranian jail. A waste of time, pointing out I've been trained in a military tradition that says you don't leave your people behind, dead or alive. No, this man won't want to know any of it. His priority is covering his ass, and he's already done that by blaming Echo Six for everything that went wrong. That drone, it's supposed to be stealth. So?

"What's with the drone, Preston?"

He stared at Talley. "I guess it's no secret, what your fuck up revealed to the Iranians. It's a Lockheed Avenger, and she's the latest VTOL Unmanned System. The vertical takeoff and landing design allows it to operate from almost anywhere, anytime. It has no exposed rotors, and the stealth aerodynamics make it almost impossible to spot from the ground at night. It's an incredible aircraft. Now that it's gone operational during daylight, the secret's out. What a total fuck-up! I'm making it part of my report. You just threw away a multi-billion dollar research and development program. You're finished, Talley!" he said again.

"Did they see it?"

"Did they see what?"

"The drone."

"Well, I don't know. They didn't tell me."

"So they may not have seen it. Probably didn't see it at all. They wouldn't have picked it up on radar, and we couldn't see it from the ground, and we knew it was there."

"What difference does that make?"

"It means you're full of shit, Preston. They don't have a clue where those Hellfires came from, do they? It happened so fast, it could have been anyone, even some rebel Iranian faction."

"Using Hellfires? No way."

"Are you sure you work in intelligence, Preston? You know that Turkey has Hellfires, and they're involved with the Iranians, especially since they share the same problems over Kurdistan. Then there are the rebels that are trying to attack Ahmadinejad's government. It's almost certain they know nothing about the Lockheed Avenger."

Preston digested that info for a short time, his habitual sneer replaced by a scowl. Finally, he nodded.

"Even if you're right, it makes no difference. I told you. I've requested your outfit is removed."

"Maybe you have, but right now, I'm here, and I'm in command, and I'll keep doing my job. Are you going to help us look for this Arash, or do we do it all ourselves?"

"You're going ahead with this crazy operation?"

"Damn right we are."

He sighed theatrically. "Okay, until you're relieved, I'll do what I can. What do you want from me?"

In truth, he had no choice. If they succeeded, and he'd stood back from offering CIA help, he'd wind up manning a CIA Station on some remote iceberg in Eskimo Land.

"The intel from Fard about that old cinema was a bust. Talk to him, and try and find out where else we can look."

He hesitated but finally nodded. A refusal to help would look bad on his career jacket. "I'll do that for you. Have him brought to my vehicle, and I'll have a chat with him on the way back into the city."

Domenico was lurking nearby. Talley told him to bring the Iranian to the SUV. He came back a few minutes later, holding the pedophile imam. Preston nodded a greeting, and they climbed into the SUV to talk, alone. He refused to have a third party present.

"No, Talley, it's just the two of us. It's an intelligence matter. There are things I don't want anyone to hear."

He waited with Domenico.

"I don't trust that man," Domenico commented after they'd been standing in silence for a few minutes.

"Which one?"

"Neither of them, but Fard goes without saying. The other guy, he's supposed to be on our side, isn't he?"

"That's true. Except that the CIA normally allies with only one side, and that's the CIA. They see everyone else as a potential enemy."

"In which case, why are we even talking with him? We should do it ourselves."

"I doubt that would get us far, Dom."

"You want to know what Shakespeare would have said?"

"No, but you're going to tell me anyway."

"Our doubts are traitors and make us lose the good we oft might win by fearing to attempt."

Talley chuckled. "How does that help us any? We don't know where to start looking."

Rovere nodded. "I've been thinking about that. There is one place that will almost certainly have some answers."

"Yeah? And where would that be, the Presidential Palace?"

"No, the Atomic Energy Organization of Iran. They're headquartered in the Amir Abad district outside Tehran."

"That's too obvious, Domenico. The guy we're looking for, he wouldn't go near that place. He keeps himself in the shadows, in deep cover."

Rovere raised an eyebrow. "Maybe. Tell me, where do you hide a tree?"

Talley grinned. "Yeah, I know the old saying, but it really is too obvious."

"Why?"

He thought for a moment. "Okay, maybe you have a point. There may be something or someone there who can help us. But my friend, that place is more heavily guarded than Fort Knox."

"That's true. We need some intel."

"You mean the CIA? But…"

"I meant your girlfriend. Let Preston take off back to Tehran with Imam Fard, and then you can ask her to find out about that place. We need to light a fire under this operation. We've been pushed around ever since we got here. I'm bored, I'm tired, and I want to start hitting back until we have what we came for. Let's get this operation moving, finish it, and go home."

Talley nodded slowly. "You could be right. I'll talk to Anika. I think I can trust her."

"Abe, she's your girlfriend."

"Domenico, she's not…"

"You trust her. That's all that counts."

"Yes."

"So talk to her."

They watched Miles Preston drive away, with Imam Fard in the passenger seat and Anika Frost in the back. Talley had talked to her alone while Preston and Fard were having their conversation. She'd agreed to rent a box truck and come back for them. While she was in the city, she'd run down everything she could find about that Iranians' nuclear facility, just outside Tehran. As the SUV disappeared in the haze of the desert, he saw Roy Reynolds jogging back with Virgil Kane. They were both smiling.

"You got rid of it okay?"

"Sure." He showed Talley a fistful of cash, Iranian rials. "A scrap dealer paid us for the metal. He crushed it into a cube the size of a small suitcase. Paid us for it, too."

"Keep it, use it to buy the men a few beers when this is done. Good work."

He sat in the shade of one of the tents, waiting for Anika to return. There was a lot riding on what the Brit managed to uncover for them, and he forced himself to keep calm as the hours dragged by. Guy brought him a plate of food, and he realized how hungry he was. As he wolfed it down, his second-in-command pressed him about how to get the operation back on course.

"I haven't a clue, Guy. When Anika gets back, we'll see what she's found out from the Tehran MI6 Station."

"You trust them?"

"That's a strange question for a Brit."

"You're American, do you trust the CIA?"

"Point taken. No, I don't trust them, not entirely, but I trust her."

"Copy that."

The day was almost over, and night was falling when he heard the sound of an engine. He watched it draw nearer, a white minivan with 'Tehran Truck Hire' written on the side in English and Farsi. It stopped nearby and Anika climbed out.

"Sorry it took so long, but I was busy. I went to the office and helped myself to a look at some of the files. I've got us a name at the Atomic Energy Organization. He's the second-in-command to the Director, a guy by the name of Javeed Zardooz. He always goes to the same bar after work, so we can pick him up there. With the right pressure, he'll tell us what we want to know. He speaks English by the way; he spent time in England. He was at Oxford University."

"Why would he talk to us?"

Talley was puzzled. *No one in this country would get to such a high level position and betray his country's nuclear secrets to an enemy.*

She smiled back at him. "He's gay, and he's terrified that if the Morality Police, the Basij found out, he'd hang from a crane in central Tehran. If we invite him to cooperate, in return for keeping his secret, it won't be a problem. But we need to move out now. He'll already be at this place, and he won't stay there all night."

"We'll move out right away. Guy, get the men moving. Domenico, make sure there's nothing left in these tents to give us away. We may not be back. Ensure everyone is in our own camo gear with armored vests. This is a night operation, so we shouldn't need to hide as students. We fight as Echo Six."

"Abe, you need to stay undercover," Anika pointed out. "You'll have to go into the bar and get him out."

"Me? Into a gay bar?" he grumbled, aghast.

"Sure, it'll be an education, and see how the other half lives. Don't worry, we know you don't bat for the other side."

"I'm quite happy not finding about the other side," he said firmly.

"In that case, it'll be part of your education," she smiled.

Is there ever a female who doesn't have the last word ready on the tip of her tongue?

The men piled into the truck, and this time Talley took the wheel. If the cops were looking for a European female driving a truck, in connection with the ambush near Evin, it would be easy for them to stop the few white females driving around the city and check them all out.

"I'm surprised they allow women to drive in this country," Talley remarked, as he threaded his way through the evening traffic. "They keep females from having any kind of equality."

"You're right. The country is pretty hard for women to make any progress in. You've noticed I always wear a headscarf?"

"Yeah, I did, all women do in this place."

"What you don't know is that the Basij run around checking, and if a woman is seen in public without her head covered, they can fine them, beat them, or imprison them; all with the enthusiastic support of the government. But at least we can drive a car. In Saudi Arabia women are not even allowed that freedom. We can't drive motorcycles inside Iran, of course."

"Why the hell not?"

She shrugged. "It offends their Islamic sense of decency."

"A pity that swinging people from cranes in a public square doesn't offend their sense of public decency."

"That's true. We're getting close. Take the next street on the left and pull up halfway down. The place you're looking for is called Bar Pourya-ye Vali."

"That's a weird name."

"He was one of their Iranian folk heroes, a wrestler. You know, naked men, sweaty bodies tussling with each other."

"That figures."

"I'll go in there with you. I've seen his photo, and I can identify him. Abe, all you need to do is act like you're keen on him and get him outside."

"Anika, I can't do that! I don't know how."

She grinned. "I suppose not. Just get him outside, anyway you can."

"Now that I can do."

He braked to a halt. Fifty meters ahead was a brightly lit neon sign, 'Bar Pourya-ye Vali'.

"Guy, I want everyone to remain in the back, out of sight. I'll stay on the commo net, in case I need you."

"Copy that. You have a good time in there, Boss."

"Guy."

"Yes?"

"Shut up."

The place had a gymnasium at the front of the building and a bar at the rear. When he walked through the door with Anika, he could immediately see a dozen sweating men, clad in trunks and working on the exercise machines. They looked up at him, saw the girl, and lost interest. He pulled Anika through to the bar at the rear. A doorman stopped him, but Anika was ready and proffered a hundred thousand rial note, about eight dollars, and he waved them inside. It was like a scene from hell, to his eyes, anyway. Through the thick, acrid smoke, he could see couples groping each other, and doing everything short of actually screwing. Many were in a state of almost complete undress, and the place stank of cheap scent, perspiration, and something else, the musky odor of sex. It was not arousing. He turned to Anika.

"This place looks like a brothel."

"Yes, it is a brothel," she replied. "They have rooms upstairs, so when the clients need privacy to do whatever they do, they can pay extra and go up there."

"Christ."

She ignored his look of horror. "Let's mingle in the

crowd. I'll see if I can find Javeed, and remember, be nice to him. We need him."

"Sure."

They pushed into the crowed. Talley ordered drinks at the bar, trying to ignore the lascivious stares from other men as they sipped their beer direct from the bottles. Anika put her head close to his.

"I see him, Javeed. He's over there on the other side of the room, the guy in the tight denim jeans and shiny black muscle shirt. He's holding the hand of an older guy."

He followed her gaze. Javeed Zardooz was very slim, very elegant. He had black hair, fashioned in elegant curls around his head. His eyes were large, almost liquid beneath huge lashes.

Artificial? Maybe he uses mascara.

But he was undeniably good looking, apart from the small, petulant mouth, shaped like a cupid's bow. The guy he was with looked older, and he wore a suit and white, collarless shirt, buttoned to the neck and no tie; a civil servant, probably, maybe even a religious man, an imam. Plenty of them were gay. They were men, and some men were just wired that way. As he watched, the older men left and walked to the bathroom. It was his chance.

"Stay here, I'll go grab him."

"Be nice to him," she smiled.

"Yeah."

He went up to the Iranian. "Javeed, is it you? Javeed Zardooz?"

The man looked at him, partly suspicious, partly appreciative of Talley's young, muscular physique.

"Who are you?"

He realized he hadn't prepared for this, didn't even have

a cover name ready.

"Uh, I'm Jack Wills." It was a name he'd seen over a store. He hoped the Iranian hadn't seen it too. "I was at Oxford. We met there."

"I see. Was it at a party, in a place like this?"

"Yeah, just like this. Listen, I'd like to talk to you about a couple of things. Could we go somewhere quiet?"

"I cannot, I am with a friend. Maybe some other time."

Talley put his hand on the butt of his Sig and managed to pull it out discreetly. He pushed it into Javeed's stomach.

"Okay, motherfucker, we'll do it the hard way. Get outside now, or I'll blow a hole in your belly and leave you here to die in agony."

"What?" The man had gone ashen. His Arab tan had turned almost white. "You cannot threaten me, I am…"

Talley rammed the barrel hard into his gut, and the man let out his breath in shock.

"It's not a threat, it's a promise. Outside! I just need to talk."

"But…"

"It beats dying in agony, mister. Move!"

He pushed the man through the revelers and out onto the street. Anika was right behind him.

"I thought you were going to be nice to him," she complained.

"I was. He's alive, isn't he?"

She grimaced as they walked to the minivan. As they reached it, the rear door opened and hands pulled the Iranian into the dark interior. Guy looked out.

"Everything okay, Boss?"

"It went fine. I'll leave him to you. Get him to cooperate. Tell him we'll kill him if he doesn't."

"Sure, I know we want this Arash guy, the Pakistan connection. Anything else?"

"That'll do for now. He has to know something, so don't take no for an answer. I'll start driving toward their headquarters at Amir Abad, in case we need to go inside to get answers. Let me know when you get something out of him."

"Sure."

He climbed into the driving seat. Anika got in the other side, and he drove out of Tehran, heading toward Amir Abad. Javeed Zardooz didn't take long to break. Guy's voice spoke into his earpiece.

"He's singing like a bird back here, Boss. He swears he doesn't know the name of the guy behind acquiring the warheads, but he has heard of the plan. They're excited about how it'll put them years ahead with their own weapons program. The only contact he's had is by email with this guy, and his emails are on a secure system inside the AEOI."

"I'm headed there now."

"It looks like someone will need to go inside and look up those emails. If we copy them to data stick, we can bring them out and get them analyzed."

"Ask Javeed if he can get us in there?"

"I already did. He was terrified, said it would cost him his life if he was caught helping us. I told him it would cost him his life if he didn't help us, and he agreed to take the chance. But the place if well protected, it won't be an easy one."

"Okay, I'll stop the truck. Bring him up to the cab. He'll have to get us past the guards on the gate."

"If there's a problem, we can take them."

"We don't want to declare war on Iran. We have to make this raid look like a terrorist hit. Ask him if there's a back way in. We can go in the front gate and let you in at the back."

Guy came back after a short pause. "He says there is a locked rear gate you could open."

"Okay, I'll stop, then bring him up."

Zardooz was shaking uncontrollably when he climbed into the passenger seat. Anika found a space behind the seats where she could crouch down out of sight. Talley followed his directions and stopped behind the high, barbed wire topped concrete wall at the rear of the AEOI.

"It is heavily patrolled, this area. You won't get away with it," Javeed whispered, his voice trembling with terror.

"Don't worry, Javeed. We'll be just fine. Anika, watch him. I'll let them out the back."

He climbed down and went around to raise the roller shutter that allowed access to the cargo area. Guy's troopers jumped down and melted into the shadows of a ruined factory opposite.

"I'll call you when we're inside," he told Guy.

"Good luck, Boss."

"Yeah, thanks. Remember to act like a terrorist, Guy."

"Sure. Salaam Aleikhum."

"Right."

They drove around to the front gate, and he tensed as they approached the armed guard standing next to the barrier. Talley braked to a halt and indicated the sentry should speak with Javeed. Anika, unseen behind the seats, interpreted for him, speaking softly so her voice wouldn't travel. Talley took out his weapon and held it out of sight, ready for use, with the suppressor locked on tight. The soldier didn't sound suspicious.

"Mr. Zardooz, why are you here so late at night?"

"I have work to catch up with in my office. Open the barrier."

"Do you have authorization from the Director? This is very unusual."

Talley could see the Iranian shaking like a leaf. He must have been convinced he was only inches away from a police dungeon and a very messy, painful death.

"No, I do not. This is urgent, open the gate, man. I don't have time for this."

"Please wait. I will check with the Chief Security Officer."

We don't have time for this shit. He makes that call and we're finished.

As he walked to the phone, Talley opened the door and jumped down. The man turned at the sound and received a double tap to the head from the Sig. Talley ran to him, lowered the body gently to the ground, and dragged him inside the guardhouse. Another guard walked into the room from somewhere out back, probably the bathroom. His eyes opened wide when he saw the stranger, and he grabbed for his pistol. Talley's Sig coughed twice, and he went down. He whirled as someone came up behind him, but it was only Anika. She frowned as she saw the bodies.

"Christ, the shit will hit the fan now."

"Open that barrier while I drag the bodies out of sight. We have to move fast, real fast."

He pulled the dead soldiers one by one into the small bathroom and closed the door. Then he ran back out to the truck. The barrier was open, and Anika stood next to it. He drove through. She closed it, and they drove through the complex. It only took a couple of minutes before they reached the rear gate. A red light showed ominously on the wall over the portal.

"Damn, it's alarmed," she said.

"Too bad. Let's get it open and let the men in. We have to locate those emails."

He opened the four massive bolts and turned the lever of the lock mechanism. As the door opened, the whole complex came alive with the sound of an alarm siren, an urgent, repetitive wail that echoed around the facility. The troopers ran inside and fanned out in a defensive position. He searched for Buchmann.

"Heinrich, we need to make this look like a terrorist operation. Try to locate some likely targets and wire them for demolition. I reckon we have five minutes, maybe ten, before they send in troops, so make it fast."

The German nodded and ran toward a building that looked as if it housed some kind of a power station, or maybe a cooling plant. Guy was behind him, holding onto the terrified Zardooz.

"Javeed, take us to your computer. How far away is it?"

"The next building, just past that one," he pointed. "But it's useless, they'll send in the Revolutionary Guard, and we'll be surrounded. We're going to die!"

"No, we're not. We've done this before, so help us out, and we'll get you out safe. Hurry it up, man. Domenico, me and Guy will go with Javeed. Prepare to receive Iranian reinforcements. We may have to fight our way out of here."

"Copy that."

"Anika, take one of the troopers and guard our truck. If we lose that, we'll be stuck here."

She nodded her understanding, and they sped toward

Javeed's office building. The door was locked. Guy fired two shots from his HK 416, shattering the glass door, and they ran in. The Iranian pointed to the stairs, and they ran up, following him into his office. He turned with a wild expression on his face.

"My computer, it's locked down at night. I forgot, it cannot be accessed," he shouted. "It's hopeless. We have to leave before they come."

"Why didn't you tell us before?" Talley asked.

"I've never been here at night. They told us about barring access after hours, but I forgot about it. We have to leave!"

Talley ignored him and examined the computer. It was a straightforward PC unit, linked to a network via cables in the back. He could see the panel of the hard drive fixed in the front of the case, which was anchored to the desk with a locked, heavy, steel security band.

"Guy, take the whole unit. Blast that lock off."

"Sure, but won't they see it's missing and wonder?"

"Not when we're finished, no." He keyed his mike. "This is Echo One. Buchmann, do you copy?"

"Ja, Buchmann here."

"We're in the office building. It's right next to where you planted your first charges. I want it to explode, and I mean a real, big explosion. Something that'll destroy everything inside."

"I can set a thermite incendiary charge. It'll torch the entire building."

"Do it fast, Heinrich." He checked his wristwatch. "I want you back at the gate in three minutes, no more."

"Copy that."

They ran down the stairs and out of the building.

Buchmann was heading toward them with Roy Reynolds helping him out, carrying a heavy pack of explosives.

"Make it quick, we're almost out of time."

They nodded as they sped into the building. Talley went back to the rear gate, noting with approval his men manning a defensive perimeter fifty meters from the exit. Then he heard the engines; trucks, possibly APCs, coming through the front gates.

"Anika, start the engine, and be ready to move out of here. Men, prepare for incoming fire. Vince, Jerry, see if you can hit them before they get near. Virgil, set up the M249 to cover our right flank. We may need it."

"Copy that."

"Valois, set up the other Minimi, and cover our left flank. Guy, take another man and get outside and cover our retreat. Make sure no one tries to sneak in behind us."

"Got it."

He watched for the enemy, but there was still no sign of them. Then the first of Buchmann's charges went off, and the entire complex went dark, security lights, street lamps, internal lights, everything. It was early. It was supposed to go off after they left.

Still, it could prove useful. Pity we didn't brought the NV gear.

Buchmann came running up out of the darkness.

"I have set the rest of the charges, but we need to be well clear before they detonate. It'll be a large explosion."

"Yeah, okay. Get to the truck. Guy's out there, help him cover our rear. Make sure we're set to go. We're pulling out in less than a minute."

"Jawohl, Herr Leutnant. The charges will explode in five minutes."

"Understood, now go."

He hurried off. Talley keyed his mike.

"Okay, everyone, we've got a big bang happening in less than five. Start pulling back out of the gate."

He saw chips of concrete ripped out the side of a building, as a stream of bullets smashed past Virgil's position. He opened his mouth to shout orders, but a dozen assault rifles opened up, and Virgil was punched back as some of the rounds hit him.

Did his vest take the impact? Dear Christ, I hope so. But the Minimi is out of action.

He ran forward and picked up the weapon, conscious that he was the only member of the unit not wearing armor, but they needed the firepower. He could see Virgil moving.

Thank Christ? His vest stopped the bullets.

"Open fire! We have hostiles coming in from the north."

He sighted on a bunch of Iranian militia rushing toward him and firing on the run. He pulled the trigger of the Minimi. The 5.56mm rounds poured out of the barrel, and he kept the trigger pressed down, spraying rounds every which way. In the light of the muzzle flashes, he saw six Iranians go down. The rest scuttled into cover.

"Vince, Jerry, try and locate those shooters on your side."

"We're on it. Jerry took off after a couple of squirters who broke away from that unit. They're working their way around our flank, and he's trying to hit them before they get any nearer."

"Copy that. Make it snappy. There's going to be one great mother of a bang in a couple of minutes. Take your last shots and get out. That's an order. Jerry, do you copy?"

"I copy you. I'm tracking them now. Just a minute,

wait." Talley heard the sound of suppressed shots. "That's one definite kill. The other one dived for cover, but I hit him in the leg as he went. I can…"

"Get out of there, Jerry, right now. And the rest of you, that building is gonna go up like a volcano in one minute. The explosion will take out the hostiles, so get yourselves out of there."

"On the way."

He looked around and saw the last of his men disappearing through the narrow gate.

Good, it's time to leave.

He picked up the Minimi and ran. He almost made it when more rifle fire slashed through the night, cutting him off from the exit. He dived for cover; aware that a single hit on his unprotected body could be fatal. He searched for the source of the incoming fire and saw the muzzle flashes of at least three assault rifles as they spewed bullets all around him. He checked his wristwatch. He had thirty seconds at most before the thermite charges went off and turned the area into a raging holocaust. He pulled the trigger and emptied the clip towards the shooters.

I hope it's enough. It has to be.

He leapt to his feet and started to run. Only ten paces until he was through the gate, and then one of the Iranian militiamen loomed around the corner. He smiled as he raised his rifle, and Talley knew he couldn't make it, couldn't beat the blast. He kept running. The building erupted as the explosion of the thermite charges ripped through it. Talley saw the walls literally bulge and begin to collapse, but it was a fleeting glimpse. The blast wave took him, hurling him through the open gate, and the breath whooshed out of his body as he slammed onto the hard tarmac; right next to Vince and Jerry, who'd been about to start back to cover him.

"You okay, Boss?" Vince asked him. "That was a spectacular exit."

Talley groaned as he picked himself up, feeling as if he'd fought ten rounds with Mike Tyson. "Yeah, I'll be fine. It's time to get out of here, let's go. What happened to…"

He stumbled as his brain refused to connect with his legs. Vince caught him and dragged him to the minivan and threw him inside. Immediately, the vehicle started moving. As they drove away, he could see the flames licking out from the destruction they'd left behind them.

"Jesus Christ," someone murmured. "When they find who did this, they'll come after us with everything they've got."

"They won't blame us," Guy murmured softly. "I was talking to Anika while we waited. She got MI6 Tehran Station to feed a rumor into the networks, some nonsense about an Israeli sponsored raid to undercut the Iranian nuclear program."

Someone laughed, "Poor bloody Israelis. They always get the blame."

"Yes, they do," he said soberly, "but we had to hit these bastards. Don't worry about the Israelis, they've been taking it for more than two thousand years. They're used to it."

Talley heard the bitter note in Guy's voice. It was understandable, coming from a man with the blood of refugees from Nazi Germany in his veins. But it was also true. It was way past time for the talking to stop, and for someone to start hitting the Iranians nuclear ambitions.

He'd no idea where they were headed, and every bone in his body hurt. He was content for someone else to make the decisions. When they eventually did come to a stop, he looked out at an odd looking building. It took him a few moments to realize it was an ancient castle or palace of some kind. They'd driven inside what had probably once been the main hall. He climbed out and was checking out the surroundings when Anika came around to the rear of the vehicle.

"What's this? Where are we?"

"It's an archaeological site, an ancient palace built by Cambyses II. He was a distant relation of Darius the Great and also a relation of Cyrus the Great. We're just on the edge of the Sohanak Park. I was involved with this excavation last year. We pulled out when they withdrew the funding, so I knew it was empty. We can stay here until we're ready to move on."

"How far are we from the other dig at Niavaran?"

"No more than ten kilometers. I'll get on to my boss, Jeff Petersen. We'll need his help. The first priority is to get rid of this truck. There'll be an APB out for it all over Iran. The second is to get hold of a laptop computer that can decrypt and read the drive inside the computer we took from the AEOI. Jeff can arrange both those things for us, unless you'd prefer to use CIA."

"No, contact Petersen and see what he can do."

She nodded. They were on their own while the rest of the unit checked out the area. Abruptly, she leaned forward and gave him a long, lingering kiss.

"What was that for?"

She stared into his eyes. "For keeping us all safe, Abe."

He grinned, embarrassed. "I'd save it for later. We have

a long way to go. We're not out of the woods yet."

"We'll get there. I know that. You'll get us there, Abe."

He felt his face was glowing red. "You'd better make contact with Petersen before I do something I regret."

She gave him a meaningful glance. "Maybe another time?"

"Out!"

She left to contact her boss. They had to decrypt that hard-won data, and pray it would take them nearer to their target, Arash.

CHAPTER SIX

Guy posted sentries and sited the Minimis to provide a withering crossfire if any hostiles tried to come at them. They had to take every precaution. They were twenty klicks from the center of Tehran, capital of Iran, home of one of the cruelest, most tyrannical regimes in the world. A regime that even now would be doing everything in its power to hunt them down and kill them. They were the enemy, to be obliterated on sight. So far, they'd achieved little more than stir up a hornet's nest. Arash, the shadowy figure behind the plan to buy in Pakistani nukes, was still not located. They had a lot of ground to cover, and the clock was ticking. Everything depended on what lay on the hard drive they'd brought out from the Javeed's office. If it led nowhere, Talley would need an alternative plan, plan B. The trouble was, he hadn't got a plan B. He knew he was stumbling along, being driven by events rather than pursuing a tightly drawn operational plan.

Echo Six had hit trouble almost from the word go. The troops they'd encountered on the way in, the search of the dig that coincided with their arrival, and the arrest of Guy's squad when they went into the old cinema in Tehran. The only part of the operation that had gone to plan was locating Javeed Zardooz and retrieving his computer, and that had been as a result of intelligence Anika had uncovered, nothing to do with CIA or even the Brit Head of Station, Petersen. He cursed the absence of their own NATO field based intelligence and their reliance on the facilities of member nations. Despite the term 'alliance' in the acronym NATO, many of the countries saw themselves in anything but an alliance with the other member countries. It was every man for himself. He looked up and saw Anika coming toward him.

"Jeffrey Petersen is on the way here. He's arranged more transport for us. He said to find somewhere around here where we can lose the truck. The whole of Tehran is hunting for it."

"I'll see to it."

She nodded. "I'll be back in a few minutes."

He called Rovere. "Dom, find somewhere to stash that truck, and ask Heinrich to set a charge to tumble some rocks over it."

"Right away."

Anika returned shortly after with a steaming, hot mug of tea. He nodded his appreciation.

"Thanks. I need to make sure the men have…"

"Already done, Abe. Guy gave me a hand, and we brewed up enough for everyone. It's been a long night. There are a few things here from when we were excavating the site, plenty of tea, powdered milk, and sugar, as well as bottled water. We expected to be back when the funding kicked in, but it never did."

"You enjoy the archaeology, or do you prefer your day job?" He looked at her keenly.

She's like a chameleon. Archaeologist one moment, MI6 spy the next. Who is the real Doctor Anika Frost?

"I'm not much of a spy," she said thoughtfully. "I see the kinds of nasty tricks people play on each other, and it's really not me. I'd be more than happy to spend all my time in places like this."

"So why don't you?"

She grinned. "One word. Money. We rely on charitable grants, and when they're not forthcoming, the work comes to a stop. Remember, that's the reason Professor Wenstrom agreed to help you out."

"Yeah, it's hard to know whose side he's on. I don't think he has much time for our Western values. I get the impression he prefers the life in Sandland."

"Only because it's a chance for him to make a name for himself. People like him, they think of themselves first, last, and all times in between."

"What about Miles Preston?"

She grimaced. "He's like Wenstrom on steroids."

"That bad, eh?"

"You'll find out, sooner or later."

They looked up as a vehicle, a battered truck with a high canvas covered back, drove into the courtyard area. Talley recognized it as a Naynava, the Iranian built troop transport and well known to NATO. He tensed. As far as he knew, they were used exclusively by the military. In the driving seat was a stranger, and even though it was still not quite dawn, it was obviously an Iranian. Before he could issue orders, the unit scattered, and Talley and Anika were alone; both in civilian clothes, they could pass as researchers. In his case, only just. The truck came to a stop, and the driver stayed in his seat.

What's he waiting for? Is the truck full of troops hidden in the back?

"Echo One to Echo Two. Guy, do you have him covered?"

"Both machine guns, Boss. Anything happens I don't like, and that truck gets blasted."

"Copy that."

The first fingers of dawn were creeping across the desert as the early sun began to appear over the horizon, chasing away the shadows. He could see the driver of the truck better now.

He's still waiting, for what? It's weird.

He was about to go and inspect the truck when he heard another vehicle approaching, this one a civilian SUV, a big Nissan Patrol. As it drew nearer, he relaxed. He could see Jeffrey Petersen in the driving seat. The Nissan stopped next to the truck, and Petersen stepped out. He beckoned to the civilian in the other truck, and the man climbed down. Petersen walked up to him, his face grim.

"I guess you know what you've stirred up in Tehran?"

"Yep."

The Brit stood there silent for a few moments and looked around the site. He turned back to Talley and indicated the driver of the truck.

"This is Ramin. He does odd jobs for me. Don't worry; he can't understand a word of English. He drove the truck out for you, and I'll take him back in the SUV. You like it?"

"I thought they were only used by the military."

"They are, so it's the perfect camouflage. No one will suspect it's being used by the enemy."

"They'll see our uniforms. That'll give it away."

"In that case only use it at night." He looked annoyed. "I can't think of every damn thing for you, Talley. If you want Iranian uniforms, go and shoot some soldiers. I gather you're pretty good at that."

Talley was about to snap back, but he realized he was tired, too tired. It had been a long night.

"Okay, we'll manage with the truck. Did you bring the laptop?"

"I thought it would be best if I took the hard drive back to my station. I could take a look at it and let you know what I find. It may need some work decrypting the contents."

"Thanks, but I'll just take the laptop."

The man pursed his lips. "Don't trust me, is that it? Listen, Talley, you're in enough trouble. Just give me the hard drive and I'll get it analyzed."

When Talley didn't reply, he shook his head, went to the Nissan, and took an aluminum case from the trunk.

"This is state of the art, and I'd appreciate it back when you're done. Anika knows how to use it. She seems to have attached herself to you."

"Okay, is there anything I need to know? Any special security precautions in place that may make our movements difficult?"

Petersen gave him a skeptical look. "You mean apart from half the Iranian Army and the Revolutionary Guard hunting down the men who attacked their atomic facility? Not really, no."

"Do they know it was us, I mean a NATO unit who was involved?"

"No, they think it was a combined Israeli air and ground

attack."

Talley nodded. "Good. We'll contact you if we need any more help. We have to make a start on that hard drive."

"Are you sure you don't want me to help you with that?"

"I'm sure."

"I have to know what you find on it. You will contact me as soon as you know what you have? It's important I know straight away."

"I'll keep you informed."

Why is he so agitated about that hard drive? It's almost as if he's worried about something we might find on it. Or is he one of Javeed's boyfriends?

Petersen stared at him for a few moments, then called to the Iranian. Ramin turned on his heel and walked back to the Nissan. He drove away in a cloud of dust, disappearing to the south in the direction of Tehran. As Talley watched them, he realized the spook hadn't spoken to Anika.

Now that's interesting. They're supposed to be colleagues, both working for MI6. I wonder what the story is behind that?

"He's not too happy with me, right now."

He looked around. Anika had come up behind him.

"Why not?"

"Because I haven't been reporting in as ordered. There are a lot of odd things happening with this operation, Abe. I don't know who to trust, so I figured it would be best kept to the people putting their necks on the chopping block."

"You think he's selling us out?"

It wouldn't be the first time a British spy worked for the people he was supposed to spy on. Ever since the Kim Philby affair, when the MI6 intelligence operative had defected to Moscow during the cold war, there'd been a stream of Brits who'd gone over to the other side.

"I doubt it, no, but it's better to be safe rather than sorry. I'll take the laptop and get started. Heinrich has removed the drive, and inside the laptop case there are a selection of cables to hook it up."

"You think you can decrypt it?"

"The laptop is loaded with the latest decryption software, so it should be possible. I'll let you know later."

"Sure. And thanks."

"No problem. I'll grab Javeed, he knows the passwords they used to protect the drive, and find somewhere quiet to go to work."

"How is he holding up?"

"He's terrified. He knows there's no going back, so I guess he'll want us to get him out of the country when this is all over."

He grinned, "I'd like someone to get us out of the country."

She smiled back as she walked away.

He spent some time with Guy, going over their next moves, but it all depended on the hard drive. He arranged for them to sleep in shifts so there'd always be two men on sentry duty. Anika refused to take a break, not until she'd made progress with the emails. So far, she was still locked out of the hard drive, and Javeed's regular passwords were useless once the machine had been removed from the facility.

"Apparently, it looks for an administrator password across the network," she explained. "Until we have it, we can't read anything."

He took the first watch. The sky was a vivid blue as

the heat of the sun seared down on the ancient ruins. The only excitement was when Heinrich fired the charge that buried the truck they'd used in the raid. It was now beneath a tumbled pile of rocks that was once part of the inner defensive wall of the palace. A sacrilege, if you were a historian, but a lifesaver for his men. Eventually, he was relieved, and he fell instantly into a deep, dreamless sleep. When he awoke, it was because he'd heard someone talking loud, as if in argument. Anika was nearby, speaking on a satphone. He waited until she'd finished and walked over to her.

"What's up?"

He could see she looked drained with tiredness. Her eyes were red, and her face still bore the smudge marks of the action the night before. She'd obviously been too busy working to clean up.

"That was Jeffrey. I managed to decrypt the hard drive and pull off some of the emails that looked promising. Javeed told me they're from someone he only knew as Archer, that's obviously Arash. This guy kept asking him pointed questions about the logistics of the operation at Amir Abad and the logistics of handling nuclear warheads. When he didn't like it, the Director overrode him and told him to give this Archer what he wanted. It has to be him, I've looked at the emails, and he continually asks for information. It's all to do with fission warheads and associated trigger mechanism, types of materials, quantities, and so on."

"That's not much help," Talley grunted. "What else?"

"I lifted the IP address from the emails. Unfortunately, it's a hard one to trace. I asked Jeffrey Petersen to run it through the Station systems, but he refused point blank."

"He what?"

"He said it was a waste of the department's resources, and that a search would reveal nothing."

"Do you believe him?"

She shook her head. "No, he's covering something, but I don't know what."

Yet again, we've hit a wall. Instead of the operation driving forward on the information we extracted from Amir Abad, we're once more at a standstill, waiting for the Iranians to uncover our hiding place, and it won't take them forever to work it out. They're not total fools. Unless...

"Petersen, you think he'd sell us out to the Iranians?"

"No, I don't believe it. There's something, some reason for him refusing to run that IP address, but he brought the truck out to us, remember?"

"Yeah, he did."

"There must be another way, someone who'll run that address through their computers."

She thought for a few moments. "There is one possibility. A guy I know in London, Adrian Featherstone. We were at Oxford together, and we used to, you know, date. Yes, I'll try him. Give me a few minutes. What time is it now?"

He checked his wristwatch. "0925."

"Right, that's just before one o'clock in London. Perfect, I'll try and get through to Adrian at Vauxhall Cross."

He recalled the odd shaped building in the heart of London on the south bank of the River Thames close to Vauxhall Bridge. Known locally as Legoland, or even Babylon on Thames. It was the home of the Secret Intelligence Service, MI6.

She was away almost twenty minutes on the satphone

link, and when she came back, she looked thoughtful.

"What is it?"

"There was no problem checking out the IP address. He put it through our experts at GCHQ in Cheltenham, and they got right back to him. The emails were sent from a coffee shop near the Gandhi Center in Tehran, the Café Yusef. Javeed says he knows it quite well, but he wasn't aware that emails came from there. They have an internet café in the rear, and that's where the emails were sent from. But it's the rest of the information Adrian uncovered that worries me. GCHQ, the Government Communication Headquarters, listens to and decrypts message chatter from all over the world. He told me something interesting. They've intercepted messages to and from VEVAK, that's the Ministry of Intelligence and Security. They're starting to check out all known archaeological sites around Tehran."

"So they know about us."

"That's not certain, but they suspect something. They're sure to come and check this place out."

"Shit! We need to get out of here. Any ideas where we can hide out until nightfall?"

"There's a derelict industrial estate to the east of Tehran about ten klicks from here. Plenty of empty buildings."

"That'll do." He stood up. "Guy!"

A few seconds later, the SAS man appeared. "What is it?"

"Could be trouble. We're out of here. Two minutes."

"Copy that. I'll get them moving."

They piled into the Naynava truck and headed out. It was a risk driving the military transport in broad daylight. They'd only just turned onto the main highway a few seconds earlier when they saw a military convoy roar past at high speed and take the turn for the ruined palace they'd just abandoned. But they reached their destination without hitting any road blocks and drove into the scarred wasteland that had once been a thriving industrial complex. Talley chose a likely derelict factory, driving into the yard. The gate had been removed at some time in the past, as had much of the buildings, leaving only a ghostly skeleton of rusting steel, clad with broken panels. It turned out to be a disused brick factory, and when they drove inside the main building, there was sufficient cover to hide the vehicle behind the old kilns. Stairs led up to the second floor where they could rest and establish a good OP. They set up the two Minimis with a field of fire that could sweep anyone approaching the building. Vince found a narrow staircase leading up to the roof. Out in the sunshine, there was a rotting platform that had once held a crane. It overlooked the courtyard and several streets beyond, a perfect sniper stand. When he was satisfied, Talley started to work out their next move. Anika, Guy, and Domenico joined him.

"We have to get to that café and take a snoop around. With any luck, it'll take us a step nearer to identifying this guy Arash, the Archer."

"That shouldn't be difficult," Anika said. "We can call a cab and arrange for it to pick us up a couple of blocks from here. I'll use my satphone."

"Not yet, we need to wait until nightfall. Guy, you'd better come into town with us, and we'll take Buchmann as well. It'll keep him and Valois apart for a while. Domenico, you'll be in command while I'm gone, and make sure you all stay out of sight." They all grinned. Every time the

Frenchman and the German were together, there was trouble, and it was getting worse as they came under increasing pressure. Each seemed to blame the other for every misfortune that hit the unit. Domenico nodded emphatically.

"I'll take care of things, Abe."

"Good."

They managed to get some rest while they waited for nightfall. There were no alarms, no patrols, and no unwelcome visitors. It reminded them of just how large Iran was. More than a million and a half square kilometers, a fifth the size of the US, much of it mountainous, and vastly bigger than its neighbor, Iraq; a difficult country to search for fugitives, but also a difficult country in which to fight a war. Talley was reminded of the importance of his operation. If they failed, and invasion became the only way to stop the Iranians getting nuclear weapons, there was the potential for a war that would devastate not only the country itself, but also the military and economies of those combatants who took part. He found a quiet piece of shade in the lee of a stone wall and dozed. Anika soon found him. She looked anxious.

"Are you okay?"

"Me?" Her eyes opened in surprise. "I'm fine. Why do you ask?"

"Something's on your mind."

She grinned wanly, "Not really. It's not easy, this operation. There's so much that can go wrong. I just wish, well, if I could, I'd like to do more to help."

She took his hand and kissed him softly on the lips. He returned the kiss, and then let her move in close to him so she could use his strength as the illusion of protection.

Soon, her breathing became regular, and he knew she was asleep.

What did that mean? She'd help if she could? What help, and what is stopping her? There's something I don't understand here, and if I ask, she'll clam up. What is bugging her?

Night fell, and they walked over a kilometer from the hideout before Anika called a cab. The company was suspicious being asked to come out to an area they knew to be derelict, but Anika persuaded them that they were surveyors. That, and the offer of double the fare swung it. Twenty minutes later, they were seated in a white Mercedes taxi, speeding toward the center of the city. When they asked for the Café Yusef, the man turned in his seat and gave them a leering smile.

"If you're out for a good time, I can find anything you want. Girls, boys, alcohol, drugs, whatever." He handed Talley a card, "Just call me on my cellphone, and I'll fix up it up."

"That's okay, buddy. We just want to relax, nothing too exciting."

"Then why do you go to the Yusef? It is neither quiet nor relaxing…oh, I see. You are there for the show. I can take you to better places. You wouldn't believe what they…"

"Just take us to the Yusef. If we need anything else, we'll call you."

"Yes, of course."

He lapsed into silence, and they looked at each other. They were beginning to get an idea of what kind of café they were headed to. The doorman stopped them, insisting they each had to pay an entrance fee of a hundred thousand rials, and then they walked into the café. In the strict, Islamic society of Iran, where women could be beaten and even imprisoned for not wearing a headscarf, where men and women could be stoned to death or hung from a crane for adultery, the Café Yusef turned the rules on their head. Put simply, it was a nightclub where the theme was sexual debauchery. They stared around in astonishment.

"This place is fucking depraved," Guy said in wonderment. "Look at them!"

Men and women in all stages of undress haunted dimly lit booths, where little was left to the imagination. It was obvious that in the darker corners, the patrons had no inhibitions about performing the sex act in a public place. It stank, of perfume, musk, stale booze, and sex. But the worst part was the young people serving the booze. There was clearly no age limit, and many looked to be no more than twelve years old, a couple of them even younger. They were all topless, girls and boys.

"It could explain why Jeffrey Petersen didn't want to identify the place," Anika breathed. "It's obvious he's a customer. If his bosses found out, he'd be sent home in disgrace."

"You're sure he's a customer?" Talley looked at her in surprise. "It doesn't seem like him."

"Hmm. He has a reputation in the Tehran Station. Some of them say he's a pervert. I've never believed it, but now I'm not so sure."

They avoided a boy who could have been no older than twelve and was trying to get them to buy him drinks. Anika led them through to a back room where the walls were lined with computers rather than copulating couples. The music was quieter, and the atmosphere cleaner. A couple of men were tapping at keyboards. The place was almost deserted. Inside a booth set just inside the door, a sad-eyed young Arab boy waited for them to rent one of the machines.

"Guy, wait here and cover us. Make sure no one comes in."

"Copy that."

He drew his pistol from under his shirt, holding it low down at his side.

"Heinrich, the two guys using the PCs. Get them down on the floor. Make sure they don't contact anyone, and tell them to keep quiet. You'd better take their cellphones."

The German nodded, his disgust with the place evident. "With pleasure."

"Anika, I want you to translate. Let's have a quiet chat with our friend in the booth, see if he's amenable to helping us."

He eased out his Sig, kept it out of sight, and pushed through the half-height door that led into the booth. The Arab looked at him, at first startled, and then his face turned to anger.

"You cannot come in here. This is for staff only. You must leave."

"Yeah, sure. Son, I want you to help us with a problem we have."

"I will call security, and you will be thrown out! Now get out of here."

His hand snaked toward a telephone, and Talley smashed the barrel of his Sig on boy's wrist. He yelped in pain.

"Now listen to me, pal. We only want a peek at your system, that's all. You cooperate, and you won't be hurt.

If not…" He looked into the room where Buchmann had the two customers face down on the floor. "You can join them. And that man, he's a killer. Hates Arabs."

The kid squirmed in terror, his face pale, "No, no, I will do whatever you want."

"Good, we need to take a look at the records on your main server. Which machine do you use for admin?"

He pointed to the nearest terminal, "That one."

"Good, let's log in and see what we can find."

He sat down and logged in as administrator. Talley saw rows of mixed Arabic and Western characters fill the screen. He looked at Anika.

"Can you understand this?"

"I think so, yes. I brought along a data stick. I'll transfer any files I find that look promising and look at them later."

"Okay." He looked at the Arab, "You, get out of there. We'll take it from here."

"Yes, Sir, I won't cause any problems. What is it you're looking for?"

"One of your clients, he used the id 'Archer', or maybe the name Arash. You heard of him?"

The Arab blanched, and his eyes shifted away, "Er, no, Sir, not that name. I never heard of it. Never!"

The kid was one of the worst liars he'd ever encountered. Talley gripped the front of his shirt and rammed his Sig against his mouth. It was harsh, and he hated himself for roughing up a kid, but if his mission failed, the consequences would be far worse.

"Last chance, kid. Who is he? Either you tell me now, or I blow your head off."

"Abe, I've got it," Anika said quietly. "He's definitely a client, and it looks as if he comes in here every evening about," she looked at her watch, "now. Eight o'clock, 2000. He's due any moment!"

Talley was still holding the Arab boy, and he jammed his pistol harder into his face. "What does he look like? Quick, it's your only chance to live! Describe him."

"Please, don't hurt me. He is a Westerner. He comes in with a message pad and looks at it to send his messages. Twice he came in with a religious man, an Ayatollah, the man who runs the Basij, the Morality Police."

"Yeah, good. Describe this Westerner to us."

"He…"

Gunfire erupted in the room. It came from a small vent they hadn't noticed on the opposite side of the room, four loud shots. Talley leapt for cover, pushing Anika to the floor, and Guy went the other way, reacting like lightning to the threat. He shouted at the SAS man.

"Guy, get out there. Find him and stop him."

"On the way."

"Anika, are you okay?"

"I'm fine."

He looked at the Arab, but it was too late. Two of the bullets had taken him, one in the chest, one in the stomach. It was obvious the wounds were fatal, and he lay on the floor, blood pumping out onto the cheap carpet. While he watched, the kid gasped out his last breath and lay still. Talley got to his feet and looked at the main server. The other two shots had ripped right through the unit, destroying the drives. He could hear shouts and screams as people reacted to the shots. Then the door opened and Guy came back in.

"He got away. There's no sign of him."

"Okay, we have to get out of here. Anika, we're leaving."

They ran through crowds of screaming customers. The rear door was open, and men and women were streaming out the back way, in case it was a police raid. They followed them out onto the street and walked rapidly away from the café. Talley knew they'd just lost their best chance of identifying Arash.

Now we're no further forward than before we first arrived in the country. Whoever shot the kid inside the café deliberately destroyed the hard drive. It could only have been Arash, or one of his people. Which means we were close, real close. But our shadowy opponent always seems to be a couple of steps ahead of us. The door of opportunity has slammed tight shut in our faces. We're no nearer to finding Arash or stopping the transfer of the warheads. We're fucked!

CHAPTER SEVEN

Anika found a cab that took them out of the city. Talley was seething with anger, how the hell could this guy always be ahead of them? And yet so far, they'd evaded capture by the Iranians. It was weird, almost like a riddle. He felt the answer was so close he could almost reach out and touch it. And touch Arash. And kill him. They walked the last couple of blocks in silence and went inside the derelict brick factory. Domenico was waiting for them.

"Did you find anything?"

Talley shook his head. "Someone shot the guy before he could tell us. All we know is he's a Westerner."

The Italian chuckled. "So we're down to only a hundred thousand people inside the country. I think we may have a problem finding him from that description. We may as well pack up and go home."

"Not quite."

They looked at Anika.

"I managed to copy some files before the server was destroyed. I'll take a look at them now. Maybe it'll help us, maybe not. Give me a half hour."

"I'll give you anything you want if you can get this operation back on track."

"I may take you up on that, Abe Talley," she replied.

He looked severely at Rovere, who was doing his best to keep a straight face. She disappeared to find and boot up her laptop.

"Love is a smoke made with the fumes of a sigh," Domenico said. "As the immortal Shakespeare once…"

"Button it!"

"Sure, sure," he replied, chuckling and then walking away, whistling another jaunty tune.

While she worked on the data, Talley prowled around the derelict factory. He climbed the stairs to the second floor and found the sentries were alert and watchful, using their NV gear to watch for any signs of trouble. He continued wandering the dusty wreckage of a once proud business, wondering how it had all gone wrong, and what had happened to those who once made their living there.

It's always the same answer. Scratch the surface of poverty and degradation in the Middle East and you'll find a mullah, an imam, an ayatollah. And still the people believe in them.

There was little more he could do but wait and pray Anika recovered something useful. If not, Domenico was right; they may as well pack up and go home. Time was running out, there were only three days before the nukes were due to be transferred across the border. He inwardly cursed this opaque, gloomy society, ruled with an iron cruelty by religious fanatics. Yet where such sick debauchery as they'd seen at the Café Yusef went almost unchecked. The major players were able to buy off the cops, while the average Joe in the street was whipped and punished to stay in line. The whole country was upside down, outwardly religious and ultra conservative, yet inwardly, as rotten and stinking as the carcass of a dead polecat. The place was just a delusion practiced on the poor long suffering populace. Then Anika emerged from the derelict storeroom she'd been using to work in. Her face was thoughtful. Then he saw her expression, and his hopes soared.

Christ, she's found it!

"What is it?"

"I think I have something."

"Thank God. Go on."

He realized the men were staring at them and listening. Domenico and Guy edged closer.

"I uncovered an ayatollah who exchanged messages both with the ID 'Archer', and with Javeed. It's too much of a coincidence. Would you bring Javeed to me? I need him in on this."

They brought the Iranian. He'd been shut inside an old brick kiln. He was filthy, covered in soot and dirt, and unrecognizable from the sleek man they'd first encountered. He could have been a coal miner, but he was calm, seemingly resigned to his fate.

Probably expects to die, Talley thought. *He could be right. There's plenty of time yet, for all of us.*

"Javeed, I need your help."

He nodded dully but didn't speak.

"You forwarded emails to and from an ayatollah. They included a carbon copy to the ID 'Archer', do you recall? There were discussions about uranium enrichment, trigger systems, and components of a nuclear bomb."

They all saw the fear in his eyes. "I had no choice. You

must understand that. The ayatollahs rule this country. When they threatened me…"

"Javeed, I don't care. You said before you didn't know, but I think you do. Tell me about this man."

The Iranian sighed, his shoulders slumped, and he started to speak. "The man you refer to is Ayatollah Faridoon Majidi. He is very powerful, many people fear him."

"What does he do, this Majidi? Is he in government?"

He looked at her as if she was stupid. "Faridoon Majidi? He is the head of the Basij, the Morality Police. He has his headquarters inside the Revolutionary Guard Barracks. He is one of the most powerful men in Iran, and the most feared. That's how he got away with coming to the Café Yusef. People were too frightened to make a complaint."

"You recall that Revolutionary Guard Barracks?" Guy interjected. "Opposite that old cinema where they came to arrest us. They took us across the road and put us in a cell before the prison transport came. It's a local headquarters for the Basij."

Talley nodded. "If he is Arash, that's where we have to go to get to him. Look on the bright side, Guy. It's not Ahmadinejad. Going after him would have been a bastard."

Guy smiled. "What about the Westerner? We know nothing about him. It could be he's on Arash's payroll, or he could be Arash himself, and this ayatollah is one of his gomers."

Talley looked at Javeed. "Have you seen this guy? He could he be an American, or maybe a Brit."

"I am sorry. I do not know him."

"Okay, we'll have to go for Majidi. He's the only name

we have. If we take him out, the operation could collapse like a pack of cards."

"How are you planning to do this, Boss?" Guy asked. The other men watched and waited for the answer; one that could seal their fate, and possibly result in their deaths.

Talley grimaced. "We have to find a way to bypass the Revolutionary Guard to get to Majidi, that's the obvious ball breaker. We need a way into their barracks."

There was complete silence as they looked at each other, as if he'd just pronounced a sentence of death on them.

"I can get us in there."

They all looked at Anika. Finally, Domenico asked the question that was on their minds.

"How?"

"The qanats."

"The qanats?" Talley was dubious, and then he recalled the nightmare. They were trapped in a qanat by rising water. Anika called out for his help, and she had died. He pushed it to the back of his mind.

"A few months ago," she continued, "I uncovered a map giving details of a previously unknown series of qanats that runs from Niavaran, taking water from the mountains all the way to Tehran. Preliminary excavations show a well at Nezam Abad, about two kilometers from the city center, which give access to the main system. It runs all the way through to Martyr's Square, and according to the map, there is a well that actually surfaces inside the Pasdaran Barracks."

Domenico for once looked unhappy.

"However we get inside, there must be a couple of thousand troops in there. It's an impossible situation. "

"No more than a thousand, according to recent

intelligence reports," she corrected him.

"And there are twenty of us." He shook his head. "It's not good odds. We'd be better off if we took this guy out when he's away from that place."

"As far as I know, he rarely ventures out of there, and when he does, it's always unannounced. The Basij is not the most popular organization in Iran, and there are a lot of people who'd like to kill him. We have to get to him while he's inside. It's the only way."

"It's crazy!" Guy persisted. "Abe, there has to be an easier way."

"I don't think there is." Talley shook his head. "Ever since we've been inside this damn country, they've been ahead of us every step we've taken. All we've managed to do is fight our way out of trouble. They were on to us before we even reached the dig, and the shooter who killed that poor guy in the Café Yusef is still running around, trying to block our moves. It's no way to achieve what we came here to do. Okay, we have a name, that's progress, but only if we go ahead and deal with this character before someone else takes another pop at us. If Majidi won't come out of the Pasdaran Barracks, we'll have to pay him a visit before he's alerted and spirited away."

"Abe," Rovere murmured, "a thousand men in there. Are you serious?"

"We can do it, Dom, but we're going to need help. First, we'll need some kind of a diversion to get those troops out of the barracks. We'll also need to lay on air cover in case we run into trouble when we're inside."

Welland nodded thoughtfully. "It could be done, but there are a lot of ifs, Boss. Will that qanat takes us in there, can you be sure about that?" he looked at Anika.

"My assessment is that the qanat will be usable, and it definitely runs under the barracks. But I can't be sure until I see it."

"So we could put this operation in place and find we can't even get inside?"

"It could happen, yes."

He looked at Talley. "Like I said, too many ifs."

"I hear you. Nonetheless, this is what they pay us for, and this could be the most important operation we've ever undertaken. It's time to finish this. We have to sneak in there, take down this fucker Majidi, and sneak out without them being any the wiser."

They worked halfway through the rest of the night putting the elements of the plan together. Talley finally pronounced he was satisfied, until he talked to Admiral Brooks and told him what he'd need.

"You're seriously asking me to station an armed drone over Tehran? Tell me I've misunderstood you, Lieutenant."

"No, Sir, you haven't. That's exactly what we need."

"You know it could start a war? If the Iranians caught on to a NATO drone over their capital, well, it's a damn good thing they're not in possession of nuclear weapons right now. They'd sure as hell have their finger on the button, and ready to launch a strike against us."

"That's why we're here, Admiral, to stop them."

Brooks sighed. "Yeah, I know why you're there, Talley, and I know the operation is critical. But I don't want to start one war to prevent another one. We sent you in there to work undercover, not park your tanks on Ahmadinejad's front lawn."

"Which is why I'm asking for the Avenger. It worked last time around."

"I damn nearly lost my job over that one, Lieutenant. That drone was one of only three currently operational in the Mid East, and it's highly secret. If the Iranians got their hands on one of those babies, we'd spend the rest of our careers counting penguins on the NATO Antarctic Research Facility."

"They won't find out, Sir. That's the idea of a stealth drone."

"Don't play games with me, Talley. You know as well as I do, things that aren't supposed to go wrong have a habit of doing just that."

"Admiral, we don't have a choice. We can't assault the Pasdaran Barracks without air support. It would be impossible. Neither could we use more men. It would attract too much attention. The only way to do this is with smoke and mirrors."

"The quickness of the hand deceives the eye?"

"Exactly, Sir."

"Yeah, let's hope so." He sighed heavily. "Very well, I'll arrange for the Avenger to be in place when you need it. God help us all if it goes wrong. Anything else?"

"No, we can handle the rest of the operation."

"How will you cope with a thousand Revolutionary Guards?"

"We've arranged a diversion. Guy Welland has an idea that should draw them away from the barracks."

"What's the plan?"

"A mock assassination attempt."

"You're posing as government assassins? That's not far from the real truth," Brooks chuckled.

"We'll stage a suicide attack, an attempted assassination on the President of the Islamic Republic of Iran.

Mahmoud Ahmadinejad."

There was silence for a few, long seconds. Finally, Brooks replied. "Yeah, I reckon that would get their interest."

But Talley felt uncomfortable, even using that single word, 'assassin', reminded him of Kay's bitter diatribe, accusing him of being a government assassin.

She knew where to stick the knife in, plum center into my sense of duty and honor. Whichever way I jump, I'm screwed, either with my family or with my unit.

* * *

It was pitch dark when they searched for the well that would give them entrance to the qanat. It was an area of waste ground lying between two decaying apartment blocks in Nezam Abad, a suburb of Tehran. The area was given over to cheap housing for the poorer section of the community. This being a Muslim country that constituted the overwhelming majority. Earlier, Guy and Virgil walked partway back into the city and hotwired a delivery truck, plain white and unwritten, to transport the unit into the city. After nightfall, they dropped off Talley's assault team close to the entrance to the qanat, and then drove away to start working on the diversionary attack. Talley smiled to himself. Buchmann had packed all their spare explosives into the truck. The plan was to drive to the Iranian Parliament building, two klicks from Nezam Abad, jam the gas pedal to the floor and aim it at the main entrance. It would be timed for when Ahmadinejad was due to appear for an important speech. Just before they struck, Anika would put an anonymous call through to the cops, warning of a threat to assassinate the President. During previous attempts by rebels to kill him, she'd told them the Pasdaran flooded the area to protect the President. Guy and Virgil were was dressed like locals. Javeed would go with them, to act as a guide and interpreter if they ran into any trouble.

"If that doesn't pull them out of the barracks, I don't know what will," Guy had smiled, enjoying the idea of tearing a gaping hole in Iranian security. "You'll hear it explode, no matter how far underground you are. Better pray it doesn't bring the roof down."

"It'll be fine. Those qanats have been standing for thousands of years. Make sure you clear the area immediately. Don't forget, we'll be out of contact while we're underground, so the timing will be critical. It's now 2030, and the President is due to arrive shortly after 2200 hours to give his speech. You have to hit it at 2200 exactly, just before he gets there. We'll be in position, ready to enter the barracks as soon as the troops start rushing towards the Parliament."

"And if you're not in position, if there's a problem with the qanat, like a roof fall, or a blockage?" Guy had asked.

"In that case, we're in trouble. We can't plan for every contingency. We'll just have to wing this one. Anything else?"

Guy had shaken his head. They'd planned as much as they could. Now it was all up to chance.

If Lady Luck is on our side, we may just pull if off. If not, well, best not think about that.

He tripped over an old bicycle that had been left on the ground, hidden by a tangle of weeds. The apartments either side of them were brightly lit, and a cacophony of Arabic music came from a score of radios, none of them tuned to the same station. Men shouted, children screamed as they played, and women called mournfully to loved ones. But the wasteland was dark, and they were using NV gear, and it didn't reveal the rusting steel of the bicycle frame and bent spokes, camouflaged by weeds.

"Anika, is there any sign of the well?"

She'd borrowed their spare NV gear to hunt for the well opening, and he smiled at her face, half hidden by the four lenses of the goggles.

"Nothing yet. It should be here, by my reckoning. Right where we're standing."

"Is it possible they filled it in when they built the apartment blocks?"

"I hope not, but they may have demolished the structure and left a cover over the shaft for safety."

He turned to the men behind. "All of you start searching for a well cover. It'll be flush with the ground."

They hunted for another ten minutes. Nothing.

"Are you sure it's here?"

"Abe, it has to be." She sounded desperate. "These qanats are important in this country. You don't just get rid of them."

"So it has to be hidden by this undergrowth. We'll have to search for it the hard way. Use your combat knives, and start tapping the ground around us until you strike something solid. You know how it's done, make it a grid search as if we were crossing a minefield."

There was a chorus of groans, but it was a token protest. The men got down on their knees and started. Ten minutes later Roy Reynolds' combat knife hit pay dirt.

"I've got it, a metal hatch flush with the ground. Has to be it."

"Can you get it open? Robert, give him a hand."

They used the blades of their knives to force the metal hatch open. The NV goggles showed up the shaft as being about six meters deep. Roy dropped a pebble, and there was a loud splash.

"We've got water. I'll drop a rope and go down to take a look."

"Make it quick."

"Boss, someone coming. It could be a cop," he heard Valois whisper.

"Everyone get down. Vince, Jerry, you got him covered?"

"We're on it," DiMosta replied, his voice a soft murmur. "Yeah, it is a cop, but I think he's been hitting the sauce. He looks a bit unsteady. I'd guess he's been partying with his girlfriend in one of these apartments."

"Copy that. Let him go past. With any luck he won't even notice us."

There was no need to kill the cop, providing he didn't pose any kind of a threat. They waited in the darkness as he came nearer. He was singing some kind of an Arabic song, and he almost made it past. At the last moment something caught his attention, probably a noise from the nearby apartments. He changed direction and stumbled over Robert Valois. The Frenchman reacted automatically as the cop sprawled over him. Talley saw his huge combat knife rise, about to slash down and through the man's windpipe.

"Stop! Just keep him quiet, knock him out. No need to kill him. We only have to keep him out of action for a couple of hours."

Valois' hand froze at the last second. He flipped the

208

knife over and slammed it down onto the man's head. The cop slumped like a sack of potatoes. He was unconscious, and when he woke up later, he'd sure have one hell of a headache. But he'd be alive. Talley searched around with his NV gear, but the area was still quiet. He keyed his mike and spoke quietly.

"Roy, how're you doing?"

"I'm at the bottom of the shaft, Boss. The qanat is here all right. I've taken a quick look inside, and it looks as if it's still in use. The water is about twenty centimeters deep. The qanat is about a meter high and about the same width. I reckon we can get through, provided the water level doesn't increase too much on the way in."

"We'll have to take a chance."

He took hold of the rope and started sliding down. Anika followed him, then Rovere and the rest of the squad. Reynolds was already partway into the tunnel, and he ordered him to stay on point. It was a long, difficult crawl, and it became even harder as the water level began to rise the nearer they got to their destination. The Pasdaran Barracks was almost two kilometers through the waterlogged passage.

Reynolds called back softly. "We got problems, Boss. It looks like the roof has partially caved in, and it's funneled the water into a narrow tube. It means we have to go forward underwater, and the blockage could be any distance."

"Can you give it a try, Roy? I'll come up and fasten the rope to you, and pull you back if you get into trouble. There won't be any way to turn around in that narrow space."

"Sure, I'll do it."

Talley shivered as he reached Roy and looked at the dark, flooded tunnel. It could easily become a man's tomb. He fastened the line to his ankle and relieved him of his weapons, handing them to Rovere, who stowed them away in a waterproof bag and passed orders for the rest of the squad to do the same with their own weapons. Talley looked at Reynolds. "You've got enough rope there for ten meters. If it's any longer than that, I'll have to pull you back."

Roy stared at him. In the dim light, Talley could see his expression and read his thoughts. If they couldn't get through, they were fucked, and Arash had won. The black trooper climbed into the water and began hauling himself through the narrow pipe. In his head, Talley began counting the seconds. He'd already decided that if Roy were underwater for sixty seconds, he'd start to pull him back in, regardless. He paid out the line as the man went further and further through the water, and then the counter in his brain told him the sixty seconds were up. He started pulling back, but almost immediately the rope slid easily back through the water. When the end appeared, it looked as if the knot he tied had come undone. He began taking off his weapons and moved toward the black water.

"No, you have to wait!" Rovere shouted. "If Roy is in there and trying to get back, you'll block the tunnel."

"Domenico, he could be drowning. I have to get him out."

"It's the wrong move, Abe. You have to give him a chance."

He checked his wristwatch, ninety seconds, a minute and a half.

How long can a man survive inside that flooded tunnel? Two minutes? Maybe three? It could stretch as far as thousand meters, or even more!

"It's two minutes. I'm going after him."

"Give him just a little more time. Three minutes, he can last that long without any major problems. Just a few seconds more, Abe."

He watched the dial of his luminous wristwatch as the seconds went by. Two minutes. Two minutes and fifteen seconds, two minutes and thirty seconds, two minutes and forty-five seconds. Three minutes.

"That's it, I'm going in."

He crouched by the narrow tunnel, took a deep breath, and went to propel himself forward. As his head was submerged in the water, something slammed into him, and he was forced back. Roy Reynolds crawled out onto the floor of the qanat, gasping and choking, but alive.

"Roy, what the hell happened? I was about to come in and after you. How the hell did that rope come untied?"

Talley waited until the bout of coughing had eased, and the man began to speak. "It didn't come untied, I did it. I sensed I was nearly at the end of the flooded section, so I untied the rope."

"You made it out the other end?"

"I sure did. It's a long haul, but it can be done. I'm not sure about the girl," he said, looking at Anika. "It's okay for us. We're trained for it, but her, I don't know. It could be a problem."

"I heard that!" she shouted. "I was a good swimmer in my time. If you can do it, I can. I won't have any problems."

Talley stared at her. "It's not a question of swimming. You'll be in a narrow, cramped pipe, unable to breathe, and not knowing how far you have to go to get to the end.

And it's pitch black. It might be worth giving this one a miss. You can go back with one of the troopers and meet up with Guy outside."

She ignored him and was already unstrapping her weapons and equipment. "Take care of that for me, Domenico. Make sure none of it gets wet. I'll see you on the other side."

Talley made a grab for her, but it was too late. She dived into the flooded tunnel, and in less than a second had disappeared.

"I'm going after her," he said to the Italian. "You can send the men in, one at a time. I'd suggest thirty-second intervals. That'll give the man in front time enough to get through."

"Is thirty seconds enough? What if the man in front freezes or gets stuck? We could build up one hell of a traffic jam inside that pipe. It might be better to give each man more time to get through."

"Time is a luxury we don't have," he replied.

He pushed into the water and almost immediately found himself plunged into a narrow, dark hell. Even though he knew Reynolds had been through to the end and back, there was the realization that the tiniest mistake could mean death, and not an easy death; death by slow drowning, trapped in an airless tube, feeling the slight pressure of the current as it pushed him inexorably through and toward the end. It reminded him that the water he was submerged in had begun its journey many kilometers away in the mountains, and here it was almost at the end of its journey. But he had done this kind of thing many times before since his days as a Navy Seal, beginning with the exacting BUD/S training that sorted out those men who had the strength, the skills and the tenacity to go on, and those who couldn't make the grade. He relaxed. This should be an easy swim, and then he could emerge the other end where Anika would be waiting. He was almost there, and there would be another man half a minute behind him. He reminded himself to get out of the pipe fast, and then he hit the obstruction and stopped dead.

It wasn't a solid mass of earth and rock. It was soft, organic, moving.

Anika!

She was trapped underwater, and her limbs were threshing, trying to break free. Her body was twisting and turning, and he sensed the panic welling up in her. He touched her, to try and reassure her that he was there to help, but already she was starting to drown. Her movements were slowing, her body starting to go limp. Then she realized someone was there, and her panic increased. She grabbed for him and managed to hold his collar, clinging to him with a manic determination, as if the presence of another human being was enough to save her life. It wasn't. Already his air was almost exhausted, and he knew he had only seconds to save both her and himself. A few seconds more would bring the next man into the submerged pipe, making a tangled blockage that would be almost impossible to clear and result in more deaths. Anika held him tighter and tighter. He knew she was gripped by a real terror, the certain knowledge she was dying. He did the only thing possible. He reached for her neck and found the carotid artery. He pressed hard, and after a few seconds, her movements ceased as she slid into unconsciousness. He had to work fast. There were three factors working against him. She was drowning, unable to prevent her body from sucking water into her lungs, he was almost out of air, and the other man was almost on him. He felt for what was holding her and found a webbing strap had snagged on a sharp outcrop of rock. It was only a few centimeters long, but enough to kill three people if he didn't free her fast. He jerked on the webbing, and at first it refused to move. The force of her panicked movements had jammed the strap into a narrow cut in the rock. He took out his combat knife and sliced through it, and immediately felt her body come free. Now he had to get her out before she died. He started to push her forward, feeling his lungs bursting with hot agony as his last reserves of air disappeared, and the carbon dioxide in his lungs tried to pressure him to take a breath. Summoning up every last vestige of strength and determination, he pushed her body in front of him, easing it through the narrow pipe and refusing to go any quicker, for fear that she would jam again. It could only have been a few meters, but it felt like the longest journey of his life. Every second was like an hour as he pushed through the pipe, beginning to despair that he'd ever make it. His brain told him insistently that it was all a waste of time. There was no point. He may as well give up and die, and submit to the torture of drowning. Everything flashed through his mind in a confusing jumble, his training in the Seals, his appointment to NATFOR to command Echo Six, and this mission to prevent the nukes from reaching Iran.

Iran! No fucking way! I accept that one day my work might kill me, and I'll die in combat in one of the world's trouble spots, but in Iran? In this shithole flooded tunnel? No fucking way!

Sheer anger and bloody mindedness drove him on, and he refused to die in such a place. He made a last despairing effort, and inch-by-inch he edged forward. His mind was blank from the lack of oxygen so that it was almost an automatic function of his muscles that pushed him on. He felt Anika's body tip forward, and it registered in his dulled brain that she had come out of the water. He made a huge, final effort, and suddenly he was out, gasping for air, just as Domenico Rovere came up behind him, and pulled himself out of the flooded pipe.

"What the hell happened?" Rovere gasped, staring at Anika's limp body.

He couldn't reply. He sucked in a few breaths of the dank stale air, and then threw himself on Anika, starting to give her mouth-to-mouth resuscitation. Domenico waited, watching him with a puzzled expression, but then Anika's chest heaved, and she spewed out a jet of water from her lungs as she started to breathe again.

"She nearly drowned?"

He explained how she snagged her webbing inside the pipe.

"You were lucky she was unconscious," the Italian commented. "I've had problems in the past with people drowning. They tend to panic and make it next to impossible to rescue them."

"Yeah, I guess I was lucky she was out."

She opened her eyes, squinting at Tally and Rovere in the beam of the flashlight. "My God, I thought I'd had it in there." She looked at Tally. "I guess it was you behind me, so you must have got me out." She massaged her neck. "That hurts, I must have hit my neck on an outcropping of rock while I was struggling to get free."

"It must have been something like that."

While she recovered, the rest of the squad came through

the flooded pipe one by one. When they were all through, he got them moving again, toward the end of the qanat, the well underneath the Pasdaran Barracks. The going became much easier, as the blockage had been holding the water back like a dam. Now, there was very little water on the floor of the tunnel. They got close to the Nezam Abad Barracks with ten minutes to spare before Guy detonated the explosives.

"How will you know when we're directly underneath?" he asked Anika.

"According to my research, the well is the last opening before the qanat reaches the center of the city. As soon as we come to a vertical shaft like the one we came down, I'm pretty certain we'll be there."

"And if we're not?" Domenico asked.

She shrugged. "Then we go on until we find the one we're looking for, but I'm sure there is only one. Dom, when we find that shaft, we'll be right underneath the Tehran Headquarters."

"Great, I've always wanted to visit that place." No one smiled. "Abe, I suggest we get our weapons and equipment ready now. We're likely to need them in a few minutes."

"Pass it on," he agreed. "Then we move on, I want to be underneath that shaft when the charges detonate. If there is going to be a roof fall, I'd like to see some sky above my head."

"I can't argue with that," the Italian smiled.

He gave the order, and they took their weapons from the waterproof bags and began the familiar task of checking them ready for action, making sure they were loaded with full clips, and in the case of the snipers, their delicate night vision sights were undamaged after the underwater swim.

Talley checked his own MP7 and Sig Sauer automatic. They'd been thorough, and everything had come through the swim undamaged. He adjusted his NV goggles, turned off the flashlight, switched them on, and the dark tunnel lit up with ghostly green light. He nodded to Anika, who had her own goggles in position.

"You'd better take the point. You know what you're looking for, but move fast. Guy's explosives will be detonating any moment now. Are you okay?"

She nodded as she squeezed past him. "I feel better, thanks. It can't be more than a few meters, I'd guess a hundred at most. We're almost on it."

She set off along the tunnel. The roof was slightly higher now, and she was able to walk bent over. The rest of them were taller and didn't have that luxury. As a result, she went ahead. After only two minutes she called back to them.

"I think this is it. There's a shaft that goes straight up with a diameter of about a meter, so there's plenty of room for us to climb. It looks to me as if there are rungs set into the side of the shaft, probably to allow for maintenance when debris collects in the qanat."

Talley came and peered up at the shaft. It was about thirty meters high, and at the top he could see a faint circle of light. He looked around as Rovere came alongside him.

"I'm going up to see how it looks outside," he told him. "It won't be long before..."

He didn't get any further. The earth trembled from a nearby explosion, and they felt the vibrations of the explosives Guy had detonated. Pieces of masonry and dirt showered down over their heads. When the debris cleared, there was an eerie silence, but only for a few seconds. Then they heard the screams and the shouts.

"It's done. I'm going up top. As soon as the troops start to leave the barracks, we'll get to work."

He climbed up the rungs until he reached the top. He squinted over the wall surrounding the well and looked into a scene like a mediaeval depiction of hell. The Pasdaran were terrified, running around the square in awed confusion. When the blast went off, it looked as if a vehicle had been approaching a gas pump to fuel up, and the blast had startled the driver. He'd collided with the pump, and a spark had ignited the fuel. Hundreds of gallons of gas were burning like crazy, and men were screaming orders, trying to cope with it and put out the flames. An officer ran out of a nearby building, shouting panicked orders as he tried to bring order to the chaos. Some of the men trying to fight the fire began to form up. The barracks gate opened, and they ran out. More of their comrades poured out of the buildings to answer the emergency. Clearly, they were taking the threat to Ahmadinejad's life seriously. He looked back down the shaft and called softly to the men.

"Another few minutes and this place will be almost empty. I'll call as soon as it's clear to go."

He watched the last of the troops pour out through the gate, and there were only a half-dozen men left fighting the blaze. It was probably as good as they'd get, so he called down the well shaft again.

"I need a sniper up here. Send Vince DiMosta up, and ask Jerry to stand by."

Vince climbed up and squeezed next to him so he could see the burning chaos of the almost abandoned barracks.

"Jesus Christ, Guy did well. That collateral damage is a stroke of luck. About time we had some. You want me to take out the rest of those guys?"

"Yeah, they won't be expecting to be hit from here. As soon as you're out of targets, climb out of the well and go over to that patch of shadow. It looks like some kind of a storeroom. It may even be the communications center, but I can't tell from here. I'll assign Jerry to cover the other side of the barracks, and then the rest of us will start searching for our guy, if he's still here."

"Copy that."

Vince opened fire, and within less than a minute, the six Revolutionary Guards went down. He climbed over the side of the well and sprinted across the open ground, disappearing into the shadows. The Polish sniper, Jerry Ostrowski, was already halfway up the shaft, and he joined Talley at the top. Abe pointed out DiMosta's position and explained he wanted Jerry to cover the other side of the barracks. He nodded and climbed out of the well to make his way to the other side. He'd almost reached his intended position when two more Revolutionary Guard troopers appeared from around the corner and almost ran into him. Their assault rifles were slung on their shoulders. They were running to fight the fire, not repel invaders. Jerry's Accuracy International rifle was too slow and cumbersome, but he snatched out his Sig and fired off two quick shots. They both found their mark, but one of the Guards was only wounded. He'd unslung his AKM and was bringing it up to fire when the 9mm round from the Sig crunched into his groin. His face twisted in agony, but he still managed to squeeze off a round at his opponent. The bullet hit Jerry square on the ballistic plate fastened to the front of his vest. The plate was enough to block the 5.56 mm round, but even so; the kinetic force knocked him flat on his back. He got to his feet still clutching his rifle, and continued to his position. But he knew, Talley knew, and they all knew that the shot might be enough to alert the remaining garrison. They were already jumpy because of the supposed attack on the President. Talley called down the well.

"Everybody out, and fast. You know what to do. Split up into pairs and start searching the buildings. And remember, if you see this Ayatollah Majidi, he is to be taken."

"You mean killed?" Rovere murmured as he climbed out.

"Only if he offers a threat. We're not assassins."

That damn word again! It seems stuck in my head.

"I take it the prospect of unleashing a nuclear holocaust on Israel would count as a threat?" the Italian asked, with a raised eyebrow.

"Yeah, I guess that'll do," Talley said tersely.

We have no brief to kill anyone, but on most operations, we don't make the rules. It's the enemy who lays down the agenda. All we're doing is responding to a threat. If that means killing a hostile, putting him down like a mad dog, so be it.

The men were pairing up and running off to begin the search for Majidi. He could be Arash, or would lead them to him. If he was part of Arash's crazy scheme, he was going down. Heinrich Buchmann climbed out of the well last.

"I've prepared a charge in the well, Boss. It's on a remote detonator, so if you want me to blow it, you only have to say the word."

"Good thinking, Heinrich. Join me and Anika, our search area is the main administration center."

The German nodded, and Talley raced off with Anika on his heels and Buchmann bringing up the rear. Lights were coming on in the buildings as the few remaining Revolutionary Guards, slower than the first responders who had chased off to respond to the threat to their President, started to go into action. As he ran, he heard the first shouts of alarm from a building a hundred meters away. It looked like it could be a dormitory. A shot cracked out, the back markers were definitely starting to wake up. The distinctive chatter of an M249 machine gun echoed around the barracks as Echo Six responded, hitting back hard. The enemy fire stopped immediately. Then more firing came from another part of the barracks, and even more from a cluster of workshops opposite, and the entire barracks became a battle zone as the Revolutionary Guard at last started to retaliate. He keyed his mike.

"This is Echo One. Keep moving. Keep moving! Remember, we have to locate and take out the target. Don't waste time on the gomers. We have to keep pushing forward. Find Majidi, and we'll find Arash. That's what this is all about."

He reached the administration block. The door was locked, but he stood back and Buchmann, the hefty German, shoulder charged it and smashed it open. Talley followed him in with the girl behind him. At first glance, it seemed empty. There were no lights. He was about to order Buchmann to conduct a search on his own, while he went to help with the firefight in the dormitory that was still growing in intensity, when they all heard a noise from the second floor; a man with an Iranian accent shouting in Farsi. The building was occupied, and the occupant was Iranian, but when the other man replied, they looked at each other in astonishment.

"Abe, that's not an Iranian. He sounds like an American, or a Brit," Anika exclaimed in a puzzled voice. "It sounds like Miles Preston to me."

He glanced at her.

Preston? Doesn't sound like him to me, but it could be. Maybe I'm wrong.

"Stay here with Heinrich and cover the entrance. I'll head up there and take a look."

He dashed for the nearby staircase and started up. When he was halfway to the second floor, he heard footsteps behind him and knew that Anika was following. He mentally shrugged.

She's a fully trained MI6 officer, so what the hell? I wonder what her agenda is for this operation? She hasn't told us everything, that's for sure.

The voices had stopped, but at the end of the passage a light was on. He looked round at the girl. She was holding her pistol, and he had no doubt she'd use it when the time came.

"I'm going to check out that room at the end, but I want you to stay right here and cover me, in case someone comes out of the other rooms and gets behind me."

She nodded and sunk into the shadows, her gun ready. Talley crept forward, careful not to make any noise. He almost missed a gun barrel that pointed out of the doorway and emptied a full clip along the corridor. He barely had time to flatten himself against the wall as bullets whistled past him. The firing stopped, and he knew he had a second or two before the shooter snapped in a new clip and started again. He threw himself forward, reached the door and rolled into the room, coming to his feet and raising his weapon to fire. But the shooter had vanished. A man sat behind a desk, a man in the iconic robes of an Iranian cleric, an ayatollah. He didn't seem to be armed, but Talley kept him covered with his MP7 as his eyes searched the room, looking for the shooter. A door was open at the back of the office, and he heard footsteps outside on metal stairs as somebody raced down a fire escape. He shouted for Anika to come and cover the Iranian cleric. Then he ran to the door and looked out, pulling back as a man who was racing away, turned and fired three shots that cracked past his head, narrowly missing him before he got into cover. When the shooting stopped, he looked back through the door and saw a figure in European clothing disappearing around the corner. There was no time to go after him, but he had secured Majidi. He went back inside, Anika had the Iranian covered. He nodded his thanks, pulled his Sig out of the holster, and pointed it at the man.

"Do you speak English?"

The man stared at him for a few moments, and then he smiled. "It matters little what language I speak. Can you hear that noise outside?"

The roar of the gun battle had increased, and it sounded as if Echo Six had run into major problems, but that wasn't what he meant. The sound of a convoy of trucks approaching the barracks told of a large number of troops returning.

"You understand what that is? As soon as your attack started, and we realized what was happening, I called for reinforcements from the Pasdaran unit to the west of the city. They have sent me two companies of troops. No matter what you do to me, you will not leave this place alive."

"Cover him!"

Anika nodded and held her gun held against his forehead, leaving him in no doubt she would use it if he did anything stupid. Talley went out onto the fire escape, in time to see the first truck nearing the main gate.

"This is Echo One. Domenico, what's your situation?"

The Italian's reply came through, accompanied by the sounds of a full on firefight.

"We are holding them in the main dormitory, but it's a close-run thing. Is that reinforcements I can hear outside?"

"Yeah, do your best. I'm calling in some help to deal with them."

"Make it sooner rather than later, Abe. We're holding on here, but only just. If those new guys join in, we'll have to make a run for it."

"Copy that. Hang in there, Domenico."

He switched over to the net that would allow him to speak to a circling P3 Orion.

The venerable four-engine turboprop aircraft had been developed for the United States Navy, and introduced in the 1960s. Since that time, the aircraft had seen numerous design advancements, most notably to its electronics packages. Patrolling on the outer edge of the Iraqi border, the Orion was able to look down over a wide area and offer command and control capability to a wide range of reconnaissance and weapons systems. Because of their proximity, they'd been handed control of the stealth drone over Tehran, the Lockheed Avenger.

"Echo One, calling Eagle One. Echo One, calling Eagle One. Do you receive, over?"

He waited for only three or four seconds before the

laconic voice of the P3 controller came back to him.

"Echo One, this is Eagle One. Receiving you strength five."

"Eagle One, I have a fire mission for you. Can you triangulate on my position?"

"Our bird is already overhead. We're looking at you right now with a live camera feed. It looks as if you've stirred things up some down there in Nezam Abad. Have you seen the convoy almost at the barracks, Echo One? There's a heap of trouble heading your way."

"That's why I'm calling, Eagle One. Can you take out that convoy? If the infantry deploy and join in the fight, we're in trouble."

"You're not kidding," he chuckled. "That's an affirmative, Echo One, we can do that. The bird is carrying a full load of Hellfires, and we're ready to launch on your order. Can you confirm that your men are all under cover? There's going to be some serious shit flying when those missiles hit."

"Give me twenty seconds before you launch the first salvo, Eagle One. We'll have our heads down."

"Confirm salvo in twenty seconds, Echo One."

"That's a confirm, Eagle One."

Talley switched to the local net. "This is Echo One. We have a missile strike inbound in approximately fifteen seconds, so keep your heads down. There's going to be some fireworks in the area of the vehicle convoy coming through the main gate."

A chorus of acknowledgements came back to him, and he rushed back inside the office.

"Everybody down. Anika, get clear of the windows!"

As she started to move, he grabbed hold of the

Ayatollah and dragged him to the floor, pressing his face into the carpet. He counted off the seconds in his head as he held the cleric's head tightly. The first indication of an attack was the sound of the missiles a split second before they hit.

The AGM-114 Hellfire was an air-to-surface missile intended originally for anti-armor use. It was a precision weapon that could be launched from air, sea, and ground platforms. Following numerous advances to the avionics, the propulsion system, and the warhead, it was more lethally effective than it had ever been.

The drone fired an initial salvo of four missiles, and they struck the convoy almost simultaneously. The blast wave smashed in the windows, and they were showered with broken glass and debris. The enormous force of the explosion lifted them off the floor, and the combination of the warheads and the gas in the convoy vehicles as they exploded was like an ammunition dump exploding. He dusted himself off and went back out onto the fire escape to check the extent of the damage. The blast radius was some two hundred meters and had flattened vast swathes of the buildings that had all but disappeared, mixed with the tangled wreckage of steel and human flesh; the remains of the infantry convoy. The main gate and the wall surrounding it either side had been pulverized, and the Pasdaran military facility was completely open to the street.

One thing's for sure, our operational window just contracted. We may have had as much as an hour without the missile attack. Now, we only have minutes. The whole of Tehran must be on alert. The threat to assassinate the President, and explosions and missiles, the city will be boiling with police and security forces determined to isolate the threat and deal with it. He keyed his mike.

" Echo Two, this is Echo One. Guy, come in. Where are you?"

While he waited for a reply, he went back inside the office.

"Majidi, get up. Anika, we're taking him with us. Secure his hands."

She nodded and delved in her pack for the plastic ties they carried as standard equipment. As she fastened his hands behind his back, he sneered at Talley.

"If you think you'll ever get out of here with your lives, you're very mistaken. How many men do you have? Ten, twenty? The Revolutionary Guard will be mobilizing even as we speak. You don't stand a chance, but if you surrender now, I may be able to save your lives."

Talley ignored him and went back outside to the fire escape. His earpiece was still dead.

"Echo One for Echo Two, Echo Two, Guy, do you read me?"

The silence seemed to mock him.

Where the hell is Guy? Have they taken him? If he's a prisoner of the Iranians, there's little or nothing I can do about it. But maybe he's okay, there's still time. What then? Majidi wasn't entirely wrong. Pursued by just about everything the Iranians can throw at us, we'll have our work cut out getting out of here. Even so, Guy is the most resourceful Special Forces operator I've ever known. If anyone can turn a bad situation around, it's him. And we have Javeed Zardooz. The combination of Guy's lethal skills with Javeed's knowledge could just give us the edge and a chance to get clear of the citywide manhunt that's inevitably already underway.

He looked across the barracks. The firefight had ended after the missiles knocked out the relief convoy. He saw movement in the yard. Four Pasdaran troopers were making for the wrecked vehicles, probably checking for survivors. Or maybe to beat it over the rubble of what had once been the main gate and security fence. They were toast. Vince and Jerry were looking for targets. They divided them between them.

"Jerry, I've got the two on the left. Can you see the other two guys?"

Ostrowski's calm voice replied, "I have a clear shot on one of them, but the guy on the far right is hidden by some of the wreckage. We have to drive him out into the open and take them all at once. Otherwise, they'll run for cover."

"We could pepper the wreckage in front of them, and that would drive them back. The second those shots strike, they'll head back like crazy."

Talley could see the gomers in front of him, about a hundred meters away. Too far for accurate shooting using an MP7, but they weren't looking for accurate shooting.

"This is Echo One, save your ammo. I can see it all from here. I'll empty a clip into that wreckage. Once they're out in the open..."

"We'll take it from there. Ready when you are, Boss."

He sighted on the still burning vehicles, pulled the trigger, and put a dozen rounds into the tortured wreckage. The sound of the bullets ricocheting off the metal was too much for the spooked Revolutionary Guards. They turned and ran back, straight into the precision sniper fire of Jerry and Vince's sniper rifles. They fired four shots each, four 7.62mm rounds. The men went down, thrown to the ground in a bloody heap by the tremendous kinetic energy of the heavy bullets.

"Good shooting, men. Everyone break off, and we'll assemble in front of what used to be the main gate and find a way out. I want you there in one minute, no more."

He took Majidi by the arm and started to propel him toward the door. He looked at Anika. She hadn't moved, and he stared at her.

"What is it? It's time to leave. In a few minutes time this place will be overrun, and I guarantee they'll be shooting first and asking questions afterward."

"Abe, how are we getting out of here? When we get through that gate, it'll be obvious we are the enemy."

"It's getting late. If we keep to the shadows, we could get clear."

"And we may not. There are vehicles inside the barracks. Why not take one of those?"

He mentally cursed himself for not thinking of the obvious.

"Heinrich you still down there?"

"Ja, I wait here, Boss."

"Can you hotwire an Iranian army truck?"

"Of course, but there is no need to hotwire them. They have a simple button start."

"That's great. Find us a couple of suitable vehicles, get someone to help you, and bring them out to the main gate. And remember, we're out of time."

"It's not a problem, I'll be quick."

He turned to Anika. "That should cover it, let's get moving."

But still she didn't move. She shook her head, "Abe, I know this may sound crazy."

He waited.

"I think we have the wrong man. We've screwed up."

CHAPTER EIGHT

He felt exasperation and anger.

"He has to be the right guy. It all points to him. It can't be anyone else. We have to get out of here now!"

She silently followed him down the staircase and out into the open barracks square, but he could feel her eyes on him. They started hurrying toward the wreckage heaped around the main gate. The only men missing were Buchmann and Reynolds, searching for vehicles. They had Majidi. Despite Anika, he was convinced they'd snagged Arash, and it was almost over.

"Why don't you ask him?"

He turned around and looked at Anika. "What?"

"Ask him if he's Arash."

He looked at her with incredulity. "Are you serious? Of course he'll deny it. We have the right man."

"I don't think he'd lie if you put it to him. Arash is hugely important to them, like a religious thing. For Arash to deny his identity, it would be like Jesus lying about who he was."

He heard the sound of an engine start. The vehicle nosed around the corner and drove slowly toward them. It was old, battered, and had certainly seen plenty of action.

"Jesus Christ," Valois exclaimed. "That's a British armored car. Where the hell did it come from?"

"It's a Scorpion," Talley agreed, smiling. "The Brits sold scores of them to the Iranians; back in the good old days before everything went crazy with their nuclear program."

Buchmann left the big diesel engine running, climbed out into the turret, and leaned down at them. "What do you think? It'll take some stopping."

"It'll do. Where's Roy?"

"He found a couple of Mercedes infantry transports. He'll bring the one with the most fuel."

"I hope to Christ he hurries. He's not buying a new model from the local Ford dealer."

Talley thought about what Anika had said.

She's wrong. We have the right man, now we have to get him out of here.

"Boss, we got company."

He looked up to the front as Valois shouted. The man had been listening for signs of any traffic approaching, and now they all heard it. And then it came into view, an Iranian police car, a white Mercedes with green stripes down the side was nosing toward them, crunching over the debris spilled over the area. Two cops in the front seats were looking at them suspiciously, although so far all they would see was a group of soldiers standing inside a barracks.

"Vince, Jerry. If they look like they've twigged, nail 'em."

"Copy that."

He could see them staring through the wreckage and the fires, trying to make sense of the chaos, and then everything seemed to happen at once. A Mercedes truck came from the rear of the barracks with Reynolds driving. He reached the Scorpion, stopped the truck, and climbed out to speak to Buchmann. But the German ran forward, climbed onto the hull of the Scorpion, and dived through the open hatch. The cops watched intently, still not certain of what they were seeing. They chatted to each other, but then one of them reached down and switched on the blue flashing roof light. The other picked up the radio microphone. Talley didn't need to give the order. Vince and Jerry readied to open fire, but before they could shoot, the driver rammed his foot down hard on the gas pedal and reversed away. The shots went wide. He watched helplessly as the two cops got further and further away. Inside the next few seconds, every car and every soldier in the city would know they were there.

Heinrich stopped them. He found the trigger of the Scorpion's main gun and opened fire. A 76mm shell flew out of the barrel, impacting on the front wall of a building fifty meters beyond where the cop car was still reversing. They reached the end of the rubble-covered street as Buchmann fired the second shot. The shell slammed into the tarmac ten meters behind them, and the car reversed straight into the newly created hole. The trunk went down, the hood went up, and the cruiser stopped dead as if it had hit a brick wall, which effectively it had. This time Buchmann had a stationary target, and despite his lack of experience with the gun, it was almost impossible to miss. He didn't miss. The white and green Mercedes exploded in a cloud of broken metal, and he was able to glimpse a body tumbling through the air over and over as the blast threw it fifty meters along the street. The thing that landed was no longer visibly human, just a shredded mass of tissue and cloth. The other cop was almost vaporized in the vehicle. He'd done well, but the question in Talley's mind was whether or not they had got out a call before Buchmann's third shot slammed home. There was no way of knowing, all they could do was get out as fast as possible and pray that this day the Gods of War would smile on them for a little longer.

They ran to the vehicles, Talley pushing Ayatollah Majidi ahead of him into the Scorpion, and Anika clambered aboard behind him. He shouted for Reynolds to join him as the rest of the squad clambered aboard the Mercedes truck. Roy took the wheel of the armored car and headed out for a gap in the broken perimeter fence.

"Which way?" he shouted urgently.

Talley looked at Anika. "You have to show him the way back to that derelict factory. I'll watch the prisoner. Heinrich, you stay on the gun, that was nice shooting."

The German nodded grimly as he fought to keep the armored car moving in a straight line. They swung out onto the main street. Before they were two hundred meters from the Pasdaran Barracks, a stream of vehicles turned in from the opposite direction, blue lights flashing. Four cop cars turned into the barracks, and then an Iranian armored car came after them, followed by a half-dozen infantry trucks packed with troops. Talley looked around the dark cabin for their prisoner and found him hanging on grimly to an ammunition locker. Up front, Anika was giving calm directions to Buchmann. He looked out of the rear vision port of the Scorpion and saw the Mercedes truck was still following.

Are we ready to exfiltrate? Until Anika spoke to Majidi, I assumed we'd achieved the primary target of the mission, Arash. Now, I'm not so sure, and we need to know. Will Majidi tell the truth if he's asked? There's only one way to find out.

He leaned across and tapped him on the shoulder. The man whirled; perhaps he thought he was about to get a bullet in the back of the head.

"Mr. Majidi, you know why we came after you?"

The man stared at him. "It is obvious, American. I know you are trying to interfere with Iran's nuclear weapons program, but it will make no difference. Take me prisoner, kill me, it is all the same. Our program will go ahead. Our warheads will be delivered on time."

"You think Arash will be able to carry on without you?"

The man nodded emphatically. "Yes, yes. Removing me from the organization will make little difference. My country will have those weapons, regardless. And in the hands of the Revolutionary Guard, we will end the occupation of Palestine, and you infidels will leave the Middle East forever."

Is the man bullshitting me, or has Anika hit on the truth?

"So you're not Arash?"

He watched the man carefully, but his surprise seemed genuine.

"Me, Arash? No, I do not have that honor. It is as I said, capturing or killing me will make no difference. He will see that the warheads arrive reach Iran as arranged, and I can assure you, Mr. American, they will be put to good use."

Anika was looking across at him, and he slid over to her.

"It looks as if you could be right."

"I'm sorry, Abe, but I have been thinking about the odd pieces of intelligence we received, and somehow they didn't seem to fit this man."

"You know what it means, don't you? The entire mission will be for nothing."

"I'm sorry, I wish that he had been the one, but somewhere along the line, the wires were crossed. Or more likely, we were deliberately led astray. It makes no difference. Even if we could locate Arash, we could hardly do anything now. Tehran is strictly a no go for us, and quite frankly, I'm amazed we got out as easily as we did."

He nodded.

Are we being driven like animals in a hunt, goaded by beaters? Pushed in the direction the hunters want us to go. Or kept away from the place where the hunters wish us to avoid?

He thought about it all the way out of the city, but the solution to the problem always seemed to elude him. Someone, somewhere, was shoving them in the wrong direction. They were getting faulty intelligence, and that was the key. And finally, he had the answer, as he narrowed the list of names down to one.

It may be incredible, but the CIA Head of Tehran Station always seems to be lurking in the background when things are going badly wrong. Miles Preston, time for a chat with the patrician intelligence head!

They left the main city areas behind them and drove out into the suburbs, past deserted streets littered with rubbish and potholes, and shabby buildings with masonry showing the dilapidation of years of neglect. They reached the derelict industrial estate, a landscape of rusting iron buildings and torn fences. Inside the courtyard of the old brick factory where they'd hidden was a four-wheel-drive SUV. He recognized it immediately. It belonged to Miles Preston. When he first saw the vehicle, it had crossed his mind that somehow Guy had made it back.

But no such luck, somehow the CIA man has second-guessed us, and if Miles Preston is the enemy, he won't be alone. But where the hell is Guy?

He keyed his mike. "This is Echo One. Close up behind the armored car. This could be an ambush."

He heard, "Copy that," from the Mercedes truck following behind.

"Heinrich, stay on the gun. We could be getting into a situation here."

"Copy that, Herr Leutnant."

Reynolds pulled up. Talley was tempted to order them to pull back and make a more careful approach, but he was also curious. If Preston was their enemy, it seemed too obvious to park his vehicle in such a way as to advertise an ambush. He heard Rovere calling from the Mercedes.

"What do you suggest, Abe? If you think it's a trap, you could cover us with the Scorpion, and I'll lead a squad into the building to flush out any hostiles. Any trouble, you can pepper them with that big gun mounted in the turret."

"Okay, we'll do it your way, but don't dismount from the truck until you're inside and out of sight. Drive straight through the doors, and be ready to open fire on anything that doesn't look kosher."

"Copy that."

The engine of the Mercedes roared as it lurched forward, smashing straight through the doors and into the empty space of the factory floor. He waited while Rovere's men deployed inside the building. Domenico came back over the commo.

"You'd better take a look, Abe. It's not what you expected."

"I'll be right in." He turned to Anika. "Stay inside the Scorpion, and keep your eye on Majidi. There's something strange going on here, and I don't want them to know we have him with us. Not yet, anyway."

She nodded. He checked his MP7, opened the hatch, and climbed out. He walked cautiously through the broken doors and into the gloom. In the middle of the huge open space, the Mercedes had stopped and the engine was turned off. Echo Six troopers were stationed around the walls, watching carefully. Sitting on an upturned wooden crate in the center was the CIA Head of Tehran Station, Miles Preston. He stood in front of him, covering him with his weapon.

"What the hell are you doing here?"

The CIA man grimaced. "I guess the real question is, what are you doing back here? It seems to me that you've brought your NATO thugs into the country and caused chaos. So far, all you've achieved is to totally fuck up everything you've touched. And I'll bet you're no further forward finding this Arash character than you were before you got here."

"Maybe, maybe not. We may have just caught the guy. We're just not sure just yet. Perhaps you can help us sort it out."

"Help you? In what way?"

"You could start by explaining to us why you've fed us the crap you've passed off as intelligence."

Preston reddened with anger. "Everything I've given you has been on the up and up. What you've done with it is bring the Iranian security forces crashing down on all our heads. Jesus Christ, going into their atomic energy headquarters, you must have been crazy. What did you get for it?"

He spoke without thinking and cursed himself for letting it slip. "We got Ayatollah Majidi. He's very close to their top man. We thought he was Arash at one time, but we were wrong. However, we have an idea who this guy is."

"Yeah? Who would that be?"

"What's your role in all of this, Preston?"

His eyes widened. "You think I'm part of this crazy nuclear plan? Jesus, you really think I'm Arash?"

He laughed out loud. "You must be crazy! Do you know where the intelligence came from that first confirmed Imam Fard's information? From my office, and without it, this operation never would have happened. You think if I was a part of this thing, I would have arranged for a SpecOps unit to be brought in country?"

Talley felt uneasy. What Preston said made sense. "I'll check out what you say. If it's true, I'll apologize. It isn't," he stared at him, "I'll blow your head off. Maybe it wasn't you, Preston," he conceded, "but it has to do be someone in the intelligence world who's involved. We've been led by the nose since we arrived in the country, and it's only been sheer luck that we've avoided the traps the Iranians have set for us."

"I'm not the only intelligence operative in Tehran, Talley. Maybe before you jump to conclusions, you should consider other people that have been close to this operation. Like her, for instance."

He looked in the direction of Anika, who was entered

the building, pulling Ayatollah Majidi along with her.

"Forget it! Doctor Frost has been with us at every stage of the operation, and she's shared the risks. It isn't her."

Preston shrugged. "Maybe not, but it isn't me, buddy. So I suggest you look elsewhere, at least if you're going to be around for much longer. I guess you know you've become a fucking liability in this town. You can bet you'll be pulled out any time."

"And that would be your doing, would it?"

"Not me, my friend, but it makes sense. You blundered into this operation and made fuck-ups at every step. We're running out of time, and our bosses are likely to send in a new team that can do the job properly."

If it's true and we're being pulled out, it'll be a disaster almost beyond belief. Don't they realize that intelligence is leaking like a sieve from somewhere in their command and control structure? Pulling Echo Six out and putting in a new team will be throwing away whatever chance is left of pulling off the mission. And I have to find out what happened to Guy and his people after they detonated the explosives. Have the Iranians taken them? Or are they hiding out somewhere, desperate for help. Perhaps one or more of them is wounded. There's no way I'm going to surrender the mission when we've come this far.

"Preston, if we don't, it doesn't matter if they send in a division of Special Forces, there's no way anyone will find him. Is this a cover your ass deal for you, move up the career ladder inside the Agency? I mean, how far would you go to stop these bastards from threatening America and the NATO allies with a nuclear strike? Which is it, your career, or your country?"

Talley could see him hesitate as he thought over the question. For a career intelligence officer, the options were straightforward. If he sided with Echo Six and the operation went down the pan, he'd wind up counting wetbacks on the Arizona border. But equally, if he pressed for a replacement team to come in, and the operation failed because they were out of time, an inquiry could find fault with the way he'd handled it. Indeed, they could put the entire blame for the failure on his shoulders, and his career in CIA would surely hit the buffers.

"You're asking me to take the gamble of my career and support you to see this mission through to the end," Preston replied, his voice low.

Talley waited while he fought to make a decision. "Miles, have you kids, family?"

He nodded. "Yeah, back home in Virginia, close to Langley. Three kids, a boy and two girls."

Talley thought about his family back home.

Joshua and James, and Kay doing her best to rip them from me while I'm away trying to defend their freedom and security.

He put the thought aside and put more pressure on Preston.

"You know that if they get their hands on a nuclear weapon, Washington is likely to be high on the target list."

"Yeah, I'm not stupid. It's just…"

He heard the faint sound in his earpiece and held up his hand for Preston to be silent. It came again.

"This is Echo One, come in."

This time, there was no mistake. It was very faint, but he could make out the message.

Guy Welland! Thank God!

"We're holed up about two kilometers from the Pasdaran Barracks. After the explosion, they flooded the place with troops and police, and we had no chance of

ECHO SIX: BLACK OPS 2

getting away. What's your situation?"

Talley explained they were at the abandoned brickworks. "Do you have transportation, Guy, any way of getting to us?"

"That's a negative, Boss, the second we put our heads outside here, they'll spot us for sure. We have to sit this one out until the heat dies away."

"We can't do that, Guy. We don't have the time. We'll come and get you. We managed to lift a Scorpion from the Pasdaran Barracks, so we should be able to reach you without attracting any undue attention. I need to get a fix on your exact location. I'll use the GPS, but are there any landmarks we can use to help us?"

"We're inside an old Christian church, so if you read the coordinates from my signal, it should be pretty obvious when you get here. There's just one problem, Boss."

"Only one?"

Guy chuckled. "Yeah, but it's a big one. We're next door to police headquarters."

Talley thought for a few moments. "Is there a back entrance?"

"That's a negative. The front entrance is the only way in or out, and it's in full view of the cops."

"Copy that. We'll think of something. Sit tight, and we'll be with you as soon as we can get there."

"Understood, Echo Two out."

Talley explained the situation to Rovere. "We have to get them out, the question is how?"

Dom grimaced. "It doesn't sound like it's getting any easier."

Miles Preston was standing nearby, listening to their conversation.

"It never does." He turned to Preston. "Avoiding a nuclear holocaust is like that. It tends to be a bit more complicated," He fixed the CIA man with a hard stare, "and it's not for cowards or the fainthearted either. Make up your mind. We're not backing off. I'm going to get my men out and see this thing through to the end. Are you with us or not?"

He nodded slowly, reluctantly, "Okay, I guess I'm with you. What do you want me to do?"

"We're taking the Scorpion back into the center of Tehran to bring Guy and his people out. I want you to interrogate Majidi. He has information, and it needs an expert to get it out of him." He smiled at Preston, "I guess it's the kind of thing they train you to do at Langley?"

"Yeah, I'll give it a shot. Believe me, by the time I've finished, I'll know what his grandmother had for dinner last night. But you should know that if he doesn't know what you're looking for, I won't be able to get it out of him."

"Maybe not, not exactly. But you're an intelligence officer, so you should be able to piece together what he tells you and come up with some ideas that will take us forward. It seems he's not Arash, but I reckon he knows, or suspects, who he is. He wouldn't be human if he hadn't been curious enough to find out at some time in the past."

"Yeah, I see where you're coming from," Preston nodded. "As soon as you leave, I'll start taking him apart. By the time you get back, if you get back, I should have something for you."

"We'll get back." He turned to Rovere, "Stay here, and make sure we don't have any unwelcome visitors. I'll take Buchmann with me. He can drive, and Vince can ride shotgun. If we get into a situation, I guess we may need a sniper."

"You'll also need an interpreter," Anika said, coming up to him.

He shook his head, "No, not this time. We haven't got the space to spare in the Scorpion, and besides, I want you to help Miles. It could well be that a different viewpoint on what he gets out of Majidi will give us the answers we are looking for."

"I still think you may need an interpreter, someone with local knowledge, but..."

"But what is far more important is extracting everything that Majidi has in his mind and piecing it all together. There's only one priority, and that's to find Arash, the Archer, and stop him getting the nukes."

"I'll do my best. Take care, Tehran is alive with security forces after your last trip into town."

"We'll be fine. They'll just take us for a Revolutionary Guard APC. Heinrich, fire up the Scorpion. Vince, get aboard. Let's go and bring our people back."

He climbed into the turret. Buchmann revved the huge diesel engine, and they roared out of the derelict factory in a black cloud of diesel fumes and smoke. He gave the German the directions as they drove, guided by the GPS that would take them to the church where Guy's squad was holed up. He estimated they were within two clicks of their destination, when he saw it at the same time as Buchmann called him.

"Roadblock ahead, Boss. What do you want me to do?"

Talley stared at the pair of cop cars slewed across the road, two hundred meters ahead. The cops manning the block didn't seem unduly alarmed by the sight of a

Revolutionary Guard APC coming toward them. They just stood and stared out of their aviator shades, waiting for the oncoming vehicle to come to a stop. When they were within fifty meters, one held up his hand for them to halt. Talley knew there wasn't a chance in a million they'd get through the check.

"Go straight through the roadblock, Buchmann. I see two cops stood there. If you can sideswipe them, it'll prevent them from calling in that they've seen us."

"Copy that."

The German stood on the gas pedal, and the heavy armored car increased speed. They should have jumped out of the way, but this was Iran, and everyone stopped for the cops in Iran, especially in the capital, Tehran. When Buchmann was level with them, he stamped on the brake, and even as the armored car was slewing sideways toward them, they were still rooted in astonishment and glued to the spot. It was inconceivable that anyone would dare to disobey their orders. The Scorpion slammed into them and collided with the police cruisers, squashing the two men between metal and metal. Both cars were flung out of the way as the massive hull of the armored car collided with them. Buchmann released his foot from the brake, wrenched on the track control levers, and brought the armored behemoth back on course through the gap that had opened when the squad cars were tossed aside like children's tin toys. Talley looked behind him, and all he could see was a litter of wreckage smeared with blood.

"That was good driving, Buchmann."

"I never did have much time for the police," the German replied.

"Right. Slow down, we don't want to attract undue

attention. We're nearly there."

He looked around him. If anyone had seen their collision with the roadblock, it was unlikely they'd be able to respond until they were long gone. Provided they moved fast.

"Vince, are you ready for some shooting?"

"Any time, Boss."

"Standby, we'll be there in a couple of minutes."

He inspected the firing mechanism for the 76mm main gun. It seemed straightforward. There was an auto-loading mechanism that would put a new shell into the breech straight after it was fired. Adjacent to the main gun was the secondary armament, a 7.62mm machine gun. He quickly familiarized himself with the controls and made sure everything was loaded and ready for instant use. The vehicle rocked as Buchmann turned into the street, and ahead of him was a large, modern office block with a half-dozen squad cars parked outside; Police Headquarters. They cruised along the smooth, tarmac roadway, and the church came into view, next door to the cops.

"Drive past, Buchmann. When we get to the end of the street, turn around, and we'll see if we can make the pickup."

Buchmann acknowledged. It was time to call Guy.

"Echo One to Echo Two. What's your situation, Guy?"

Heinrich reached the end of the street and began making a wide turn to bring them back to the church. The communications net was silent. He called again and still silence. Vince poked his head up into the turret.

"What do you think, Boss? Could they have been taken?"

"It's anyone's guess. Ordinarily, I'd just stop nearby

and we could go in and check the building out. But we're wearing camo gear and we'd be picked up instantly. We need to think of something more subtle."

"I have a better idea," Buchmann called from the driver's position. "I think it will work." Talley was about to object, but the German picked up speed until they were almost adjacent to the boarded-up church. He wrenched on the steering levers, and the Scorpion swerved to the left, its tracks ripping up the sidewalk, tearing up pieces of masonry, and hurling them left and right. He smashed the APC straight through the enormous double doors guarding the entrance. Talley barely had time to duck and cling on grimly as they struck. Broken timbers rained down over his head. Buchmann drove forward and kept the vehicle moving, through thick curtains hanging down to separate the foyer from the main area of the church, and then they were inside. It was dark, with only one ray of light piercing the gloom from a narrow window set high up above the altar. The sole movement was the dust motes swirling in the light's beam. Talley reached forward, clicked on the searchlight, and played it around the cavernous building. There was nothing. No sound, no movement. The pews had been removed, together with all the other furnishings and ornaments that would normally be present in such a building. It was just a dark empty space; a testament to the politics of bigotry practiced by Muslim countries the world over. They were quick to protest against any perceived slight or discrimination, yet even quicker to destroy any religious body they felt to be in competition with their own.

"Buchmann, keep the engine running and turn the vehicle around. We need to be ready for a fast exit. I doubt we have more than a couple of minutes before the cops arrive from next door. Vince, come with me, we'll look around and see if there's any sign of them."

He climbed out of the turret and stepped down to the flagstone floor. There were doors to the left and right of what had once been the high altar.

"Vince, you check inside the right door, and I'll take the left. Make it quick."

"Copy that."

Both troopers ran forward, their MP7's ready to fire. He put his hand on the tarnished brass handle of the small oak door, just as it started to open.

"Vince, cover!"

He dived to one side and waited, his gun pointed at the widening crack in the door. A man peered out and then stepped through.

"You made enough noise coming in to wake the dead."

Talley stared at Guy Welland's smiling face. "Guy! Christ, man, what happened? We've been trying to contact you."

His number two grimaced. "We hit trouble, Boss. We were pulling out after we set off the charges, and Javeed led us to this place when the cops flooded the area. I know it's next door to Police Headquarters, but he reasoned it was the last place anyone would look. Then our radios packed up for some reason, maybe interference from the transmitters next door."

"Javeed is here?"

Guy shook his head. "He said he would go out and try and find transportation to get us back. That's the last we saw of him."

"Copy that. It's good to see you, but they'll be swarming

around here like flies on a turd. We need to get out now. Climb aboard the Scorpion, and we'll pull out."

"What about Javeed? He could come back at any time," Guy pointed out.

"There's nothing we can do. It may be that he just split and has decided to lie low somewhere. We'll worry about him later, but for the time being, we have a job to do."

They boarded the Scorpion and Buchmann drove forward. As the vehicle nosed out through the wrecked front doors of the church, he stopped. The place was alive with police. To the left the street was blocked with a half-dozen squad cars, and to the right they'd commandeered a big, articulated semi-trailer rig. A cordon of armed men was arranged in a semi-circle in front of them, and in the center of their ranks an officer stood with a loudhailer. He shouted something in Persian that echoed up and down the street. Talley ignored him and measured the situation to the right and left. He figured the weak spot was the rig to the right of them.

"Buchmann, I'll clear a gap past that rig. Get ready to move as soon as you have enough room to squeeze through."

"Copy that."

"What do you want me to do, Boss?"

He looked down at Vince and grinned. "Nothing. If this doesn't work, about the only option we are left with is prayer."

He climbed down inside the turret and slammed the hatch shut. He shuddered. The clang as iron hit iron was loud, like a death knell, the lid of their coffin closing. He put his head to the optical sights of the 76mm main gun, and the huge semi-trailer came into view. He used the elevation control to bring the barrel down. It was a difficult shot. The join between the tractor and the trailer was a narrow target, and he knew as soon as he opened fire, the cops would call in their heavy artillery. Iran, like most Muslim dictatorships, had no shortage of heavy artillery ready to use against their own people. The cop was still shouting into the loudhailer. He pulled the trigger and winced as the shell crashed out of the barrel, deafening him with the crash of the shot. It was well aimed, and a small space opened between tractor and the trailer. Buchmann stamped down on the pedal, and the Scorpion lurched forward, gaining momentum. The police opened fire, and small caliber bullets peppered the hull so that the interior of the armored vehicle was like being inside a metal box caught in a raging hailstorm. He ignored the cacophony. They were safe enough inside the armor-plated cabin. At least, until the Iranians brought up something heavier, which would be soon. Through the viewport he could see the gap he'd hit with the shell, but the unit still partially blocked the way through, badly twisted and broken, but still joined.

"Boss, what do I..."

"Hit it, Heinrich. It's our only chance. You have to go through it and smash the trailer apart from the tractor. If you stop, we're dead."

The German grunted and concentrated on pointing the APC exactly at what he estimated to be the weakest point. The tracks hammered on the tarmac as the Scorpion rumbled forward, faster and faster, churning up chunks of roadway as it gathered pace. Talley heard a shouted, 'Hold on' from Heinrich, and he gripped the breech of the gun to steady himself as they hit. The forward momentum of the armored vehicle smashed into the wreckage and almost broke through. Almost, but it held, and Buchmann had to reduce power to the tracks as they skidded on the tarmac, digging deeper and deeper ruts that may as well have been their grave. Then the first shell cracked out from behind them and exploded on the semi-trailer. He whirled to look behind and saw the Iranians had reacted fast. Too fast, they'd brought up a light anti-tank gun, a wheeled artillery piece that was enough to destroy the Scorpion with a single hit.

"Heinrich, reverse, reverse! Get us out of these ruts and go forward slowly. You should be able to climb over the remaining wreckage using the tracks."

"Ja, ja," he shouted. Talley felt the whiplash as he jerked the vehicle into reverse and slammed it backward, up and out of the deepening ruts he was creating. He didn't wait to come to a stop, slammed the gears into forward with a crunching noise of tortured metal, and the Scorpion started forward once more. Another shot cracked out from the anti-tank gun, hammering into the road only two meters to the side of them.

"Boss, you want me to do something about that gun?" Vince called up to him. "There's the auxiliary 7.62mm machine gun. That should scare them off."

"Not now, Vince. We have trouble enough. We don't want to escalate it by starting a shooting match. Let's hope this baby has the guts to climb out of here."

Buchmann then hit the wreckage. This time the Scorpion was traveling slower, and instead of burying its nose into the twisted metal, the tracks scraped and bit onto the torn metal and started to climb. Up, up, even further, the nose went up and the rear went down until they were almost perpendicular. Talley opened his mouth to shout to Buchmann to stop before they overturned, and then slowly, very slowly, he felt the tracks begin to bite again, and the APC started to tip forward and climb over the shattered semi-trailer. The Scorpion went up and over, and they were almost there when the anti-tank gun scored its first hit. The shell hit the thin rear armor and crashed through the cabin. Every man inside waited for oblivion, but instead, the shell smashed through the side armor and exited the vehicle. It whistled across the road and impacted on the wall of an apartment block opposite, skidded to the ground, and hustled across the street. It buried itself in the center of a tangle of rubble and weeds that had once been a house. By a miracle, they'd been hit with a dud, or perhaps the gunner in his excitement had loaded a training round. It was a reprieve, probably the only one they'd get that day. Then they were over the blockage, facing an open street.

"Get us out of here, Heinrich," he shouted. "They'll be after us, so try and lose them in the back streets."

Even as he spoke, he realized how ridiculous it sounded; several tons of tracked APC trying to disappear in the center of the city, but they had to try. Buchmann accelerated away and hurtled through the streets, ripping up the tarmac roadway as he slowed the tracks to take bends and corners at the last moment. Talley opened the hatch and looked behind, surprisingly there was no sign of a pursuit. The parlous state of the city's back streets helped them. They were so damaged, littered with missing flagstones and potholes, that the damage caused by the passage of the Scorpion wasn't obvious. Buchmann managed to navigate through to the eastern outskirts of the city, and they made it back to the derelict factory. The men started to shout with joy at it came into view, but Talley was still worried.

That escape was too easy, as if whoever's charged with chasing an armored car, using only a cop car and armed with light weapons, decided to play it safe and not pursue us with too much enthusiasm. There is another possibility. They were called off, but why?

Buchmann charged straight into the dark interior of the factory and stopped the Scorpion out of sight of the road.

"Jesus Christ, that was one hairy rescue!" Guy exclaimed, climbing out. "We didn't rate our chances of getting out of there too highly. Thanks."

Talley nodded. "Anytime."

Rovere ran out and shook hands with Guy. Anika walked out and examined the holes in the hull of the armored car.

"It looks as if you've been in a fight."

"Yeah, it was a tight one, but we were lucky. Did you have any luck with Majidi?"

She nodded. "Some, we're still working on him. He's a tough one, but I feel we're starting to wear him down. Miles is in there with him now. He was…"

She stopped abruptly. The scream coming from deep inside the building was blood chilling; a strangled cry of agony and terror. Talley ran forward, followed by Anika, Guy, and Domenico. He pushed through into what had once been a maintenance workshop, littered with the remains of rusting machinery still bolted to the floor. Miles Preston was there, standing over Majidi who was stripped naked and strapped over the skeleton of a drilling machine. His back bent backward at an unnatural angle, and the CIA man was holding a long, thin drill bit that he was forcing into the man's urethra. Majidi was groaning in agony, sweat pouring off him, and his eyes weeping with fear and pain.

"Miles, what the hell are you doing to him?"

Preston looked around casually and nodded a greeting.

"What I'm doing is uncovering the identity of the guy who's trying to turn the world into a nuclear-armed terror camp."

"You can't do it like this. I'm sorry, Miles but that kind of torture is excessive. There has to be a better way to get him to talk."

"There's no need. I think I got what I wanted out of him. He just needed that final incentive to give me a name. That last little bit of encouragement."

"You mean you know who it is?" They all stared at him. It seemed incredible that he'd had been holding back all along.

"Yeah, I think so. He didn't give me a name, but I got enough loose data to put it all together."

They waited, but he was determined to have his moment of drama, and they were going to have to ask for it.

"So who is it?" Anika asked.

"Your boss. Jeffrey Petersen."

CHAPTER NINE

She stared at him in utter astonishment. "Jeffrey?" She shook her head, "No, it's impossible. Is this some kind of a joke?"

"It's no joke. I put it together from the pieces and bits of information I did get from him."

"Yeah, we heard you getting that information out of him," Talley said grimly.

Preston shrugged. "I was almost finished anyway. If he didn't want to get hurt, he shouldn't have held out on me. He's been singing like a canary for the past hour."

"So what brought you to the idea that it's the MI6 Head of Station, Tehran?" Anika questioned him. "Frankly, Miles, you'd better have some solid evidence for making that accusation."

"Have you seen your boss lately?" he asked.

"No, not recently, but that's not unusual."

"Maybe not, but plotting to import nukes from Pakistan is unusual."

His expression challenged her to refute what he was

saying.

"So Majidi did identify him?"

"Not by name, no, but the description tallied. There's no doubt, look at some of the evidence. First off, we know that this guy, this Arash, is a keen student of Persian classical history. Otherwise, why would he have chosen the name Arash, one of their ancient warrior heroes?"

Talley wanted to say there were any of a score of reasons for him choosing that particular name, but he waited for more.

"CIA has been worried about leaks of information over the past year, and we suspected someone inside the intelligence community was passing information to the Iranians, specifically the Pasdaran, the Revolutionary Guard. One of our chief suspects was Jeffrey Petersen, and he sure was in a position to pass on details of your mission to prevent the Pasdaran obtaining the nukes."

Anika shot him an irritated glance, "And how many others had that information?"

He inclined his head in agreement. "That's true. There were maybe four or five people who had the entire package. Except for the one piece of information, the location of that abandoned cinema opposite the Pasdaran Barracks. I've checked to make sure, because I knew nothing about it when I heard your guys had been captured. I spoke to Jeffrey, and he mentioned the old cinema and said you'd been caught inside. Of course, only three of your guys were taken, but he didn't know that at the time. He told me your entire unit was ambushed and taken prisoner by the Pasdaran. How did he know that?"

Anika was shaking her head. "I still don't believe it," she murmured. "I've always admired Jeffrey. He's one of the old school, the professionals who are a legend in the MI6 community in London."

"Like Kim Philby," Preston sneered. "You know as well as I do, the one thing MI6 is famous for is the number of leaks that have occurred over the years."

Kim Philby, the infamous traitor who betrayed MI6 before escaping to Moscow.

"Did Majidi describe Jeffrey Petersen in detail?" Talley pressed him. "You're certain it was him?"

"Oh, yeah. I showed him a photo I've been carrying of Jeffrey Petersen. At the time, we thought he may have been giving secrets to the enemy, but we didn't know he was Arash himself. I showed the picture to our friendly Ayatollah, and he clammed up completely. That's when I piled on the pressure. He didn't know the name but confirmed the man in the picture is Arash. Something else you may not be aware of, not only is he fascinated by everything Iranian, but his wife was killed recently. She was Iranian, and with connections to some of the senior guys in their military, so you can imagine the potential there for a nice flow of information. Unfortunately for us," he smiled ruefully, "the information was flowing from the UK, the US, and NATO into Iran, not the other way as we thought."

Anika went to interrupt. Talley was surprised to see her face had reddened, and she seemed angry, very angry. Preston stopped the interruption and held up his hand.

"If you need anything more to go on. I told you his wife was killed, but it's the circumstances of her death that are interesting. She was visiting her relations in Pakistan, traveling to Islamabad cross-country and supposed to be a sightseeing trip. It was just one of those bad coincidences.

A US drone sighted the SUV she was in, identified is as hostile, and destroyed it. We were all sorry for him, but we didn't know it turned him in that way."

Anika nodded. "He was devastated. It changed him completely."

"He may have been helping out the Iranians already," Preston pointed out. "Given his pro-Persian views, it made them more extreme, and he looked for a way to get revenge. Using his contacts inside Iran, as well as his wife's family in Pakistan who were just as intent on revenge, it wouldn't have been difficult to set up the operation."

Anika was shaking her head, near to tears.

"I still don't believe it, not Jeffrey."

Talley looked at her closely.

What is it that's stuck in the corner of my mind? Something about her, something about the way she looked and the things she said is making me suspicious. I'll have to put it aside for now, but there'll be questions to ask after.

He looked away from her.

"I've heard enough. I'm convinced, so let's go find this bastard and stop him."

"No, please, let me find him and talk to him," Anika exclaimed.

They all stared at her. Talley shook his head.

"The time for talking is over. We have to take the bastard down." He stared at Preston. "You know so much about this, maybe you can tell us where we can look for him."

Preston smiled. "I may be able to do better than that. I know he keeps a sizeable yacht moored in the Gulf. Apparently, he's a keen sailor and diver. The boat is called the Rostam, and she's fitted out as a diving and research vessel. We believe he's been using her to hunt for underwater ruins and relics of ancient Persian civilizations. The boat even has an underwater hatch. They call it a moon tank that can be accessed from inside the hull, so divers can leave and re-enter the boat in bad weather. We had a report that she sailed recently down through the Gulf and out into the Indian Ocean. I'd bet the ranch that's where he went."

"Pakistan," Guy exclaimed, "it had to be his destination. So the bastard is bringing them in by sea, when all the time we figured they would come overland."

"I understand his boat left the harbor in Pakistan late last night," Miles informed them. "She is due to make landfall back in Iran in forty-eight hours."

Talley thought fast.

Everything's falling into place. Even the timescale corresponds to the intelligence we received. It's only the means of transportation that's a surprise, and the man behind it. Arash, the Archer, Petersen, that's incredible! Except the mythical Arash never wielded arrows with the power of the nuclear weapons that Petersen has under his control.

"What about Ahmadinejad? Is he behind any of this?"

"Absolutely not," Preston replied emphatically. "In fact, I can tell you that Ahmadinejad is totally opposed to this lunatic's game."

"How do you know that?" Talley asked him suspiciously.

The CIA man spread his hands wide and grinned. "Because I've been talking to him."

They all stared at him, astonished. Guy started forward angrily and snatched hold of his collar. "You're telling us that you have been collaborating with that little fucker all this time?"

Preston was unmoved. "I took my orders from the

Director of Central Intelligence, and he took his orders from the Commander-in-Chief, the President of the United States. And I can tell you, buddy, when he says jump, us foot soldiers on the ground have to jump."

Talley put his hand on Guy's arm. "Let him go, Guy. We need to hear what he has to say."

The SAS man removed his hand from Preston's collar. The CIA man moved to straighten his shirt. "We knew there was a leak of information coming from somewhere, and we knew it wasn't CIA. Therefore, it had to be either NATO itself or one of the NATO partners. Our President contacted Ahmadinejad directly and talked to him about the whole scheme, threatened him with the fires of hell if he carried it through. As you may imagine, he's keen for his country to get hold of nuclear technology, but this if different. But Ahmadinejad said it was news to him, and the idea of a rogue branch of the militia possessing nuclear weapons worries him almost as much as it does us in the West. So the two Presidents agreed to cooperate to try and put a stop to it. Obviously, Ahmadinejad can't come out openly and say he's against it because that would fly in the face of what he tells his voters. Neither could he admit he was cooperating with the US, the Great Satan. So they kept it all under wraps."

"You seem to know everything, Preston, so where is that vessel right at this moment?"

The American grinned. "I wondered if you'd ask. While you were out bringing back your people, I used my satphone to call Langley and give them the heads up on Petersen, and his boat. There's a US submarine in the Gulf, and they tasked the Pentagon to give the order for it to locate and shadow Petersen's boat. The Rostam is apparently heading for its home port of Bushehr."

"So why don't you just instruct your submarine to sink her? Then we can all go home."

"Because we can't be a hundred percent certain the nukes are on board. The only way to be sure is to get on the boat to check it out. While I was making the call, they looked up the latest satellite images. She has an escort of ten Revolutionary Guard fast patrol boats. It'll need someone with expertise of clandestine search and destroy missions."

Talley nodded. He could see where it was going. "I get the feeling we've been used as puppets all along, hung out to dry while people like you play your wiseass games. You want us to finish this."

"Don't be bitter, Talley, but yeah, as it happens, I do have a plan for getting you out there."

Miles Preston made a half dozen calls with his satphone, and within a few minutes, a tourist bus arrived at the factory gate.

Almost as if it had been preplanned? But how?

"That's your transport. It'll take you to Tehran International Airport, and you'll find a chartered aircraft waiting for you there. It'll carry you to Kuwait City. From there, you will find arrangements for the next stage of your journey."

Talley stared at the CIA man in disbelief. How he'd put it altogether was astonishing, except he'd forgotten one important factor.

"Preston, you know as well as I do that half the cops in Tehran are hunting for my unit. We'll be stopped and arrested before we get even halfway to the airport."

"It won't happen. Take it from me, Lieutenant, it's all

arranged. You have a clear run all the way through the city and out to the airport. No one is going to stop you."

How can CIA arrange to hold off the Iranian police after the shitstorm we've kicked up? There's only one possibility. Ahmadinejad!

He walked out to the gate where the bus waited. It was a modern, air-conditioned vehicle that would have been used to transport tourists around the historical sites of the city. He squinted as he saw movement in the distance.

Shit!

Two police cruisers were approaching, but they braked to a halt a hundred meters away and sat waiting. The cops stayed put. He turned to Miles Preston.

"I thought you said it was all arranged? There are two cruisers out there. For all we know, there could be a whole heap more waiting out of sight. It has all the makings of an ambush."

Preston smiled. "There are no more cops waiting around the corner, Talley. The cruisers are there to escort you to the airport, and to make sure you don't have any problems on the way."

"That's all?"

"That's all. You have my word on it."

I wonder how much the word of a CIA agent is worth? There's no answer to that. One thing's for sure, the Iranian cops know exactly where we are, so if there's going to be an ambush, there's nothing we can do to stop it happening. Our best and only chance is to go along with the CIA plan.

"You say that Ahmadinejad is in on this?"

"Yep, he sure is. I know it looks crazy, but from an intelligence perspective, he has nothing to gain and everything to lose by allowing the Pasdaran to acquire nuclear weapons. The politics of this country are incomprehensible to us, but as much as we don't like Ahmadinejad, if he falls and the Pasdaran takes over, it will be only weeks or even days before the missiles start hitting Israel. You know the old saying, the enemy of your enemy is your friend?"

Talley nodded. "I've heard it, yeah. I don't always believe it."

"Well, believe this, the real enemy here is the Pasdaran, and they are Ahmadinejad's enemy too, which I guess makes him our friend."

"For now," Talley murmured. He turned to Guy. "It seems we don't have a choice. You'd better get the men aboard that bus, Guy. We're going on a trip."

He nodded and gave the order. Talley turned to the CIA man before he left.

"Preston, just a word before we go. If this is some kind of a CIA setup, I'll come back, I'll find you, and I'll kill you. And then I'll go find Ahmadinejad, and he gets a bullet too. Clear?"

"Yeah, no worries, but there's no setup. This is a straight deal, all the way down the line."

Talley boarded the bus. The men were quiet and tense. All of them had unslung their weapons, and he heard the clicks of clips being checked and snapped in ready to fire. The driver, an elderly Arab man looked around fearfully. Clearly, he wasn't used to having his bus loaded with armed troops who looked mean enough to shoot him at the least provocation.

"Is it all right to leave now?" he asked, his voice betraying a slight tremor.

Talley looked around.

We're as ready as we can be, short of smashing out the windows front and rear, and mounting the Minimis ready to fight off an attack. Not a good idea. Not yet, anyway.

He nodded to the driver. The man closed the door and drove the bus away. One of the cop cars went ahead of them, and the other waited until they had passed and fell in behind. Guy raised an eyebrow.

"Anything you want us to do about them, Boss?"

He shook his head. "Best leave them alone. If this is an ambush, they'll hit us with more than two squad cars. We have to hope Miles Preston hasn't set us up."

His number two shrugged and sat down, clearly uncomfortable with the enemy so near. Anika sat next to him but said nothing. Her face was pale, and she was clearly as unhappy about the arrangement as the rest of them. Talley sensed there was much more she was upset about.

Whatever it is, no doubt she'll level with me later.

The bus took them through the derelict and rusting factories, passing shabby housing estates that littered the outskirts of Tehran. Gradually, the quality of the buildings improved as they neared the airport. There were a few luxury villas with pools, multi-story office blocks, and a general air of prosperity surrounding the wealthier area. They tensed as they reached the airport security barrier, which was manned by half a dozen cops. Parked close by, Talley could see several trucks loaded with Iranian infantry. It may have been they were normally stationed near the airport, but he doubted it. He gripped the butt of his MP7 and waited for the ambush, and for a tank or an armored vehicle to suddenly block the road. They'd be faced with a score of heavy weapons pointed directly at them. But to his astonishment, the barrier rose, and the bus driver drove straight through and out toward the apron. He parked at the foot of the boarding steps of a charter jet, a twin engine Canadair CRJ-200. He recalled they carried around fifty passengers and were commonly used for hopping between city airports. The bus driver opened the door and gestured at the aircraft stairs. Talley mentally shrugged.

If this is an ambush, it's a peculiarly complex and expensive way of doing it.

"We may as well get aboard," he called to Guy. "It looks as if Preston may have been on the up and up."

"Unless they worked out another way to get rid of us, Boss. Maybe they've put a bomb on board the aircraft."

Talley smiled. "It's possible, but I don't think so. Everything about this operation stinks. I bet if we check the charter on this aircraft, we'd find it was signed before we even arrived in Iran."

"How do you figure that?"

He'd been thinking of nothing else ever since they returned to the derelict factory and found Miles Preston waiting for them. Incredibly, he'd come to the conclusion they'd been left blind by their bosses, right from the moment the operation began. There were too many questions that couldn't be answered, too many coincidences that weren't coincidences at all, and too many escapes that were a little too easy. He looked back at Guy.

"I haven't worked it all out yet, but I think I know someone who does have some of the answers."

"Who is that? I'd sure like to talk to him."

Talley looked at Anika, and then back at Guy.

"Ask her, I reckon she can fill in some of the blanks for us."

He noticed the way she paled as she looked back at them.

"I don't know what you mean."

"I think you do. You have a lot of explaining to do later."

"I can't tell you everything, but I'll tell you what I can," she said slowly, "when it's all over."

I wish I could believe her.

They strapped into their seats, the engines fired up, and the stewardess closed the door. Then she came to check on her passengers, giving them the regulation airline smile of welcome. There were no objections. She was a trim young girl, probably in her mid-twenties, with a row of bright, white teeth and huge moist eyes that were almost an invitation to ravish her. Talley had little doubt if he had any questions about the mile high club, she'd be well placed to answer them. The Canadair picked up speed and roared off the tarmac and up into the clear blue skies of Iran. The pilot immediately set course for Kuwait City, a thousand kilometers due west. The stewardess wheeled a trolley along the aisle laden with sandwiches and soft drinks, and the men were able to relax and eat a meal for the first time in days. When they'd been in the air for half an hour, Anika stood up.

"I have to go to the cockpit. I need to make a call."

She walked away, and Talley murmured, "I bet you do."

Guy looked at him with a puzzled expression. "What gives, Boss? Is she working for the other side?"

"I don't know, but she has a lot of questions to answer."

The flight took almost ninety minutes, and then they heard the grinding of the hydraulics as the undercarriage came down ready to land at Kuwait International. He looked out of the window and could see a US Navy Chinook sitting on the tarmac. As the CJR-200 slammed down onto the runway, he could see the twin rotors of the Boeing CH 47 beginning to turn as the pilot started the engines. Their aircraft braked to a halt, and only seconds later the stairs were being maneuvered into place. The stewardess smiled as they filed off the aircraft. A naval officer was waving at them to head in the direction of the Chinook. They piled on board the 'flying bus' and immediately the engines roared as the craft lifted off, heading southeast into the Persian Gulf. It was only fifteen minutes later when the big helo banked over and swooped in and touched down on a golden beach, right on the edge of the Gulf; next to four RIBs that were pulled up on shore beside the sparkling waters.

"Good to see you again, Lieutenant."

Talley nodded a greeting to the petty officer waiting to push off from the beach. "You too. I guess it was just our luck your boat was in the vicinity when it was needed."

The man nodded absently as he checked the members of Talley's team on board, started the powerful engines, and reversed away from the beach. He spun the wheel, increased to full throttle, heading out to sea before replying.

"Luck, Sir? I don't know about that. We were told our destination was the Persian Gulf two weeks ago. We've been creeping around the Indian Ocean ever since, waiting for that boat the Rostam to show up."

It was two weeks ago when Admiral Brooks went through the operation with me. Once again, it feels like powerful, shadowy forces I have no control over are pushing me along. I wonder if there are any more surprises on the way. When I get back, if I get back, I'm going to have a long chat with Vice Admiral Brooks. First they want to give me some Mickey Mouse promotion, and remove me from command of my platoon. And to add insult to injury, they keep my men and me in the dark. It could easily have resulted in all our deaths. Okay, the nukes are critical, but so are my men's lives.

The dark sail of the USS Virginia loomed in front of them, appearing out of the night like a dark and threatening monster of the deep. Which he supposed was not an unreasonable way to describe a vessel with the power to destroy entire nations at the touch of a button. He stepped onto the deck and saluted the flag, climbed through the hatch at the base of the sail, and went through to the control room. The Skipper, Ed Dawson held out a hand.

"Welcome back, Lieutenant Talley. I gather they've got another hairy one for you."

"It looks that way, Cap'n. Do you have a location on that yacht?"

Dawson smiled. "We'd have to be blind if we couldn't follow her. She's got herself an escort of Iranian patrol boats, ten of them. They're Revolutionary Guard vessels, and they make enough noise to wake up old Neptune himself. The convoy is still about fifty kilometers offshore, heading straight for the port of Bushehr. I take it you're intending something pretty nasty for them?"

"We are that. As soon as my squad is aboard, would you make all possible speed in that direction, while we put together a plan to take the yacht."

"Those are my orders too, Lieutenant."

He looked around the control room, and his exec caught his eye.

"We're all aboard, Skipper, and they've stowed the RIBs. Hatches are all closed and the board is green. We're ready to dive."

"Very well, you have the con, dive the boat. Make your depth two hundred meters. I understand the navigator has a course to take us to that convoy, so get us there as fast as you can. Full ahead."

"Aye, aye Skipper, I have the con, depth two hundred meters, full ahead."

He picked up the broadcast microphone. "Standby to dive the boat. Make your depth two hundred meters. Dive."

Talley felt more than heard the surge of water as it entered the buoyancy tanks spaced along the hull of the submarine. The forward part of the boat tilted down, and the USS Virginia entered the dark depths of the Gulf. He went to the exercise room where his unit was busy preparing the equipment for the coming assault. The Revolutionary Guard patrol boats would be no pushover; intel had reported four of them were armed with surface-to-surface and surface-to-air missiles, and the remaining six craft carried heavy machine guns, as well as a crew of well-armed fanatics. His first choice would be a clandestine boarding of Petersen's yacht to confirm the presence of the nukes, and then arrange to destroy them. The alternative would be to tangle with the patrol boats, but with each of them carrying a crew of ten men, it would mean attacking a large and well-armed force. The potential for disaster was huge. In the end, what he came down to was what Special Forces were best at, a sneaky, underhand approach, followed by maximum destruction while the enemy was looking in the opposite direction. He changed into one of the spare wetsuits the Virginia carried and began to prepare. Buchmann would take charge of the explosives, although the need for a powerful blast meant they would each carry additional charges in their waterproof packs. They had their personal weapons, mainly MP7s and Sigs, in waterproof bags. The Virginia carried DPDs, diver propulsion devices, combat diving vehicles designed to transport two fully equipped combat divers and additional equipment on long range missions. The units, like small torpedoes, would pull them through the water at high speed. For the plan to be successful, they had to catch up with the yacht, but after that the help from the submariners would be limited. Although the Virginia was there to assist them, under no circumstances could it become involved in any kind of a firefight; especially so near to the coast of Iran, and with the fanatic Revolutionary Guard close at hand. Captain Dawson had put it clearly and succinctly.

"You men, when you go out of that hatch, you're on your own. I can't help you, not with anything. Those are my orders, and I've been warned to obey them on pain of court martial and a long prison sentence."

No one replied. What was there to say? Nothing. They were on their own. The normally silent nuclear submarine went to full power as it hurtled through the water to cut off the pleasure yacht, the Rostam. The feeds from the overhead surveillance aircraft showed Petersen's convoy cruising through the water at a steady ten knots. The USS Virginia plunged along in excess of thirty knots, but even so, they were almost out of time before the yacht reached Iran. Dawson called them to the control room, and Talley went along with Guy and Anika.

"We're going all out, and my chief engineer tells me he's fired every single knot a man could get out of this vessel.

But even so, it'll be close. At current course and speed, my navigator estimates we'll only be twenty klicks off the coast when we make the intercept. Those are disputed waters, so you should be aware the Iranians will feel within their rights to open fire without warning."

"That's pretty clear," Talley replied. "So the only way we can play this is to shoot first and ask questions after. How long before we reach the intercept point?"

Dawson looked at his navigation officer who replied, "About thirty minutes, Skipper, assuming they don't increase speed."

"Very well, you guys had better make your way to the tubes. You need to be ready as soon as we are in position."

"Copy that, Captain."

Talley left them. The Virginia was equipped with a nine-man diver lock out chamber for rapid deployment of swimmers directly from the submarine. The plan was simple; they would go out in groups of seven with the propulsion units, launching as close to the convoy as possible. While they trailed the convoy, the Virginia would go ahead and surface between the boats and the coast of Iran, under the pretext of conducting antipiracy operations. Petersen would be suspicious, of course. Carrying that particular cargo, he would be worried about any kind of interference, but there would be little the Iranians could do when faced with the awesome power of the USS Virginia. While they argued, Echo Six would close underwater and board the Rostam. If the nukes were on board as they supposed, they would sink the yacht, and the Virginia's divers would recover the warheads from the seabed, safe from the view of the Revolutionary Guard. It was a good plan, but like all plans, things could go wrong.

And where nuclear weapons were concerned, there could be no margin of error. None!

Talley was leading the first group. They packed into the chamber, and he adjusted his mask and mouthpiece. When the rest of his squad was ready, he pressed the button fixed to the bulkhead. Immediately, the engineer outside began to flood the chamber. He felt his pulse start to race as his heartbeat increased. They were close to the objective, extremely close. The next few minutes would decide the outcome of the entire operation and possibly the future stability of the Middle East. Water flooded over his head, and he forced himself to control his breathing and relax as he waited for the overhead hatch to open. There was a panel in front of him with a status board and lights. The status light was red. Then it changed. He sensed the darkness of the water lightening as the hatch began to open. He started the electric motor of the DPD and swum out, followed by the rest of his squad. Anika was with them. He'd argued against it, but she insisted it was important she represented the interests of British intelligence, especially after Petersen's treachery. Finally he relented, nobody knew Jeffrey Petersen better than she did. If things went wrong when they boarded the yacht, she just might have something useful to offer.

His squad stopped their ascent five meters below the surface and began to head east, in the direction the convoy was travelling. The DPD had a built-in miniature sonar system, and he could easily track the eleven vessels, the Rostam with its ten guard boats. The DPD was too slow to keep pace with them, but all that would change when the Virginia surfaced and forced them to stop. He turned his head, sensing movement from behind, and saw Guy's squad coming up behind him. They pushed on slowly for another minute, and then Domenico brought up the rest of Echo Six. Talley immediately went to maximum power, and the DPD surged forward, chasing the convoy. It was pulling ahead as it neared the Iranian coast.

What's gone wrong? Has Petersen's convoy refused to obey the order to stop? Unlikely, it would draw attention to them, but it's something we have to bear in mind. Has the worst happened?

Dawson had considered the idea of launching a torpedo to sink the yacht, but a torpedo designed to take out a large naval vessel with an armored hull, hitting a mere hundred-foot pleasure yacht would blow it into small pieces. The possibility of some kind of a nuclear accident or even plutonium being blasted into the atmosphere to spread over hundreds of square kilometers was a nightmare that didn't bear thinking about.

They plowed on while he ran through the options. They had enough range with the DPDs to follow Petersen's craft to the shore where they could attack them as they made harbor, but that would bring them within the range of the guns of the escorting gunboats. They had to hope the Virginia would be successful; it was their only chance. He looked at the visual readout on the scanner. They were still dropping back, approximately three kilometers from the convoy and the gap was opening. As he watched, the range stabilized and started to narrow as they closed on the convoy.

The Virginia did it. The convoy has stopped!

They surged on, feeling a new hope. Finally, they caught up. The water was clear, with just enough of a light breeze to ripple the surface and hide the underwater approach of Talley's unit. They looked up to see the underside of eleven vessels, only two hundred meters ahead. A further two hundred meters away was an enormous black hull, the underside of the USS Virginia. The Rostam was obvious to them; a hundred foot long pleasure yacht twice the length of the Revolutionary Guard boats. Talley led the way down deeper, until they were eighty meters below the surface and underneath the Rostam. He abandoned the DPD, by switching off the motor and allowing it to slowly sink to the bottom of the Persian Gulf, its work done. The others did the same, and Echo Six began their ascent until they were directly below the hull of the Rostam. The next step would be difficult. It was daylight, and there was no way they could sneak aboard. All they could hope for was that all eyes were on the giant submarine barring their path. Talley swum to the rear of the yacht, looked around to check that his squad was ready, and rose to the surface. The boarding ladder, which they had established in advance was fastened to the rear of the craft, was where it should be. He dumped his weight belt and fins. He kept the small air cylinders strapped to his chest and tugged his mask down around his neck, as he climbed the ladder. The rest of his squad followed close behind. As soon as he was clear of the water, he shook his MP7 clear of the waterproof bag clipped to his belt and stepped onto the aft deck of the yacht. He could hardly believe his luck. All the Iranian crew were staring at the awesome sight of the nuclear submarine in front of them. He knew it couldn't last, and they had to take over the yacht quickly before the Iranians turned to sweep their surroundings. Speed was the only way they could protect themselves from the awesome firepower of the gunboats. In their favor, the Revolutionary Guard would not fire on a craft carrying their precious nuclear weapons. But first, they had to secure the Rostam. Talley clicked on the commo as he ran along the deck.

"Echo Two, take the starboard side and secure the crew. I'll take the port. Echo Three, use the aft hatch to get inside and secure the cabin areas. Guy, as soon as the bridge is secure, I want you to hold it against all comers. I'll start searching the cargo area for the nukes."

A series of acknowledgements came to him, and he kept on running toward the door that gave access to the bridge. A door in the side of the superstructure opened, and a militiaman stepped out, carrying a folding stock AKM. He was young and fast. Perhaps something had alerted them that they had been boarded. He brought up his assault rifle to fire just as Roy Reynolds, coming up behind Talley, fired past him and shot the Iranian with two rounds from his Sig. The pistol was fitted with a suppressor, and the two rounds would have scarcely been audible outside of a few meters, but the militiaman had his finger on the trigger. As he was flung back by the force of Roy's bullets, his finger closed on the trigger and the AKM opened fire. The weapon kept firing as he slithered over the narrow lip at the side of the deck and went over the side. His body hit the sea with a loud splash, but it was the noise of the shots that did the damage. Heads popped up on the gunboats as every man stared at the Rostam, and a crackle of rifle fire peppered the superstructure around Talley's squad. It had started.

"Everybody, get inside and take cover," he shouted to his men. "Guy, how are you doing?"

"We just came onto the bridge, Boss. There were five of them here. We shot three, and the other two are taken care of."

"Copy that. Contact the Virginia, and tell them we're on board. Then try and stop those gunboats from getting any nearer."

He'd noticed that the boats had reacted fast and were edging towards the Rostam. Another Iranian militiamen stepped out of a hatch in the center of the deck, saw Talley and his squad, and raised his assault rifle. Talley snapped off a shot from his MP7, and the man's face exploded in a shower of blood and tissue as he fell back. Then they were through the door onto the bridge. Valois had taken the wheel, and Rovere was disappearing down the ladder into the bowels of the ship.

"Robert, get this boat turned around and head back out to sea, full ahead."

Valois spun the wheel, and the big yacht curved around, heeling over sharply as it altered course through a hundred and eighty degrees and went to full speed.

Talley nodded to Guy. "Keep her full out. We won't lose the gunboats, but at least it'll give them something to think about if they have to chase us. Contact the Virginia and advise them what we're up to. I'm going below to suppress any hostiles still on the boat and help locate those nukes. Is there any sign of Petersen yet?"

"Not yet, but he's aboard somewhere."

"We'll find him. Do your best with those gunboats. I'm going below."

Guy nodded. They were acutely aware of Dawson's warning. The submarine was expressly forbidden from offering them any help. Even if Dawson wanted to help out, the Virginia carried no short-range weapons. Her armament consisted solely of Mark 48 torpedoes and

Tomahawk missiles. Apart from that, there were only the crew's personal weapons, assault rifles, pistols, and at best a couple of light machine guns. Even so, the sheer size and power of the massive warship may be enough to hold back some of the gunboats. Hopefully. He plunged down through the companionway leading to the lower deck. As his feet hit the floor of the narrow passageway that ran through the boat, a volley of shots whistled past his head, and he flung himself down. He shouted to the men behind him to take cover, and then fired a three-shot burst at the shooter. The man had taken cover inside a cabin ten meters from where Talley crouched, ducking out of sight as his shots ripped chunks out of the woodwork next to him, and then leapt back out to fire again. This time, Talley was ready for him. He hit him in the stomach with another three-shot burst, and then fired a single shot into his head to make sure. It was never certain whether or not a hostile wore an armored vest. The man was thrown to the floor in a bloody ruin, but Talley ended his screams with a final shot to the brain.

"Move, move," he shouted at the men behind him. "Take one cabin each, and look out for Rovere's squad, he's down here somewhere. If you see the Englishman, Petersen, try to take him alive. There are a lot of questions we want him to answer."

He heard the shouts of acknowledgement and rushed forward, pushed open the door of the nearest cabin, and stepped back. No one fired at him, so he looked inside to see the room was empty. His men were pushing open the doors of cabins further along. He ran past them and down a set of stairs at the end that led to the lower deck. Domenico's squad was grouped at the bottom of the stairs.

"What's going on? Why aren't you searching the boat?"

"It's Petersen," he replied. "He's in the cargo area at the end of this passage with a half-dozen Revolutionary Guards. He said if we try and take him, he'd explode one of the nukes."

"Shit! Do you think he's serious?"

"I think anyone crazy enough to do what he's done, is crazy enough to explode a nuke, even when he's sitting on it. Besides, he must know he's finished. All he has to face is a lifelong prison sentence."

A thought occurred to Talley. "Do you know if he's in touch with those gunboats?"

"Yes, he is. He must have a short-range handheld radio with him. I heard him talking to them."

"That means he could be playing for time."

He keyed his mike. "Echo Two, this is One. What's the position of those gunboats?"

Guy replied immediately. "They're all around us, Boss. They just moved closer to box us in. The Virginia is holding station. She's about five hundred meters south, but the Iranians don't seem too intimidated by her. They're obviously planning something. I guess they intend boarding us. I'll get back to you. There's a message coming in from the submarine."

A voice shouted out loud. Petersen, the upper class Brit accent was unmistakable. "Is that you, Lieutenant Talley?"

He turned to Domenico and murmured, "Anika is on the bridge. Get her down here. She may know how to deal with this bastard."

Rovere nodded and went back up the stairs to the bridge. He shouted to the man inside the cargo area.

"Mr. Petersen, I am speaking to Arash?"

The Brit laughed. It was like a cackle, and the maniac was sitting on top of a nuke only a few meters away from them. They exchanged glances. There were only two possible outcomes for this stand off, and one of them was bad, very bad.

"Yes, Lieutenant, I am Arash. You are talking to the man who will put Persia back to its rightful place in the world. A country that is feared and respected, no derided as the home of a bunch of sand niggers."

"What do you want?"

What do I want?" The voice was sneering, with a heavy dose of hysteria. "I want you to get off my boat. I guess you're familiar with the word 'piracy'?"

"You know we can't do that, Petersen. If you hand over those warheads, we can strike a deal. We can all get out of this alive, and I can arrange for you to avoid a long prison sentence."

"It isn't going to happen, Talley. Here's what I'm offering. Either you get off my boat now, or I trigger one of these missiles."

"Don't be stupid, you'll..."

Petersen interrupted him. "It's you who's being stupid, while I hold all the cards. You have fifteen minutes to get off this boat. If any of your men are still aboard after the deadline, you'll all be blown to hell."

"Listen to me," Talley shouted desperately. "We have to talk about this."

"There's nothing to talk about. Fifteen minutes, Lieutenant, and the timer is running. If you want to live, I suggest you get moving now. This discussion is over. The next move is up to you."

Anika came running down the companionway and joined him. He rapidly explained the situation.

"Do you think he's capable of it? I need to know what kind of a man we're dealing with."

She was aghast, and astonished. "Petersen is Arash? That's incredible." She looked thoughtful. "He is obsessive about everything to do with Persian history. I have a feeling he sees himself as some latter day Persian super hero, so yes, he's potentially capable of anything."

Talley stared at her. "But surely he's British. Why would he feel that way?"

"You know about his wife. Her family was descended from the Iranian aristocracy, and there were links to the Shah. I think he's just got caught up in it, rather like Lawrence of Arabia. He sees something romantic about the supposed great days of the Persian dynasty and plans to recreate them. I think he could do it."

"You know a lot about him. How come? I know you're holding out on me. What is it?"

She looked away and didn't reply. Talley checked his wristwatch.

Two minutes have gone by already, and I have no idea how to deal with Petersen. We could try storming the cabin, but that won't deactivate the nuke.

"Twelve minutes, Lieutenant," he shouted. "If you're going to make a decision, I suggest you make it fast. Unless you want you and your men to die, I'd start getting off this boat, right now."

"We got company, Boss," he heard Guy's voice over the commo. "The Virginia has just reported a light frigate about three kilometers away, and she's heading toward us at high speed."

"Iranian?"

"It's the Jamaran, a Moudge class guided missile boat. She carries missiles, torpedoes, a 76mm DP rapid fire auto-cannon, 40mm AA gun, and Noor missiles, as well as triple 324mm light torpedoes and SAMs, enough to hurt us badly. Wait, the Virginia. She just crashed dived. It looks like she's clearing the area. I'm not surprised. The Jamaran could do her a lot of damage if it caught her on the surface."

"So we're on our own."

"It looks that way, yeah, and the gunboats are pressing in even closer."

"Copy that. Be ready to abandon ship. If Petersen won't surrender, his other option is to detonate the nuke."

"We won't get far in a few minutes," Guy pointed out.

"I know that. Give me a minute. I have an idea."

He looked around for Buchmann. The German was at the foot of the ladder, putting together his charges to sink the Rostam.

"Heinrich, leave that. I don't think this boat is going to need much help to sink. You see that cabin door next to where Petersen is holed up in the cargo hold?"

Buchmann nodded.

"I want you to get in there and plant a small charge that will take down the partition between the cabin and the cargo hold."

"Jawohl." He picked up his pack and ran into the cabin.

"Are you sure this is the way to play it?" Domenico asked him. "That madman is quite likely to detonate early if he thinks we're trying to attack him."

"If this works, Domenico, he won't be in any position to detonate anything."

"Even so, that still leaves the nuke. There's no way any of us can disarm it, at least, not in the few minutes we have left."

Talley nodded. "That's probably true. How big would you say that weapon is? I mean, what would you say it weighs?"

Domenico shrugged. "I don't know. It's designed as a warhead for a relatively small missile, so I would guess fifty kilos, not much more."

"That's what I thought. And how deep is the water here?" Domenico's face that had been so serious suddenly broke into a smile. "It's pretty deep, at least a thousand meters, I'd guess."

"That's my guess too." He keyed his mike to contact the bridge. "Echo Two, this is Talley. Contact the Virginia, and tell them to clear the area. They're to get out fast." He checked his watch, "Tell them they have nine minutes before the nuke explodes."

"Copy that. What about us?"

"Just do it, Guy. With any luck we'll be okay, but get the Virginia clear."

"Copy that."

Buchmann came out of the cabin and nodded, "It's ready to blow."

Talley turned to the men. "When that charge blows, we're going into the cargo hold through that cabin. They'll be watching the door, so with any luck we should surprise any of them left standing. As soon as they're all dead in there, we're going to abandon ship."

"What about me," Anika asked. "What do you want me to do?"

"Yeah, I want you to check that nuke and make certain

the time is running like he said. That's really crucial. For this to work, it has to blow."

She stared at him doubtfully. "I hope you know what you're doing, Abe."

"Yeah, me too." He looked at Buchmann. "Hit it!"

The German shouted, "Fire in the hole!"

They crouched down away from the blast, and he triggered the explosive charge. The detonation was surprisingly small, and even before the smoke had cleared, Talley was charging through the cabin door. Buchmann's explosive had torn a huge hole in the partition wall. They were in the cargo hold, which held six militiamen; four had been catapulted to the floor by the force of the blast. Two others were still standing and beginning to level their AKM assault rifles. Petersen was there too, semi-conscious, and as Talley watched he slid to the floor, stunned and battered by the explosion. He took the first militiaman with a single tap to the face that spun him around. Vince charged in behind him and fired several short bursts from his MP7, raking the other militiaman and cutting down the four who were trying to get to their feet.

Petersen finally recovered his wits and saw Talley standing in front of him, surrounded by his men and Anika.

"You must be mad," he croaked, "You know you're going to die?"

"Maybe," Talley replied, "but I'll have the satisfaction of knowing that I've stopped you, Petersen. Your scheme is over, so why don't you disarm the nuke? At least you'll live."

"Never! I'm going to stay here and watch you die when that warhead explodes."

"I think not, Petersen. I have other plans."

The rest of them watched in horror as he fired two shots into the man's chest and head. The man's body was torn apart by the high-tech bullets.

"What the hell did you do that for?" Domenico shouted in dismay. "He could have disarmed the warhead."

"He wouldn't have helped us. He wanted us to die. Contact Guy, tell him to meet us at the underwater hatch, it'll be in the lower compartment at the rear of the boat, and to send a signal to the USS Virginia to let them know we're leaving. If we survive the blast, we'll need a lift home."

Domenico shook his head, "I hope you know what you're doing."

"Do it!" Talley shouted.

"There's something wrong here," Anika exclaimed. She'd been staring at the time of the bomb. "When he said…"

"Not now! Is the bomb set to explode, yes or no?"

"Well, yes, it is, but…"

"We're almost out of time, so tell me later. The rest of you, follow me. We have to get that hatch open ready to leave."

He led the way out of the hold and back along the passageway toward the back of the boat. They came to a door with a sign that said ' Diving Operations, Caution - Do not enter'. He kicked the door open, and they rushed after him into a room five meters square, with racks of diving equipment fastened to the bulkheads.

"Everyone, grab what equipment you need. We're leaving."

He snatched a weight belt from the racks of equipment

and strapped it around his waist.

"Hurry, we probably don't have much more than five minutes left."

Guy came rushing through the door with his squad, and Talley pointed to the equipment racks.

"Get kitted up, weight belts, fins, anything you ditched when you came aboard. We're leaving now."

Reynolds pulled aside the moon tank cover. The sea churned and boiled below; a reminder that the entry was only intended for use when the boat was stationary. Guy had left it on autopilot, and it was running at its maximum speed of fifteen knots. It was the only way. Leaving the boat by going over the side, they'd be in full view of the Iranians. If they weren't machine-gunned in the water, the Revolutionary Guard would drop depth charges, which would be enough to kill any divers caught in the open sea nearby.

"Five minutes won't do it," Guy pointed out. "Is it worth being slaughtered in an underwater atomic blast, or would quicker to end it here?"

"That's not the full story," Anika shouted to him. She was standing by the sea hatch, possibly contemplating jumping into the roaring maelstrom kicked up by the propellers. "I tried to tell you, but I didn't get a chance. After Abe shot Petersen, I checked the time on the warhead. Petersen lied to us, probably to give him more time to negotiate. He set it for thirty minutes, so we have about twenty minutes left."

He made a quick calculation in his head. It meant they would be ten kilometers away when the device detonated.

It's still painfully close, but we have a chance.

He shouted at the men, "Let's go, move. Swim away on

the opposite bearing to the yacht's course. Follow me, and forget the weapons and equipment. All we need is to get out of here and fast."

He pulled down his mask, bit onto his mouthpiece, and jumped into the sea. Immediately, he was caught in the roaring turbulence kicked up by the two powerful Caterpillar diesels pushing the yacht through the water at maximum speed. He was spun around like a spinning top, and he felt his mask being wrenched off. With a huge effort, he kicked away from the swirling water and managed to fit his mask back into place. He swam further from the vessel, looking around to watch the rest of his people tossed around by the angry turmoil of the twin screws, and then they were all clear. Now all they could do was swim as fast as possible and hope to get enough distance between them and the yacht. Guy swam right behind him, and Rovere brought up the rear to make sure there were no stragglers. Anika was a surprisingly strong swimmer, and she swam along right next to Guy. As he fought his way through the water, he made the calculations. Of course, there was no way of knowing what kind of warhead the Pakistanis had supplied to Petersen, but it had to around ten kilotons. The underwater shockwave from the explosion would be enormous. There was no doubt it would create a tsunami that would travel for many hundreds of kilometres. The Revolutionary Guard vessels would be totally destroyed in the blast, as well as the frigate that had arrived in the area.

That's too bad. If these people want to play with nukes, that's the risk they have to take.

But he also knew that the sledgehammer effect of the underwater shockwave would almost certainly kill his entire unit. It would be like being hit by a truck. The enormous pressure would explode their lungs and every other organ in their bodies. They would become lifeless corpses, hanging in the water as ruptured lungs and stomachs slowly filled, until they all sank to the bottom.

Better to go that way, better to lead my people in a last desperate surge of hope than to sit around waiting for death, like animals in a slaughterhouse.

He checked his wristwatch, six minutes to go, and he kicked his fins harder, spearing through the water to put as much distance between the yacht and the swimmers; and to give the men behind him the illusion of safety.

They swam on. His lungs were bursting, his muscles aching, but it was worth one final effort, worth going out in a blaze of hope. The effort was so great he sensed everything was going dark, and he wondered if he was suffering from oxygen depletion.

That's strange. I'm a former Navy Seal, a trained combat swimmer.

He looked down and saw it wasn't darkness that had engulfed them. It was the great black hull of the Virginia that had appeared beneath them. The underwater hatch was open in an obvious invitation. Hope flared, and he pointed with his arm, turning to make sure the rest of them had seen the sub. They swam down a few meters, and the first group went into the hatch. Talley pushed Anika inside, and then Reynolds, Valois, DiMosta, until ten troopers were packed in the tight space. He pulled the lever that closed the watertight door and looked around him. As he guessed, Guy was still outside, with Domenico, Buchmann and the last of his squad. There were eleven of them remaining, a tight squeeze. But they still had to get the first batch inside the submarine and flood the compartment again for the second batch. He checked his watch again, expecting at any second to feel the effect of the blast as the weapon detonated, but they still had fifty seconds. He counted down, forty seconds, thirty seconds. It wasn't enough, but then the hatch reopened, and they crammed inside. Eleven swimmers in a compartment design for only nine, but it was the most luxurious feeling in the world, the slightest chance of life. Guy pulled the lever to close the door, and immediately the pumps started emptying the water from the compartment to enable them to enter the submarine. They were still knee deep in water when the warhead detonated, and everything went black.

CHAPTER TEN

A bright light shone over his head, and his mind wandered as he tried to make sense of where he was.

Is this the afterlife, some kind of heaven?

" Lieutenant! Can you hear me?"

Something floated over him, a dark shape that was blurry and indefinable.

"Talley!"

This time it was a human voice. He fought to clear his brain and focus his eyes. The blurry shape swam into focus, and it was nothing unworldly. A man's face, a corpsman wearing the uniform of the United States Navy.

"Where am I? What happened?"

"When the nuke detonated, you were tossed around inside the outer chamber. We got you out of there mighty fast, but there were some injuries from the blast wave."

"What about radiation?"

He shivered as he waited for the answer. Every man feared radiation when from nuclear fission, invisible but deadly after any kind of explosion or nuclear accident.

The corpsman reassured him they'd conducted a number of tests, and all of them were in the clear, but Talley could see that it wasn't the whole answer.

"There's something you're not telling me. What is it?"

The man shook his head. "Not everyone made it, Sir. There was one fatality, a Robert Valois. I'm afraid the concussion hit him too hard. He was just in the wrong place at the wrong time, one of those things. He died straightaway. It's a miracle he was the only death. One of your people has been pestering me to see you, a Sergeant Guy Welland."

"He's my second-in-command. I'd like to speak to him."

When Guy came into the sick bay, he was wearing a bandage over his head. He smiled ruefully.

"I banged my head against the hatch. How are you feeling?"

Talley tried to nod, but the effort almost made him pass out, and he closed his eyes momentarily to keep conscious.

"I've been better."

"You heard about Valois?"

"Yeah, that's a bummer, to have come this far and then get killed within feet of safety. I wish to Christ I could have done more. Maybe I should have moved faster. There must have been something."

Guy shook his head. "There was nothing you could do. What saved us was the Skipper of the Virginia. He brought his boat back into the danger zone to pick us up. If he'd obeyed orders and hightailed it out of Dodge, we wouldn't be having this conversation. Standing orders for any kind of a nuclear explosion are to go to flank speed and clear the area. He shouldn't have stopped for anything. We're just lucky he had the guts and initiative to stick around for us."

"Yeah, I'll have a word with him. I reckon we owe him a lot. I only hope to Christ he doesn't hit trouble for helping us out."

"If he does, I suggest we stage an operation on the Pentagon and take out the bastards responsible."

Talley smiled. "Let's hope it doesn't come to that. We have enough problems as it is. What about Anika? Was she injured?"

"Not badly, no. She sustained a couple of cuts and bruises, but she came through okay. I take it you still have concerns about her?"

He nodded. "I'll talk to her another time."

Guy was about to reply, but the corpsman came back into the sick bay and told him to get lost. Talley objected, but the man ignored him and thrust a needle into his arm. Seconds later, he once again drifted into oblivion.

When he awoke, he was strapped to a gurney, which two burly sailors were carrying to the submarine's cargo access hatch. He was only half aware of the transfer to a United States aircraft carrier that involved him being winched on board a helo hovering five meters above the deck. The aircraft carrier, the USS George Washington, was stopped in the water five hundred meters from the Virginia. Even in his semi-comatose state, Talley was aware of the immensity of the Nimitz class nuclear powered carrier, as the aircraft controller guided the helo to a touchdown on the deck. They handed him over to a pair of corpsmen who were waiting to receive him, and they carried him down to the carrier's well-equipped hospital. A doctor attended him immediately.

"How are you feeling? I gather you took something of a bump back there, some kind of an underwater explosion?"

His mind screamed a warning. The physician was unaware there had been a nuclear explosion. That meant there was a complete information blackout. It was understandable, but pumped full of drugs, he reminded himself to be mighty careful.

"Yeah, something like that."

"You know what caused it, Lieutenant, were you attacked? Or was it an old mine floating around from World War II?"

"We're not too sure of that, Doc. I guess they're looking into it right now."

The medical officer nodded absently as he gave Talley a thorough check over. He finished and nodded to Talley, "I reckon you're in pretty good shape, son. We'll be running some more tests, ECGs, MRIs, that kind of thing, but I'm confident you'll be fine."

Before he could go on, there was a knock on the door, and Anika walked into the room.

"Ma'am, this patient is not up to visitors just yet..."

"It's okay," Talley said quickly. "Could you give us a few minutes, Doc?"

He nodded and left the room, calling, "A few minutes is all you get, feller. Then you need to get some rest."

They stared at each other for a few moments.

"You were hurt badly when the warhead exploded, Abe. Did you learn about Valois?"

"I know. Are they shipping his body home, or will there be a funeral?"

"Apparently, his last wish was to be buried at sea. It's due to take place at midday tomorrow."

It reminded him he'd completely lost track of time.

"How long was I out?"

"Almost twenty-four hours. Abe, I was really worried. When you blacked out in the compartment, your mouthpiece slipped out, and I tried pushing it back in for you. Guy helped to support you until they opened the hatch. For a time, it looked as if you'd stop breathing. I started mouth-to-mouth on you. It took a while, but then you started breathing again. What worried us was whether you'd suffered any permanent damage." She gave him a tired smile. "It seems you're okay."

"Yeah, I'm okay." He caught her eyes. "I haven't lost my memory either. I guess you know there are a few things we need to clear up."

She stared back at him without speaking for a couple of minutes, but he waited.

Seems she's trying to make up her mind about something. Telling me the truth, maybe?

"I guess you want to know about Petersen."

"Amongst other things, yes. I know that you passed him information about our movements."

She went pale. "How? How did you find out?"

"Too many coincidences, I guess. Too many things were going wrong right from the start, and as you know, I suspected Miles Preston, at first. It was a long and complicated trail, and then it became clear that Miles wasn't double-crossing us. It was Petersen all the time, and I didn't have to look too far for the next part of the puzzle. I had to ask myself, who was uniquely placed between Echo Six and the MI6 Head of Station to pass back information about our movements? I didn't believe it at first, but I had to look at the obvious. There was only one candidate, and that was you."

"It's not the whole truth. I did pass on a couple of things, but I had good reason."

Before she could go on, the physician bustled back into the room.

"You'll have to do get out of here, Ma'am. He needs treatment and rest. Come back tomorrow if you want to see him again."

She nodded and moved toward the door.

"What reason?" Talley shouted after her.

She turned back to stare at him. Her voice when she spoke was almost inaudible. "He was my father."

He lay back with his mind in turmoil as the Doc attended to the lines feeding drugs and saline into him. As his consciousness began to recede, he still couldn't work it all out.

Her father! It doesn't seem possible. It sure was an odd relationship, with each appearing to conspire to bring about the death of the other.

When he awoke, it was still at the forefront of his mind. But he had little time to think about it, as Guy and Domenico entered the room dressed in borrowed uniforms.

"It's the funeral service for Robert Valois. We thought you'd want to come."

He looked for his wristwatch, but of course it had been removed. Even so, he knew that it was still only evening.

"I thought that was supposed to be at midday tomorrow. What is it now, around midnight?"

Domenico grinned, "You've been out for a while, it's 1130 hours. Daytime."

1130 hours! That means I've been unconscious again for almost eighteen hours.

"Get me a uniform! I have to be there."

"Anika managed to borrow some stuff for you, and she'll be here in a moment."

He grimaced as Guy mentioned her. His number two stared at him.

"You still have a problem with her?"

"Let's get the funeral over with. I'm not sure if there's a problem or not."

They both went silent, and a few seconds later Anika brought an armful of clothes into the room. They helped him out of bed while she pulled on his pants and shirt, and buttoned on a jacket. He looked down as she was lacing his shoes and realized he was wearing the uniform of a full commander of the United States Navy.

"It seems I've been promoted," he said dryly.

"It was all I could get you."

He nodded his thanks, and then felt a spell of dizziness. He almost collapsed, but Guy and Domenico took an arm apiece and kept him on his feet. They helped him along the narrow companionways that led up to the flight deck. A contingent of the crew of the George Washington was drawn up in full dress uniform, along with an honor guard of marines with rifles. To one side, and looking totally out of place in their ill fitting, borrowed gear, were the men of Echo Six. He went to join them. To his astonishment, Heinrich Buchmann was almost in tears. He was astonished but touched.

"We are all soldiers, Heinrich. We all have to take the same his chances, and next time it could be you or me. Besides, I thought you and Valois hated each other."

The German nodded. "Yes, we hated each other. Do you know why?"

He shook his head.

"We were serving in Afghanistan, a joint special operations mission to target Taliban bomb makers. You know, the IEDs that cause us so many casualties over there. We went into a hostile village, and our mission commander, a German who was also the commander of my unit, ordered an immediate frontal assault on the enemy to hit them before they had a chance to pick us off one by one. There was no way of knowing what else they had in store for us, traps or ambushes around the village, and he decided not to take the risk. We charged in and overran their positions, but we took heavy casualties. Three of our men were killed and five more were wounded. But the French, there was no sign of them. Eventually, they arrived, and it turned out their leader had disobeyed the order to charge and had kept his men, the French Special Forces, behind cover while we went in and did all the work. When I joined Echo Six, I recognized Robert Valois as one of that French unit, and I'd have liked to take him apart piece by piece. But I had second thoughts during this mission. He fought like a hero, and it wasn't him who gave that cowardly order. It was the French squad leader who refused to charge. All he did was follow orders. I guess if anything, I should look up that officer and take him apart, but it's too late now. I lost some good friends in that attack, which I guess is why I felt so bad about Valois, but lately I thought I should have talked it out with him, and maybe come to an understanding. Perhaps he disagreed with the order to stand back while the attack went in. Now I'll never know."

Talley nodded. "I understand, my friend, but you have to realize it's all in the past. What killed Valois was that lunatic Petersen and his plan to acquire nuclear warheads for the Revolutionary Guard. And what killed your men in Afghanistan was another bunch of fanatics. If we're to do the job we're paid to do, we need to keep our sights fixed firmly on the enemy, and not on our own men."

"Ja, I think you could be right."

"Tenhut!"

They came to attention as the Admiral in command of the carrier battle fleet came onto the deck. He went to the rail where Valois' coffin was shrouded in a flag.

It's a nice touch, Talley reflected.

They'd searched through the ship's stores and located a French flag, the Tricolor, the red, white, and blue standard of France. The carrier's chaplain said a few words over the coffin, and the Admiral gave the eulogy. An aide came to Talley and asked him if he wanted to say a few words as the man's commander, but he declined, feeling unable to keep on his feet for even the few minutes it would require. Then it was all over, and the bugler played the Last Post as the coffin slipped over the side. The Marine Detachment fired a three-volley honor salute. The shooting took him back to those final desperate moments on board the Rostam when they were engaged in an almost apocalyptic struggle to take control of the yacht. His mind started to slip, and he felt his legs going rubbery. The next thing he was aware of was when he woke up in the sick bay. Guy and Domenico were both in the room with him.

"What happened?"

"It was too early to get back on your feet," Domenico asserted firmly. "If she was still here, I would have recommended some leisure time with the lady."

"She's gone? You mean Anika has left the ship?"

"You didn't know?" He looked puzzled. "Apparently, she was needed back in London for a debrief. She spoke to the Captain, and he arranged for a helo to take her to Dubai International for a transfer to a London flight."

Talley closed his eyes. *So she managed to slip away. If I'd been conscious, I would have stopped her. There are far too many questions for her to answer. Until I have all the answers, I wanted to keep her within reach, but now it's too late. Her colleagues in MI6'll protect her, and my chances of questioning are almost non-existent.*

He spent two days recovering in the hospital of the USS George Washington. During this time there was a complete news blackout on the events surrounding the decimation of the warheads. One peculiarity of a submarine is that the crew is of necessity out of contact with the outside world, apart from the official communications channels. There was no possibility of any information leaking out, and by the time the sub docked, the crew would no doubt have been warned to keep silent on penalty of the direst punishments. Not that they would need any threat, the crew of a nuclear submarine is, like the Special Forces, the elite of the world's military.

They were allocated transport to take them back to NATO headquarters in Belgium, and Talley's squad was lifted off the deck of the George Washington by a pair of SH 60 helos, the Sea Hawk variant of the venerable Black Hawk. The two aircraft flew them to Kuwait International Airport where they transferred to a Kuwaiti Airlines Boeing 757, on a direct flight to Brussels. On arrival at NATO, Rovere led the men away for debrief, but Talley and Guy were summoned before Vice Admiral Carl Brooks. His greeting was cold. There were no handshakes, no preliminaries.

"I called you both here to find out about the fuck-up in Iran."

"Hold on there, Admiral," Guy exclaimed, "The mission was a success. You sent us there to prevent the Pasdaran from getting hold of Pakistani nukes. That's exactly what we did. Not only that, the guy who was running the show is doing an Osama bin Laden, feeding the local fish population."

Brooks didn't smile. If anything, his face became even grimmer. "I guess you're aware of the complaints we've had about the Iranians cops who were killed during the mission. As well as an indeterminate number of Revolutionary Guards, and the kidnapping of the number two man in the Iranian's atomic energy facility. Which, by the way, has been almost totally destroyed. It's true you achieved your objective, and a lot of people are breathing a sigh of relief right now, but the head of NATO, SACEUR, is going ape over the collateral damage the Iranians suffered. And the UN! Don't mention the UN. For Christ's sake, why did you have to leave such a trail of destruction? You men are trained to operate in the shadows, not to park a squadron of tanks on Ahmadinejad's lawn."

"We didn't fully achieve our mission objective," Talley interjected quietly.

Brooks swiveled to stare at him, "What the hell are you talking about, Lieutenant? I saw the overheads from the Gulf, and there was no doubt those warheads were atomized, along with the Rostam, the guy who was running the show, Petersen, and the Revolutionary Guard boats."

"That's true, Sir, but one of the players managed to escape."

He explained to him about Doctor Anika Frost, and his

suspicions about the part she'd played in helping Petersen evade Echo Six while they were hunting for Arash. When he informed the Admiral she was Petersen's daughter, his jaw dropped open in astonishment.

"You're shitting me, Lieutenant? His daughter? We don't have anything like that on record."

"No, Sir, I guess not, but that's the way it is. Maybe she was adopted, maybe she changed her name somewhere along the line, who knows? They were both British intelligence officers, and so they would have had every opportunity to cover their tracks."

"You're sure about this?"

"I am, Sir. The only question I have, is how deeply she was involved?"

"How do you mean?"

"I mean that because of their relationship as fellow intelligence officers in the Tehran Station, as well as presumably father and daughter, she passed on intelligence to him. But how far that went, I don't know. There's a lot I need to ask her."

Admiral Brooks looked thoughtful, "Yeah, I bet you do. You know she's back in London?"

"So I heard. She was recalled to MI6 Headquarters."

"That's true, but she's also doing some work for the archaeologists you were with in Iran." He grinned. "I happen to know that tomorrow evening she's giving a talk on the Persian era archaeology at King's College in London."

Talley and Guy looked at each other.

"Then I guess we'll be headed for London," Talley murmured.

Brooks gave him a sharp look. "Remember, Lieutenant,

she's a serving officer of the British Secret Intelligence Service. You're not going there for an assassination. I expressly forbid it."

"There's no question of that," Talley replied. "What we're looking for is answers. Then you can decide where we go with it."

Brooks nodded and appeared to be satisfied. "Very well, but keep me informed. I want to know every move you make before you make it. My office is still trying to pacify the Iranians after Echo Six tore the country to shreds, not to mention SACEUR. I don't want to have to deal with the Brits as well. They can be damn awkward when they put their minds to it." He looked at Guy, "Present company excepted, of course."

The SAS man nodded, but Talley noted Guy's expression, and he was not paying attention.

Something about the operation is bugging him.

"Before you go, Lieutenant, remember I want you to think about that promotion. As you know, it would give you the rank of Lieutenant Commander with an early jump to full Commander. It's a big deal, you know. You'd be a fool not to give it some serious thought."

"I appreciate it, Admiral," he nodded, "but I have the best job in the world, leading a Special Forces unit in the field. I don't think an extra stripe and a few more bucks in my pay packet would compensate for losing it."

"Well, think about it, son. I intend to make some noises about you, Sergeant Welland. How would you feel about…"

Guy was already shaking his head, grinning, "If you're talking about a commission, Admiral, you can forget it. In the SAS, we were organized into four man squads, and they weren't officers. Like Lieutenant Talley, I don't think I'd want to lose that kind of action."

"It could mean command of your own unit, Sergeant. You've done good work. I think you could be wasted as second-in-command."

Admiral Brooks had to be content with that. "Fair enough. Just be careful what you do in London. It's not a Third World shithole, so they won't put up with the kind of mischief you got up to in Iran."

Both men smiled. "Don't worry, Admiral," Talley replied, "we'll behave."

"And make sure I'm informed of everything you do. I don't want to see it on CNN before I hear about it from you."

Sergeant Williams was waiting for them in the outer office. Admiral Brooks' aide produced, as if by magic, tickets for the Eurostar that went direct from Brussels to London.

"How the hell did you manage to do that so fast?" Guy asked him in disbelief. "The only way would be if you had the Admiral's office bugged."

"Bugged? I wouldn't dream of it. If you gentlemen would like to follow me, I'll take you to the Eurostar terminal."

He led them to the Admiral's luxurious Mercedes, and they were treated to another ride through the Belgian capital, this time to the bustling railway terminal. Williams explained it was the fastest way to get to central London, particularly as they were on official NATO business. He winked as he told them it avoided the need for travel through airports, and airport security.

Talley smiled. "Yeah, I was wondering how we could

get our hardware into England. I thought we'd have to leave it with you, but I guess it won't be a problem."

"I wouldn't guarantee it, Lieutenant. There's always the possibility you could be stopped and searched, but it's not very likely, especially as you are travelling in uniform."

"Understood, we'll just have to take the chance. I hate to go on a mission unarmed. It feels as if I'm not wearing my underwear. Not that this is a mission, not exactly. We're going for a friendly chat."

Williams smiled. "I've kept up with the reports of Echo Six in the field. All I can say is whoever you're going to have a chat with, would be well advised to wear a flak jacket. Just my opinion, of course, no offence."

"None taken," Talley replied dryly.

He left them at the terminal and they boarded the Eurostar almost immediately. Williams had done them proud, their tickets were booked in the business class section of the train. In less than two hours, they were exiting the Channel Tunnel and rocketing through the English countryside en route for London. As they enjoyed their first decent meal for a long time, brought to them by an unusually attentive and attractive waitress, they discussed how they would handle Anika Frost.

"Are you sure she's crooked?" Guy asked him. "She seemed committed to the operation, and put her life on the line more than once. She doesn't strike me as someone working for the other side."

"She was working for her father," Talley replied. "I know about Petersen's wife, her mother, being hit by a drone strike, so maybe that was enough to turn her against everything she believes in. Neither of them looks like the usual Muslim fanatic."

"You think there's another motive? The usual reason, money?"

"The British Secret Intelligence service has a record of high-level treachery," Talley pointed out. "Most of them, people like Philby and Anthony Blunt, betrayed their country for their beliefs, but more than a few had their own bank balances in mind when they actually did it. My guess is that he got bitter going around the world from posting to posting, seeing how well other people did. The death of his wife was the final straw, and he would have found it easy to go over to the people he was so obsessed with, the Persians."

"But nukes? That's taking it to extremes."

"It is taking it to extremes, although the rewards would be massive. But now that Petersen is dead, my concern is with Doctor Frost. How deeply was she involved? She could still hurt us."

"I noticed you called her Doctor Frost, and not Anika," Guy observed. "It looks as if you've made up your mind. Not using her Christian name is putting some distance between you and her before you take action. It's as if you've already decided she's guilty."

Talley didn't reply.

Maybe he's right, and deep down I know she passed information to Petersen that was enough to get men killed. She betrayed us.

In his world, it didn't require a person to pull the trigger or drop the bomb to kill someone. It was enough to pass on information that would enable someone else to do the killing. In the shadowy world of SpecOps, there was generally only one punishment, death.

They watched the green fields and farms of the county of Kent rush past the fast moving train, and gradually the pastoral landscape gave way to the grimy and sprawling suburbs of London. Soon, the train slowed and they pulled into the soot-covered Victorian splendor of St Pancras Station. Thankfully, they had not seen any customs officials on their journey, and the weapons they brought in their luggage had passed undetected. They took a taxi into central London and checked into the Dorchester Hotel, with NATO paying the tab. When they were safely in their room, they were able to prepare for their confrontation with Doctor Anika Frost. Talley unstrapped the false bottom of his carry on bag and removed his Sig Sauer P226. He pulled out the clip and checked the ammunition load, slapped it back in, and attached the sound suppressor to the end of the barrel. Guy sat on his bed and watched him.

"What? What's the problem, Guy? Something has been bothering you since we talked to Admiral Brooks in Brussels."

Guy seemed to come to a decision, and he sighed. "It's just this, Boss. I'm still not sure about the way this was handled. It's the involvement of that bastard Ahmadinejad. You know my ancestry, and although I'm not a practicing Jew, most of my family are Jewish, so he's the archfiend as far as we are concerned. Yet it seems as if that nasty little shit has manipulated us all along the line. We're helping him out, can't you see that?"

"Guy, what about the warheads? You were there, man! We were nearly killed, and you know that Petersen was behind it. President Ahmadinejad just tried to put a stop to it."

"Yeah? Or did he have something else in mind, like using us to prop up his regime? I don't know, Abe. All

I do know is I don't like being pushed by a guy like him. For a long time, I've harbored an ambition to put a bullet between his eyes. And here we are helping him out, so he can keep threatening Israel and anyone else he takes a disliking to. It doesn't seem right."

Talley fixed the SAS man with a hard stare, "Guy, I know where you're coming from. Just because the enemy of your enemy is your friend, doesn't mean that he's any less of an enemy."

Guy nodded, "Yeah, that's about it."

"Think about this. We've prevented a massive threat to the West and to Israel itself. If the time comes when it's right to put a bullet between Ahmadinejad's eyes, I'll be right behind you, lending you a hand. But in the meantime, we have a problem to deal with here. If she did sell us out to the Pasdaran, then she has to answer for it, and I don't give a fuck about what the Brits feel. We lost a good man in Valois, and someone has to pay. Here's the deal, Guy. Do your job, see this through, and we'll talk about the other thing afterward."

"Okay. Let's see what the little lady has to say, but as for the other thing, someone has to take him down."

Talley could see he was still reluctant. He thought about the repercussions that would follow a hit on the President of the Islamic Republic of Iran.

One thing's sure, the tens of thousands of Islamic fanatics who pose such a problem to the security of the Western world would likely mushroom into tens of millions. It's true the world would be a better place without him, except that killing him could have the opposite effect and tip the politics of the Middle East into a conflagration engulfing most of the world. World War Three!

He watched his second-in-command begin to carry

out the checks on his own handgun, prior to putting it out of sight under his coat. Until their conversation, he hadn't given a great deal of thought to Guy's attitude to Mahmoud Ahmadinejad. But he felt a shiver as it came to him that the SAS man showed all the signs of becoming a loose cannon. A loose cannon that could potentially be almost as much a threat to security as the nukes they had just taken care of. If he did go on a mission to assassinate the Iranian President, the Iranian Head of State would die. Talley realized his options were limited. If he thought it was about to happen, he would have to be stopped. And in the case of Sergeant Guy Welland of the SAS, stopping him would mean having to kill him.

Would I have the cold resolution to shoot and kill a man I've grown to like and trust?

He flinched as he heard a click behind him, almost as if his partner had read his mind and had decided to make a preemptive strike, but when he turned around, Guy had merely opened the door ready to go out. He noted Talley's reaction and raised an eyebrow, but didn't comment.

"If we're going to that meeting, Boss, we ought to head out now."

Talley nodded. "Let's go see what she has to say."

They walked through the busy streets of the capital of the United Kingdom. It had been raining, and the downpour had stopped. The streets and sidewalks were wet, reflecting the feeble glow of the streetlights trying to penetrate the gloom. London teemed with scores of people of different nations. In ten minutes he heard as many as a dozen different languages.

"I thought this was supposed to be England," he chuckled to Guy. "I've hardly heard an English accent since we left the hotel, apart from yours."

"I grew up in London," Guy replied, "but it's not the place I once knew. It's become something of a melting pot for the world's populations."

"Including terrorists?"

"Oh, yes, there are plenty of those. The Islamic lunatics seem to make a beeline for this place. We can be sure of one thing, sooner or later, when we've cleared out the cesspit of Iran and the Middle East, we'll have plenty of trade in this city."

There it is again. The focus on Iran, so obviously he's thinking of Ahmadinejad. God help us if they find out that a member of an elite NATO force is targeting their President.

They reached the beautiful old buildings of King's College, London and read the sign outside which gave directions to the lecture to be given by Doctor Anika Frost. People were already going through the doors, and unsurprisingly, considering the subject of Persian history and archaeology, many of them were obviously of Middle Eastern descent. They entered the building and walked along the corridor to the lecture theatre. As they pushed through the doors and walked inside, a girl with her back to them turned, and they came face-to-face. Her eyes widened, and her jaw dropped before she managed to control her expression.

"So you came."

Talley nodded. "Didn't you expect us?"

"Yes, I suppose I did expect to see you London, but not here." She made a joke, "I thought you'd had enough Persian history to last a lifetime." Neither of them returned her smile. Slowly it faded.

"So why are you here?"

Still neither of them answered. What was there to say? Finally she nodded.

"I guess you've come here to kill me, is that it?"

Talley shook his head. "All we want to do is talk, Anika, that's it. Can we meet up afterward? You know that we have to tie up a few loose ends."

"And then kill me?"

He stared into her eyes. Those beautiful, deep brown eyes that he'd once seen filled with passion as they made love. That was a lifetime ago. Yet with a start, he remembered that it was only a matter of a few weeks.

"I guess it'll depend on your answers."

She thought for a few moments. "Okay, when I've finished speaking, you'll find me in the green room at the rear of the lecture theatre. I should be on my own, and we can talk as much as you like."

She waited a few seconds. Talley nodded, and she turned on her heel and disappeared into the backstage area. He turned to Guy.

"You'd better wait out back in case she tries to make a run for it."

"And if she does?"

He hated himself for giving the order, but knew that if she did run, it would be all the proof they needed that she was bad.

"If it comes to that, kill her."

CHAPTER ELEVEN

The lecture began, and Talley listened for a short while but quickly became bored. She was passionate, totally absorbed in her subject. For the first time, it was clear how deeply involved she was with the history and archaeology of Persia, now the Islamic Republic of Iran. To stop himself from falling asleep as she droned on about the technical measurements of rural qanats, he let his eyes wander around the imposing room. It was a throwback to the Victorian era; high ceilinged, with walls clad in dark oak paneling. He was seated, like the rest of the audience, on hard wooden benches that were elevated like the seats in a cinema. Sadly, they were not as comfortable. When the place was built, learning took precedence over the comfort of the listeners. He examined the audience, most of whom were students, checking for any potential hostiles. But they all looked completely innocent, and he began to relax. She talked for almost ninety minutes non-stop, illustrating her lecture with a video projection from her laptop computer; showing digital images she had picked up in Iran. He smiled as he recognized many of the places on the screen, including the dig where they'd hidden when they first arrived in the country. Finally, the lecture came to an end. She smiled to acknowledge the applause and ducked out through the door that led backstage. Immediately, Talley got up to follow her, though he was confident she was going nowhere until he'd talk to her. Guy Welland would stop her, should she be inclined to try and make an escape. He pushed through the door into the room behind the stage. There were a couple of closets, a table and four chairs, and mirrors around the walls. At the rear, there was a door marked 'fire exit'. It was slightly ajar, and the room was empty. Anika had gone, and there was no sign of Guy.

He realized it had been less than a minute since she'd left the stage. He rushed out through the door and found it led into an alley, lit only by a feeble lamp. It was enough to backlight him as he exited the building, and he recognized the sound of a suppressed pistol as a shot chipped stone out of the masonry behind him. He rolled to the ground, dragging out his Sig. He couldn't make out the target but pointed the gun forward into the darkness and shouted to her.

"Anika, don't be stupid. Stop shooting. We need to talk."

Her voice came back, grating and sarcastic. "Talk! Do you take me for a fool, Abe? You came here to kill me. You think I don't know that? It's too late for talking. I'm leaving now. So don't try to follow me. If you do, the next shot will be in your head.

"Is that what you did to Guy? Did you kill him?"

She laughed, "You don't know a thing, Abe Talley. No,

I didn't kill Guy. He has his own agenda, and killing me is not part of it "

He understood with a chill. Guy had decided Ahmadinejad was the man responsible for everything that had gone wrong with their last operation. Could it be true? He reminded himself it was only the word of the CIA Head of Station in Tehran, Miles Preston that had insisted the Iranian President was hostile to the acquisition of the rogue Pakistani missiles. Guy's family was either Jewish or of Jewish descent, so the depth of his hatred for Ahmadinejad was no surprise. The wily Iranian President was on record as repeatedly stating that Israel should be wiped off the map. Nonetheless, the Brit SAS Sergeant was Talley's second-in-command, and he felt responsible for his actions. Somehow he had to stop him. He flinched as another shot almost parted his hair. He was surprised and thankful that Anika was such a lousy shot, but even as he had that thought, her voice called out to him.

"Don't think that I couldn't have put that one between your eyes, Abe. If I wanted to hit you, you'd be dead from my first shot. You can take it as a warning. If you follow me, the third shot won't miss."

"Where are you going? You know damn well you can't get away with this."

"Can't I? You've forgotten where I work. At MI6, we specialize in the art of the illusion, smoke and mirrors. Forget about me and get on with your life."

"Anika, why are you doing this? Can't you see that what you're doing is crazy?"

"Crazy? He was my father, Abe. I know now, he was a true believer. He devoted his life to Persia and everything Persian. When he thought America was planning an invasion of Iran, it drove him to despair. He saw what had happened in Iraq, the destruction of their heritage, of their culture, and civilization. He couldn't allow that to happen in Iran."

Her father! Jesus Christ. That meant when the drone killed Petersen's wife, it killed Anika's mother. It explained a lot.

"I'm sorry about your mother, but it was an accident. And Iraq was a dictatorship that threatened the west with WMDs. They had to get rid of Saddam Hussein. He was a threat to the security of the West, and if Iran gets nukes, they'll be worse."

She chuckled. "A threat to security? You're talking about the infamous WMDs, I suppose. But there never were any WMDs, were there? All they've done is replace one bloodthirsty regime with another, and as a result, more people are dying today than there were before Iraqi was invaded."

"So you think helping the Pasdaran get hold of those warheads was the solution?"

"I don't know, Abe. But my father did, and maybe he had a point. It wasn't the Revolutionary Guard who killed his wife. Whatever the reason, I only tried to help him without harming your operation."

"It didn't work, Anika, did it? At least one of my men was killed, and many more people died as a result of collateral damage."

Her laugh was bitter. "I won't argue with you. It's too late for that. I'm leaving, and remember, don't try and follow me. This is your last warning. If you want to stay alive, stay away from me."

He tried to pierce the gloom at the other end of the alley that was in complete darkness; aware he was still washed by the light outside the fire door. He heard nothing and saw nothing, so he cautiously climbed to his feet and crept along the narrow passage. With every step his shoulders tensed, waiting for the shot that would end his life, but when he reached the end and peered around the corner, she was nowhere in sight. He mentally went through his options.

Where the hell will she go? There's only one likely place, the headquarters of SIS at Thames House, Vauxhall Cross. If she gets there, she'll disappear completely.

He started to run, remembering he had to reach the River Thames and find the street known as the Embankment. It followed the course of the river all the way to Vauxhall Cross, which was on the opposite bank. He turned into Lancaster Place and powered along the street, scattering shoppers and bystanders, some raised their fists and shouted abuse. He ignored them, seeing ahead the wide ribbon of the river reflected in the moonlight. He didn't hear the shot, but a pistol round creased his arm, glanced off, and buried itself in some innocent who was in the wrong place at the wrong time. He ignored their cry, and ignored the pain of his wound. There was no time. In the distance, turning onto the embankment, he saw Anika. She was tucking her pistol out of sight as she disappeared around a corner. He kept running past rows of historic London buildings that held no interest for him. He was entirely focused on one target.

I have to stop her resurrecting her father's crazy plan. Damnit, she caused the death of one of my men. Am I bitter about being used by this woman, a woman I thought I was falling in love with? So bitter I'd hunt her to death? No, she's a target, just a target.

Then he saw her fall. It was probably a loose or misplaced

paving stone, but she tripped and went sprawling from the sidewalk and into the road next to a parked vehicle, a London taxicab. He picked up speed, feeling relief that he may be able to take her alive. He closed on her, twenty meters, fifteen meters, ten meters, but then she raised her hand and squeezed off a shot. He felt a hot agony as it lodged in the top of his leg, and he almost toppled over. He managed to stay upright and ducked behind a stone statue on the sidewalk, as more shots spat toward him. She fired off four more rounds, and the first three missed, but it was the fourth that did the damage. The bullet from her small pistol took him in the right hand, the hand that held his Sig Sauer. The weapon dropped uselessly to the concrete and skidded away, three meters from him; three meters of exposed ground lay between him and his pistol. There was no cover, and the pedestrians had scattered like confetti in the wind. There was just him and Anika; and the yawning gap lying between him and the only means of defense from her murderous onslaught.

"I told you to leave it alone, Abe," she shouted as she got to her feet and started toward him. He measured distances and angles. In the second it would take him to fling himself across the open space, she could put three or four more shots into him. Already, his leg was going numb with the shock of the wound, but even without being slowed by the agony in his leg, he knew he couldn't make it. She hadn't fed him a line. She was a crack shot. And then hot rage and anger welled up inside him.

No way! She'll probably drill him me with several shots before I'm halfway there, but I have make the attempt.

He tensed himself, ready to leap, but first he tried to persuade her give it up.

"It doesn't have to end like this, Anika. If you shoot me down here, there are a hundred witnesses. There's no way you'll get away with it, even with the help of your friends at MI6."

She was nearer, walking forward slowly and steadily; her little pistol held at arms length and pointed rock steady at the center of his body. She laughed, a cold, bone-chilling laugh. At that moment, he realized the Doctor Anika Frost he'd known and slept with, even started to fall in love with, was just an illusion. She was just as much a sociopath as her lunatic father, and the raving President of Tehran, Ahmadinejad. Despite their pretensions of civilization, they had the morals and intentions of the gutter; people who would murder women and children if it furthered their cause, without so much as blinking an eyelid.

"Oh, but it does have to end like this, Abe. They killed Petersens's wife, remember, she was my mother. And I know you won't stop hunting me for what happened in Iran. I know it, and you know it. I'd be looking over my shoulder for the rest of my life, waiting for the moment when you and your bunch of assassins come gunning for me. You killed my mother and my father. You're not murdering me as well. So yes, it does have to end here."

Assassins. Kay's word yet again!

He saw her body tense, and he prepared his muscles and sucked in oxygen for that final, last second surge that would carry him to his Sig Sauer lying so near and yet so far away. He was watching her intently and saw the faint narrowing of her eyes as she prepared to fire, but he didn't even begin to catapult himself off the ground and make a grab for his pistol. Two shots rang out, a double tap, the mark of a trained professional. It was over.

He'd closed his eyes. Now he opened them, wondering why he couldn't feel the shock and agony of the bullets that must have slammed into his body. Yet all he saw was a red London bus trundling innocently past on the embankment, crowded with astonished passengers looking down on the bloody scene. He looked across to where he'd last seen Anika, and she no longer stood there. She was lying on the ground, her body torn and streaked with blood. She was obviously dead. Guy Welland stood over her, still holding his Sig Sauer to cover the body. Guy knelt down and put his fingers to her neck, checking for a pulse. He looked across at Talley and shook his head. She was gone. In the distance, he heard the wailing of police sirens. Guy came over to him, held out his hand, and pulled him to his feet.

She's gone. Despite everything, we shared some precious moments together. Why didn't she surrender? At least she'd have lived.

He felt an overwhelming sense of loss and misery as Guy came helped him up.

"You'd better put your arm over my shoulder, and I'll help you get away from here."

"Why, Guy? Why did you do come back? I thought you'd decided…"

"To go over to the dark side?" Guy smiled his piratical grin. "I won't deny it had a certain appeal. Somewhere along the line, that oily little bastard needs someone to take him out."

"But not you," Talley murmured.

Guy shook his head. "Not yet. I guess when it comes down to it, Boss; I have a job to do. We have a job to do, and it's doing something I've wanted ever since I was a kid. People laugh at notions of duty and obeying orders, but somehow it's become ingrained in me. As long as I'm your number two, I'm paid to back you up."

Talley glanced down at the body lying on the sidewalk. There was a large, red stain, as her blood seeped out of her body, and with every drop that left her, he felt a part of his humanity draining away with it. People were starting to edge closer now that the shooting had stopped, to see what the excitement was all about. After all, it wasn't everyday you saw a shooting on the streets of London.

"I guess I ought to say thanks, Guy, but somehow it doesn't seem enough. I honestly thought I was going to have to follow you to Heathrow, and find you waiting for a flight to Tehran."

Guy raised an eyebrow. "And then what? Would you have killed me to stop it happening?"

"I don't know," Talley replied quietly. "I guess it's what you said. We have a job to do, and it's a job that gets under your skin and ingrained in your system."

"That doesn't answer my question."

"It's all the answer you're going to get, Sergeant, and that's an order. Leave it at that."

"Yes, Sir," he grinned, "I reckon we ought to get out of here. I mean out of the UK. The cops will be here any moment, and when her intelligence colleagues find out what happened, they're going to be sore as hell. I'd sooner not be around to take the flak."

"We'll have to deal with it sooner or later."

Guy nodded. "Let's make it later. They can send us an e-mail if they want any answers."

Talley smiled. "That will do for me. Let's go."

CHAPTER TWELVE

They'd fixed the event in one of the conference rooms in NATO Headquarters, Brussels. Talley's unit was present to watch the promotion ceremony. He felt uncomfortable wearing his US Navy dress uniform, with the bars of a full lieutenant. And he did his best to stand at attention, the wounds to his hand and leg were still sore, although they were healing fast. Guy Welland stood next to him, resplendent in the number one full dress uniform of the Welsh Guards, an elite regiment and part of the Brigade of Guards. Understandably, neither the SAS nor the Navy Seals were inclined to distinguish themselves with individual uniforms. As they spent most of their working lives working in hostile countries, they didn't intend to make life any easier for those who wanted to hunt them down afterward and kill them. They came to attention as Vice Admiral Carl Brooks entered the room, and then there was a stir, as the Commander of NATO appeared; the SACEUR, Admiral James Stavridis, and a rare honor for one of the most senior military men in the world to make an appearance. Even the men's rigid discipline couldn't stop them from glancing nervously around them.

Why is Stavridis here, just for a routine promotion? Talley thought.

"Ladies and Gentlemen, the Supreme Commander of NATO, Admiral James Stavridis."

The Admiral nodded to his aide as he walked up to the lectern.

"I guess you men above all would know that Special Operations go unremarked because of the need for secrecy. However, a recent operation, which need not be mentioned, was carried out with a bravery and dedication that went beyond the normal call of duty. Lieutenant Talley, step forward. You are promoted to the rank of Lieutenant Commander. Admiral Brooks has made it clear to me that you wish to stay with Echo Six, and I'm happy to go along with it, especially in view of your record in the field."

They shook hands, and the newly promoted Lieutenant Commander Talley shook hands with the Admiral and stepped back. Then it was the turn of Sergeant Guy Welland who was promoted to Warrant Officer, and given the obligatory handshake. Both men cringed at the round of applause, and Talley was just waiting for the moment when it was all over and he could stand the men a round of drinks in the bar.

"Lieutenant Commander Talley?"

He looked around and saw a NATO officer looking at him. The guy wore the uniform of a Lieutenant Colonel and was olive skinned. Turkish, probably, Talley supposed, an important NATO member nation.

"What can I do for you?"

"Would you come this way, Commander? There is somebody who needs to speak to you."

He shrugged and followed the man out of the room, along the labyrinth of corridors until they came to an unmarked door. The officer knocked the door. There was an inaudible reply from inside, and he held it open for Talley.

"If you would go in, Commander, I'll leave you here. Good luck."

Talley walked in, surprised and puzzled. He didn't like surprises or puzzles. Neither did he like the person he came face-to-face with. He was staring at the President of the Islamic Republic of Iran, Mahmoud Ahmadinejad.

What did Guy called him, the archfiend? Yeah, that's about right.

He stood with several of his assistants bunched up behind him. Another man standing with him was obviously his interpreter. Ahmadinejad offered him a handshake, but Talley stood rigid, waiting.

"What can I do for you, Sir?"

The President spoke in Farsi, and the man next to him translated.

"I want to thank you for stopping the enemies of the Islamic Republic from overthrowing my government."

Strange, or is it my imagination the way the President is smiling at me suggests he's hiding something?

He nodded.

"I was in Brussels for a meeting with ministers of the European Union, and my army chief of staff suggested I came here to thank you personally," he continued.

Talley nodded again, seeing through the veneer of civility.

"I didn't do anything for you, Sir, but I guess you know that. It's a pity that so many of your people had to die."

The President shrugged. The meaning was clear, a few people dead being of no consequence. He was still looking at him with that faint, enigmatic smile, and if Talley weren't in NATO Headquarters, Brussels, it would have been in his mind that somewhere around the corner a trap was waiting to close on him. An aide whispered in Ahmadinejad's ear and he nodded.

"I'm told that I am needed elsewhere, Lieutenant Commander Talley. Perhaps we will meet again."

"I hope not." He gave the man a cold, hard stare.

Guy was right. Whatever the operation required, aiding someone like Ahmadinejad was wrong. He needs someone to put a bullet in his brain.

The entourage swept out of the room, but Talley realized he still wasn't alone. Two men remained, both Iranians, and they had that hard, competent look of Special Forces, or maybe intelligence operatives. One of them, he had a scarred and pockmarked face that looked as if he'd been in one too many fistfights, nodded to him.

"I wonder if you would come with us, Lieutenant Commander. There's something outside I want you to see."

Talley grinned and shook his head. "Not in a million years, buster. If I were carrying a loaded assault rifle, maybe I'd take a look. You know I don't trust you, my friend, and I don't trust your people."

The man gave him an understanding nod, "Of course, I expected nothing else."

He looked behind Talley, who realized that somehow the second man had maneuvered into a position behind his back. He saw the faintest change of expression from Scarface and started to whirl around but felt a sharp stab of pain in his left shoulder as the man behind him fired.

He was holding a pistol in his hand. Talley leapt forward to wrestle it away from him, but he only managed to take one short step before his legs turned to rubber and his brain started to go fuzzy. The two men lowered him to the floor, and just before everything went black, they dressed him in an unfamiliar uniform. On the brink of unconsciousness, he noted the uniform wasn't unfamiliar after all. It was the uniform of the Iranian military; the same as Ahmadinejad's guards wore. They'd disguised him as an Iranian to spirit him out of NATO with Ahmadinejad's entourage.

When he awoke, it took all of his strength to push himself off the floor and struggle to his knees. He promptly vomited onto the hard concrete, and then two men grabbed him and pushed him into a chair. He was so weak with the effects of the drug they had pumped into him that he couldn't stop them strapping his wrists and ankles to the chair, leaving him powerless. His vision slowly cleared, and he looked at a face that was slightly familiar, Scarface, one of the Iranians who ambushed him inside NATO Headquarters. He was astonished they'd dared to put into place such a bold ambush, in the very heart of NATO. The security headquarters of the Western world, and they'd penetrated it to kidnap a NATFOR officer. The Iranian, Scarface stood in front of him, staring at him with an expression that was both violent and angry.

"You thought you could devastate my country and bring about the deaths of many of our people?" he snarled at him. "You do not realize the people you are dealing with.

You may think you can get away with it, but believe me, our memories are long, and our reach is even longer."

His head dropped as the drug swirled through his brain, but he managed to look up and stare at his captor.

"So Ahmadinejad is reduced to kidnap?" He realized he was slurring his words. "I knew he was a low down piece of scum, but I didn't think he'd stoop this low. I imagine the EU and NATO will think twice before they invite a piece of shit like him inside their doors again."

The man chuckled. It wasn't a pleasant sound, more of a harsh grating noise, like two pieces of metal rubbing together. "Ahmadinejad? He knows nothing of this. The fool genuinely wanted to thank you. He's just a puppet. Don't you realize? Inside the Islamic Republic, my people have all the power, and the good Mahmoud jumps to our tune."

"So you're Pasdaran. I should have known by your stink. Have you run out of women and children to torture and hang from cranes in the main square?"

Scarface scowled and smashed his fist into Talley's face. He felt one of his teeth break, and thought, *'there goes my dental plan'*. Maybe if he could keep a sense of humor about this, he could survive long enough to figure a way out. The man put his face close to Talley's, and he spat out the broken tooth. It hit him in the eye, and he reeled back, astonished that his prisoner would dare to resist. Talley had known since he was a kid; the last thing bullies expect is for their victim to retaliate. But his satisfaction was brief, and all it earned him was another punch in the face. He felt warm blood trickling down from his lips.

"You may as well know in advance that I'll see you in hell before I tell you anything."

Scarface nodded. "Yes, I'm sure we will meet in hell, but I will have the satisfaction of knowing you get their first. Save yourself a deal of pain, Commander Talley. All I need to know is how you uncovered our plan to bring the warheads in from Pakistan. It is important we find out who betrayed us. It makes no difference now, except that your death will be easy if you tell me the truth. If not, you will die over a long period. I can keep it up for several hours, and you will shriek in agony for every second that you wait for the blessed relief of death."

Did this fucking raghead seriously think I'd tamely give it all up in response to a few threats?

Just as Talley, like other military men, failed to understand the cruel and brutal rationale of the Arab world, so the Arabs didn't understand concepts of decency and loyalty. He thought of Javeed, the homosexual Deputy Manager of the AEOI. Doubly damned, both as a gay man and for helping Echo Six, even if he was given no choice. How could these people have any concept of decency, when every last piece of malicious agony they inflicted on their people could blithely be explained away as, 'the will of Allah'? The Christian world had once been as bad, true, but they'd got over it. It seemed incredible in the age of mass information and communications that anyone could be so naïve as the Islamic nutjobs.

"There's one thing I can tell you," Talley murmured through his broken and bleeding mouth.

Scarface leaned forward eagerly, "Good, now you're being sensible. Tell me, quickly!"

Talley stared him straight in the eye, "You can go fuck yourself, shithead. And when you're done, go fuck the camel that brought you here."

The man's eyes narrowed in fury and his face reddened. He lunged forward and smashed him on the side of the head with a punch so hard Talley was rendered unconscious.

He came to a few minutes later. He'd achieved his objective, for while he was unconscious, there was no way he could answer any questions. He knew he was in a shut ended situation, and there was no way out. All that awaited him was death, and all he could choose was the manner of his going. He could choose the easy way or the honorable way. He was a soldier, who'd never sacrificed the honorable for the easy. He heard Scarface talking and couldn't make out what he said, but it had something to do with a cell phone. He looked around the room and saw his tormentor speaking to one of the other men who was fiddling with the phone. Then his hopes soared. They'd taken his cell.

The stupid bastards!

Scarface saw the direction of his gaze and sneered.

"You see. We have your phone, and we can find every person you have called from its memory, everyone, from your contacts in Tehran to your own family. Believe me, we will be paying them a visit, and they will suffer badly. Talk to us, Commander."

He was only half listening. If Guy and Domenico were half the men he knew them to be, they would already be aware something was badly wrong, and one of their first actions would be to triangulate the signal from his cellphone. He had to hold out for a little longer, and with luck they would arrive to rescue him. Except that when they got there, there may be only a bloodied corpse left to rescue. It all depended on how he could hold up against the brutal interrogation, and how long he could string them along for.

"Leave my family out of this!" he shouted. "Does it turn you on, making war on women and children? Is that where you get your kicks, you sick psycho?"

"We are soldiers of Allah," Scarface screamed back at him, "Everything we do, we do in his name. If people have to suffer, it is for His greater glory."

He raised his fist to strike again, but Talley had only one card left in the deck. He had to play for time. It was time to produce the carrot.

"If you leave my family alone, maybe we could strike a deal."

The man stopped and considered for a few moments. He turned and snapped out an order, and one of his men came to stand directly behind Talley. He took hold of Talley's hand and gripped it hard against the solid wood of the chair arm. There were two remaining Iranians in the room, and one of them opened the door and shouted to two men on guard outside.

Guy, where the hell are you?

"If you play any more games, I have told the man standing behind you to use the butt of his pistol to smash your fingers."

Talley looked down and saw the steel butt of a Russian Makarov held over his right hand like a hammer.

"Then he will smash the fingers of your other hand and then start on your toes. I have also ordered the men outside to begin noting the numbers on your cellphone. We will soon know everything about your family, their names, their addresses, and we will send our people to visit them. This is your last chance. Tell me who you contacted while you were in Tehran."

So he'd run out of time. He knew he was about to suffer the long, agonizing descent that would lead to a painful death. So be it, he was a soldier, a warrior, and he'd always known, ever since the day he signed on, that it could come to this. He was out of options. There was nothing more he could say, no more insults to throw, or broken teeth to spit out. All he could do was grit his teeth and try to bear the pain. He watched Scarface steadily, waiting for the nod that would be the order to smash the butt of the Makarov down onto his right hand, and start hammering at his fingers until they were a mangled ruin. There were no more excuses, no more delays, nothing to be done. It was finished. He watched and waited for the start. As if in slow motion, he saw Scarface nod. It was almost like a film reel being undercranked. He could smell the dampness of the atmosphere in the room, meaning it was an underground basement. What a place to die! He would never see blue skies again or the faces of Joshua and James. To feel the breath of warm, California wind on his skin. All he could see was the flaking white paint on the ceiling. He felt a faint tremble as a white flake fell down, and then another.

What was that?

Scarface turned, still in slow motion, to look at the door. His mouth opened to speak to one of his men. It was like a gently choreographed ballet, and in his head Talley understood he was already on a different plane, his mind and body steeled to cope with the agony that was to come. And then Scarface was tossed across the room like a piece of broken rag, as an explosion blew the door in, and the shockwave sucked the breath out of his lungs. The room filled with choking white smoke, and he fought to suck in the last of the precious oxygen that remained. A group of men crashed through the door, all of them heavily armed and armored in vests and helmets, and wearing respirators against the choking gas. He recognized the first man in immediately.

Guy Welland rushed forward, strapped a mask over his face, and started to cut him loose. Half a dozen more Echo Six troopers were in the room, and they knocked down the Iranians with a few well-aimed shots from their MP7s. Outside, Talley could see more of his men setting up a defensive position. It was magical, a clockwork precision ballet, just as they'd practiced a hundred times before.

"Are you injured?" Guy asked, his voice mirroring his concern.

"I'm okay, there's nothing broken." He got to his feet and felt his legs wobble, but Guy steadied him.

"You sure?"

"I'm fine. How do we stand?"

More gunfire cracked and whistled along the passage outside the door, and it was obvious that wherever he was held captive it was well guarded and fortified. Guy started to explain they were in the basement of the Iranian trade delegation, and a unit of the Revolutionary Guard was staying in an annex at the rear as part of Ahmadinejad's protective detail.

"How many are we facing?"

"We estimate about thirty of them. We've knocked out a half-dozen, but we have a fight on our hands."

Talley was about to reply when the awesome, mechanized drumbeat of a Minimi drowned everything out, and the gunner raked the passage.

"That was Roy," Guy explained. "He's covering the

entranced to this part of the basement.

"They're bunching for a direct assault," Reynolds shouted, dependable as ever in a tough situation.

"Use grenades, all of you," Talley shouted. "Kill the bastards."

"You sure, Boss? It'll cause a lot of damage. This is a diplomatic mission, so we're pushing the envelope as it is. You want us to wreck the joint?"

"Roy, I don't give a fuck for diplomacy. They're the ones who caused it, not us. Toss the grenades!"

"You got it."

The basement shook as four of his men lobbed their grenades. They weren't a moment too soon. The Pasdaran had bunched up for a fanatical charge on the enemy who had dared to invade their territory. Talley felt recovered enough to poke his head outside the door and look along the passage. He was in time to see a closely bunched squad of soldiers hurtle toward them. They were all firing AKMs on full auto, and the hurricane of gunfire swept the passage in a torment of lethal, hot metal. Two of his men took hits, one on his helmet and the other on the shoulder of his armored vest. Reynolds grunted as two shots hit him in the hand, and he was forced to drop his Minimi. Talley and Guy grabbed him by his boots and hauled him inside the room. The other men lobbed more grenades and dived through the door as they exploded.

The room was filled with smoke and dust. Flakes of plaster continued to drift down from the ceiling. Guy looked out again through the doorway.

"They're coming back through the smoke," he shouted, as he scooped up Reynolds' Minimi. He worked the action and looked at it in dismay. The bullets that struck Roy in the hand had smashed the breech. "Shit, it's useless," he snarled, tossing it to the floor. He looked out through the door again and jerked his head back inside as a hail of bullets ripped along the passage, narrowly missing him.

"We underestimated them," Guy snarled. "I guess I should've known they would have more of their people here to guard Ahmadinejad. There must be as many as forty or fifty of them out there, judging from the incoming fire."

"Grenades?" Talley asked.

Guy shook his head. "If you recall, we were attending the promotion ceremony in our dress uniforms. When we guessed you'd been taken, we only had time to grab some basic equipment and go after you. Those grenades were all we could find at short notice."

They heard shouting from along the passageway. It was obvious the Pasdaran commander was preparing his men for a new assault. Talley assessed the situation, and it was grim. The men had torn off their respirators and were checking their remaining ammunition. They looked at him, waiting for a solution.

"Hey, this is some kind of a rescue," he smiled, trying to ease the tension. No one smiled back, "If you hadn't come, I would have been dead by now. So I owe you one, men, all of you. As soon as they mount the next assault, I want Guy and three other men to dive out and lie flat in the passageway, emptying their clips into their first wave. Four more men will be standing in reserve. As soon as the first four have emptied their clips, they're to come back inside, and the second group will dive out and do the same. That should blunt their enthusiasm. Soon as they start to fall back, the remaining men will charge out and meet their attack head-on. We'll see if we can push them back to where they came from."

"I guess that was the Devil's asshole," one of the men remarked.

That did raise a chuckle, but they quietened down as they heard the Iranian commander bellow the order to attack. Talley nodded to Guy.

"Get your men out there now, and let them have it."

Guy's group flung themselves low through the doorway onto the floor, and as the hurricane of gunfire crashed over their heads, they emptied their MP7s into the onrushing Pasdaran and slid back inside the room. The second group of four launched themselves outside and repeated the attack. They heard multiple screams of agony from the Iranians torn to shred by the unexpected resistance.

"You men! Back inside now and reload. The rest of you, let's go. Charge!"

He didn't have an armored vest, but he didn't care. They were heavily outnumbered and in a situation escape from seemed unlikely. Their only chance was to take unexpected action, to shock and awe the enemy with a ferocious attack that would hopefully get them on the run. They were low on ammunition, and some of the men fired single shots and short bursts as they ran. They had the satisfaction of seeing some Iranians fall, and the rest turn on their heels to try and escape the ferocious and accurate gunfire that was tearing them to bloody ruin. As Talley reached the corner and looked around, a machine gun opened up and fired a long burst at him that echoed and ricocheted along the concrete walls. He snatched his head back, but not before he'd seen the machine gun blocking their exit from the basement. Low on ammunition, out of grenades, it was only a matter of time before they were overcome by the seemingly limitless supply of men and ammunition the Pasdaran had at their disposal.

Guy ran up behind him, and Talley rapidly explained the situation.

"Dom was hit," he said ominously, "It looks bad."

Talley looked around to see Rovere lying on the floor in a pool of blood. Buchmann was working on him, pressing a dressing down hard to staunch the flow of blood from a volley of bullets that had taken him in the stomach. Domenico's healthy tan had faded to a pale gray. He rushed over to him.

"How bad is it, Buchmann?"

The German looked up at him. "He needs an ER room, and fast. He's all torn up. I estimate he was hit by at least three bullets, all in the same area. I think they missed the lungs, but his abdominal area, the intestines are going to need major surgery. If he makes it that far."

"Shit!"

Rovere was unconscious, perhaps a mercy. At least he wasn't suffering any pain.

"We'll get you out, Dom, that's a promise," he murmured to him. "Guy, we have to get past them. If we don't, Dom is going to die."

"Yeah, I know. It'll have to be frontal assault. Do or die," he smiled.

Guy sounded as calm and laconic as ever. There was no sign that any of the men of Echo Six realized they were facing defeat. Yet Talley knew no matter how they played it, the enemy had them trapped. An eerie silence descended on the basement as the Iranians ceased fire. Guy looked at him with a raised eyebrow.

"You reckon they're out of ammunition?"

Talley shook his head. "No, but let's see what ammunition we have left."

Guy stared back at him. "So it's to be the final charge?"

Talley grinned. "Yes. Maybe they'll turn and run when we hit them."

He grunted. Whoever the Iranian commander was, he was no patsy. He'd regrouped his men after they fled in panic and got them back in the fight. Yet the one word that might have saved the lives of Echo Six, the option that troops faced with defeat often considered, 'surrender', was not voiced. It was not part of their training, not part of their vocabulary. As long as they had a gun in their hand and breath in their body, they would fight.

"Are you ready?" Talley asked them. "Buchmann, stay with Dom. We'll need the rest of you for the attack."

They all nodded and tightened the grip on their guns. Their expressions were calm but determined. The action had come down to the very essence of what they were paid for, trained for, and selected for. They were the best of the best, and no one would make them give up the fight. Talley opened his mouth to give the order to attack, and closed it as he heard a new voice shouting orders. The voice switched to English.

"It's over! You can stand down."

They looked at each other. Guy shook his head.

"No fucking way is this over, not until we finish it."

"No, wait," Talley stopped him, "there's something else. Listen!"

The man shouted again, in English but with an Iranian accent, "My President wishes to speak to you. Hold your fire!"

"We're listening," Talley shouted back. He heard footsteps approaching, and he risked a quick look around the corner and blinked, in case he was dreaming. The President of the Islamic Republic of Iran was walking toward them; Mahmoud Ahmadinejad, the archfiend, despised enemy of America, Israel, and at times it seemed like the whole world. His interpreter accompanied him.

"I have ordered these men to stop shooting," the man passed on his President's words, "This should never have happened. I offer you my apologies. You may leave."

They stared at him, wondering when the trap would spring. But how could it be a trap? The President of the Islamic Republic had put his life in danger to call off the fight. Talley turned to his men.

"It looks kosher, men." He smiled as he saw Ahmadinejad flinch at his use of the Jewish word.

Interesting, you understand English. Or maybe the word is the same in Farsi.

"It's genuine. We're out of here."

As he walked past Ahmadinejad, the man held out his hand again, and once more Talley refused to shake it. He stopped and stared at him.

"I don't know what your involvement is, Sir, but I do know that if you could have killed us all, you would have done so."

He could hear the interpreter translating his words, and he continued.

"I won't shake your hand. There's too much blood on it. But I'll do you a favor instead. This man," he turned and indicated Guy Welland, "wants to kill you. I'll keep him away from you until such time as you are safely back inside your own country. After that, all bets are off."

The President spoke a few words. His eyes were cold, glacial, and Talley had a glimpse of the ruthless fanatic that terrorized the Middle East.

"You are correct. All bets will be off."

The Iranian President stood to one side, allowing them to walk past and up the staircase that led to the first floor and the street exit; and freedom. Four of the men gently carried Rovere, who still had not regained consciousness.

The Iranian trade delegation building was surrounded by a cordon of cop cars, ambulances, and a detachment of NATO troops, and in front of them stood their boss, Vice Admiral Carl Brooks.

So that's why he had to stop it. He couldn't allow the Revolutionary Guard to take us out, not with the cavalry parked up here.

"Medic! We need help here! Make it fast, you people!"

Two Belgian paramedics ran up to him, and he directed them to Rovere. They worked like lightning. Seconds later, he was transferred to a gurney, and they hung drip stands over his inert form and put needles into him to transfer the drugs that might save his life.

"Is that all of you?" Brooks asked, counting Talley's men as they filed out.

"That's it, Sir, all of us."

"Any other casualties?"

Talley indicated Sergeant Roy Reynolds' broken and bleeding hand. "We need to get him to an emergency room, and fast."

"He can go in the ambulance with Rovere. What happened in there?"

Talley answered with one word. "Pasdaran."

"And they let you go?" Brooks continued, his face reflecting his surprise.

"They didn't let us go, Sir. It was the Iranian President, Ahmadinejad. He intervened."

"He intervened?" Brooks said, astonished. We didn't even know he was inside the building."

"Yeah, he was there, and he called off the dogs."

Brooks shook his head. "If that don't beat all. That bastard helping you out of a nasty situation."

Guy intervened. "Only after he'd helped put us into it in the first place. He must have been behind it."

Talley shook his head. "I don't know, Guy. But remember that Iranians' politics are a strange business at best, and he's no friend of the Pasdaran. He just used us against them."

"How do you mean?" Brooks pressed him.

Talley grinned. "Remember the old saying, Admiral. The enemy of your enemy is your friend. When we went into Iran, we were the enemy of the Pasdaran, and the Pasdaran are making a play for power, trying to overthrow Ahmadinejad. They're his enemy, and I reckon that made us his friend. For now."

"I'd still like to shoot the fucker," Guy murmured.

"I reckon you'll get your chance," Talley replied, "It was a setup."

He turned to Brooks. "Did you know any of this, Sir?"

"I don't know what you mean, Talley."

"We've been going around and around in circles ever since this mission started. It looks to me like NATO discovered the Pasdaran faction inside Iran was trying to snatch power. That would make open warfare in the Middle East almost inevitable, especially between Iran and Israel. Admiral, those nuclear warheads the Rostam was carrying, I noticed they had American trigger mechanisms.

Care to comment, Sir?"

Brooks looked away.

"Son of a bitch," Guy murmured. "Are you telling me that we were set up by our own people right from the start?"

"We'll never know," Talley replied. "All I do know for sure is that someone got the idea to mount the biggest smoke and mirrors operation in the history of NATO. It was very clever. Set up the Pasdaran to challenge Ahmadinejad, and send us in to stop them. He had no choice except to support us behind the scenes. So the Pasdaran got a bloody nose, and I've no doubt he's already called for the arrest of their senior people. I'll bet it's like the night of the long knives over there. It means Iran doesn't get nuclear weapons, the Pasdaran is fucked, and Ahmadinejad owes us a few."

"But the nukes! What if we failed?"

"You remember Anika said Petersen had lied to us about the timer? She was wrong. The timer was already set to explode after thirty minutes, just before the Rostam hit the coast. There was no way those warheads were ever going to reach Iran. It was a win-win. Either we took down Petersen's alliance with the Revolutionary Guard, or they'd explode anyway and take a few of the bastards with them. It meant a lot of scores could be settled, both on our side and the Iranians. When the dust has died down, I can guarantee the Iranians will start making noises to the West about new trade agreements. That's the way the game is played, isn't it, Admiral?"

Brooks looked at him for long moments and then turned away, but his eyes said it all. At least he had the grace not to lie. Not anymore.

"So who do I kill?" Guy grumbled.

"Right now, I couldn't say," Talley replied, "but as soon as I do know, you'll be the first one I tell. First, I'm going to visit Domenico and Roy at the infirmary. I won't be able to relax until I know Dom's okay.

"I'll go with you," Guy nodded. "They may need an incentive to do their best work on Domenico."

Talley nodded, but he didn't smile. He thought of Anika, of her bleeding and dying in the London gutter.

Once again, I'm alone in this world.

"Hey, Boss, what's the problem? We pulled it off, and we're about to go and celebrate. Where should we go?"

And in that moment he realized he wasn't alone.

I do have a family, a family of the most highly trained and deadliest killers in the world yet they depend on me. Some may call us assassins, true. But we'd give our lives for each other. Isn't that enough?

"After we're done at the hospital, and provided Dom is okay, I'll make some calls. We're going to find the best beer and the best women in this city!" Talley exclaimed.

A chorus of cheers rewarded him. He'd made the right call, and for that night and many nights to come, he wouldn't be alone. So why did he feel the empty hole in the pit of his stomach? Too many deaths, Robert Valois and Anika Frost, and Domenico Rovere may well be on the danger list for a long time to come. Countless civilian and military casualties inside Iran, many of them innocents, men, women and children going about the normal business; all for what? He wasn't sure, not sure at all.

Talley made an effort to push it all to the back of his mind. Yet there was another huge, gaping hole in his life, his children, Joshua and James. Would he win them back? His thoughts turned once more to the letter, kept safe and hidden in his locker. The lawyer said his wife Kay had asked the court for sole custody of his kids, and would no doubt do everything in her power to justify it. He thought about his wife's statement.

'You're never there, Abe, you're a stranger to them. And besides, look at the kind of work you do. I don't want my kids to be brought up by someone who's little more than a government assassin.'

No, that wasn't true. Men like him risked their lives to prevent the assassins from turning the West into a bloody warzone. But that was another fight, one he'd give his all to win. There'd be time to worry about that later. Right now, his other family needed him to help heal their wounds.

"The operation is finished. Let's go."